Also by Marian D. Schwartz

Realities

The Last Season, The Story Of A Marriage

Harry Danced Divinely: Collected Giffort Street Stories

War on Giffort Street, a novella

Sara Barefield

THE WRITERS' CONFERENCE

A NOVEL

MARIAN D. SCHWARTZ

Gristmill Publishing, L.L.C.

The Writers' Conference is a work of fiction. The characters and events portrayed in this book are the product of the author's imagination. Any resemblance to actual persons, living or dead, events, or places is entirely coincidental and not intended by the author.

The Writers' Conference

Marian D. Schwartz

Copyright ©2012 by Marian D. Schwartz

All rights reserved.

ISBN 978-0-9886076-4-4

Gristmill Publishing, L.L.C.

*Dedicated to the success of aspiring writers, who work against
almost impossible odds.*

Contents

Prologue
1998

They were in a drab classroom facing each other on oversize student desks, a slight man whose large head gave him the appearance of a gnome, and a middle-aged woman whose dark roots were beginning to show beneath her ash blond hair. The only light in the room was filtering in through two narrow rain-spattered windows. The man's name was John Warrenton. He was a published novelist on the staff of the Clymer Workshop, and he'd had the unhappy task of telling the woman sitting opposite him, Rose Ann Bethune, that in his judgment her novel simply didn't work. Their conference, for which she had paid a substantial fee, was nearly over.

"I'm sorry I can't encourage you with this novel," he said. "Family sagas are difficult to write, and the characters in the family you've chosen to write about are so… so despicable, to put it bluntly, that they're almost unbelievable. I can't imagine that anyone would want to spend time reading about them."

"Faulkner's characters weren't exactly sweethearts," she said in a soft drawl that contrasted sharply with the hard consonants in his Yankee speech.

But you're no Faulkner, he thought, checking himself before the words flew out of his mouth. He rose to indicate that the conference was over. Then, feeling that he had to give her something positive to take away from their meeting, he said, "You've written some fine sentences."

She took the manila envelope from him that contained her manuscript, ignoring his outstretched hand. *Don't cry*, she kept telling herself, *don't cry, don't cry, don't cry…*

And she didn't cry until she was outside in the rain.

Rose Ann walked with her head down so no one would see her weeping. Privacy, she wanted privacy; she hadn't had a private moment since the conference had begun with the exception of time in the bathrooms, and then almost always pressured by the awareness of people waiting their turn on the other side of the door. She knew that her roommate, Francine, was in the room waiting for her. She couldn't face Francine, she couldn't face anyone.

She started down an unpaved road behind the theater that she'd noticed yesterday. The novel had taken up her whole life. It had become the reason for her existence, the only thing that truly mattered. The novel had given her something to look forward to, the promise of a new beginning where she wouldn't have a husband who cheated on her, children who didn't call unless they wanted something, a mother whose demands were unending. She could free herself from all of them.

Writers were supposed to write about what they knew. That's what the books said. Warrenton said her characters were so despicable that they were almost unbelievable. He was wrong! She had depicted them as they were, generations of liars, cheats, petty thieves—mean-spirited people who inhabited the twisted branches of her family tree.

Rain started coming down heavily. She saw a large garage ahead that had a green tin roof and two sets of double doors, one of which was open. Hurrying toward the building, she slid on a muddy patch and lost her balance, landing on her side. She got up slowly, testing to see if anything was broken. Then she looked at her blouse and khaki slacks, slick with mud, and broke into choking sobs at this final insult.

Ordinarily the pattering of the rain against the tin roof would have soothed her, but her sobbing was wild now, beyond containment. She walked around the equipment in the building—a tractor, riding lawnmowers, a snow blower, a large blade for snow removal—without any of it registering. But when she saw a coil of rope hanging on a metal hook that was attached to a sheet of pegboard behind a long workbench, she stopped. *That was it*, she thought, *that was it.*

It was all there for her: the rope, the exposed beams, and a stool next to the workbench that she could stand on.

Her weeping stopped as she concentrated on making the slip-knot noose, convinced that fate was telling her what to do.

Frank Stryker, the caretaker at the Clymer Workshop, found her less than a half hour later. He had come in to get a snake to unplug a toilet in the main building, the Tabard Inn. The color vanished from his ruddy face when he saw her hanging from an overhead beam near the workbench. "Jesus," he said, backing out the door. A heavy-set fellow, he half-walked, half-ran to the director's office in the Tabard Inn, forgetting about the snake and the plugged toilet.

The director of the conference, Colin Rafferty, insisted upon going back to the building with him. "Aren't you going to call the police, the rescue squad?" Stryker said, still out of breath.

Rafferty looked at his watch. It was five fifteen. If he waited to call, the people attending the conference would be in the dining room when the police and rescue squad arrived. He could direct their vehicles away from the Tabard Inn so conference members wouldn't be aware of anything amiss. "Frank, I take your word for what has happened, of course," he said. "But it's my responsibility to see the tragic incident before making the calls."

Stryker understood. The director was going to do his best to keep the incident quiet, like other incidents that had been quickly swept away.

Rafferty almost succeeded. Rose Ann Bethune's body was circumspectly removed, and the only people the police questioned were Stryker, the writer John Warrenton, and her roommate Francine Shaw. All three were cautioned by Rafferty not to discuss what had happened with anyone because of the upsetting effect it would have on the conference, but it was impossible for Francine. She was close in age to Rose Ann, and the two roommates had bonded from the first day of the conference; not only did she find it impossible to hide her grief, she didn't feel right lying to people when they asked for Rose Ann, so she told a few of them. Those few told a few more, who told a few more, until finally everyone at the conference knew that Rose Ann Bethune had committed suicide by hanging after her conference with John Warrenton.

The following year there was a new director at the Clymer Workshop, Roy Talbot. The novelist John Warrenton wasn't asked to return.

> *"I was always my own teacher."*
> Eudora Welty

Chapter I

Roy Talbot, the director of the Clymer Workshop, walked to his office window, which faced the driveway that looped in front of the Tabard Inn. He looked out, then glanced at his watch and looked out again, his pale gray eyes straining to see down the road. He had been repeating the same ritual for hours—walking to the open window, glancing at his watch, straining to see down the road—each time he had heard a car approaching. It was now one o'clock in the afternoon, and there was still no sign of the Workshop's star fiction writer, Michael Pierce. Talbot's spare body felt leaden from lack of sleep. He had awakened before dawn, his skin coated with perspiration, his heart pounding. He had dreamed that the trustees were demanding his resignation because Pierce hadn't come to the Workshop: the trustees were shouting at him and waving their fists until his eyes had popped open in panic.

The vehicle that had summoned him to the window was a red Volkswagen Beetle with a mangled front fender. A fellow who appeared to be in his late twenties emerged from the car feet first, head next, to an amazing height. If he hadn't been so tense, Talbot might have chuckled with amusement at seeing the giant get out of the undersize car, but in his present mood the startling image was of no more significance than a black horsefly that was crawling up the screen outside his window. The entire staff had arrived on Tuesday except for Andrew Cox and Aaron Greene, who would be coming shortly, and Michael Pierce. He hadn't communicated with Pierce since a telephone conversation they had had in the spring: Pierce had called to resign, furious because Eric Nettles, a novelist whose work he detested, had been hired to teach at the Workshop.

Talbot sank into his desk chair and wiped his high forehead with a sodden handkerchief, remembering the conversation. Although he had tried every appeal he could think of to get Pierce to change his mind, the novelist had been adamant. Finally, in desperation, he had suggested to Pierce that by not coming to the

Workshop he would be relinquishing his forum to Nettles. Pierce had hung up without replying; they had not communicated since.

Talbot sighed. In a few hours he would know. He heard a car motor and leaped up again. His office door opened when he reached the window. Startled, he turned and snapped, "What is it?"

Dolores Durkin, called Dee Dee by everyone who knew her, jumped as if she'd been stung. "I knocked first."

"Sorry."

"Why don't you keep your door open to get some air circulating? It has to be a hundred degrees in here. How can you stand it?"

"I'm managing quite well," he said after he peered out the window to look at the latest arrival. It was a dark blue Volvo, definitely not Pierce. "Is that why you're in here—to check the temperature?"

Ordinarily his caustic remark would have devastated Dee Dee, but the heat, the pressure of overseeing the arrival of over two hundred people, the burden of supervising a temporary staff, plus other responsibilities, which included writing the conference newspaper, the *WORKSHOP BULLETIN*, had made her temper as short as his. In the five years that Talbot had been the director of The Clymer Workshop, he had managed to heap most of the work of running the conference onto Dee Dee's ample shoulders. She had been infatuated with him since she had been in his classes at Axton College, a heavy, bespectacled, frizzy-haired coed gazing at him adoringly; there was nothing she wouldn't do for him. But lately her feelings had begun to change. "Douglas Webb is here," she said testily, "and he's objecting to filling out the health form and signing a release."

"Tell him that he has to if he wants to attend the Workshop."

"I did. He won't sign."

"Try again," Talbot said, returning to his post at the window. The last thing he needed now was a problem with Douglas Webb. Webb's poems were extraordinary, the work of someone exceptionally gifted, but the poems were filled with references to madness and suicide. People who attended the Workshop were all screened for potential problems through the health form; the intensity of the conference could precipitate a breakdown, or worse, a suicide. Webb hadn't returned his form.

Dee Dee followed him, the gathers in her cotton-print skirt

billowing over her hips, and thrust the health form and release into his unwilling hands. "I've done all I can with Douglas Webb."

"It wasn't a request, Dee Dee," he said, shoving the papers back at her. "If you had followed up on his health form, we wouldn't have this mess."

She dropped the papers on his desk. "You accepted Webb," she said. "And if you don't get him in here soon, we'll have a bigger mess. Douglas Webb is neither inconspicuous nor retiring. He's huge—I'd guess almost seven feet tall—and he's as explosive as his poems. When I asked him to fill out the health form and sign the release, he seemed willing to cooperate until some people came to the front desk. Then he refused to even look at the papers. It was almost as if he were deliberately trying to make a scene to draw attention to himself. There's a small crowd out there now, and he's in the center of it playing to them like they're his private audience."

"Send him in here."

Douglas Webb's entrance into the director's office was as threatening as the weather. "I demand to know why you're putting me through this!" he said, his eyes, nearly black in color, boring down at Talbot from an impressive height.

"I'm not putting you through anything," Talbot replied, recognizing Webb as the driver of the Volkswagen. "A completed health form is required of everyone who attends the Workshop. You neglected to return yours, so we're asking you to fill it out here."

"It's an invasion of my privacy! What right do you have to ask questions about medications I've taken, any hospitalizations I've had?"

"Every right. People who attend the Clymer Workshop live on this property, which belongs to Axton College, as paying guests. Therefore, Axton has the privilege of denying residence to anyone who may pose a threat to the community as a whole."

Webb's eyes sparked at the word threat. "What does the college think I'm going to do, chop down the trees?"

Talbot's thin lips twitched with impatience. "I don't have time for nonsense," he said, trying to get a fix on the agitated young man. If it weren't for Webb's unusual height and magnetic eyes, he would be considered rather ordinary looking, a deeply-tanned, cleft-chinned fellow wearing jeans and a yellow knit shirt, no different from thousands of American males.

Webb thrust the release at him. "Is everyone given one of these to sign?"

Distracted by the sound of a car coming up the road, Talbot went to the window, but by the time he got there the car was beyond his range of vision. The car, the heat, Pierce, and now Webb straining the limits of his patience. "I don't have time to argue with you," he said firmly. "Either you complete the health form and sign the release or you leave. It's as simple and final as that."

"You've accepted my money."

"It will be refunded."

"All right," Webb said, his attitude becoming as cooperative as it had been hostile. "Do you want me to fill these out here?"

"No," Talbot said, anxious to be rid of him. "Go back to the front desk. Dee Dee, the woman who gave you the papers, will take care of you."

After Webb left, Talbot closed his office door and went to the window. The sky was overcast, heavy with storm clouds that had been gathering for hours, growing darker and thicker in the oppressive heat. He hoped the weather would hold until the welcoming reception was over. There was a distant, teasing clap of thunder, then another, as if in response to his thought. The air steamed like a pot of scalding soup. He knew he should go check Webb's health form, but he remained at the window. It was too late to do much about Webb anyway.

***

Agatha Risley walked down a long corridor in Buffalo Niagara International Airport looking for the gate to make her plane connection. Nearly six feet tall, with legs so thin they appeared barely capable of supporting her angular body, she resembled a long-necked bespectacled bird carrying a blue tote bag and a woven-straw summer purse. Today, perhaps for the first time in her adult life, she was not self-conscious. Too excited to sleep, she had gotten up at dawn to shower, dress, and finish packing. At nine o'clock she took a flight out of Lincoln, Nebraska to Chicago, the first of three airplanes she had to take to reach her destination. It was a tedious trip but one that she hoped was well worth the effort:

after years of wanting to attend, within hours she would formally register at the Clymer Workshop.

The waiting area at the gate was empty. Agatha perched on a chair near the end of a row so she could watch the people walking past, an occupation she found fascinating. There were so many clues people gave—the expressions on their faces, the energy or lack of it in their strides, the clothes they wore, the luggage they carried—that told her something about them.

Soon a slender woman who had strawberry-blond shoulder-length hair and flawless skin took a seat on the opposite side of the aisle. Agatha recognized her—she'd been on the plane from Chicago—and smiled tentatively.

"It looks like we're heading for the same place," the woman said, setting a black bag that held a laptop and a large white-leather handbag on the seat beside her.

"The Clymer Workshop?" Agatha said, mentally guessing that the woman might be in her late twenties or early thirties. At forty-seven, she found it more difficult to estimate people's ages than when she was younger.

"I'm Laura Belmont," she said with a warm smile. "Have you ever been to a writers' conference?"

"Agatha Risley," Agatha said, smoothing the blue jumper she was wearing over her bony knees. "This is my first time."

"Then it's a first for both of us. I'm a little nervous."

"Why would you be nervous?" Agatha said, unable to imagine anyone as attractive as Laura being nervous about anything.

"I just made the decision to attend the other day," Laura said. "I wanted to come as a participant, but there wasn't an opening. The woman I spoke with in the Workshop office seemed to think I could get someone on the staff to read a sample of my novel, but I'm starting to have doubts."

"Oh, I'm sure someone on the staff will read it. I know I would feel honored if you asked me," Agatha said. "Have you finished the novel or is it still a work-in-progress?"

"It's done."

"I'm impressed. Writing a novel takes commitment. It's an act of courage."

"Or a testament to hope," Laura said.

"Don't minimize your accomplishment," Agatha said, thinking of her own poems. She had been writing poetry for as long as she could remember. Her childhood poems were wistful, filled with creatures that talked, magical kingdoms, and beautiful princesses and handsome princes who lived happily ever after. As she grew older and more self-conscious, detesting her odd, old-fashioned name which had been cruelly changed in the schoolyard from Agatha to *Hagatha*, the emphasis on *Hag*, and becoming increasingly dismayed as her face and body grew homelier and gawkier, her poems became formal and stilted, the lines dragging with self-conscious alliteration, the subjects reflections on nature, on books she had read, on anything and everything but herself. To define her pain in words would be unbearable. She had never submitted her poems anywhere.

"Are you attending for prose or poetry?" Laura asked.

"Both. I'm an English teacher," Agatha said, too modest to add that she taught all honors classes.

"Then you'll be an observer?"

Agatha nodded a bit too vigorously; her wire-framed eye glasses slipped. With a long forefinger, she pushed them back on the bridge of her beaked nose.

A slight man wearing jeans, a green polo shirt, and a baseball cap that partially obscured his face took the seat next to Laura. "This is the gate for Jamestown?" he said before setting down his laptop and backpack.

"Yes," Agatha said excitedly, recognizing his narrow jaw line and prominent nose from a picture in the Clymer Workshop brochure. He was the novelist Andrew Cox.

"Am I right in assuming that we're all heading for the same place: the Clymer Workshop?"

"Yes," Laura and Agatha said in unison.

After they introduced themselves, Cox said, "I understand that the country around the Workshop is beautiful. Have you been there before?"

"No," Agatha said, leaning slightly forward so she wouldn't miss a word the novelist said.

"It's our first time," Laura said.

Cox gestured at the book she was holding. "What are you reading?"

"*The Awakening*, by Kate Chopin," Laura said. "A friend loaned it to me."

"Hmmm, sounds familiar. Isn't that a women's lit book?"

"It's beautifully written," Agatha offered. "By today's standards it would be considered modest, though it was really shocking for its time."

Andrew Cox smiled at Laura, revealing a slight overbite that accentuated his large front teeth. "So tell me what you've written,"

"A novel," Laura said, tucking her slender legs as far under her chair as she could. Although his cap hid his eyes, she could feel them on her, probing audaciously.

"What do you do when you're not writing novels?"

A fellow wearing an airline uniform came up to them. "The commuter to Jamestown will be boarding now," he said. "You can go through the gate after I check your boarding passes."

Agatha hung back, rummaging through her purse as if searching for her boarding pass, while Laura, Andrew Cox, and two men wearing business suits went through the gate. The boarding pass was where she had placed it, safe in a center compartment, but she couldn't think of another excuse to allow them to dump her gracefully. It wasn't as if she hadn't had experiences similar to this one, she told herself in an effort to stop tears that were threatening to surface as she inched her way toward the gate, still pretending to search for her boarding pass.

Cox stopped and turned before climbing the steps to the plane, realizing that Laura hadn't kept pace with him. "Aren't you coming?" he called.

"I'm waiting for Agatha," Laura said.

He shrugged and started up the stairs.

Agatha blinked with surprise when she came out of the terminal and saw Laura. "Why aren't you on the plane?" she said.

"I was waiting for you."

"Oh… how thoughtful… thank you."

"Don't thank me," Laura said. "After all, aren't you my oldest Clymer Workshop friend?"

"Why, I believe I am," Agatha said, her myopic eyes sparkling with tears of gratefulness.

***

Doug Webb was assigned to a room in Dickens, one of three brown-shingled structures built during the nineteen fifties when Axton College, like the rest of America, was enjoying a period of prosperity. The three buildings—Dickens, Tennyson, and Thackeray—were constructed to house males attending the conference, an ideal solution, it seemed to the trustees at the time, to curb sexual promiscuity that had flourished in the Tabard Inn despite the segregation of sexes into separate wings. Distance, they soon learned, did not provide a solution to the problem. If anything, the people attending the conference in subsequent years were more promiscuous than those who had attended previously, and certainly more open about it. The trustees remained adamant, however, that Dickens, Tennyson, and Thackeray house only men, overriding objections that the buildings were monuments to pretense.

Webb had walked halfway across the Workshop campus when he realized that he had left his pills in the Volkswagen. Skipping one pill wouldn't make a difference, he thought. He felt fine, amazingly good considering the hassle he'd just been through with the release and the health form. There was no way he could avoid stating that he had been hospitalized for psychiatric problems—if they had read his poems, they knew—but he wasn't obligated to tell them the number of hospitalizations he'd had, the medication he was taking, or the name of his doctor. It was none of their damn business. Besides, he was no longer seeing Dr. Bateson. The eight Eskalith Bateson had prescribed had given him diarrhea and dry mouth, and had caused tremors in his fingers like an old man's. Even worse, the high dosage had killed his poetry, leaving him feeling lightheaded and empty. Eliminating five out of the eight pills was the smartest thing he could have done; three pills a day were just enough, the perfect dosage. He'd get the pills later. He couldn't take an Eskalith until after he ate dinner anyway. The important thing was that he must remember to take it.

Eskalith, the magic pill that kept him steady. In the years before he was diagnosed as bipolar—time wasted because doctors blamed his first depressions on his mother's suicide—his mood swings from deep depression to wild, irrational exuberance had destroyed every relationship that had been important to him and had alienated what little family he had. He had been expelled from Yale, had been hospitalized more times than he could remember, and had been homeless for a time, wandering the streets wild-eyed and ranting. With the pills he had managed to put his life back together: he had a steady landscape maintenance business and he had time to write. He missed the friends he had lost, but eventually he would make new ones. Now all of his effort had to go into his poetry. Yale wouldn't re-admit him, but here at the Clymer Workshop he would have the opportunity to learn from Aaron Greene, who was probably the best living poet in America. Finally, he was in a good place.

Whistling, he covered the remainder of the campus in long, easy strides, his duffel bags balanced on his broad shoulders.

He found his room near the center of a narrow corridor that branched off a steep staircase. The room, like the rooms in the Tabard Inn, was barely large enough to contain two beds, a small chest of drawers, a nightstand, and a desk. A compactly-built man came in as Webb was setting down his duffel bags. "Hi, I'm Dan Hecker," he said, extending a manicured hand.

"Doug Webb."

"Glad I caught you before I went to look around," Hecker said. "It might be a good idea for us to make some… uh… plans for the use of the room."

"Plans for what?"

"The fairer sex," Hecker said. "We both can't bring women in at the same time, so we'll have to arrange some kind of signal for each other. I was thinking of a handkerchief tied around the doorknob, unless you have a better idea."

"A handkerchief is fine."

Hecker pulled a spotless white handkerchief out of a back pocket of his jeans. He grinned, revealing a set of perfectly-capped teeth. "If my instincts are right, this will be in tatters by the time the Workshop is over," he said, tossing the handkerchief onto the dresser. "I don't know why I didn't think of coming to a writers' conference before. There is no recreation except for readings and screwing."

"Are you a writer?" Webb asked dubiously.

"I'm a dentist."

"Then what are you doing here? This place is for people who are serious about becoming writers."

"I've written some poetry. Women love it. They're crazy about the idea of going to bed with a sensitive artist," Hecker said. "Dentistry has no charisma."

Webb's dark eyes flashed. "Then poetry is a game to you."

"Hey, don't get upset," Hecker said, stepping back. "Look, I'm a realist. I know damn well I'll never be a great poet, so why should I chase after something that's impossible for me to achieve? If I use the poetry I write to attract women, what difference does it make? I'm not hurting anyone."

"You're using poetry as a cover, pretending to be something that you're not."

"What kind of sex life do you think a lame guy like Byron would have had if he'd been a farmer or a blacksmith?" Hecker said.

"Byron could have been a tax collector and women would have fallen for him. But he didn't pretend to be anything other than what he was—a poet!"

"Neither do I. I'm a dentist who occasionally writes poetry, no competition for you serious fellows. Fair enough?" Hecker said, holding his hands up in a gesture of peace.

Webb stared at Hecker's hands for a moment. "I suppose," he said.

Hecker stepped in front of a wood-framed mirror that was hanging over the chest of drawers and expertly smoothed strands of brown hair over his receding hairline. "I'd better get going," he said. "With all the real poets around, I'll have to move fast. By the way, am I right in assuming that you're a poet?"

"Yeah," Webb said, opening a duffel bag.

"Women go for tall men. You've got a winning combination— height and poetry. You should have a great time here," Hecker said, heading for the door.

"Don't worry, I didn't come to the conference for sex, so I won't give you any competition," Webb said, adding with a smirk, "and I sure as hell won't claim that I'm a dentist!"

***

A young woman wearing a white shirt and navy slacks was standing in the center aisle of the reception area in the Chautauqua County Airport holding a white cardboard sign on which CLYMER WORKSHOP was lettered in black. Laura, Agatha, and Andrew Cox, who was feeling the after-effects of a turbulent descent and landing, walked toward her with their luggage. "You might as well sit down," the driver said when they told her they were going to the Workshop. "We have to wait for another plane."

She remained standing after they were seated, studying the trio of travelers with open, although not impolite, curiosity, as if their destination made them somewhat unusual and deserving of special attention.

"How long will it be?" Cox asked. His skin below his baseball cap was distinctly pasty in color.

"Just a few minutes," she said.

Cox excused himself and headed toward the restrooms. The plane they were waiting for landed before he returned, depositing four additional travelers to the group: a fair-skinned woman whose long black hair made her appear younger than her twenty-four years; a well-built, middle-aged man who was looking around with interest; and a white-haired couple, the man walking with a pronounced limp and a cane. The driver pulled a list out of her shirt pocket, then silently counted her passengers. "We're missing one," she said.

"He's here," said Laura, gesturing at Cox, who was coming out of the restroom.

They followed her through wide glass doors and set their luggage on the pavement. While they waited for the van Agatha approached the elderly gentleman, thrilled to be in such close proximity to the famous poet Aaron Greene, who was leaning on his cane. "Excuse me, Mr. Greene," she said, extending her hand. "My name is Agatha Risley. I want to tell you how much I have enjoyed reading and teaching your poems."

Greene nodded and shook her hand perfunctorily, his heavy lids moving slowly over glazed brown eyes, and then turned his head away without uttering a word.

A gray van pulled up. "Our ride is here," Laura said, trying to maneuver away from Cox, who had placed himself firmly at her side.

The driver opened the passenger doors, then walked to the back to open the rear doors for the luggage. When she started loading the suitcases, the well-built fellow offered to help after he saw Cox follow Laura into the van. "It's okay," she said, struggling with a bulging black suitcase with zippered outside compartments that looked ready to explode. "It's part of my job."

"I won't tell anyone," he said, helping her hoist the bag. "Whew! This one must be stuffed with rocks."

"Thanks," she said when they were finished. Then she hesitated.

"Are you a writer?"

"I'd like to be. Why do you ask?"

"I don't know. You don't seem like the rest of them, I guess."

"Is that good or bad?"

"Good," she said, her cheeks rosy with embarrassment. "What are you going to write?"

"A novel."

"What's your name?"

"Jerry Hofstrand."

"I'll remember it," she said.

Hofstrand took the empty seat next to the long-haired young woman, glancing appreciatively at her breasts, which were bulging extravagantly against her blue sweater; then he quickly looked away, guessing that she was approximately the age of one of his daughters. He introduced himself after the driver started the engine.

"I'm Diana Rothenberg," she said with a smile. "Are you in the military?"

"I was," he said. "How did you know?"

"When I was in graduate school, one of the visiting writers talked about training yourself to be observant if you want to be a novelist, so I've been working on it. You have perfect posture."

"Thank you for the compliment," he said, "and for the tip. I've learned something already!"

The van turned left on Main Street, traveled a short distance, then made a right on I-86 going east. Agatha had taken a seat in the back, wanting the extra room; she also felt a need to recover from Aaron Green's disinterested response to her praise of his work, which she considered bordering on rude. As they approached Cattaraugus County the land became noticeably hillier, lush green hills that dipped and swelled endlessly across the horizon as far as she could see. The van sliced through the mid-afternoon heat, finally turning off the interstate at the exit to the town of Randolph.

They were out of Randolph almost as quickly as they had entered it, moving southeast on narrow country roads that twisted over and around the hills like roller coaster tracks. Farms became sparser and more widely spaced; on a few there were Amish farmers wearing black hats tending their fields with their sons, the young males somberly-dressed miniatures of their fathers. It was difficult to see ahead. The road, swallowed by trees, seemed to unwind reluctantly. "We've really left civilization," Cox said nervously.

It's beautiful, Agatha thought, gazing out the window.

"Did anyone see a restaurant in that town we passed?" Cox said. "Or a movie theater?"

No one replied.

After they had traveled for miles between walls of dense forest, the van turned sharply left onto a dirt-and-gravel road. The air was still, soundless except for the van's tires crunching against the small stones. There was nothing to see but towering trees that blocked the sun until, finally, the darkness lifted. Ahead, the timber-and-stucco Tabard Inn loomed in Tudor splendor. "Good God!" Cox said. "We're in the wilderness. We're in the middle of nowhere!"

***

Laura pulled her suitcase up an oak staircase to the second floor of the Tabard Inn, her muscles straining with every step. By the time she reached the top, her blouse and shorts were damp with perspiration. Resting a moment, she looked down the hall, squinting to read brass numbers on dark doors spaced unevenly along yellowed-plaster walls. The corridor had a musty, mildewed smell despite an open window at the far end. Wrinkling her nose with distaste, she started down the hall, wondering as she had so many times during the past few days if she had made the right decision to come here.

Attending the conference had been her best friend Gretchen's idea. Gretchen was the one person in the world whom she trusted and relied on above all others. Their friendship began when they were assigned a room together as college freshmen. Toward the end of their freshman year her mother died; the death certificate said the cause of death was a ruptured intracerebral aneurysm, but she knew her mother really died from an explosion of loneliness and grief. Her father had died suddenly six years earlier. An only child, she felt unbearably alone and believed she couldn't have gotten through that time without Gretchen and the Strait family. The Straits opened their hearts and their home to her; they became her surrogate family, Gretchen as close as a blood sister.

After she'd finished the novel, which she'd written as a challenge to herself, she gave it to Gretchen, who was unreservedly enthusiastic. She'd quit her job and her lover of ten years, who was also her boss, finally putting to rest any hope that he would marry her. She was thirty-four years old and beginning to feel the pressure of time. She wanted a husband, children, a satisfying career. She wanted her novel published. But when she started researching the best way to accomplish this, what she learned was discouraging: there were thousands of people like her who couldn't get an agent to represent them; all they received for their efforts were form rejection letters. Even writers who had already been published received form rejection letters. The more she researched, the grimmer it looked. She read that agents and editors were looking for specific genres—thrillers, mysteries, women's fiction, crime novels—and her book was about two young orphans who struggle to stay together and survive in the early twentieth century, which didn't fit into any of the categories. When she told Gretchen that she'd decided to concentrate her efforts on looking for a new job, Gretchen convinced her to attend a writers' conference first to see if she could find a publishing connection there. The Clymer Workshop had a last minute opening and she took it.

The room she was assigned was the second last on the right. There were no locks on the doors. She knocked, waited, and knocked again before stepping inside. The room was crowded with furniture: mismatched maple beds on either side of a single window, a maple table that served as a night stand, a chest of drawers, and a small desk and chair consumed most of the floor space. The bed to her right had been made; the other bed had a pillow, sheets, two gray blankets, and two white towels piled on the mattress. She heaved her suitcase onto the unmade bed.

After she started unpacking, she was in no mood to meet her roommate. All but two hangers in the closet were hung with the stranger's clothes—expensive clothes, Laura noted as she draped her shorts and jeans, one on top of the other, onto the remaining hangers. She would have put the rest of her clothes in the chest of drawers, but there wasn't room; four out of the six drawers were stuffed with her roommate's knit tops, sweaters and lingerie, including the two deep bottom drawers. Maybe the clothes horse isn't used to sharing space with anyone, she thought, angrily setting her suitcase on the floor so she could make the bed.

The door opened as she was stuffing her pillow into the pillowcase. A blond woman approximately her age wearing khaki shorts, a pink knit top embroidered with a Ralph Lauren logo, and brown leather sandals breezed into the room. "Hi," she said, throwing a towel and a purse on the other bed. "You must be my roommate. I'm Gwen Eggleston."

"Laura Belmont."

Gwen pushed her damp towel aside and sat down. "Have you seen the bathrooms?"

"Not yet. I just arrived."

"You won't believe it! There are only two bathrooms in this wing, and one hasn't been modernized; it doesn't have a shower."

"How many bathrooms are there on the floor?"

"Six. Can you imagine? Six bathrooms!

"Six are better than two."

"I counted the rooms. If there are two people sharing each room, sixty-six people will be sharing six bathrooms," Gwen said, running her fingers through her frosted-blond hair as if to emphasize the gravity of her findings. "That means eleven people to a bathroom. It's horrendous!"

"It'll be uncomfortable but not impossible if everyone is considerate," Laura said, putting as much stress on *considerate* as she dared. "I don't think people come to a writers' conference expecting to relax in luxury."

"I suppose you're right," Gwen said, "but I didn't expect it to be *this* primitive—eleven people sharing one bathroom. Maybe they deliberately planned it this way so we would all know what it is like to suffer before we become artists."

Laura smiled. "If they really wanted us to suffer, they wouldn't have bothered with indoor plumbing."

Gwen grimaced, then laughed. "You remind me of my husband. Whenever I tell him about something awful, he always points out how it could be worse."

"He sounds terrific. It's hard to find a man who's an optimist."

"I don't know if I'd call him an optimist. He's a lawyer. They see things differently. He's always projecting what could happen, what might happen."

"That's what writers do. Does he write?"

"Just legal stuff. I'm going to be the writer in the family. He agreed to take care of the kids so I could come here."

"How many children do you have?"

"Three, two boys and a girl. Our housekeeper will watch them when they get home from day camp; he'll take over at night."

"How old are they?"

"The boys are ten and eight; my daughter is six," Gwen said, opening her purse. She withdrew her wallet, pulled out a picture, and handed it to Laura.

Laura gazed at three blond children whose faces smiled back at her. They were all handsome. The little girl was especially beautiful, her full face glowing with innocence that Laura responded to with longing. "They're gorgeous. I don't think I could leave them if they were mine," she said, returning the picture.

"You could if you were really serious about becoming a writer," Gwen said. "I'm totally committed. I went back to college to finish getting my degree when my daughter was two, and I'm not stopping now."

"Do you ever worry that she might resent it someday?"

"I can't be concerned about that now. My energy has to go into my writing. And if I make it, she'll have the satisfaction of seeing her mother's name on a shelf full of books.'

Your satisfaction or hers? Laura thought. "What do you write?"

"Fiction," Gwen said. "I've written short stories, and I'm working on a novel. What about you?"

"I just finished writing a novel."

"Good, then you're a participant like me. I didn't want to room with an observer."

"No, I'm an observer," Laura said, walking to the door. "And one of the things I've observed is that you've taken most of the hangers and drawer space. I'm going to count the bathrooms now. While I'm gone, you can clean your stuff out of one of the bottom drawers and rearrange your clothes in the closet so I can have a few more hangers."

"I didn't realize," Gwen said, her face clouding under her bottled blondness. "I guess we got off to a bad start."

"It could have been worse," Laura said, although she couldn't quite imagine how.

***

Agatha removed the last of her lingerie from her suitcase and carefully placed the items—a modest blue summer nightgown and a heavier gown in a soft shade of peach to wear on cool nights—in a dresser drawer. She had scrupulously divided the hangers in the closet and the drawer space so that her roommate wouldn't think she had taken advantage of her earlier arrival. There was no decision involved in her action; always grateful for acts of kindness she received from others, she had made consideration a habit, aware that thoughtful actions can be more eloquent than words.

Her suitcase wouldn't fit into the closet. She surveyed the room, looking for a spot to store it. There was no available place other than under one of the beds. Although she didn't care which bed she slept in, it might be important to her roommate. She shoved the suitcase into the closet as far as it would go and proceeded to make both beds, pulling and tucking the sheets as tightly as she could over the sagging mattresses.

There was nothing left to do except to look for Laura Belmont or read *THE WORKSHOP BULLETIN* while she waited for her roommate. She had concealed her disappointment when they were given room assignments: hers was in Tabard II; Laura's room was in the Tabard Inn. It would have been pleasant to have been able to share a room with Laura. She wondered how she would be received by others at the conference, whether they would be as nice to her as Laura had been or as indifferent as Andrew Cox. Like facing new students each year, new social situations were always difficult. It would be better, she decided, to stay in the room and read the conference newspaper, *THE WORKSHOP BULLETIN*. Laura had her own reasons for coming to the Workshop, and providing companionship to a homely, middle-aged spinster schoolteacher wasn't one of them.

A buxom woman of about fifty whose wrists were covered with gold bracelets appeared in the doorway as Agatha was reading about participants requesting specific staff members to read their work. "Excuse me," she said breathlessly, "is this room forty-five?"

"Yes," said Agatha, rising off the bed she'd been sitting on. She hurried to the door and extended her hand. "I'm Agatha Risley. You must be my roommate."

The woman, who was a head shorter, peered up at Agatha, her gray eyes more critical than friendly. "Claire Saxon," she said, briefly clasping Agatha's hand. Her over-sweet floral perfume was nearly overwhelming in the humid air. "I had an awful time getting my luggage up the stairs. You'd think they'd provide people to carry our bags for the prices we're paying."

Claire hoisted the larger of her two suitcases on the bed opposite the one Agatha had been sitting on. "The room is tiny," she said, glancing around, "and the wallpaper doesn't help. Brown is so depressing."

Agatha hadn't noticed the wallpaper, a nondescript print in beige and brown that was mottled with age. "I doubt that we'll be in the room much," she said. "I just finished reading THE WORKSHOP BULLETIN. There will be lectures and workshops all day, every day."

"Are there any social activities planned?"

"There is a reception today at five o'clock."

"I hope I'll have time to finish unpacking," Claire said, walking to the closet with an armful of clothes. She paused at the opening, looking with annoyance at Agatha's suitcase.

"Oh, I'm sorry," Agatha said, hurrying to remove the offending valise. "I would have put it under one of the beds, but I didn't know which one you wanted."

"There aren't enough hangers."

"Why don't you layer your things temporarily," Agatha suggested. "Later we can ask for more at the reception desk."

"I suppose." Claire sighed, her expression as blue as the eye shadow that was caked in the creases of her eyelids.

"Would you like me to go ask now?"

"Yes, thank you."

Claire was removing a bulging, oversize pink-flowered cosmetic bag from the smaller suitcase when Agatha returned. "They didn't have any hangers," she said. "I'm sorry."

"I should have expected it," Claire said, touching her forehead as though she were experiencing the onslaught of a severe headache. Her hands were plump, her nails polished in a bright shade of metallic pink. Scowling, she yanked the zipper tab on the cosmetic bag. The overstuffed bag popped open, shooting its contents in every direction: bottles containing Ambien, Motrin, buffered aspirin, Immodium, Correctol, Pepcid, penicillin tablets,

Claritin, Prozac, glucosamine, calcium, and black cohosh rolled on the floor with corn pads, Rolaids, Visine, sun screen lotion, Band-Aids, Cortaid ointment, Bactine, and a thermometer in a plastic case.

Agatha stared at the explosion of medication, amazed. There were enough supplies to stock an infirmary, she thought, stooping to pick up a roll of adhesive tape that had landed at her feet. "Are you ill?" she asked with concern.

"Certainly not," Claire said, taking the tape.

"But," Agatha said, blinking at her roommate, "all this…"

"I never go anywhere unprepared. My late husband and I did a considerable amount of traveling—Europe, South America. We always took everything we could possibly need with us."

"Oh," Agatha said, still impressed by the quantity of medication despite Claire's explanation. "Did your husband suffer from ill health?"

"Not until he got cancer. We were planning to go to China this summer. I didn't want to go by myself, so I decided to come here. I think I've made a mistake."

"Why do you say that when the conference hasn't even begun?"

"The accommodations, for one thing. Two people sharing a room that's the size of my walk-in closet at home," Claire said, gesturing at the walls with irritation. "Not enough hangers or drawer space, no private bathroom, no privacy anywhere."

"I'm sorry," said Agatha, beginning to feel like an intruder. "Maybe you'll feel differently when you go to the reception. It's starting in ten minutes."

"We'll probably be the oldest people there."

"There are a number of people our age, really," Agatha said in the earnest, coaxing tone she used when speaking to a recalcitrant student. "I saw them in the reception area."

"Men?"

"Yes," Agatha thinking of Jerry Hofstrand. Although he didn't seem to notice her, she had been aware of him in the van, his direct, no-nonsense attitude and easy humor. She hadn't dared check to see if he was wearing a wedding band. Whether he was married or not wouldn't make a difference; no man had ever looked at her without turning away.

"I'd better hurry," Claire said, stepping over pill bottles and corn pads on her way to the closet.

Agatha bent down and began picking up the fallen medical supplies. "Aren't you going?" Claire said, removing a purple blouse from a loaded hanger.

"I'll wait for you," Agatha said, rising with bottles and bandages in her hands.

Claire's gray eyes traveled from Agatha's bespectacled face to her bony ankles in a sweeping, critical glance. "Go ahead without me."

"I don't mind waiting."

"I get nervous when someone is waiting for me," Claire said firmly. "I'm sure you understand."

Agatha's chin trembled. "I believe I do," she managed to say before she left. Regardless of the countless times she'd been rejected, whether subtly or openly, each time it happened it still came as a cruel surprise. There was something about Claire, she thought as she walked slowly down the hall, a demanding self-centeredness that reminded her of her mother, the source of her most painful early memories of rejection. Her mother had often lamented that she looked like her father's side of the family, tall and ungainly, which was most unfortunate. No matter how hard she tried, she had never been able to please the woman who had given birth to her, not even when she had cared for her during her last, lingering illness: her mother had complained that the soup was too hot, that it was too cold, that nothing Agatha did was ever, ever right.

When Claire descended the staircase fifteen minutes later, she was irritated that no one was at the reception desk to take her request for a room change. She had no intention of tolerating that homely Agatha hovering around her, scaring away eligible men.

***

Michael Pierce's silver Maserati crossed the exit ramp of the interstate in seconds, car and driver moving forward as if constructed out of a single, sleek unit built for speed. At the end of the ramp Pierce braked to a stop, looked at his watch, and checked the odometer. He had made excellent time, averaging over seventy-five miles per hour without being stopped by the state police. Smiling, he patted the dashboard as if it were a partner sharing his pleasure in speed, an ally in his race with time. He turned onto the road that led to Randolph and looked sideways at his wife, Leila, who was sleeping in the passenger seat. Dressed in beige-and-white shorts and a white knit top, her head was tilted away from him, her mouth slightly open. As always he was stirred by her beauty, her glistening black hair and smooth tanned skin that stretched tautly over her high cheekbones. She was the most exotic-looking woman he had ever seen, fine-boned and perfectly-formed, her body a contradiction of softness and surprising strength. Even in the winter when she wasn't tan, her olive skin and bone structure made her appear slightly foreign, almost Indian or Eurasian. He resisted the temptation to touch her thigh and instead briefly rested his hand on the black leather seat.

Leila sighed, then moaned as if she were having a dream in which she was being hurt. The moan was low and plaintive, aimed, he felt, directly at him. He began to think about the subconscious, how the mind, released from inhibitions, expresses emotion openly—people crying in their sleep whose pride would not allow them to shed a tear when they were awake. His father, stoically waiting for death, weeping in his sleep, always surprised and embarrassed that his cheeks and pillow were wet with tears when he awakened. Characters in his books sleeping fitfully, screaming, thrashing, their dreams a tool to enhance the fiction. But the tool could quickly turn into a trap, technique substituting for plot, the risk of writing junk.

Leila moaned again, this time the moan a deep cry of longing that Pierce felt as if it were an accusation. He debated whether to awaken her or let her sleep until they arrived at the Workshop. It might be better to let her sleep, he thought, remembering the fight they'd had when he told her he'd decided to go to the conference after all, her justifiable anger, which he had accepted—somewhat begrudgingly, he realized now—both aware and unwilling to acknowledge that the Workshop wasn't what they were really arguing about. A baby. She was moaning for his child, for the infant he refused to give her. And he could not, would not, tell her why. He'd tried to make it up to her in other ways—the new house in Connecticut, a decorator to help her chose furniture, rugs, anything she desired. Money was meaningless now. His books were earning more than he could ever spend. Material things had never been important anyway. He had the only luxury he wanted—the Maserati. He didn't give a damn about the rest. His work, his books were all that mattered. And Leila. Her constant demands to have a baby were destroying their marriage. Why couldn't she be content? Why, when he had told her before they were married that he would never have children, she had not only accepted it but had seemed relieved?

When the Maserati's tires hit the dirt-and-gravel road leading to the Workshop, Leila opened her eyes and stretched her arms. "Sorry I dozed off," she said. "The ride must have seemed endless without company."

"I turned the radio on for a while hoping to get a local disc jockey."

"Any luck?"

He shook his head. "There was talk radio on every station I could get, bombastic white men appealing to the meanest instincts in people."

"I wonder if disc jockeys knew how important they were to novelists, keeping them tuned in to pop culture."

"I doubt that they'd care. If we all listened at once, we wouldn't make an appreciable difference in their ratings."

"I wouldn't be too sure about that. Half the people in America dream about writing a book."

"Dreaming and writing aren't the same thing."

"True," she said, "but the Workshop is filled every year."

He smiled. "With the most ambitious dreamers."

Leila didn't smile. "The sky is almost black. It looks like we're heading straight toward the center of a storm."

"We probably are," he said, turning into the Workshop campus.

***

People started gathering for the welcoming reception before five o'clock. Most came singly or in pairs, the pairs newly acquainted roommates bolstering each other so they wouldn't be venturing into strange territory alone. They walked through a grass-and-concrete courtyard nestled between the horseshoe wings of the Tabard Inn, down a sloping expanse of sun-browned grass to a wide flagstone terrace. The terrace was ringed with white Adirondack chairs; on one end a long table was set up, where young waitresses were placing stacks of clear plastic glasses next to three capacious punch bowls.

Laura, still dressed in the shorts and blouse she had been wearing all day, started down the grassy slope. She would have liked to shower and change, but returning to her room meant the possibility of another encounter with Gwen. Seeing women wearing sundresses and cool cotton skirts reminded her of her roommate's selfishness, and her lips compressed with irritation.

It seemed to Laura that a majority of the people on the terrace were middle-aged women, most of them standing stiffly, their faces fixed in self-conscious smiles. Rather than approach them, she found an empty chair near the punch table. "Is this taken?" she asked a fellow sitting in the next chair.

"No," he said without looking up.

"I'm Laura Belmont," she said, sitting down.

"Stan Dynarski."

"I guess we're early."

He nodded.

"Have you been to a writers' conference before?"

He nodded again.

You aren't a conversationalist, she thought, looking sideways at him. She guessed he was somewhere in his thirties; he was blond and muscular and obviously tense, sitting hunched forward as if he were waiting for someone. His profile would have been attractive if it weren't for the exceptionally thick-edged lenses in his eyeglasses, which were exposed in rimless frames. "Do you write prose or poetry?" she asked, trying again.

"Fiction," he said, turning to look at her. His face was full and rather flat, his features strongly Slavic. "And you?"

"I brought a novel," she said. "I applied too late to come as a participant. I hope I can get someone on the staff to read it."

"You and everyone else."

"You're not very encouraging," Laura said with a nervous laugh.

"Do you really want to know what this place is about?" he said. "Courting favor. Hustling. Everyone, including the staff, is trying to make the right connections. Look around: what do you see?"

The terrace had filled with people while they were talking. Groups had begun to form, each group gathered around one person like planets clustered around a sun. Although she didn't recognize some of them, she guessed that the individuals who were surrounded were all staff members. "It isn't unusual for people who want to become writers to be anxious to talk to published novelists and poets."

"They're not just talking," he said. "They're fawning and hustling, like I told you."

"Why are you so bitter?"

"See that guy in the green shirt?" he said, pointing. "That's Andrew Cox. He's the same age I am, thirty-three. I'm as good a writer as he is, maybe better, and I can't get published because I don't have the connections he has, or the WASP name, or the hook." Dynarski's voice rasped with barely controlled anger.

"What do you mean by a hook?"

"When Cox was eleven years old, he saw his father murdered during a bank holdup. It was big news at the time, and Cox refreshed everyone's memory with his first book—a novel about a boy who sees his father murdered in a bank holdup. Nothing in the damn book, not even the title—*Holdup*—was original, but he and his New York publisher called it fiction and made it news all over again."

Laura had her own reason for disliking Andrew Cox, but she thought Stan Dynarski was being incredibly naive. "There is nothing unusual about a writer drawing from his life for his fiction. It's done all the time."

"Drawing from your life is one thing; describing your father's brains spewed on a marble floor is something else. It takes a certain kind of person to do that—a vulture."

"Has he written anything since?"

"Yeah," Dynarski said bitterly, "his second book came out in the spring before 9/11. It was on the bestseller list for over a year."

"What is it about?"

"Terrorists," he said. "The critics call him a 'master of mindless violence.'"

"Why did you come here if you feel so negatively about this place?"

"To see Michael Pierce," he said. "I want him to read my novel."

"Which one is Michael Pierce?"

"He isn't here yet," Dynarski said.

Stan Dynarski wasn't the only one on the terrace looking for Michael Pierce. Talbot had been fielding questions about Pierce's absence since he had arrived at the reception. He would have preferred to remain in his office, standing by the window, but his presence at the gathering was mandatory. He moved mechanically through the crowd, glancing anxiously at the grassy slope, praying that Pierce would appear.

Dan Hecker was also looking for someone, but as he told Doug Webb, the connection he was interested in making was definitely not literary. There weren't as many prospects as he had anticipated. Although he had recently celebrated his fortieth birthday, he felt closer to thirty and preferred women who were younger, in their mid-to-late twenties. As he moved between groups on the terrace, he saw to his disappointment that most of the females were over thirty; a few looked older than his mother, who had just had her face lifted at the age of sixty-five. He noticed Webb talking to a creamy-skinned young woman who had long black hair and breasts that he mentally labeled *outstanding*. Webb was doing well for a guy who professed that he was here strictly for his poetry, Hecker thought, spotting a brunette on the lawn who looked like she might be a possibility.

The reception was half over when it became windy. Women's sundresses billowed above their knees, and the waitresses struggled hopelessly with the plastic cups on the punch table, which tumbled down and rolled hollowly across the flagstones. Leaves on the surrounding trees were flipped upward, their silver undersides shining like new coins. An unusually strong gust briefly parted the black clouds. The hum of conversations stopped as people looked up, startled by the sudden brightness of the sun. At that moment a man and woman began descending the sloping lawn, their slender frames bathed in golden light. The wind whipped the woman's gleaming black hair; the man's iron-gray curls shone in the spotlight of sun. Several people gasped; others stared open-mouthed at Leila and Michael Pierce as if the pair had materialized out of a surrealistic painting.

The opening between the clouds closed by the time the Pierces reached the terrace, murky light once again settling over the reception. Talbot was the first to greet them. "You're as beautiful as ever," he said, kissing Leila on the cheek. He extended his hand to Pierce. "Thanks for coming. I knew you wouldn't let me down."

Pierce's eyes flickered with amusement. "We didn't decide to come until yesterday."

Talbot's pulse skipped; the bones in his legs felt like paper straws. "Oh… well… I'm glad you did."

"I haven't seen a schedule," Pierce said. "Who is lecturing first, me or Nettles?"

"Nettles, on Friday. You'll be lecturing Saturday morning. I thought you'd prefer it that way."

Pierce nodded his agreement. "I see him over there. I guess it's as good a time as any to meet the opposition."

"I'll introduce you," Talbot offered quickly, anxious to circumvent friction between the two men. Getting Pierce to come to the Workshop years ago had clinched his job as director; now he needed Eric Nettles to help him get his poems published.

"I'll introduce myself," Pierce said.

"Remember, you're both here for the same reason, to teach…"

It was too late. Pierce was already working his way through the crowd.

Eric Nettles was sitting on a lawn chair, talking animatedly to conference members. Pierce stood on the fringe of the group and waited until the novelist was finished. Then he stepped forward, saying, "Excuse me."

Nettles stood up as people moved aside. The two men faced each other, pausing for a moment before they shook hands. Although Pierce was appreciably taller than Nettles, the older man's leonine head and barrel chest made him appear the more powerful of the two. "That was quite an entrance you made," Nettles said. "A bit contrived though, don't you think?"

"It was rather Gothic," Pierce agreed, smiling wryly. "But I have no argument with the elements when they work that effectively."

Before Nettles could reply, there was a tremendous clap of thunder followed by a flash of lightening that flooded the Workshop campus with brilliant light. The people on the terrace blinked as though temporarily blinded. The light vanished as quickly as it came, plunging them into darkness. There was another clap of thunder so intense that the flagstones beneath their feet vibrated. Then, without so much as a few warning drops, it began to rain.

There was a rush toward the Tabard Inn. Dry and hard after days without moisture, the parched lawn couldn't absorb the sudden downpour. Women struggled to scale the slick grass and slid, pushed back by the wind and driving rain, their wet clothes clinging to their bodies. Agatha, barely able to see through her rain-streaked glasses, floundered like a bird with broken wings until someone grabbed her hand and pulled her up the slope. "Thank you," she gasped. She removed her glasses to look at her rescuer and saw Jerry Hofstrand, who was starting down the slope to help someone else. How nice, she thought. Still holding her glasses, she trudged to her room squinting like a waterlogged, myopic crane.

***

The tables in the dining room, Hackett Hall, were filled when Diana Rothenberg came downstairs for dinner. She stood beneath the arched entrance debating whether or not to go in. The bathroom where she had showered had killed her appetite: steamy and water-spotted, the tiled floor covered with webs of strangers' hair, she'd had all she could do not to gag. Even after she had showered, she still didn't feel clean. It was as though the previous occupants' grime had not only settled in the room, but on her.

She couldn't decide. Hackett Hall was both appealing and formidable. Light from a massive wrought-iron chandelier suspended from the vaulted ceiling reflected on the leaded glass windows, making them glisten like sheets of cut crystal; rough beams on the walls added to the room's charm. But the Hall was huge, and the only empty seat she spotted was at a table where her roommate, Marsha Pratter, was sitting. Marsha had been one of the first in line for a bathroom; she had talked compulsively while she waited, asking questions that were prying and tactless. Embarrassed for the woman, and for herself because she was Marsha's roommate, she had left to wait at a different bathroom, taking the last place in a longer line.

Webb saw Diana, stood up, and crossed Hackett Hall in long strides. She could feel his presence before he reached her, a hypnotic energy that was as incredible as his size. Her stomach growled. "How was dinner?" she asked, hoping he hadn't heard.

"A waitress said it's Salisbury steak, but it looks like cow chips and tastes worse. I'm not sticking around for dessert."

She grimaced. "I think I'll get a sandwich at the Shed."

"I'll go with you. I have to get something from my car."

They walked to the back entrance of the Inn. It was overcast and drizzling. "Would you mind waiting while I run upstairs to get an umbrella?" she asked, looking at the threatening sky. "I don't want to take any chances after that last downpour."

His dark eyes followed her as she ran, her overfull breasts bouncing provocatively under her plum-colored summer sweater. He had been so absorbed in their conversation at the reception, both excited by her intelligence and relieved that she wasn't a fraud like Dan Hecker, that he hadn't focused on her figure. Blood rushed to his groin as he remembered Hecker's white handkerchief.

They went to the parking lot first. Diana glanced at the Volkswagen, then at him, and smiled at the disparity in their sizes. He crouched and slid onto the front seat; although his movements were quick, she saw him open the glove compartment and remove pills from a bottle. After he got out of the car, he stuffed the capsules into a pocket of his jeans. "Allergies," he said.

They started talking about allergies, a topic that led them to writers who were physicians. "Chekhov," she said, "but he never really practiced. It would have been a waste if he had."

"William Carlos Williams, a general practitioner from New Jersey," Webb said excitedly. He began reciting:

"so much depends
upon
a red wheel
barrow..."

By the time he was finished, he had completely forgotten the capsules in his pocket.

***

When the waitress came to remove the dinner plates from the table where Laura, Gwen, Agatha, Marsha Pratter, Stan Dynarski, Dan Hecker, and Marshall Stoddard were sitting, there was a temporary lull in conversation. Gwen had rushed to take a seat at the table when she had spotted Laura, who was sitting opposite Stoddard. Gwen hadn't connected with anyone she'd encountered at the welcoming reception. Unable to get near the staff members, most of the people she'd met were older women who were either divorced or separated or in unhappy relationships, all of them hoping that attending the conference would somehow change their luck in life. Talking to them had left her with an unsettled feeling that she couldn't seem to shake. Although their initial meeting hadn't gone well, at least she knew Laura, and she was certain she would have an opportunity to talk to Stoddard.

She was wrong. From the start of the meal Marsha, a mousey-looking woman whose curly hair had frizzed in the humidity, had been relentlessly questioning everyone at the table, much to Stoddard's relief. A bearded, rotund man whose shaved scalp exposed a sausage-like ring of fat at the base of his head, he was the only non-fiction writer at the Workshop. He found dining with conference members a chore; every year he wrote Talbot suggesting a separate dining room for the staff. While Marsha asked everyone where they came from, what they did for a living, what they wrote, were they published, were they observers or participants, he was relieved of the necessity of speaking to them.

There was an exhausted silence at the table when the waitress, a thin girl in her teens whose expression was frazzled, returned with a loaded tray. Laura was one of the first to be served her dessert, a brownie sitting in a puddle of melting vanilla ice cream. "No, thank you," she said. "Would it be possible for me to just have a dish of ice cream?"

"I'll try," the waitress said, her bony shoulders drooping in response to the special request.

"Don't you like brownies?" Marsha asked after the girl left.

"I like them," Laura said.

"Then why didn't you want it?" Marsha said.

"The brownies have nuts in them," Laura said, exasperation creeping into her voice. "I'm allergic to nuts."

Seeing Stan Dynarski start to snicker, Agatha said, "Marsha, are you here as an observer or a participant?"

"An observer," Marsha said. "Last year I had a short story published in a local magazine. I've written more stories since, but they haven't been published yet. I'd like to have enough for a collection. I don't come in contact with writers. I teach the sixth grade…"

Agatha's intention was to distract Marsha so she wouldn't notice Dynarski's snicker. She didn't expect Marsha to start talking about herself nonstop. Laura was the first to get up to leave. "I guess that ice cream isn't coming."

Stoddard followed, then Hecker, Dynarski and Gwen. Agatha excused herself, thinking as she hurried out of Hackett Hall, that she had never encountered anyone as lonely and starved for attention as Marsha Pratter.

***

Laura was putting a sweater into the bottom dresser drawer when Gwen came into the room. "I hope you can fit all your stuff in," Gwen said. "I had to put some things back in my suitcase, but my husband says I always take too much."

"It's tight but manageable," Laura said, slipping her feet into sneakers so she could leave as quickly as possible. She did not want to go to the evening reading with Gwen.

Laura saw Agatha on the path that led to the theater and called to her. Agatha turned and, smiling broadly, stopped and waited, holding a black umbrella in one hand and her blue canvas tote bag in the other.

"I didn't get a chance to talk to you at dinner," Laura said. "Are you all settled?"

"Yes," Agatha said, stepping around a puddle.

Laura leaped over a wide patch of mud and landed gracefully. "I wish we could have roomed together. I'm beginning to think we're the only balanced people here."

"It is more intense than I expected, but that could be because it's the first day, and everyone is adjusting," Agatha said. "Your roommate Gwen seems pleasant."

"She's making an effort. We didn't get off to a good start."

Laura paused. "Agatha, at the airport you said you'd be willing to read my manuscript. Is that offer still open? I'd like to give you a few chapters. Please, don't hesitate to say no if you feel it's an imposition."

"I would be delighted to read it!" Agatha said, beaming.

"Thanks. I'll give it to you after the program tonight," Laura said. "Tell me about your roommate. You haven't said a word about her."

Agatha's pace quickened. "I hope we get good seats," she said, blinking rapidly.

"Is she that bad?" Laura asked gently.

Agatha's lower lip trembled. "She made it quite clear that she doesn't want to associate with me."

"What is her name?"

"Claire Saxon."

"Claire Saxon is a fool," Laura said, patting Agatha's arm as they entered the Circle Theater.

They chose seats in the center front, several rows back from an elevated platform on which stood a lectern and microphone. The platform, like the walls and floor of the semi-circular building, was constructed of wide-planked wood that had darkened with age. If it weren't for sophisticated track lighting suspended from wood beams and row upon row of wood folding chairs, the rustic building could easily have been mistaken for a peculiarly-shaped, oversize hunting lodge rather than a theater.

Talbot, dressed in jeans and a short-sleeve striped shirt, leaned against a wall near the double-door entrance, watching the theater fill. Chairs scraped; the steady hum of conversations rose in volume, then subsided, each time a staff member entered; moths, lured inside by the brightness, circled the overhead lights in a death dance. When almost every chair was taken except for a few in the back, he started to close the doors and happened to glance at Dee Dee, who was sitting at the end of the front row. She shook her head and gestured, as if wiping her brow. As usual, she was right: it was too hot to keep the doors closed. He left them open, briefly nodding his thanks as he walked past her to the steps of the platform.

It wasn't necessary to ask for their attention. A prolonged squeal from the microphone when he turned it on silenced everyone in the theater. His eyes traveled up and down the rows of people, pausing briefly as he located various staff members—Eric Nettles, Marshall Stoddard sitting large and lumpy in an aisle chair, Andrew Cox, Aaron Greene, frowzy Sara Newkirk, Phyllis Baran—while he removed papers that were under a heavy plaque on the lectern. The air felt thick on his arms and face, dense with humidity and expectation. They were all waiting. Waiting to be officially welcomed. Waiting despite the heat and their weariness for the program to begin. Over two hundred people waiting for him to unlock the door to their dreams. Deeply moved, he forgot for a moment all the work, the planning and scheming that had brought him to this place. Suddenly the speech he had prepared seemed trite. Slipping the papers beneath the plaque, he began…

"While he was clearing brush from the side of the road to the Inn this past spring, our caretaker, Frank Stryker, hit a hard object. Excited, he called to tell me that he found a plaque. He guessed it had probably been on the property since the Workshop had opened seventy-four years ago, and that it had been obscured by dense vegetation for so long that no one remembered it. I asked him to send the plaque to me.

"It arrived a few days later, black and encrusted with dirt. I took the plaque home, and my wife and I cleaned it. As the letters emerged, we began to feel as though we were uncovering a mystery. But when we were finished, I realized that we knew only part of the story. The plaque said: *The Clymer Workshop, Gift of Benjamin Clymer in Memory of Garnet and John Clymer.*

"Who was Benjamin Clymer? Who were Garnet and John Clymer? Benjamin's parents? His children?

"Curious, I tried to find out as much as I could about Benjamin Clymer, the man who donated the land and money to establish this conference, and his family. My hours of research yielded nothing. There was no mention of him in Axton's archives, no record of a Clymer having attended the college. It was strange, I thought. Why would a man who was not an alumnus of Axton College give the school such a generous gift?

"Then I turned to Otis Hackett's papers. Otis Hackett was the president of Axton College at the time the gift from Benjamin Clymer was received. He was a legend in his own right, an imposing man who is still regarded as the greatest of Axton's administrators. Dr. Hackett is credited as being the moving force behind the Clymer Workshop. His accomplishment is as awesome today as it was in 1930, for he managed, by the sheer force of his commitment and conviction, to clear this land and build the Tabard Inn in a matter of months, in the throes of the Depression. Although his accomplishment was quickly recognized and frequently praised, he remained strangely silent and, one must suppose, characteristically modest about what he had done until his retirement. At that time, he simply said when pressed in an interview, 'The Clymer Workshop is the result of one man's dream and another man's tenacity.'

"I searched through Otis Hackett's papers without success. Although he had had a strong sense of history—he had kept all of his records and correspondence, which he had generously donated to the school—there was no mention of Benjamin Clymer in any of them. It was as if someone had gone through the papers, deliberately removing anything that pertained to Mr. Clymer and the Workshop. Why? I wondered. Why, when Benjamin Clymer had given a substantial gift which had become, in a very real sense, a living legacy, had he remained almost anonymous, as elusive as a ghost?

"Unfortunately, I had no time for further research. All I have to offer you is Otis Hackett's statement: *'The Clymer Workshop is the result of one man's dream and another man's tenacity.'*

"I think we can safely assume that the tenacity Dr. Hackett spoke of was his own. As for the dream, I would like to believe that it was Benjamin Clymer's.

"If I were a novelist, I would be tempted to construct Benjamin Clymer's life. There are so many possibilities that could be explored, so many ways in which he could be imagined. But since I am not, I offer the story to you. All I ask is a percentage of your royalties."

Smiling, Talbot paused while the audience chuckled. "Instead, I would like you to think about dreams and tenacity, the material out of which art is made. Without them, we wouldn't have poems and short stories, novels and plays. Without them, we wouldn't be here tonight."

Talbot lifted the brass plaque and held it for the conference members to see. The raised letters gleamed, reflecting the overhead lights. "Tomorrow morning this plaque will be placed on the Tabard Inn, next to the front entrance. I would like to think that, if Benjamin Clymer were here with us, he would be pleased. On his behalf, on this beautiful land he generously gave for our use, I welcome you to the Clymer Workshop with these lines from Coleridge's poem, *To Nature*…"

Still holding the plaque, he recited from memory:

"So I will build my altar in the fields,
And the blue sky my fretted dome shall be,
And the sweet fragrance that the wild flower yields
Shall be the incense I will yield to Thee,
Thee only God! And Thou shalt not despise
Even me, the priest of this poor sacrifice."

There was a moment of silence before the audience applauded. The silence was tender, almost reverent, as if over two hundred souls were paying quiet homage to a benefactor they knew only by name, a man many of them had already begun imagining. Dee Dee gazed at Talbot through a mist of tears, forgetting her anger and the many times he had disappointed her, in love with him all over again.

Talbot swallowed, as moved by his eloquence as his audience. Then, lowering the plaque, he acknowledged their applause with a smile before speaking again. "It is now my pleasure to introduce Terence Hill, whose reading will officially open the seventy-fourth Workshop. Mr. Hill is the author of two books of poetry, *Hear Me, Brother* and *Catch The Day*. Critics have praised his strong sense of craft, his sensitivity to language, his eye for detail. A recipient of a National Endowment fellowship, he teaches at Berkeley. Please welcome Terence Hill."

Hill and his wife, a stunning woman who had tawny skin and elaborately braided hair, were sitting in the front row, the only African Americans in the theater. The poet rose and, carrying two slender books and a folder, walked up the steps to the platform.

The conference members watched Hill intently, particularly the women, as he arranged his materials for the reading on the lectern. Dressed in white slacks and a navy broadcloth shirt open halfway down his muscular chest, exposing his rich brown skin, he had features that looked sculpted; a broad forehead, high cheekbones, and a strong jaw line made him exceptionally handsome. But when he began to read, first giving each group of poems a pithy introduction that was neither self-serving nor self-conscious, it was clear that his poems were as carefully crafted and lyrical as the critics had noted.

Talbot listened to Hill with a mixture of envy and relief. He had invited the poet to come to the Workshop hoping to draw African Americans. Sensitive to criticism that the staff and attendees at the conference were overwhelmingly white, the trustees had insisted that this change. Although there were still no African American applicants, Hill's picture appeared prominently in the Clymer Workshop brochure, giving the sought after impression of integration. And as Talbot pointed out to the trustees, there would be eight Asian Americans attending this year, which was certainly progress.

When Hill finished reading at nine fifteen, Talbot clapped as enthusiastically as anyone in the audience, grinning like a man who had ordered an item from a written description in a catalog to find, upon its delivery, that it exceeded his highest expectations.

The outside air provided little relief from the stickiness inside the theater. Although it was no longer drizzling, it was still warm and humid. A stream of people headed toward the Shed to buy soft drinks at the snack bar; others lingered inside waiting to compliment Terence Hill on his reading; some straggled to their rooms, exhausted after a day of traveling and meeting new people. Two black-haired, beautiful young women waited for their husbands—Cheryl Hill, seated inside the theater, and Leila Pierce, leaning against a tree watching conference members milling around Michael.

Leila looked at the people surrounding her husband, unable to distinguish their faces in the darkness. It was the same every year, she thought, at every conference, at every college they visited. So many people paying homage to Michael Pierce. Six years ago she had been one of them, a college senior eager to talk to the famous visiting writer. She had sat in his seminar, committing to memory every word he uttered. She had waited to speak to him before class, after class, at his office. He was the only man she had ever wanted. Just to be with him, to share his life would be the fulfillment of her life. She had chased him shamelessly. Two years later he divorced his wife and married her. Now, four years after they were married, the constant repetition of crowds surrounding him had made them all look the same. Still, among them there might be a young woman like herself, as obsessed and determined as she had been.

She sighed and shook her head. Even her thoughts were infected with repetition. Why had he changed his mind, deciding at the last minute to come to the Workshop when he had been so adamant about not going? The new house was shaping up nicely since their return from England. Why did he want to leave to come here? What could he possibly hope to accomplish? To discover another Tolstoy? To teach as he had taught for years, spreading his gospel of strong plots and strong characters, trying to fix what he felt was wrong with American fiction? It certainly wasn't for the five thousand dollars he was being paid.

The group around him started to disperse. She saw him jogging toward her, his white shirt a lantern in the darkness. "I'm sorry," he said. "I couldn't get away. You know how it is."

They walked down the hard-packed dirt road that ran between the Tabard Inn and Tabard II. "That was quite a welcoming speech Roy gave tonight," he said. "I didn't think he had it in him. It was the first time he didn't sound like a cheerleader delivering a rah-rah Clymer Workshop pep talk."

"He really got me interested in Benjamin Clymer. Even the man's name is appealing."

"Do you want to do some digging?"

"What for?" she said, beaming the flashlight she was carrying away from them so he couldn't see the defensiveness in her face.

"You're usually bored here after a couple of days."

"I detest library research. You know that."

"I have a feeling that the library isn't the place to look."

"Where, then?"

"If it were me, I'd start with the neighboring farms, then move on to Randolph. I'd talk to people whose families have lived around here for generations."

"What could they possibly know? Benjamin Clymer has been dead for years."

"Oral history," he said, "people passing stories down from one generation to the next. It has always been an undervalued resource."

"Do you honestly think anyone around here would know about Benjamin Clymer?" she said skeptically.

"There's a strong chance. These are rural people, farmers, and they pass their land to their children. I doubt that there are many outsiders around."

"I suppose," she said, wondering if he were humoring her by suggesting busy work to keep her occupied so she wouldn't be miserable for the next week.

They turned left onto a road that led to the staff buildings, which were separated from the rest of the campus by a wide stream. At sometime during the first twenty years of the Workshop's existence, the stream had been dubbed Barrier Creek by a disgruntled participant, who acidly observed that, in its irregular path, the creek neatly separated the published writers from the unpublished writers. As they approached a wooden bridge, she said, "Let's stop at Clemens for a drink."

"I think I'll pass. I want to keep my head clear."

The boards on the bridge creaked, as if protesting their weight. "You know what working at night does to you," she said, unable to keep disappointment and frustration out of her voice. "You can't turn it off. You'll be tossing all night, writing and revising in your head."

"It won't happen this time, I promise."

"Don't make promises you can't keep."

"I never do, at least not knowingly."

"Really?" she said. "What about your promise that we wouldn't be coming to the Workshop this year? Are you telling me that I'm in Connecticut now?"

"That wasn't a promise, Leila," he said, putting his arm around her. "It was a statement. I said I wasn't going, and then I changed my mind."

The windows of Clemens were beaming welcoming rectangles of light. "See you later," she said, pulling away.

***

Gwen was sitting at the desk in their room when Laura came in. "I'm requesting Michael Pierce first," Gwen said, her pen poised over a clean sheet of paper, "but I imagine everyone else is, too. I'll put Eric Nettles second, even though I really don't understand his books."

"Then why are you requesting him?" Laura said, pulling her suitcase out from under the bed.

"Because his work is important, because it's literature," Gwen sputtered, "and *literature* is what this place is about."

"Really," Laura said, taking her cell phone from the suitcase.

" I can't decide between Phyllis Baran and Marshall Stoddard. It's an important choice."

"What about Merle Ackerley?"

"Merle Ackerley!" Gwen said with such disgust that she looked as if she'd been told to eat worms. "No one wants Merle Ackerley! His stories are in *Redbook*!"

Laura was tempted to ask what was wrong with *Redbook*, but she could see from Gwen's expression that her question would place her in the same category as the magazine. "So I've heard,"

50

she said.

Gwen's cell phone, which was on the desk, rang after Laura left. It was her husband, Tom. "The kids were hoping you'd call," he said.

"I couldn't. There was dinner, then a reading; there isn't a lot of free time here. The place is almost primitive—hardly any bathrooms or closet space. I feel like I'm camping out."

"Then you'll appreciate home more," he said. "When is Michael Pierce going to read your stuff?"

"I'm not sure I'll get Michael Pierce. I'm going to request him, but I have a feeling everyone else is, too. He's the most sought-after writer here."

There was an uncomfortable silence before he spoke. "You told me that you absolutely had to go to this conference because you needed Michael Pierce to criticize your work. You said he'd know what you needed to do to get published. So now who's going to look at it?"

"I don't know. It could be Michael Pierce, but there are no guarantees."

"You need to come home with something, Gwen. You've been writing for over two years, treating me and the kids like we come last on your list of priorities, and you have nothing to show for it."

"I got a *glowing* rejection letter from *The New Yorker*."

"It was still a rejection," he said.

The connection started breaking up. "Make sure you call tomorrow so the kids can talk to you. Jess misses you terribly. She keeps asking for Mommy."

Then the connection was gone.

Laura was having better luck outside with her cell phone. "Gretchen?" she said. "I hope I'm not calling too late."

"I thought about you all day. How is the conference? Are you enjoying it?"

"I'm surviving," Laura said. "It's pretty intense here. The participants are uptight about who is going to criticize their work."

"Have you met anyone on the staff who you can ask to read your novel?"

"Just Andrew Cox, and I'm staying far away from him. He's a pig."

"What?"

"He took the seat next to me on the van coming here and wasted no time trying to work his hand up my thigh."

"What did you do?"

"The only thing I could do: I removed it. If we'd been alone, I would have slugged him."

"At least your day wasn't boring."

"It certainly wasn't, except for endlessly telling people my name and that I'm an observer," Laura said, laughing. "There are a lot of guys here looking for sex. But I did meet an exceptionally nice woman, Agatha Risley. She's a high school English teacher. I gave her the first chapters to read. I brought a couple of sets."

"Shouldn't you be trying to give the chapters to someone on the staff?" Gretchen said. "The goal is to make a connection that will help you get published, or at least show you the way."

"I couldn't get near anyone on the staff today except for Cox."

"Maybe tomorrow you'll have an opportunity. Call me if you get a chance. I want to hear what's happening."

"Gretchen… in case I never told you, you were a terrific roommate."

"What inspired this?"

"The roommate I have here is a piece of work. She talks about literature like it's a religion spelled with a capital L."

Gretchen laughed. "You're going to have an interesting time."

"It's looking that way," Laura said, thinking that the word *challenging* could be substituted for interesting, which is what she suspected.

***

Hecker climbed the stairs casually, resisting an impulse to take them two at a time. He was afraid he would blow it if he appeared too eager. The brunette he'd met at the reception was willing. Even better, she was married so he wouldn't have to deal with guilt or recriminations later. At the end of the Workshop they would go their separate ways. It was a damn good thing he'd thought of the handkerchief so Webb wouldn't walk in on them.

He peered down either side of the dimly lighted hall, feeling the beginnings of an erection as he imagined her naked. The corridor was clear, but…

Hecker raced down the hall, stopped in front of the closed door to his room and stared slack-jawed, his penis shrinking in his bikini briefs. There, looped around the doorknob, was his white handkerchief!

****

Growing up in Lincoln, Nebraska, Agatha was accustomed to the sound of trains. But the distant sounds of the locomotives west of town were no competition for Claire Saxon's snoring. Claire's snores were long and loud, complete with an ear-splitting whistle that filled their stifling room.

It was a wonder Claire hadn't wakened everyone at their end of the corridor, Agatha thought, wearily hauling herself out of bed. She put on a robe and her glasses, took her flashlight and Laura's manila envelope, and quietly left the room.

There was a desk with a lamp and chair at the far end of the hall. Agatha settled in and started to read.

It was a matter of chance that Galen Riordan saw Duff O'Reilly kill his mother. Galen woke with an earache not long after he went to bed. Gritting his teeth from the pain, he went into the hallway and heard voices. He stood at the top of the stairs to listen, a sandy-haired fourteen-year-old whose long, skinny legs looked vulnerable below his nightshirt, until he was sure that the person his mother was talking to was Duff O'Reilly. He wasn't about to present himself to a stranger in his bed clothes.

They were arguing about money from his father's livery business. O'Reilly and his father had been partners. After his father's death a year ago, O'Reilly said he would buy out his father's share of the business in monthly payments. The first couple of payments were regular, but then there were missed payments. He knew his mother was worried about money. He also knew that she was afraid of Duff O'Reilly. He was a big, fierce-looking man who had bushy black eyebrows that rose up at the ends like dark wings, and he had the florid complexion of a hard drinker.

They were in the kitchen. He could hear them clearly despite his throbbing ear. "Ed's share of the livery is worth more than the payments you've given me."

"You've gotten yer fair share," O'Reilly said, the words coming out slurred.

"I'll have to hire an attorney then. There's no other way for me

to handle this."

"You'll do no such thing!"

Galen had just reached the doorway when he saw one of O'Reilly's large, hairy hands holding his mother by the neck. With his other hand, he pushed her head back. There was a horrible cracking sound. O'Reilly let go of her and she slid to the floor.

From the odd angle in which her head was laying Galen knew that O'Reilly had killed her. He froze when O'Reilly turned in his direction and started lumbering toward him.

Galen ran though the hallway, grabbing coats off hooks to throw in O'Reilly's path. He was about to knock over the table by the front door before he raced outside when O'Reilly stumbled and crashed to the floor.

O'Reilly was out cold, either from drink or a gash on his head that was dripping blood. Galen knew he had to move fast. More than anything he wanted to go into the kitchen to his mother but he couldn't, there wasn't time. Choking back tears, he hurried upstairs, pulled on a pair of wool pants, and ran to his mother's room. Quickly, he opened the top drawer of her dresser, took out a small black leather purse, then rushed to his little sister's room. He found her sleeping on her back, her face framed in blond ringlets, her lips curled in a smile as if she were enjoying a sweet dream. "Betsy, you have to get up," he whispered as loud as he dared, pulling back the red-checkered comforter that was covering her. "We have to go now."

Her eyelids fluttered. "Go?"

"Stand up," he whispered urgently. "I'm going to carry you."

Betsy fastened herself to him like a clam, her arms around his neck, her legs around his waist. He grabbed the comforter and wrapped it around her, flipping a corner over her head so she wouldn't see O'Reilly. He stopped only once—to step into his galoshes—before rushing out the door into the snowy night. To his relief he saw that O'Reilly had come with a horse and an open two-seat buggy that belonged to the livery. "We're going for a ride," he said, feeling Betsy's breath, warm and trusting, against his neck as he brushed snow off the seat.

"Where's Mama? We have to get Mama."

What could he tell her? She just turned seven. He couldn't think. The frigid air had sharpened the pain in his ear. A tear escaped from the corner of his eye; he shivered beneath his nightshirt. "Mama's resting," he said as they started off into the night.

Despite the late hour and her exhaustion, Agatha finished the chapters she'd been given, wanting more.

***

In Hawthorne, the staff residence between Whitman and Melville, Pierce lay awake beside his sleeping wife. They were both naked, lying uncovered on the double bed. Although the windows were open, there was no breeze. Leila was sleeping on her stomach, breathing deeply, her black hair damp with perspiration. He rolled from his side onto his back and put his hands under his head, staring into the darkness. The chapter still wasn't right, he thought, going over what he had written, sentence by sentence. His legs moved restlessly, mirroring the activity in his mind. Suddenly he smiled and sat upright. Leila stirred. He glanced at her shadowy figure guiltily, remembering what she had said earlier in the evening: *You can't turn it off.* He rolled onto his stomach, his feet itching to cross the room to the desk. Maybe he could take the laptop into the bathroom, close the door and do the revision now. But it might wake her. It would have to wait until morning.

The middle of the mattress sagged. He felt as if he were slipping onto a trough and moved closer to the edge. The sensation of slipping triggered a memory of his father, who in the last weeks of his life was too weak to adjust his body on the hospital bed that had been set up for him in the living room. He father's body would slip to one side, his head and shoulders angling toward the floor; he or his mother would straighten him, and his father's eyes would flicker with embarrassed gratitude. Such a strong man reduced to a baby's helplessness, he thought, that once powerful body nothing but bones and flaccid skin. It would happen to him. Accelerated atherosclerosis, his death sentence written in his genes. No Pierce male had lived beyond the age of fifty-three. The lucky ones, his grandfather and Uncle Lionel, had died quickly of ruptured aortic aneurysms. But his father and Uncle John, robust, healthy men until their heart attacks, had lingered for months, pale, skeletal, short of breath, so weak they couldn't climb the stairs to die in their own beds. Inheriting his small frame from his mother's side, the Maitlands, was no protection. He had the Pierce body chemistry. He knew when his hair started turning gray at twenty, like all the Pierce males. Even with by-pass surgery and heart transplants, there was no guarantee. He watched his weight, stopped eating red meat, jogged for miles in winter slush and summer heat. How many years would it all give him? Maybe ten with luck. Ten years to complete a body of work, to race with the thickening of his vessel walls. So little time, so little time…

***

❧ WORKSHOP BULLETIN ❧

VOL. 74, NO.2   THE CLYMER WORKSHOP   AUGUST 12, 2004

GOOD MORNING!

The local weather forecasters predict a warm, sunny day with the temperature and humidity beginning to drop early in the evening to give us a refreshingly cool night.

MORNING PROGRAM

9:30 A.M. Poetry Lecture
(Roy Talbot)
10:30 A.M. Fiction Lecture
(Phyllis Baran)

Roy Talbot's lecture, "Striving for Organic Unity," will focus on Samuel Taylor Coleridge's theory that the poem be approached as a "work of nature." Phyllis Baran will discuss "The Writer's Life as a Source for Fiction."

AFTERNOON PROGRAM

2:00 P.M. Poetry Lecture
(Terence Hill)

3:00 P.M. Guest Lecture
(Ross Girvin)
4:30 P.M. Mixer in the Shed

EVENING READING

Andrew Cox will read his fiction. Mr. Cox is the author of *Holdup*. His latest novel, *Sequence Of Terror*, was on *The New York Times* bestseller list for over a year.

GUEST

We are privileged to welcome Ross Girvin, editor and book critic for *News Break* magazine. Mr. Girvin will discuss reviewing and will give tips to the would-be reviewers among us.

REMINDER

All participants must deliver their manuscripts to the Workshop office by 9:00 A.M. today. Manuscripts must be contained in boxes or manila envelopes. Loose papers in open folders will not be accepted due to the difficulty of handling and the risk of loss. Requests for specific staff members may be attached: list first, second and third choices. It is assumed that participants have copies of their submitted work.

The manuscript assignments will be posted at 4:00 P.M. on the bulletin board opposite the Workshop office and on the bulletin board near the entrance to the sitting room.

PHOTOCOPYING

A limited amount of photocopying can be handled in the Workshop office. Work to be photocopied must be given to a member of the office staff who is authorized to use the photocopy machine. The charge is fifteen cents per copy.

TIDBIT

"I don't know what to do. I thought I'd be able to submit my entire novel. It's impossible to select an excerpt from an epic!"

"Envy is not unknown among writers..."
Mordecai Richler

Chapter II

The glacier that slowly inched its way across the land that was to eventually belong to Benjamin Clymer scooped out the property like the inside of a teacup, the valley enclosed by gently sloping hills rising to meet the sky. In the winter, the hills formed a protective barrier that cut the force of biting winds. But in the summer, the same hills trapped moist air within the valley for hours, condensing it into thick gray fog. Known as valley-fog phenomenon, the opaque gray air would lay in the valley like a fallen cloud until the sun burned it off.

At dawn Douglas Webb left Dickens dressed in a gray T-shirt and deeper gray jogging shorts. He had been up most of the night, his mind racing from one thought to another like an over-wound clock ticking hours away in the space of minutes. He was exhilarated, for he had composed three poems, writing and revising them line-by-line in his head, while his roommate, Dan Hecker, slept. His accomplishment was marred only by a nagging awareness that his supercharged mental activity was a warning signal that he was entering a mood swing he might not be able to control.

Curious as to where it led, he ran on the path that followed Barrier Creek, the gray of his T-shirt blending with the fog so completely that at a short distance all one could see of him was his head, arms and legs moving steadily through the mist. His head and neck appeared to be floating, free and independent from his body, as if carried on a cloud.

His breath was effortless and even as his sneakers hit the damp earth. The foggy landscape reminded him of a tunnel, cool and dark and mysterious. He thought of Diana. She had asked if she could read his poems. He had promised to give them to her, but now he wasn't sure. The history of his life was in his poetry, his very soul was exposed. She would know everything—his expulsion from Yale, his suicide attempt, his hospitalizations, his mother's suicide. Diana was brighter and more sensitive than any female he had ever met. What if her attitude toward him changed? People would forgive almost any illness as long as it was physical; they would accept a failure of the body but not of the mind. He'd have to explain it to her before she read the poems. He wanted her to understand that his problem was a metabolic disorder, but he would have to figure out how to explain it without revealing that he had to take lithium carbonate, a natural salt that controlled manic-depression. He'd also tell her that it was hereditary. But he wouldn't stress the genetic aspect, just mention it to explain his mother's suicide. Instead, he'd tell her about his medication, which was as easy to take as aspirin. Maybe he'd take two Eskalith after breakfast to make up for yesterday. He could feel a high building. Sex with Diana and three poems in one night! A damn shame to cut that energy. He'd take one pill, then wait to see how it worked. What if she wanted to know the name of the illness? It was as risky to tell her that he was bi-polar as it was to say manic-depression. Maybe she wouldn't ask.

Webb ran until he came to an area that was roped off. Jogging in place, he debated whether to continue on or go back. He decided to explore the area the next time and turned back, running as if weightless in the fog, his head floating in the mist above his damp gray T-shirt.

***

Marshall Stoddard was waiting on the porch at Clemens to ambush another jogger, Michael Pierce. After years of attending the conference with Pierce, he knew the novelist's habits well: Pierce ran every day, either early in the morning or late in the afternoon, regardless of the weather. Stoddard wasn't happy being out early in the day. He much preferred the evening, when he could sit with a glass in his hand. He was fond of saying that his favorite sport was walking from the bar in his den to his easy chair.

At least he had freedom this year; his wife was taking a cruise with her sister, who was recently widowed. In the past she had always accompanied him to the Workshop, watching for potential transgressions though her zealousness puzzled him since they hadn't had sex in years. Their marriage could best be described as a prolonged affair of accommodation. Her money was the lure that had caught him; at the time he believed that love and children would follow, but he soon learned that money wasn't the soil from which happiness sprung. The marriage was barren in every respect, and the fortune that he assumed would last indefinitely was nearly gone, thus an additional source of worry and bickering. His books hadn't brought the financial success they needed, so he had come to the conference again out of necessity, glad to renew old contacts while at the same time disdainful of the job he was hired to do. He was not interested in the scribbling of would-be writers; nor did it bother him that he didn't possess even the most basic of teaching skills. He thought of himself as a critic and writer, far above such pedestrian concerns.

The fog had begun to dissipate. Squinting through his eyeglasses, he finally spotted a slim figure wearing a white T-shirt at the bend in the road. With surprising speed for a man of his size, he hurried off the porch, hoping as Pierce approached that it would look as if he'd been walking nonchalantly. The unaccustomed exertion left a telltale film of perspiration on his bald scalp that he swiped at with a handkerchief.

"Marshall," Pierce said, slowing to a trot as he approached, "What brings you out so early?"

"Insomnia," Stoddard said. "*Places At The Table* isn't doing well. I called my editor on Monday. He says the book is moving slowly."

"Sometimes slow starts, if they're steady, can be positive. Books that build on word-of-mouth recommendations can do exceptionally well. Did he say they're going to continue advertising?"

"He wouldn't make any promises. When I asked, he reminded me of every ad they had taken out. He sounded like he was reading from a completed shopping list. They've also postponed my book tour." Stoddard paused, pursing his fleshy lips. "But you don't have these problems."

Stoddard's tone was accusatory. "I've had my share," Pierce said defensively. "My first novel had only eight reviews and one small ad in *Publisher's Weekly*. People didn't know the book existed, and my publisher didn't give a damn."

"Ah," Stoddard said, raising his index finger as if he had made a point. "I thought you might have forgotten about that."

"Marshall, what exactly are you trying to say?"

"Your second book might have suffered the same fate as your first if it weren't for my review in *Sir*."

"You know I'm grateful and always have been. After so many years, I don't see the point in bringing it up again, unless…"

"Unless what?" Stoddard coaxed.

Pierce looked at him, incredulous. "Are you intimating that my review of *Places At The Table* is to blame for the problems you're having?"

"You said it, I didn't."

Pierce's eyes flashed. "But you believe it!"

"The review could have been more enthusiastic," Stoddard said in a high-pitched whine of resentment.

"That review was positive! I overlooked more than I should have. You're so out of line it's pathetic! I'm going to try to forget we had this conversation, but it won't be easy!"

Stoddard didn't move after Pierce trotted off. Pierce had no reason to react that way, he thought. He was the one who'd been injured. Nothing was working out the way it should—not the book, not the conference. That woman last night, refusing him. Stupid broad had acted like she'd been insulted. She wouldn't have refused Pierce. If Pierce had even hinted an interest, she would have been quick to oblige him. He'd handed Pierce the world and now the guy was angry. Ingratitude! Now he supposed he'd have to apologize. Well, he wouldn't, not unless it became necessary. There was a problem with his reading. He'd read from *Places At The Table* last year and the year before, but that was pre-publication so it was considered new work. Other than the raw beginning of a manuscript that wasn't going anywhere, *Places At The Table* was all he had to read from this year as well. The people attending the conference wouldn't know the difference, but his colleagues would. Reading from *Places At The Table* again would be a public admission that he hadn't been able to create anything new, and reading from the manuscript he'd been struggling with would mean public embarrassment. He should have considered that before agreeing to attend. Pierce would probably dazzle everyone by reading from a new novel as he did year after year.

Stoddard trudged to the Inn for breakfast, adding more resentment and envy to an already packed emotional storehouse of the same.

Pierce was also rattled by the confrontation. He didn't want to be reminded of what Stoddard's review of his second novel had done for his career. As he showered and dressed, he thought about his first novel, how the sparse reviews it had received had been scattered, coming every once in a while like afterthoughts instead of close together to get the public's attention. He had watched other novels that he knew weren't as good as his, some that were nothing but trash in his opinion, propelled by some mysterious force to the bestseller lists. At the time he was teaching a few classes at a small college in the mid-West; his first wife was supporting them working as an admissions counselor at the school so he would have time to write. So much hope had been invested in that book. Although the disappointment had been devastating, he continued working on his second novel, believing this novel was better than his first. Still, when the book came out he steeled himself for another round of disappointment. Instead, the weight of Stoddard's early review praising the novel seemed to draw a rush of other laudatory reviews, the reviewers all following the critic's lead as though they were eager to be included among the discerning who recognized a brilliant new talent. At the time he'd felt grateful to Stoddard, aware that without the critic's review his second book would have suffered the same fate as his first novel. What he hadn't anticipated was that at their first meeting at a publisher's party, Stoddard made it clear that he expected payment in kind. Twice he'd felt obligated to write reviews of Stoddard's books that he'd felt were dishonest, reviews that he'd managed to forget until he'd been reminded of them. It would take some effort not to let this latest reminder spoil his day.

***

Marsha Pratter stood between the beds in the room she shared with Diana, alternately glancing at her watch and her roommate. It was seven forty-five; people were starting to go downstairs for breakfast, and Diana was still sound asleep. Marsha pursed her lips, debating what to do. Her expression, pinched with irritation and indecision, accentuated her weak chin and close-set eyes. She had seen Diana sitting with an unusually tall fellow at the reading. When the reading was over, she had watched the pair leave together, talking earnestly. She had tried to catch up with them, hoping they might include her in their conversation or accompany her to the Shed (she had gone to the reading alone), but by the time she was outside the theater, they were gone. It was difficult enough coming to the Workshop knowing no one; at the very least she had expected a companionable roommate, someone in their mid-to-late thirties or early forties. Instead, she had gotten Diana, who was young and self-contained, almost aloof.

Some people have everything, Marsha thought, looking at Diana. The young woman was sleeping on her stomach; her fair skin was slightly flushed, her long hair flowed across the pillow like a skein of black silk. Marsha touched her own sensibly-short hair in a wistful, sub-conscious gesture. Even as a teenager she wasn't able to wear her hair long; it bushed out and made her look like a clown. She sighed enviously. Where had Diana gone last night? She had searched for her everywhere; she hadn't seen the tall fellow either. Could they have been…? Her eyes bright with curiosity, she said, "Diana, Diana, you'd better get up."

"Mmmmm," Diana said, burying her face in the pillow.

"It's seven forty-five. If you don't hurry, you'll miss breakfast."

Diana raised her head and looked at the aged brown wallpaper as if she hadn't seen it before. Then she focused on Marsha and remembered. "Where were you last night?" Marsha said.

The hungry curiosity in her roommate's eyes forced Diana into full consciousness. "Around," she said, suppressing a smile as she recalled her evening with Doug Webb.

"Around where?" Marsha asked greedily.

"Around here."

"Where around here? I looked everywhere. What time did you get in? It had to be after one o'clock because I was up. I had trouble falling asleep."

"That's a shame."

"What's a shame?"

"That you had trouble falling asleep."

"I still don't know when you got in."

"Does it really make a difference?"

"Yes, of course it does."

"Why?"

"Because," Marsha said, "because…"

Diana sat up. "Marsha," she said kindly, "I'm a big girl. I can take care of myself. We're roommates, but we have to give each other some privacy."

Marsha's receding chin retreated into her neck. "Well, if that's how you feel," she sputtered, starting for the door.

"Please, don't misunderstand me, it's just that…" Diana said, struggling for a tactful way to reclaim the situation, "most people don't like to be questioned. It's better if you wait for them to volunteer information."

Marsha turned, her sallow complexion coloring. "Are you saying that I should mind my own business, that I ask too many questions? Are you telling me that I'm nosey?"

Exactly, Diana thought, remembering Marsha's relentless quizzing of everyone in line to use the bathroom after yesterday's storm. But from the injured expression on Marsha's face, she knew that her agreement would be disastrous. "Just try to relax," she said lamely. "This is a new situation for all of us. It takes time to adjust."

"I suppose," Marsha said, somewhat mollified.

After Marsha left, Diana lay back on her pillow thinking of Doug Webb. She had never met anyone as magnetic, as alive. She closed her eyes, reliving their evening together. They had made love twice; his energy had seemed inexhaustible. The second time he had lasted longer than she had thought possible for a man, bringing her to climax over and over again, which had never happened to her before. When he had first entered her she had stiffened, afraid that her body couldn't accommodate him. Now she wondered if she could ever be satisfied with less.

***

Agatha took a copy of THE WORKSHOP BULLETIN off a pile stacked on a carved mahogany table that was next to the arched entrance to Hackett Hall. Although she would have liked to scan it, she folded the paper and slipped it into her tote bag, wanting to be seated at a table before her roommate came down to breakfast.

"Are you waiting for someone?" a trim, freckled woman asked as Agatha peered inside the dining room.

"No, I was just looking for a spot at one of the tables."

"I see some places at a table near the window. Shall we take them?"

"Yes," Agatha said, instantly warming to the woman's friendly manner. "I'm Agatha Risley."

"Nan Abington," she said with a smile.

They crossed Hackett Hall and took two empty chairs at the far end of the table. "I usually don't eat breakfast, but I'm starving this morning," Nan said after they gave their order to a curly-haired waitress. "Either it's this country air or that awful dinner they served us last night."

"It's probably both," Agatha said. "I always eat breakfast. I couldn't get through my morning classes if I didn't."

"Do you teach English?"

"Yes," Agatha said, "to high school juniors and seniors."

"You're brave. I'd be afraid to face a classroom filled with teenagers."

"I teach honors classes. My students are very bright and conscientious. Sometimes I think they'd learn as much or more if I weren't there."

"I doubt it. You must be a great teacher to be given the best classes."

"I've just been at it for a long time," Agatha said, hoping that Nan didn't think she'd been bragging. "Do you work?"

"I was a social worker until our son was born. Then I had a second son and was a full-time mom until they were in school all day. I worked in my husband's business until I started writing."

"A novel?"

"Yes, and an agent accepted the manuscript a month ago. I think my husband and sons are even happier than I am," Nan said, smiling. "They're relieved to have the book out of the house."

The waitress returned with granola for Nan and French toast for Agatha. Their conversation was so pleasant that Agatha hardly noticed that the French toast was soggy.

***

After he ate a quick breakfast, Jerry Hofstrand went back to the room he shared with Stan Dynarski. He had put off delivering his manuscript to the Workshop office because he hadn't decided which writers to list as his first, second, and third choices. His first choice was Michael Pierce, but from the talk he'd heard since he'd arrived, Pierce was everyone's first choice. A recently retired career officer in the Air Force, he knew that the odds of having his request granted were against him. Experienced in the acceptance and denial of requests, both as an applicant and as an administrator evaluating them, he had learned to calculate risks and act accordingly. It would be wiser, he thought, to list Pierce second, putting another writer first whom he wouldn't find objectionable. He mentally ran through the list of fiction writers on the staff: Pierce, Eric Nettles, Phyllis Baran, Marshall Stoddard, Andrew Cox, and Merle Ackerley. Nettles was definitely out despite his big name; he had tried to read one of his books and had found it impossible to understand. He knew nothing about Baran and Ackerley other than what he'd read in the Workshop brochure and wasn't willing to take a chance with either one. That left Stoddard and Cox, neither of whom he could work up any enthusiasm for. Of the two, he supposed Cox would be the better choice; he'd read *Holdup* and had found it gripping though too graphically violent for his taste. Also, Cox's second novel about terrorists had been well-received and had made it to the best-seller list. Stoddard's books hadn't gone anywhere, and of the three he had written, only one was a novel. That settled it: he'd put Cox first, Pierce second, and Stoddard last. It wasn't a list he could get excited about except for Pierce, but he'd have to accept it. If he'd known he would be this far along in his novel, he would have applied to Bread Loaf early in the spring, where the staff was probably better.

He was standing at the maple dresser, where he'd left a piece of paper and a pencil next to a large manila envelope, when the door opened. It was Dynarski. "Haven't you turned your manuscript in yet?" Dynarski said, eyeing the envelope.

"There's time."

"Who are you requesting?"

"Cox or Pierce."

Dynarski sat down on his bed. The faded jeans and white T-shirt he was wearing accentuated his over-developed biceps and powerful thighs. "What have you got there?" he asked, gesturing at the envelope.

"A novel."

"What's it about?"

"A man who works at the Pentagon. He stumbles onto a conspiracy that's funneling millions of dollars into private hands."

"A thriller?" Dynarski said, his voice tinged with condescension.

"I suppose you could technically call it a thriller," Hofstrand replied. Actually, he hoped to chronicle a man's disillusionment with the system he had believed in and the moral dilemma with which he would ultimately struggle.

"Then you'd probably be better off with Cox."

"Why?" Hofstrand said, his pencil poised over the paper.

"Pierce is a serious writer. I don't think you'll have a chance at him with a commercial manuscript."

"Is that so?" Hofstrand studied Dynarski as if trying to decide something. "What makes certain subjects serious and others commercial?"

Dynarski's eyes shone like iridescent gray beads behind the thick lenses in his glasses. "You're kidding," he said.

"No, I mean it. Why would a novel about a man working in the Pentagon be considered less worthy than a novel about, say… an eccentric family?"

"The genre, for one thing. Thrillers are escapist reading."

"Do you mean that if a novel is entertaining, then it isn't art?"

"Serious fiction has to do more than just entertain," Dynarski said impatiently. He shook his head, looking at Hofstrand as if the older man had no business coming to the Workshop.

"I think I understand. What you mean by fluff could be a novel that's written for serialization in a newspaper or a magazine."

"Exactly."

"Maybe someone should have told that to Isaac Bashevis Singer."

"What are you talking about?"

"Singer's novels were originally published as serials in a Jewish newspaper."

Dynarski scowled. "Where did you hear that?"

"On television," Hofstrand said, writing rapidly. "Years ago Singer was interviewed. He said the weekly deadline kept him going."

"I don't believe it!"

"Why would he lie? He'd already won the Nobel Prize in Literature," Hofstrand said, removing the top sheet of his manuscript from the manila envelope. Smiling, he attached the list to the typed page with a paperclip. The list read:

Pierce

Pierce
Pierce

Hofstrand was still smiling when he delivered his manuscript to the Workshop office. But as he walked to the Circle Theater to hear the first lecture, his victory began to lose its shine. In his eagerness to prove Dynarski wrong, he had succumbed to the moment, surrendering his carefully calculated odds at getting a staff member of his choosing. He won the battle, he thought with regret, and lost his perspective on the war.

***

When Leila came back to their bedroom after breakfast, she found Pierce at the desk typing on his laptop. Despite the open windows, the air in the room was still close from yesterday's humidity. "We have to go," she said.

Pierce turned at the sound of her voice. Although he was less than ten feet away from her physically, she knew from the distant look in his eyes that his mind was miles away, his consciousness planted in a fictional world known only to him, impossible for her to reach. "Roy's lecture will be starting soon," she said. "If we don't leave now, we'll be late."

"Go without me."

"Why should I have to suffer through another boring Coleridge lecture? If you're not going, I'm not going, either."

"One of us has to go."

"Since you're being paid, you're elected!" she said, her voice rising.

"Be reasonable, Leila. I don't want to argue with you. I've already had trouble with Marshall this morning."

"What kind of trouble?"

"He ambushed me after my run. He tried to make it look like we met accidentally, but he must have been waiting for me on the porch at Clemens because he was sweating from exertion when he met me on the road. He probably ran from the porch, which would be a year's worth of exercise for him. His book isn't selling and he's blaming my review. He feels that I haven't paid him back sufficiently for his review years ago in *Sir*."

"You gave his book a better review than it deserved."

"That's what I told him, but he'll never believe it. He thinks he's responsible for my success. I've never felt such resentment! He's blaming me for every book he hasn't sold."

She recalled clumsy advances Stoddard had made to her in the past. On one occasion, when he was drunk, he had confided that his wife was frigid; another time he had confessed that the editor of his first book had been more interested in his reputation as a critic than in his manuscript. He had been more annoying than threatening, almost pathetic, but he got nasty when she politely rejected him. "Probably he was just venting. If you pretend it didn't happen, he won't be embarrassed and maybe it'll pass," she said, hiding her concern. Marshall's ego bruised easily; Michael shouldn't have told him the review was generous. "Really, we have to go now."

"I told you, I'm not going. I want to finish this chapter."

"Then finish it!"

She quickly crossed the room, grabbed her purse off the dresser, and started fishing inside the canvas-and-leather bag for her keys. "Where are you going?" he said.

"I'm taking your suggestion. I'm going to track Benjamin Clymer's ghost."

He watched her walk to the door, her tanned legs long and elegant beneath white shorts. "You'd better change."

"Why?"

"You'll be knocking on the doors of farmhouses. When the farmers' wives see those sexy legs, they might not want to introduce you to their husbands."

"What should I wear? It's hot."

"Put on something modest that will give you credibility," he said, wondering if he should go to Talbot's lecture. His absence would be noticed and probably resented. But Roy owed him, he decided, scrolling to an earlier page he had typed.

She threw her purse on the bed and pulled off her top and shorts, which she stuffed into a dresser drawer. Walking to the closet in her low-cut bra and bikini underpants, she was aware that he was lost again. If she stood at the desk and ripped off her bra and pants he wouldn't notice, she thought, snatching a blouse in a rich shade of coral and beige linen slacks off hangers. She watched him as she dressed. He was hunched over the laptop, his fingers moving rapidly, as if all of his energy, every fiber of his being was concentrated in the machine.

***

Dee Dee sat in her usual seat at the end of the first row near the double doors, watching Workshop members file into the Circle Theater. It was already uncomfortably warm and would soon be unbearable from the additional heat given off by several hundred people. She had at least a half-dozen excuses for not attending Talbot's lecture, not including the most justifiable reason—that she knew every word he was going to say because she had typed the entire speech—but she sat, perspiring in a pink blouse and matching capri pants (a new outfit that a sales woman had assured her did not make her look like Petunia Pig), her hair frizzier than usual because of the humidity, her round face lit with anticipation. It did not matter to her that she had heard him deliver a similar lecture last year or the year before or the year before that. If pressed, she couldn't have told when she had begun feeling protective toward him, aware that his obsession with Coleridge had become a staff joke; nor would her loyalty allow her to admit, even to herself, the real reason for his continued dependence upon his scholarly work: Roy Talbot talked about Coleridge's poetry because he was not a recognized poet in his own right; he lacked the credibility that comes from accomplishment, the respect granted to men of talent. Her love for him more than excused his deficiencies. This year she had taken the bold step of assigning herself the room next to his in Melville, knowing that she couldn't wait much longer. After suffering through his affairs with other women, it finally had to be her turn!

Laura slipped into an empty seat in the back of the theater next to Webb as the lecture was about to start. She had stopped at the Shed to get orange juice because she couldn't drink the juice served at breakfast, which was watery and had a metallic taste.

Adjusting the microphone, Talbot cleared his throat. "I would like to begin with a quote from Samuel Taylor Coleridge's *Biographia Literaria*, also known as *Biographical Sketches of my Literary Life and Opinions*. 'Poetry', Coleridge wrote, 'even that of the loftiest and, seemingly, that of the wildest odes...'"

As the lecture continued, Webb began to move restlessly, shuffling his oversize feet, crossing and re-crossing his legs, rubbing his hands, twiddling his thumbs. Diana, who was sitting on his other side, kept glancing at him as if admonishing him to sit still. "What a waste of time," he muttered.

Laura nodded her agreement, then put her finger to her lips, a gesture for which Diana mouthed *thank you.*

"Think of the poem as a work of nature, as complete unto itself as a tree or flower," Talbot went on, unaware that people's eyes were glazed with boredom. When he finally concluded with a lengthy quote, the audience clapped politely at first, then more vigorously, as if collectively embarrassed by their lack of enthusiasm. Interpreting the swell of applause as a measure of the success of his lecture, Talbot stood behind the lectern beaming with the thought that Coleridge had never failed him. After he left the platform he watched people file out, his expression becoming increasingly cold as the theater emptied. His eyes were the color of frost when Dee Dee, who had remained in her seat, walked up to him. "Have you seen Michael?" he said. "Or Leila?"

"I don't think so," she said, trying to remember. "The lecture…"

He accepted her compliments on his speech without hearing them, nodding automatically like an over-wound mechanical toy. Pierce has gone too far this time, he thought, seething. He wouldn't let this insult go unacknowledged! But he wouldn't confront Pierce; that would be the wrong move, an admission that he'd been wounded by this public slight. There was a better way. For every decent manuscript Pierce got, he'd be given another that was a piece of junk!

Outside the theater, Laura introduced herself to Webb and Diana. "It's good to know that I wasn't the only one who was bored in there."

"That guy babbled for almost an hour about nothing; it was all literary nitpicking. Not one of Coleridge's daemonic poems was even mentioned!"

"I gather you're a poet."

"Yes," Webb replied, but before he could say more his roommate came up to them. "I'd like to talk to you," Hecker said to Webb, so agitated that he didn't acknowledge Laura and Diana.

"Alone," Hecker said assertively.

Laura and Diana started to walk away. "You don't have to go," Webb said.

"We don't mind," said Diana.

As the two women headed for a large oak to get some shade, Diana said, "I think he's Doug's roommate. He's a dentist who writes poetry to attract women. His theory is that poetry has more charisma than dentistry."

Laura laughed. "Theories don't always work. I met him last night. He was so obviously on the make that it would have been funny if it hadn't also been irritating."

Hecker waited to speak until he felt Diana and Laura were a good distance away. "Look, that handkerchief idea isn't going to work."

"It worked fine last night."

"For you," Hecker growled. "Not only were you using the room when I came up with someone, but you didn't remove the handkerchief until after two o'clock. I was wandering around half the goddamn night with no place to sleep!"

"Sorry, my mind wasn't on the time."

"The handkerchief arrangement is off! Finished!"

"What do you suggest, then?"

"Alternate nights," Hecker said. "Last night was yours and tonight is mine. But within limits. By midnight the room has to be free."

Webb's eyes glinted with amusement. "What if one of us runs over the time limit?"

"Either it's midnight or the deal is off!"

"All right," Webb agreed.

Hecker looked at the tall poet and frowned, as if the matter still weren't settled. "Don't you sleep? You weren't in the room when I finally got to bed, and you were gone when I got up."

"Some people need less sleep than others," Webb said before walking away.

***

The second lecturer of the morning, Phyllis Baran, a slender, brown-haired woman approaching forty whose prettiness had begun to fade, took her place behind the lectern at ten thirty. While she adjusted the microphone with efficiency that belied her nervousness, her eyes happened to focus on a lean fellow sitting in an aisle seat. His chiseled features and distant, dreamy expression reminded her so strongly of her former husband that her breath caught in her throat. It had been years since their marriage had been annulled and he had been committed to an asylum, years since she had re-lived that traumatic time in the pages of her first novel. No, it isn't an omen, she told herself, it's just a coincidence, nothing more.

She fingered the typed pages of her lecture, fighting panic while the conference members waited expectantly. She had to go through with this, she thought, a public confession that her fiction was autobiographical. It would be her absolution for years of denying the source of her work. Then she would be able to write again. It wouldn't matter that she had used up her life, as a hateful critic had said in his review of her last book. She would prove him wrong, she would prove everyone wrong who had ever doubted her.

Phyllis Baran gripped the edges of the lectern with trembling hands. "I would like," she began, "to tell you the story of my life."

It was a perfect opening, for there are no words more beguiling than the promise of a story. The audience listened intently as she led them through her impoverished childhood in Johnstown, Pennsylvania, her college years at Duke University, and her failed marriage to a young, aristocratic Southerner who had concealed from her his long struggle with mental illness. She told her history well, recounting her life with humor that she had failed to recognize while she had lived it. The detested smokestacks of her childhood became comforting objects in a lost landscape, her college years infused with romance instead of grinding work to keep her scholarship…

Talbot, who had been about to leave to work on the manuscript assignments, stood in the doorway stunned as he listened to Baran's admission. Why had she chosen to reveal this at the Workshop? he wondered. He didn't like surprises, though he doubted that it would have any effect on the conference.

Sitting toward the back of the theater, Pierce nodded imperceptibly. He had long suspected that Baran's fiction was autobiographical and had considered her a lightweight, a writer lacking an imagination, which was, in his opinion, an insurmountable weakness. Still, he was puzzled as to why she was giving a lecture that was a public confession, not that he believed even half of what she'd said.

The thoughts of other writers on the staff were similar to

Pierce's. Although they were surprised at her admission after her years of denial, they all clapped heartily at the end of the lecture. Baran accepted their applause with relief, believing it meant their approval of what she had done.

Leaving the theater with a stream of people, Laura met Agatha, who was with the trim, freckled woman she had met at breakfast. "This is Nan Abington," Agatha said, introducing them. "Nan is a novelist like you, Laura."

"I'm delighted to meet you," Nan said warmly. "Agatha told me that you've written a wonderful novel."

Laura responded with a modest smile.

"What did you think of Phyllis Baran's lecture?" Nan asked as they started walking toward the Inn.

Laura thought of her parents' deaths, of her long affair with her boss, Greg Towbridge. "I don't think I could use my life as the basis for a novel. Could you?"

"I did, sort of," Nan said. "My novel is about a woman in her forties who has an unexpected pregnancy. It actually happened to me. I was forty-two. At the time it was a shock. My husband and I didn't tell anyone, not even our sons, who were fourteen and seventeen at the time, which turned out to be a good thing because I miscarried at the end of my second month. Afterward, I kept thinking *what if I hadn't lost the baby*? How would our boys have reacted? Our parents? Our friends? How would our marriage have stood the test of a late-in-life unplanned child? My novel sprouted out of those questions."

"Nan has an agent," Agatha said, "and an editor is reading her manuscript now."

"How did you get an agent?" Laura asked, relieved to have finally met someone who had succeeded in getting representation.

"It's a long story."

"I like long stories," Laura said.

"This one didn't begin well," Nan said. "When I first started looking for an agent, I used Google. The agents I found were big names. They had impressive web sites and specific criteria for submissions; nearly all of them stated that they wouldn't consider multiple submissions, which meant that I could only submit to one at a time. This didn't bother me because I naively believed that they would get back to me in six to eight weeks as they stated on their web sites. But the first agent I contacted didn't get back to me for almost four months, the next one for over two months. Each time I received a form rejection letter; in one of them the agent stated that she received over four hundred queries a week. It was daunting. Half a year had lapsed and I was getting nowhere. My husband joked that at the rate I was going, I'd be sending out query letters from the old folk's home.

"So I did more research and found a publication at the library called the *Literary Marketplace*. All of the agents are listed in there. I looked for agents who represented authors who wrote books that seemed to be in the same genre as mine, and sent them query letters along with a synopsis of my novel and couple of sample pages. I ignored what I'd read about multiple submissions and sent out six queries at a time. Then the rejections came, one after another. I stopped counting when I reached thirty. Some didn't even bother to return my stamped, self-addressed envelope. I don't know what bothered me most, my disappointment or their lack of basic courtesy. Then, finally, an agent was willing to read my novel. I was ecstatic until she sent it back with a letter saying she didn't think she could sell it. That's when I wanted to quit. I felt as though I was drowning in rejection, but my husband wouldn't let me. He was so convinced someone would want to publish my novel that he said he'd send the query letters himself if I wouldn't. So I half-heartedly sent out another letter and got the agent I have now."

"You must be so glad you didn't quit," Laura said.

"Yes," Nan said. "My roommate did something similar here. She's an observer, but she wants someone on the staff to read one of her short stories. She asked Michael Pierce, and he told her to leave a note with a synopsis in his mailbox. He said he'd get back to her if he has time."

"Really," Laura said, wondering how many others had come to the conference with the same idea she had.

***

As Leila steered the Maserati into the circular drive, she saw Frank Stryker, the Workshop caretaker, nailing a brass plaque to a wide beam in front of the Inn. The sight of the shining plaque added to her feeling of frustration. Her morning had been fruitless. Of the people she had spoken with at the seven farms where she had stopped, only one held the hope of possible information about Benjamin Clymer. It was by far the most prosperous of the farms, the farmhouse and outbuildings old but well-kept. A boy who came to the door told her that his parents weren't in, but they might know something about the Clymers because their farm had once belonged to his great-great grandfather. The only positive discovery she made was the result of a wrong turn she had taken. After driving for several miles on a narrow two-lane highway thinking that she was heading in the direction of the Workshop, the road started winding up unfamiliar hills. Realizing her mistake, she was about to turn around when she saw an escarpment ahead. She pulled onto the shoulder and walked across the highway to the edge of the rocky cliff. The sight below was breathtaking—a wide curving river with tiny, tree-covered islands floating on it like lily pads. The river was cradled on each side by green hills. She stood on the escarpment for a long time, gazing at the river, the tiny islands, the hills, moved by the raw beauty and aching to share it. Michael had to come with her to see this, she thought, he had to come.

She parked the car and got out to look at the plaque as Stryker was driving the last nail through a pre-drilled hole. "It adds a nice touch, don't you think?" he said, stepping back to view his handiwork. He was a balding, thickset man who had a ruddy complexion and large red calloused hands.

"It's dignified," she agreed. "Roy said you found the plaque accidentally. Have you learned anything since about Benjamin Clymer?"

"Nope," he said, rubbing his bristly chin. "But I bet he'd be surprised if he was here today and saw what his money's come to. There's been summers when I've had to take a drive into the hills to get back to what's real. It can sure get crazy around here, a weird kind of craziness that you can't put your finger on, like a change in the air pressure—you can't see it but you can feel it working on you."

"I know what you mean," she said, imagining how the people attending the Workshop must appear to him.

"The safest guess is that Clymer was a farmer. In fact, I'd put money on it."

"A farmer?" she repeated doubtfully. She had been imagining Benjamin Clymer as a reclusive philanthropist who had a love of literature, who was perhaps a frustrated writer.

"Sure," Stryker said, as if it were as obvious as the plaque he had just nailed up. "This land is as good as any in Cattaraugus County, as good as any in the state, I'd wager. I once heard a professor from Cornell give a fancy talk about a glacier coming through these parts, dumping fine silt as it went along. This piece of land got its share and then some. Clymer was a farmer, all right."

"It's hard to believe that a farmer would leave his land and money to establish a writers' conference," she said, immediately regretting the phrasing of her response.

Stryker pulled his shoulders back. "Why not? Farmers read books."

"Of course," she said.

She walked back to the car annoyed with herself for having asked him about Benjamin Clymer. Frank Stryker's conjecture was not only farfetched, it was absurd.

Pierce came into their room as she was changing. "Any luck?" he asked.

"Not really. The only lead I got was from a boy who said that his parents might know something. I'll go back in a few days, maybe around dinnertime."

"You missed Phyllis's lecture. It was more like a confessional: she admitted that her fiction is autobiographical. It's strange, especially since she's denied it for so long," he said. "Sara asked about you. She noticed that you weren't at the lectures and wondered if you were ill."

"What did you tell her?" she said, doubting that Sara's motivation was concern for her health. She had disliked Sara Newkirk from the moment she had first met her years ago. Michael, like the rest of the staff, was crazy about Sara. It was as if Sara had some kind of hold on them; she was everyone's buddy, and they treated her as if she were the president of their private club.

"That you had some research to do."

"I found something wonderful today. I took a wrong turn and ended up on an escarpment overlooking the Allegheny River. It was beautiful, Michael, absolutely beautiful! Will you go there with me this afternoon?"

"Maybe," he said. She looked so earnest, so lovely, that he

couldn't bring himself to tell her that he'd already planned to spend whatever free time he had in the afternoon writing; it would be the last chance he'd have to work on his novel before he was given participants' manuscripts.

***

Dee Dee knocked on Talbot's office door when she returned from lunch. "How is it going?" she said, stepping around stacks of boxes and manila envelopes.

There were two rows of papers on his desk, one sheet for each staff member. "I'll have the lists ready for you to type by three o'clock," he said, taking off his reading glasses. She should get rid of that outfit, he thought. It made her look like Miss Piggy.

"Do you want me to get you something from the kitchen?"

"I had a sandwich from the Shed."

"Do you need any help?"

"Thanks, but it's a one-man job."

"Did anyone request Merle Ackerley?" she said, stalling.

"No, not even as a third choice," he said, putting his glasses on.

He was back at work before she left, scanning a master list he had compiled months earlier. His eyes rested near the bottom of the list on the name *Diana Rothenberg*. Next to her name there was the symbol of a plus, which meant that the original submission she had sent to the Workshop with her application was superior. Of the one hundred five participants on the list, a total which included both prose writers and poets, only sixteen had a plus next to their names; the rest had either checks or minus signs. The checks and minuses were almost equal in number. He glanced at Diana Rothenberg's note, which requested Pierce first, followed by Baran and Nettles. Her selection of Baran over Nettles surprised him; Nettles was by far the better known and more respected of the two writers. He quickly read the first page of Rothenberg's manuscript. The sentences were sparkling, clean and strong, written with the confidence of a writer who has found her voice. He reached automatically for Pierce's assignment sheet, then compressed his lips, remembering Pierce's absence at his lecture. He had already given Pierce three of the best participants, more than the bastard deserved. Diana Rothenberg would be assigned to Baran, he decided, jotting her name on the writer's sheet before picking up the next manuscript.

***

After lunch Agatha and Laura decided to walk on the path along Barrier Creek. Clumps of pearly everlasting with iridescent blossoms were growing along the stream in random bouquets; pale yellow-and-white butterflies flitted between the lavender flowers of Joe Pye weed. "It's beautiful here," Agatha said, the sun hot on her face and arms. "The water is so clear I can see straight to the bottom. It's such a good feeling to be in a place that has been untouched by pollution."

Laura spotted a used condom caught on a low branch of a bush. "Look," she said, pointing to where random, flat-topped stones rose invitingly above the water, hoping to divert the older woman's attention. "I'm going to try to cross."

"Some of those stones seem quite far apart," Agatha said as they got closer.

Laura was already untying her sneakers. "The worst that can happen is that I'll fall in, which will feel good in this heat."

Agatha watched as Laura leaped from rock to rock, impressed with her athletic grace.

"What great balance you have," Agatha said after Laura returned grinning, having clearly enjoyed the challenge.

"I guess you never lose what you learn. I did gymnastics until I was twelve."

"What made you stop?"

"I had a growth spurt and I got breasts. I was so much taller and more developed than the other girls that I was self-conscious. Also, my dad died that year."

"I understand. My father died when I was nine, and nothing was the same afterward," Agatha said. "But now I want to talk about your novel. I found it compelling. I was immediately drawn into the children's lives, into caring about them. And the scenes you created are so vivid, particularly the children's arrival at the old woman's farm on the bitter winter night they had to flee."

"Crazy Gertie's?"

"Yes!" Agatha said enthusiastically. "The hulk of the old house, the shadows on the snow playing tricks, the owl hooting, the wild-eyed old woman sitting on the porch with her shotgun, the children's terror. I can see myself teaching your novel, having a wonderful time with that scene. You're a born writer."

"Thank you, Agatha," Laura said, feeling a rush of gratitude. She had begun to seriously question whether coming to the Workshop was a wise decision. "Meeting you at the airport was the luckiest thing that has happened to me at this conference!"

"Oh, my," Agatha said, flustered at the unexpected compliment.

Soon they came to an area that was roped off; there was a DANGER sign nailed to a tree. "I can see a path," Laura said, ducking under the rope. "I wonder where it goes."

"Maybe we're not supposed to venture beyond this point."

"I don't know why we shouldn't. It can't do any harm to look."

With some misgivings, Agatha followed. They walked through woods, then came to a clearing. Ahead the land dropped sharply into a gorge; the stream followed, trickling down rocks to boulders below. Beyond the gorge, thickly-forested hills swept across the horizon. "I never expected this!" Agatha said. "It looks like a picture postcard. This place is full of surprises!"

Laura noticed that Agatha's nose had gotten quite pink. "I think you've had too much sun. We'd better start back and stay in the shade as much as we can."

When they came to the path that separated the Inn from Tabard II, Agatha reached into her tote bag. "You'll want this," she said, handing Laura the manuscript.

Dynarski, who had come out of the Inn, walked up to them. "That envelope looks important," he said.

"It certainly is," Agatha said. "It holds the first chapters of Laura's novel, which are most impressive. I couldn't stop reading."

"You can't get a better recommendation. I'd like to read it."

He looked at Laura expectantly. She supposed there was no reason why he shouldn't read it—she had a duplicate set in her suitcase—yet she didn't like feeling boxed in. Unable to think of a refusal that wouldn't be insulting, she said, "Sure," though she wasn't sure at all.

"I'm not going the lectures this afternoon so I'll have plenty of time to read it. You'll have it back before the reading tonight."

***

When Laura left the Circle Theater after the first lecture to stretch, she was surprised to see Dynarski holding her manuscript. "I thought you weren't coming to the lectures," she said.

"I'm not," he said. "I wanted to tell you that I finished reading your chapters."

"That was fast."

It was the first time Laura saw him smile; with the habitual intensity in his expression gone, he was actually quite handsome. "It's excellent," he said, giving her the envelope. "If you've sustained it, you have a hellava novel. I'd like to read the rest."

"It's all I have. The rest is on a CD. I thought I could have it printed here if I needed to, but at fifteen cents a page, it's too much."

"Do you want to go out to dinner tonight? We can go to Jamestown. They should have a Kinko's there, and you can get the rest printed."

"Maybe just a few more chapters," Laura said, thinking aloud. "It would be good to have a decent meal, as long as we go Dutch."

A shadow of disappointment passed over his face. "Uh… sure," he said. "What time do you want to leave?"

"I'd like to go to the mixer for a little while, just out of curiosity. Do you want to meet me there or at the Inn?"

"Let's make it for five fifteen in the lobby of the Inn."

Laura went back inside the theater and took her seat next to Agatha. "I glimpsed you talking to Stan. I bet he's as enthusiastic about your manuscript as I am," Agatha said.

"Yes!" Laura said, with relief. Any doubts she'd had about the novel were gone. "He's driving me to Jamestown later to get a few more chapters printed."

"I think he's interested in more than just your book."

"I'm not encouraging him," Laura said firmly.

***

Leila walked into Clemens at three thirty. Usually she avoided the place during the day because she found its dark wicker furniture, dull beige walls, and clubby alcoholic atmosphere depressing. At night Clemens resembled a friendly local bar, its flaws hidden by dim lighting and nocturnal conviviality. But now she wanted a drink. Upset because Michael had refused to go to the escarpment, she had left him sitting at his desk and had wandered aimlessly over the campus for better than an hour, seeing nothing but his shoulders hunched over his laptop, oblivious to the world beyond the screen in front of him.

She went directly to a long trestle table which was placed against a wall between two open windows. Set on a green plastic tablecloth were bottles of gin, vodka, rye, scotch, and vermouth, pitchers of orange and tomato juice, a jar of olives, stacks of plastic glasses, two large metal ice buckets, and bottles of ginger ale, tonic water, and club soda. She made herself a gin and tonic, then crossed the room, stopping to speak briefly to Phyllis Baran and Sara Newkirk before taking an isolated chair in a corner facing a window.

The frosty bitterness of the gin was pleasing. She sipped it slowly until she became aware of someone standing near her. "You make that drink look irresistible," he said. "I don't believe we have been formally introduced. I'm Eric Nettles."

"Leila Pierce."

"Yes, I saw you arrive yesterday with your husband. That was quite an entrance you made. Do you mind if I pull up a chair and join you?"

"Sure," she said, gesturing for him to sit.

They talked about the sultry weather, then about creative writing programs and writers' conferences, sharing their general observations. Nettles had taught at a number of workshops and, like Michael, was frequently invited to be a guest writer at colleges. He conversed easily, and well. Prepared to dislike him, she instead found him engaging, his leonine head and the mischievous twinkle in his eyes attractive. Although he was less than ten years younger than her father, there was nothing paternal about him. He reminded her of an aging lion, his white hair falling from the balding crown of his head to his shoulders like a mane, his burly upper torso hinting of power and virility. Perhaps, she reflected later, his appeal came from the way he had looked at her, as if savoring her femininity, making her feel deliciously attractive. She couldn't recall when Michael had last looked at her like that.

He offered to refill her drink. "No, thank you," she said, rising. "I'd better be going."

"Your husband is probably wondering where you are," he said, walking her to the door. They were nearly the same height, Leila slightly taller.

"I doubt it. He's lost in his fiction. He's been writing all afternoon."

"Dedicated fellow," Nettles commented with a wry grin. "If I had his temptations, you wouldn't find me sitting in front of a computer."

"Yes, I would," she said. "If I've learned one thing being married to a novelist, it's that there is no woman alive as beguiling as the muse. But thanks for the compliment."

Nettles remained at the door as she walked down the path to the road, his gaze fixed on her long legs and perfectly-proportioned body.

***

There was a rush toward the Inn after the lecture on reviewing. Barely managing to extricate herself from the crowd, Laura watched the people sweeping past her with a mixture of relief and envy as they hurried toward the bulletin board. As much as she would have liked to be a participant, she didn't have the stress of worrying about which writer on the staff her manuscript would be assigned to.

When she finally got to her room, she couldn't get the door open. "Gwen," she said, rapping, "I need to get in there to change."

There was no response.

Again, she knocked on the door. "Please, Gwen, open the door."

Still no response.

Laura looked at her watch. It was four fifteen. She's probably upset over her manuscript assignment, Laura thought, banging on the door. "Gwen, I have to get in there!"

"I want some privacy," Gwen said in a tremulous voice that was nearly inaudible. "Don't you have any consideration?"

The word *consideration* snapped Laura's patience. "EITHER YOU OPEN THE DAMN DOOR OR I'LL GET A MAINTENANCE MAN UP HERE TO BREAK IT DOWN! IS THAT CLEAR?"

Laura was conscious of women's heads poking out of doorways to see what the shouting was about. "Is there a problem?" asked the woman in the room across the hall.

"Not anymore," Laura said, hearing a scraping sound from behind the door.

When she entered the room, Gwen was lying on her bed facing the wall. "You could have given me some privacy," she sobbed.

"No, I couldn't. I want to go to the mixer, and I'm going out to dinner. I barely have enough time to change. And aren't you being a bit over-dramatic? The news you got couldn't have been *that* bad," Laura said, taking black linen slacks out of the closet.

Gwen rolled over and propped herself up on her arm. Her eyes were red, her face tear-streaked. "Merle Ackerley," she wailed, "I got Merle Ackerley!"

"Really, he can't be incompetent or he wouldn't have been asked to teach here. Why don't you give him a chance?"

"You don't understand," Gwen said, breaking into fresh sobs.

But Laura did understand. She knew it was the upset of the assignment itself, the rumor she'd heard that the best manuscripts were given to Pierce and Nettles, the very worst to Ackerley. Unable to think of anything to say, she pulled out her suitcase from under the bed. It was unlocked. She tossed in the manuscript and removed a CD from a side compartment. Gwen was still weeping when she left.

***

Laura collided with Webb as she was leaving the Shed. "What's your hurry?" he said.

Her face was flushed. "You might not want to be seen talking to me."

"Why?"

"Some people were passing around a copy of a recent *New York Times Book Review* in which there was a great review of Marshall Stoddard's new book written by Michael Pierce. When I questioned if it were ethical for Pierce to write a review of Stoddard's book since they were both staff members here and probably friends, everyone looked at me as though I had committed a terrible blunder. I'm not exaggerating," she said, gesturing with an open hand. "One-by-one they walked away from me until I was left standing by myself. They made me feel like I had a communicable disease."

"Good for you, Laura! I was beginning to think I was the only one at this conference who isn't afraid to speak out," he said. "I'm looking for Diana. Did you happen to see her in there?"

"No, I didn't."

"I might as well go in anyway," he said.

Andrew Cox was leaving the Inn as she was coming up the walk. He was clean shaven and dressed in a striped button-down shirt, leather boots with heels that made him two-inches taller, and what looked like a new pair of jeans. He wasn't wearing his usual baseball cap, and she could see his scalp through his thinning brown hair. "You look like you've got plans for tonight," he said. "Are you coming to my reading?"

"Is there another show in town?"

He laughed. "Maybe we can meet afterward," he said, adding, "in the Shed."

There was no way she'd be anywhere near the Shed after his reading, she thought, entering the Inn.

Dynarski was waiting for her dressed in a red polo shirt and khakis rather than his usual T-shirt and jeans. "We're going to Olean instead of Jamestown," he said as they walked to the parking lot, which was at the far end of the campus behind the tennis courts. "Olean has a Staples that does printing. I asked the woman in the office. She gave me the names of some restaurants, too."

His car looked new, a huge, shiny black SUV with dark tinted windows that made Laura think of a hearse. "What do you do for a living?" she asked after he turned on the ignition.

"Uh… construction," he said, opening a map. "You can be the navigator."

When he gave her the map, she noticed that his hands weren't rough looking or calloused, his skin and nails too smooth and even, it seemed to her, for someone who worked in construction. She was about to ask him what kind of construction when he abruptly changed the subject. "What are you planning to do with your novel when the conference is over?" he said.

"I honestly don't know. I was hoping to get some guidance here."

"This is the third writers' conference I've attended, and if it's anything like the first two, the only guidance you'll get is a lot of generalities. You need to watch out for scams."

"What do you mean?"

"There are agents who advertise that they'll read your manuscript for a fee; if they like it, they'll represent you and waive the fee. Like a jerk, I fell for it. The agent charged me a one-thousand-dollar reading fee and returned my manuscript with a page of criticism, full of misspellings, that was written on a high school level by someone who wasn't very bright. A stupid secretary criticized my novel!" he said bitterly.

"Ouch! Thanks for the warning."

He seemed so angry that she wondered how she could defuse him. "You didn't tell me who is going to criticize your novel," she said, immediately regretting she'd asked in case it was Ackerley.

"Michael Pierce."

"Congratulations, you must feel relieved."

"No," he said. "That was the deal. I told Talbot I wouldn't attend unless I was guaranteed to be assigned to Pierce."

Before concentrating again on the map, she wondered if there were any others at the Workshop who had made a similar deal.

***

Gwen didn't go to dinner. Unwilling to be seen with her eyes red and swollen, she waited until the hallway was quiet before she went to one of the bathrooms to wash her face. Then she ran a washcloth under cold water, planning to lie down with it over her eyes when she returned to the room.

Soon the washcloth was warm and she was up, fighting panic. There was no mistaking the message she'd been given: her assignment to Ackerley meant that her work was considered to have little, if any, potential. Tom wouldn't be aware of this when she told him, but she had to leave the conference with positive news. She had put her ambition to become a successful writer before him and the children, and he knew it. If she didn't succeed here, she could no longer expect him to be overlooking. They had fought about it: what she termed *focused,* he called *selfish and self-centered.* During one of their fights, which had become more frequent as she had became more determined, she had made the mistake of telling him about the famous sculptor, Louise Nevelson, who gave her son to her parents to raise because she felt she couldn't devote herself to her art and be a good mother at the same time. The look on his face, the shock and disappointment, still

87

haunted her.

She had always been focused, she thought, pacing. And she'd always gotten what she wanted, which included Tom, who had been married to someone else when she met him. She would leave this conference with something positive; she just had to figure out how to accomplish it.

***

The Italian restaurant they went to after Laura had three additional chapters printed was nicer than she had expected; the tables were covered with white cloths and had small vases with sprigs of fresh flowers in them. She ordered chicken Marsala; Dynarski, spaghetti and meatballs. "Finally, decent food," she said, wanting to talk about something other than writing. His intensity was enervating.

But Dynarski seemed unable to talk about anything else. He told her that he had an MFA from Iowa. "Some of my classmates have been published," he said, ignoring his dinner. "They were favored by the instructors because they were likeable and funny in the workshops. They knew how to call attention to themselves, and they cultivated the established writers on the faculty like politicians, making contacts that would help them. I didn't know how the game was played until it was too late. I'm a better writer than any of them, and they've gotten published!"

Laura doubted that it was as simple as he was making it sound, so she concentrated on her food, nodding occasionally at what he said to indicate she was listening while he went on and on. By the end of the meal, he drank more than he ate, washing his bitterness down with three beers.

"We're not going to make it back in time for Cox's reading," he said as they were leaving the restaurant.

"I wasn't planning on going anyway," she said, exhausted from his endless stream of resentment.

It was dark when they reached the Workshop campus. Laura thanked him after he parked the SUV. "You just finished your first book, so you're probably wondering why I keep doing this," he said, shifting in his seat to face her. "Wanting to be a writer is different from wanting to be anything else. If you're a success, if you get published and the critics like your work, people will read your books and know what you think and how you feel about life. No matter how careful you are at trying to conceal them, your deepest feelings will be exposed for public scrutiny, for approval or scorn. You take the risk because you want this more than you have ever wanted anything. It's crazy. Maybe all writers are a little crazy, some more than others. But if you're rejected, the risk you've taken isn't even acknowledged. It's as if someone is telling you that your best effort, the finest work you can produce, is worthless."

Laura couldn't see his eyes; it was dark and the lenses in his glasses were thick. But she knew there were tears in them.

Then, what she hoped wouldn't happen, happened. "I have some wine in my room," he said, reaching to put his arm around her. "Vodka, too, if you want something stronger."

She desperately tried to think of something to say that wouldn't add to his wounds. "Maybe another time. These past few days have been harder on me than I expected. What I need right now is a good night's sleep. I hope you understand."

He withdrew his arm. "Yeah," he said sourly, "I understand."

It wasn't too late to call Gretchen, she thought, shivering in the chilly night air as she hurried to the Inn. But she had nothing to report, which shouldn't make her feel as if she'd failed, although somehow it did. All she could do was try again tomorrow. At some point she had to get lucky.

An unexpected weariness settled on her as she walked down the hallway to her room. Steeling herself for another encounter with her roommate, she opened the door. Gwen wasn't there. Realizing that she hadn't seen people in the hall waiting to use the bathrooms, she hurriedly undressed, got into her bathrobe, and grabbed her towel and toiletry bag, briefly energized by the promise of a hot shower and a good night's sleep.

***

The temperature had dropped considerably by the time Andrew Cox's reading was over. Agatha and Nan decided to go to the Shed for hot chocolate. "What did you think of the reading?" Nan said.

Agatha frowned. "I don't know what disturbed me more, the tone of the fiction or the way the females were portrayed, almost as shells, hollow beings more like puppets than people."

"The protagonist's decision to kill every member of his bosses' family, starting with the children, as revenge for having been fired is what gave me chills. Someone full of anger could read it and think it was a good…" Nan paused. "Here he comes. He's heading straight toward us and he doesn't look happy."

"Excuse me," Cox said. "Have you seen Laura?"

"No," Agatha said.

"Did either of you see her at the reading?"

"We were sitting near the front of the theater, which isn't a good spot to see who's coming in."

He gave them a perfunctory nod, then walked away.

Agatha took a sip of her hot chocolate. Although she knew intellectually that one shouldn't confuse a writer's work with his life, after hearing Cox read his fiction she was surprised to find herself hoping that he couldn't locate Laura.

Webb and Diana had also gone to the Shed for hot chocolate. It was Webb's suggestion when he noticed that Diana was shivering, though as soon as he mentioned the drink he remembered that he hadn't taken an Eskalith after dinner.

Diana found an empty spot in a corner of the cavernous room while Webb waited in line at the snack bar. He had gotten his first choice, Aaron Greene. She hoped he hadn't noticed how disappointed she was that she had been assigned to Phyllis Baran, her second choice. She forced a smile when she saw him coming toward her with two steaming paper cups. "Be careful," he said. "It's hot."

"Good, it'll warm my hands."

He studied her for a moment. "What's bothering you?"

"Pierce was my first choice," she said, swallowing hard. "Baran was my second. I picked her over Nettles because my work is nothing like his. Also, I read her novels and enjoyed them. I just… expected to get Pierce."

"Maybe you'll feel differently after you go to one of her study groups. Pierce has a big name, but that doesn't mean he can teach. Trust your instincts."

"Thanks, you made me feel better," she said, giving him an honest smile this time.

He returned her smile, wickedly. "I can make you feel *really* good. Hecker has the room tonight. Can we use yours?"

"With my roommate to keep us company?" she said, laughing.

"I don't think so."

***

Hecker was on his way to the room he shared with Webb with the woman he had attempted to bring there the previous night. They had been together most of the day, meeting for meals and sitting together at lectures. Being in her company had been wearing. She had talked incessantly about poetry; she was fixated on the subject, obsessed with becoming a recognized poet. He had been supportive and sympathetic, listening to her go on endlessly though he was thoroughly bored. But he had too much time invested in her to start looking for someone else. And she was attractive. She was slender and petite, and she had fabulous teeth—even, beautifully shaped and sparkling white, which more than met his standard for dental perfection.

He suggested going to his room so he could give her his poems. They walked briskly to Dickens, eager to escape the cold, damp air. She followed him up to his room without hesitation, but when he closed the door behind them her eyes widened, as if she were surprised at finding herself there. "It's freezing in here," she said nervously.

He put his arms around her. She wasn't much larger than a child and her size excited him. She tried to push him away. "Aren't you going to show me your poems?"

"Later," he said. "Let's get warm now."

"I can't… I'm married."

"If we don't seize this moment, we'll hate ourselves. It's been torture for me being with you. You must have sensed how I feel. And I know that you're attracted to me."

"But my husband…"

"He won't be hurt unless you tell him. Besides, it's different for us—this place, poetry. In a sense, our lives are in suspension while we're here."

"*Our lives are in suspension,*" she repeated, playing with the phrase. "That's nice."

"Inspiration," he said, putting his mouth on hers.

She didn't resist him. Hecker undressed her, marveling once more at her diminutive size; she was fine-boned and had high, firm breasts. At first she seemed to be holding herself back, but he took

91

his time, playing with her breasts and clitoris until she climbed on top of him, more than ready. He came groaning with pleasure, feeling compensated for the hours he'd spent listening to her talk about her poetry.

"I have something to tell you," she said after they separated.

Oh God, he thought, *she has herpes*! *AIDS*! He couldn't breathe. "What?" he managed to croak.

"I was here last year."

He couldn't speak. Either he had misheard her or he was having a coronary.

"Aaron Greene criticized my poems," she said as if she were sharing her deepest secret. Her eyes were closed. "When I got home, I went to bed and stayed there for a month. I couldn't get up. I guess I wanted to die. Greene nearly destroyed me."

"Oh," he said, starting to breathe normally again.

"Aaron Greene is a heartless bastard!"

"Then why did you come back?"

"To prove that he was wrong. I threw out almost everything I had. I worked nonstop for months. I never told anyone what Greene said, not even my husband."

"But Terence Hill is criticizing your poems."

"Yes," she said. "And now that I've met you, I feel that I did the right thing by coming back. You really understand me."

Those were dangerous words. This was a mistake. "Uh… you'd better get dressed before my roommate gets back. I'll walk you to the Inn."

He half-walked, half-ran with her to the Inn, using the cold as his excuse for the rush.

***

Pierce was in bed reading when Leila, wearing a red flannel nightshirt, settled in beside him. "How are the manuscripts you've been assigned?" she said, eyeing a short stack of manila envelopes on his night stand.

"So far, with the exception of one, they're junk. Some of them don't even know the meanings of the words they're using," he said, reaching for the top envelope. He pulled out a manuscript and flipped through the pages. "Listen to this sentence, it's a prize. A male character says, '*I built a wall around me that she could not impregnate.*'"

He returned the manuscript to the envelope and put it back on the nightstand. "Roy really stuck me. He probably figured he would pay me back for not going to his lecture. He won't do it again, though. We're not coming back."

"Seems I've heard that before," she said dryly.

He picked up the manuscript he'd been reading. "This one has potential, but the guy is so intent on telling the story that he isn't allowing his characters to do it for him. He's reporting instead of dramatizing. It seems as if he's afraid of the issues he's raising. If he can fix it, he'll really have something."

The excitement in his voice stirred feelings in Leila that she thought were gone. Once she had envisioned their marriage as a literary idyll, each working in separate studies, then meeting at the end of the day to read aloud the results of their labors. Although she had long ago reconciled herself to the fact that her efforts couldn't compensate for her lack of talent, there were still moments when the memory of that hope rose without warning, quick and cutting. "What's the writer's name?"

"Gerald Hofstrand," he said, slipping the manuscript into the envelope.

Yawning, she rolled away from him.

He turned off the light, then nestled his body next to hers. He slid his hand under her nightgown, moving it up her thigh to the cleft between her legs. She rolled onto her stomach. He tried again, now caressing her back and buttocks, the flesh firm and satin-smooth beneath his hand. She didn't respond. Usually she was eager for him, moist and ready as though she had anticipated his desire. "Is something wrong?" he said.

"I'm tired."

"That's when it's best," he coaxed, pulling open his pajama bottoms.

"No, Michael," she said.

He rolled onto his back, stunned by her refusal. She rarely denied him, and never this firmly. Damn, he thought, wondering what had set her off. The last thing he needed now was trouble that could affect his work.

He shifted onto his side, thinking of the last catastrophe in his life—his divorce—the results of which would forever haunt him. The legal bickering had caused him to lose control of the novel he was working on. The reviews had been devastating: *Michael Pierce's fiction has lost its bite... Pierce has settled into mediocrity... an easy read that will outrage no one...* The money he had made, more than he had ever dreamed of earning, was no compensation. His next novel had proved that he was still a writer to be reckoned with, but the reviews were reserved, the critics unwilling to fully reinstate him to his former place after his huge commercial success. This new novel would do it. All he needed was to preserve that delicate balance...

***

❧ Workshop Bulletin ❧

VOL. 74, NO.3   THE CLYMER WORKSHOP   AUGUST 13 2004

GOOD MORNING!

The weather forecast promises a sparkling day, warm and sunny, with the temperature dropping in the evening.

MORNING PROGRAM

9:30 A.M. Fiction Lecture (Eric Nettles)
10:30A.M. Poetry Lecture (Sara Newkirk)

Eric Nettles will discuss "Innovative Fiction." Sara Newkirk will talk about "Poets: The Keepers of Language."

AFTERNOON PROGRAM

2:00 P.M. Panel on Little Magazines
3:00 P.M. Study Groups
5:00 P.M. Cocktail Party— Lower Terrace

EVENING READING

Roy Talbot will read from his poems. His books of poetry include *Slivers Of Sun* and *Pipe Dreams*. He is a professor of English at Axton College. This is his sixth year as the director of the Clymer Workshop.

GUESTS

We are pleased to welcome Janice and Grant Barker, co-editors of *Willows*, a magazine of prose and poetry, and Lorraine Appleton, editor of *Artmark*, who will participate in our afternoon panel on 'little' magazines. Included in the discussion will be practical pointers such as the length of submissions and knowing the magazine. Phyllis Baran will moderate.

STUDY GROUPS

Each participant should report to the study group led by the staff member assigned to criticize his/her manuscript. Observers may attend the study groups of their choice. See the bulletin boards for study group locations.

MESSAGES

Please check your mailboxes several times a day. Staff members will be setting up schedules for manuscript conferences and will contact you with messages placed in your mailbox. If you have lost or forgotten the combination to your mailbox, please don't force it open. The combination can be obtained at the Workshop office.

EVENING BUFFET

To alleviate congestion at tonight's buffet, there will be two tables set up instead of one. The food on each table will be identical. We would like to remind you that the buffet is not a smorgasbord. One trip to the table only, please.

BOOKSTORE

After an unavoidable delay, the bookstore is finally open! We have a wide selection of books written by your favorite authors, as well as toiletries and other sundries. Bookstore hours are:

8:00-9:00 A.M.
12:00-2:00 P.M.
4:00-6:00 P.M.
7:00-8:00 P.M.

LIQUOR ORDERS

Saturday morning our chief engineer, Frank Stryker, and a member of his staff will be driving to Jamestown for some important supplies, not the least of which is you-know-what. You can place your orders for the BYOB mixer on Sunday (and any nightcaps you are contemplating) in the sitting room immediately following lunch. Sorry, checks cannot be accepted. Cash only.

MISSING!

Copies of *The New York Times* have mysteriously vanished from the sitting room. It would be appreciated if the parties who inadvertently removed the papers would return them so they can be enjoyed by others.

TIDBIT:

"Oh! If I ever write a good book, I will really have earned it."

- Gustav Flaubert in a letter to his mistress, Louise Colet

*"Three-fourths of philosophy and literature is the talk of people
trying to convince themselves that they really like the cage
they were tricked into entering."*
Gary Snyder

Chapter III

Refreshed after a good night's sleep, Laura was one of the first
people to go into the dining room for breakfast when it opened at
seven. Without so much as an encouraging smile at the other
people who were entering, she immediately headed for a table at
the far end of the cavernous room, where diamonds of sunlight
were coming in through the leaded glass windows. She didn't want
to appear to be deliberately rude, but the prospect of being able to
eat a meal in silence without having to introduce herself or feel
obligated to ask polite questions to strangers was too tantalizing to
jeopardize. One of the things she had learned about herself since
arriving at the conference was that during the years she had lived
alone she had developed an appreciation for solitude, for quiet
moments when nothing and no one intruded on her thoughts.

Before she had finished reading the first page of the *BULLETIN*,
Dynarski was at her table, taking the seat opposite hers. Andrew
Cox wasn't far behind him. "I looked for you last night," he said,
taking the chair next to her.

"She was with me," Dynarski said.

Cox's expression darkened. "Really."

At that moment Marshall Stoddard spotted Cox as he stood in
the arched entrance, and he went straight for the table. Networking
never hurt, he thought, especially adding someone new. And the
luscious strawberry-blond was there, which was another
enticement.

Gwen followed soon after. When she entered the dining hall
and saw the two writers at Laura's table, she hurried across the
room to join them, greeting Laura as though she were a long-
treasured friend.

A sturdy-looking girl of about sixteen who wore her hair in a
thick brown braid came to take their order. "We have orange or

tomato juice," she said, "and granola or pancakes."

"Does the granola have nuts?" Laura asked.

"I think so," the waitress said.

"Then I'll have pancakes and tomato juice."

Cox turned toward Laura. "Don't you like nuts?"

"She's allergic to them," Dynarski said, sounding noticeably proprietary.

Gwen, who had been waiting for an opening, said, "My daughter was allergic to milk."

The conversation drifted from allergies to the morning program until their food arrived. Laura's pancakes were rubbery, which gave her a perfect excuse to escape. "Does anyone know if the Shed is open?"

"Are they that bad?" Stoddard said.

"Like old tires."

Stoddard checked his watch. "The Shed should be open. If you're lucky, they'll have muffins from The Flour Bin. It's a bakery in Olean that makes the best muffins I've ever eaten. They take special orders if you call in advance. I used to order a dozen of their banana muffins—some with blueberries and some with chocolate chips and walnuts—to pick up before I went home at the end of the conference."

Laura thanked him and excused herself.

She walked briskly across the campus and met Pierce coming out of the Shed carrying a brown paper bag in one hand and a plastic glass filled with orange juice in the other. "Mr. Pierce," she said, delighted to finally be able to approach him alone. "I'm Laura Belmont. Could I speak with you a moment? I'm sure you want to eat, so I won't keep you long."

"Sure," Pierce said.

"I applied to the Workshop too late to be a participant," she said, the words sounding stale to her after having repeated them so many times in the past two days. "I just finished writing a novel before I came here. It's a story about two children who are orphaned after the older child, a fourteen-year-old boy, accidentally sees his mother murdered. I know how busy you must be, but is there a chance you could look at a chapter?"

"What happens to the children? Do they go to live with mean relatives?"

"They're left on their own. The story takes place at the turn of the century before the social service system that we have now was in place. Some horrible things happen to them, as well as some good things."

"Then the novel is about good and evil."

"Yes."

"It sounds interesting. Put a note in my mailbox with your name, a brief synopsis of the plot, and your mailbox number. I can't make any promises: if I have time, I'll get back to you."

"Thank you," Laura said, so elated she practically skipped into the Shed, a large wood structure that had a single enormous room. In front of the snack bar—a long counter that had a small kitchen behind it—there were tables and chairs. Worn, over-stuffed sofas and chairs scattered randomly around the room were dwarfed by the space.

The girl behind the snack bar counter told her that they'd just gotten a delivery of muffins from The Flour Bin. She bought a blueberry muffin that was huge and so buttery and full of fruit it tasted sinful. For the first time since she'd arrived at the Workshop she felt glad that she had come.

***

Agatha had had a difficult night. Claire's snoring had been thunderous, like a train roaring through a tunnel with a whistle to scare cows off the tracks. To add to her misery, the sunburned skin on her face and arms hurt when it brushed against the coarse bed linen. She'd slept fitfully and had stayed in bed longer than usual. Now it was seven fifty-five and she was supposed to meet Nan for breakfast at eight o'clock. Her bed was made and she was showered and dressed; she had been waiting for fifteen minutes for her roommate to relinquish the hazy mirror over the dresser so she could put on lipstick and re-comb her hair. "This mirror is terrible," Claire said, stepping back to take yet another look at her makeup. "I don't know how they can expect us to tolerate such primitive living conditions."

"Would you mind if I use it for a moment? I just want to put on some lipstick and comb my hair."

Claire stepped squarely in front of the dresser. "I'm almost finished," she said, picking up a mascara wand.

Agatha picked up her tote bag and left wordlessly.

Agatha's silent exit had the effect of a rebuke. "She could have been patient," Claire muttered to herself, putting a final coat of mascara on her lashes. For some reason she felt defensive. It must be this place, she thought. Oh, how she wished she had a different roommate, though she couldn't imagine who it would be; she still hadn't found anyone whose friendship she wanted to cultivate. Everyone was so intense, and their attitude toward her because she was an observer was not only snobbish, it was deprecating, as if she were lacking in ability. A lot they knew! All of them pining to be published, and she had been earning money from her writing for years. Her trips, her jewelry, even this conference was paid for with checks from her stories. She could tell them a thing or two! She'd been published in the best of the confessionals—*True Romance, True Confessions, Modern Romances.* But they were such snobs, everyone making snide remarks about *McCall's* and *Redbook*, especially *Redbook.* There was nothing wrong with *Redbook*; it was a perfectly respectable magazine. It was a good thing she had used pen names. If they were aware she wrote for the confessionals, they'd snicker at her like they snicker at *Redbook.* Maybe her stories weren't masterpieces, but they were filled with characters and plots that a woman could identify with. The money she'd made was proof of it! She'd show them! She'd give the manuscript of her novel to the director and ask to have it criticized. She'd tell him that she wanted to become a participant. As soon as he started reading her work he would immediately recognize her as a professional. Then she'd request Pierce and get him.

With that last satisfying thought, she gave herself an extra spray of perfume.

***

The skin on Agatha's face was flaming when she entered the Inn. "Something got your blood circulating," Nan remarked.

"Please, don't get me started," Agatha said, following Nan into the dining room. She realized too late that she was being led to a table where Jerry Hofstrand was sitting. Her fingers tightened around the handle of her tote bag. He probably wouldn't remember her, she thought.

Nan took a chair directly opposite Hofstrand. Agatha perched awkwardly on the chair beside her, as if she were uncertain she would stay. A waitress came over to tell them there were pancakes or cold cereal for breakfast. "I'll have orange juice, granola, a banana and coffee," Nan said.

The girl looked uncomfortable. "I'll look for bananas, but I'm not sure there are any."

"They haven't served fresh fruit once since we've been here," Nan said after Agatha ordered pancakes. "I didn't expect gourmet meals, but I would like a piece of fruit every day."

"They're trying to fill us up with starch," Hofstrand said, holding his spoon above a bowl of granola. "It's economical and satisfying."

"You mean cheap and fattening," Nan said, laughing. She introduced herself and Agatha to him.

"I believe we have already met," he said, his steady brown eyes focusing on Agatha with recognition. "Weren't we in the same van coming here?"

Agatha nodded. She was happy that he remembered and would have liked to speak but was unable to move her tongue. It was, she thought anxiously, paralyzed.

The waitress returned with their breakfast. "Are you enjoying the conference?" Nan asked.

"So far it has been interesting. I'm not getting much out of the poetry, though."

"Fortunately, Agatha has helped me with the poetry or I'd be lost."

He focused on Agatha. "Do you write prose or poetry?"

"Poetry," Agatha managed to say, "but I'm just an observer."

"A very knowledgeable one," Nan interjected.

"I'll know where to look when I need an interpreter."

"Have you been writing long?" Nan asked.

"Since January," he said. "I retired from the Air Force in December and thought I would give it a try."

"Were you a pilot?"

"No," he said with a smile. "Most people in the Air Force don't fly planes. I spent the last eight years at the Pentagon."

"That's a place I'd like to know more about."

"I hope there are thousands of people like you, including some editors."

"Are you going to reveal the Pentagon's secrets?"

"None that are classified, but I intend to expose some accepted practices that I feel should be examined."

"It sounds interesting," Nan said.

After he left Agatha sat holding her coffee cup, lost in the joy that he had remembered she was on the van. But her next thought completely crushed her happiness: he probably remembered her because she was so homely.

"Are you all right?" Nan asked, noticing that Agatha's head seemed to be sinking into her neck.

"Oh, I'm fine," Agatha said hollowly, "just fine."

***

Eric Nettles, the innovative fictionist described by critics as... "a virtuoso of style… a veritable magician with language," sat in the front row of the theater while conference members filed in to hear his lecture. There was no hint of nervousness in his manner, no aura of apprehension. His demeanor was that of a profoundly confident man of fifty-four who has succeeded in all he has set out to do.

The theater filled rapidly. After a final few stragglers found seats in the back, Nettles ambled up the steps to the platform. He set his speech on the lectern and put on a pair of reading glasses. Then, pitching his burly upper torso forward, he began.

"At this very moment, while I am speaking to you in this sylvan setting, somewhere a person has just been murdered. During the time that lapsed since I rose from my seat, walked to this lectern, put on my glasses, and spoke of the murder, someone was raped, a child perished in a senseless accident, people died needlessly of starvation and disease, unsuspecting victims were mugged, and terrorists were setting explosives to intimidate by killing and maiming.

"I didn't recite this litany of horrors to scatter the last traces of sleep from your minds, although as writers I am sure you appreciate the effectiveness of shock to rivet the attention of others. My purpose was to describe, as briefly as possible, the chaotic, senseless world in which we live. There is no grand design for life on earth, no meaningful pattern that controls what happens on this planet with the exception of the orbit in which we hurtle through space, a path governed by natural law. And even this planet could disappear like a ball in a magician's hand as the result of human ingeniousness. Man has built sufficient nuclear warheads to reduce the earth to pebbles in less time than it would take us to eat lunch.

"Still, we go on living our daily lives as best we can, struggling with our work, raising our families, forming new relationships, eating, sleeping, making love, doing all the things that human beings do in their attempt to lead a well-ordered existence. But even there we encounter problems. Few of our days are memorable; most are repetitions of the day before, and the day before that. One week mirrors another. We are bound by schedules, by responsibilities, by our bodily needs. Our lives blur into incoherence, one year blending into the next with infrequent demarcations—marriage, the birth of a child, the purchase of a home, a change of jobs, the death of a family member or a friend.

"What I am leading up to," he said, "is the heart of the challenge that faces a writer of innovative fiction. Since experience is the material out of which fiction is made, what should the novelist write about? What can he write about when he is living in a world filled with chaos, and at the same time, his daily life, as he is living it, is essentially a repetitious blur? How can he make sense out of the senselessness that surrounds him, particularly when he understands that experience cannot be self-sustaining on its own? How can he fashion fiction that meaningfully unifies both chaos and incoherence?"

To answer the questions he raised, Nettles expertly led his audience through the evolution of the novel from the eighteenth century to the post-modernists, as though each development were an inevitable progression on the path toward innovative fiction. "What a writer of innovative fiction is doing," he said, "is taking the final step, eliminating plots because they are no longer necessary or relevant."

Pierce had all he could do to remain in his seat. He had been listening to Nettles with intense concentration, his antipathy of the man's fiction giving way to grudging admiration for Nettles' carefully constructed arguments. The man was intelligent and persuasive. Too persuasive. His was a voice both strong and enticing, as seductive as a siren's. But for Nettles to blatantly state before this audience of neophyte writers that plots were neither necessary nor relevant was totally irresponsible!

Pierce's gaze swept around the theater, taking in the

mesmerized faces of the Workshop members. They were all listening to Nettles as if bewitched. He felt Leila's restraining hand on his arm, silently admonishing him to stay calm, not to overreact. Without glancing at her he knew that her face was apprehensive, that she feared he might march to the platform and interrupt the lecture. He lightly squeezed her hand to reassure her, though with each word Nettles uttered it became more difficult to restrain himself. His pulse was rapid; each quick breath he took was a gasp of silent rage. He would have to wait twenty-four hours to undue Nettles' damage, he thought, if it could be undone!

While Nettles continued to eloquently expound his theory of innovative fiction, Pierce began mentally formulating his rebuttal. Sitting with his legs thrust into the aisle and his chin resting on his fist, he remained so engrossed until he heard the post-modernist speak the name of Vladimir Nabokov.

"In a lecture to college students, the late Vladimir Nabokov cautioned them to… *bear in mind that art is a divine game,*" Nettles said. "It is our responsibility as writers to play the divine game as best we can, challenging both ourselves and our readers within a framework that will hold the most intricate schemes, while at the same time acknowledging that it is all a game, perhaps one of the most serious games we will ever be engaged in."

Talbot applauded as enthusiastically as anyone in the audience as Nettles left the platform. The novelist was his last chance to get his poetry manuscript placed without having to circulate it among publishers he didn't know, which would be opening himself to the possibility of repeated rejection; editors would realize immediately that the publishers of his previous two books weren't supporting his work. Nettles' position as adviser to the University of Wisconsin Press could give him the boost he needed. If Nettles pushed his manuscript, it would be accepted. He was cultivating the novelist as much as he could without being obvious; if Nettles detected even a hint of his desperation, all would be lost.

Rising from his seat, Talbot rushed to congratulate Nettles. He pumped the novelist's hand, praising the lecture effusively

Pierce watched the two men with disgust, Nettles beaming while Talbot fawned over him. Pierce's arms were crossed, his jaw set. Like hell art was a game! Tomorrow was his turn. If Nettles wanted to play games, he'd better be prepared to lose.

***

Sara Newkirk walked across the platform, her stride as forthright and solid as her short, wide frame. Dressed in a drab, loose-fitting long cotton shift, she pushed her lank brown hair off her damp forehead and, stretching to see over the lectern, looked at the audience squarely, demanding their attention before she began reading an article she had written that she intended to publish, with some modifications, in a literary journal for which she was the editor. A staff member for years, she found the Workshop an ideal place to test new work; her colleagues' comments had proved to be excellent feedback.

"Poets," she said in a voice which was soft and cultured, surprising in contrast to her appearance, "are supposed to be the guardians, the preservers and protectors of language. I say *supposed* because that is what I was taught and what I believe."

During the next forty-five minutes, Newkirk alternately educated and chastised her audience. She talked about the rich heritage of poets, hundreds of years of the work of hundreds of men and women, describing this legacy as a foundation upon which new poets must build. Envisioning the foundation as a brick wall to be preserved and protected, she then described the wall crumbling under the weight of the drivel being currently published. She talked about gibberish masquerading as poems, about flippancy and self-indulgence, about a disregard for order and rhythms. Wondering aloud if the latest generation of poets had ever bothered to read poetry other than their own, she told them that few of her students could recite a line of Yeats from memory. She slammed a pudgy fist on the lectern, demanding to know how people could hope to become poets if they were unwilling or unable to be taught by Shelley and Keats, Whitman and Dickinson, Yeats and Stevens. As the lecture progressed, the people in the theater began to look as if they were not only seeing Newkirk's metaphorical wall but were having their heads banged against it.

She concluded by reading a portion of T.S. Eliot's essay *Tradition and the Individual Talent*, which she exhorted them to read. There was a lengthy pause before they applauded, as if they were so chastened that they feared to clap without permission. Most of what she had said wasn't new to them, but they had never been made to feel personally responsible.

Newkirk was not dismayed by their hesitation. She looked at the dazed expressions on their faces with a satisfied glint in her eyes, like a schoolmistress awarded respect from students whom she knows can't love her.

"That was some lecture!" Laura said to Nan and Agatha outside the theater. "I feel so ignorant. Do either of you know anything about that essay by Eliot?"

"It is famous for an analogy in which a filament of platinum is put into a chamber containing two gases," Agatha said. "The platinum acts as a catalyst, causing the gases to combine into a new substance, an acid, I believe. I can't recall which gases they were, but I do remember what Eliot said: *The mind of the poet is the shred of platinum*. What he meant is that the greater the artist, the better he will be able to transform his insights and experiences into the images and phrases of art, creating something entirely new from the raw materials he is working with."

Laura looked at Agatha as though considering a possibility that hadn't occurred to her before. "Do you have a doctorate?"

Blinking rapidly, Agatha turned her head from side to side like a bird whose nest has been discovered. "Well... yes... but I don't use the title. I'm really just a schoolteacher. The degree was for my own pleasure. Selfishness, I guess. I enjoyed the reading and attending the lectures."

"I'm sure you did," Nan said with a gentle smile.

***

After lunch Laura went to her room to prepare the material she was going to put into Michael Pierce's mailbox. She'd had the morning to think and had decided to include the first two pages of the second chapter of her novel. Agatha's enthusiasm for the scene in which the children arrive at Crazy Gertie's farm was her guide. If Agatha, who had a doctorate degree, had been impressed, then it might persuade Pierce to take a deeper look. She should have guessed that Agatha had a doctorate, not that her education made any difference. Agatha was a treasure, someone she wanted to keep as a friend after the conference was over.

She made her note to Pierce brief.

Thank you for reading the synopsis of my novel. The orphans' story is, as you said, about good and evil. I am enclosing two manuscript pages from the start of the second chapter so you'll have a glimpse of my writing.

Laura Belmont

She was about to fold the papers when she decided to make it look like a regular submission by putting them in a manila envelope instead; an envelope drew more attention and was less easily lost.

Gwen came in as she was leaving to put the envelope in Pierce's mailbox. "Did you get someone on the staff to look at your manuscript?" Gwen said.

"Not really."

"Well, don't waste your time asking Michael Pierce," Gwen said. "He's refusing to read any manuscripts other than those assigned to him."

"How do you know this?"

"I… I just know it," Gwen sputtered.

Gwen must have asked him, Laura thought as she headed downstairs. She felt lucky when she put the envelope in Pierce's mailbox.

***

Merle Ackerley strode down the hall to the Workshop offices, his gangly stride purposeful, his long knobby neck thrust forward as if he were fighting a stiff wind. He had spent nearly four days mulling over every explanation he could think of for the snubs he had encountered from his fellow staff members since he had arrived at the conference. Of all the reasons he could some up with, which included being a Southern-Appalachian writer, his newness in a group of people who were old friends and acquaintances, his lack of the credential of a prestigious literary prize or grant, and the recent publication of one of his short stories in *Redbook* (although their disdain for *Redbook* not only surprised but angered him), one explanation eclipsed the others to the point of rendering them insignificant: Roy Talbot had singled him out for the treatment he was receiving by scheduling him for the only afternoon reading. Until he heard Talbot's lecture, he hadn't thought about the schedule. Talbot's performance was the clue. He

108

was like a hound dog when it came to sniffing out a second-rater, and Talbot's speech on Coleridge had put him directly on the man's track. The director was a parasite, a man living off his position and the creativity of others to enhance his own name. There was nothing in that lecture worth a damn; it was all high-blown rhetoric, the talk of a fellow who had nothing to say, as unnecessary and nonproductive as a new reading of *Moby Dick*. He didn't have to read one of Talbot's poems to know that the man didn't have the talent of a stone buried in a creek bed. Talbot used Coleridge, and now he was using him by taking his rightful evening reading. It took some pondering, but he finally decided how he would handle this.

Grim-faced, Ackerley brushed his wheat-colored hair, an even mixture of gray and blond, off his forehead, and approached Dee Dee's desk.

"How can I help you?" she said, looking up from her computer screen.

"I want to speak to Roy Talbot."

"He's on the phone," she said, looking up, "long distance."

"I'll wait."

Instead of sitting on one of the high-backed wood chairs lined up against the wall, Ackerley started pacing back and forth in front of her desk, each stride impatient and insistent, spelling trouble.

His pacing made Dee Dee glance nervously at the lighted button on her telephone. She stepped inside Talbot's office and closed the door as soon as the light went off. "Merle Ackerley is waiting to see you," she said, keeping her voice low. "He's steaming about something."

Talbot's eyes briefly met hers, communicating the same thought: Ackerley's reading. Surprised at her perception, Talbot refocused first, glancing at his watch. The panel started in twenty minutes; since it took eight to ten minutes to walk to the theater, anything Ackerley had to say would have to be said quickly. "Send him in."

Ackerley ignored Talbot's outstretched hand, keeping his fingers firmly entrenched in the pocket of his jeans. "In that memo you gave to the staff when we got here," he began in a slow drawl, "you mentioned that we should notify you if we anticipated any difficulty with our schedules."

"Is there a problem?" Talbot forced himself to ask.

"I won't be able to give my reading on Sunday afternoon."

When he had originally put Ackerley in the Sunday afternoon slot, boldly giving himself an evening reading for the first time in his years as the director of the Workshop, Talbot had assumed that the novelist would accept the assignment without protest; Ackerley was an outsider who wouldn't know the difference. Dee Dee's warning had alerted him to trouble, but he hadn't expected this. "Wh… Why can't you read on Sunday?"

"It's the Sabbath," Ackerley drawled. "As a practicing Baptist, I really can't see my way clear to work on the Lord's day."

"But reading isn't work, not in the sense that you'll be doing something new. All you'll be doing is reciting, the same as a preacher does on Sunday when he reads his sermon."

"A preacher's Sunday work is sanctioned because he's in the business of saving souls. As God's surrogate, his place is on the pulpit. I'd be reading for my bread-and-butter."

"I would have gladly switched times with you, but my reading has already been announced in the *BULLETIN*. It's too late to change the schedule now."

"Oh, I didn't intend that you should switch with me," Ackerley said, aware from reading the previous year's brochure that Talbot had taken the afternoon reading. "It's early enough so that you can switch me with someone else."

Talbot had all he could do not to groan aloud. "Why did you wait until now to tell me?"

"There are plenty of nights left. It shouldn't be a problem," Ackerley said. "Or will it?"

"I don't know," Talbot said, his mind rapidly running through the list of staff members who hadn't read.

Ackerley stepped toward the door. "It seems fairly simple to me. Unless the Sunday afternoon reading isn't desirable for some reason."

"No, no, one time is as good as another."

"Then changing my reading should be easy," Ackerley said, slipping out of the office without waiting for a reply.

Before Talbot could blink he was facing a plump, middle-aged woman holding a bulging manila envelope. "Your secretary said you were busy, but I'll only take a minute," Claire Saxon said, setting the envelope squarely in the center of his desk. "I've decided that I want to become a participant. I'd like you to read my manuscript—it's a novel—and I want Michael Pierce to criticize it."

"The manuscript assignments have already been made," he said, furious with Dee Dee for allowing the woman to barge in.

"One more manuscript won't make a difference," she said. "And after you've read my novel, I'm sure you'll agree that it was a mistake for me to enroll as an observer."

"I'll let you know," he said curtly.

"Thank you." She paused in the doorway. "Now remember, I want Michael Pierce."

Talbot sank into his chair holding his head. Moments later Dee Dee appeared. "I'm sorry. She bulldozed her way in before I could stop her."

"How many people does Ackerley have on his list?"

"I'm not sure."

"Well, he may have another one," he said, hoping the manuscript was as bad as he suspected it was.

As he walked to the Circle Theater, he thought about Ackerley's refusal to take the Sunday afternoon reading, which would create unpleasantness and hard feelings no matter whom he chose to switch. Phyllis Baran was the logical choice. Her last book had mixed reviews, and her lecture was a mistake. After years of denying that her fiction was autobiographical, her public confession made her look like a fraud. It would have been smarter to admit it from the beginning; people find it hard to forgive a liar after they've been duped. Damn that Ackerley! Telling Phyllis was going to be difficult. She'd probably blame him because he hadn't taken the slot for himself.

***

Webb was waiting for Diana when she came out of the Studio, a rustic two-story cedar-shingle structure that had weathered into a grayish-brown. Wearing white shorts and a red tank top, Diana looked uncomfortably warm and not at all happy. "How was your study group?" he asked after they started walking down the dirt road toward the center of the campus.

"A waste of time. The air in the room was stifling, and we just sat there, discussing what we were going to discuss until the time was up. I don't think Phyllis Baran even cared. She seemed as bored as we were and did nothing about it. All she did was occupy space and perspire daintily."

"Since you're so unhappy, why don't you talk to Talbot? Tell him that you got nothing out of Baran's study group and want to be switched."

"I'm not comfortable making waves like some people," she said pointedly. "Why did you press that woman on the panel so hard this afternoon about the work she accepts? She gave you the answer you wanted with her first reply."

"No, she didn't. Talking about competing for grants and wishing people would buy her magazine before submitting their work was skirting the issue. I wanted to hear her admit, straight out, that the material she publishes is a reflection of her personal taste."

"What could you hope to gain from it other than embarrassing her and the other panelists?"

"They came here on an ego trip and to get publicity for their magazines. The panel was their moment in the sun, so if they paid for it by being embarrassed, it was a risk they should have been prepared for. Together, the editors of little magazines—of all magazines—have tremendous power. They sit like gods deciding what is published. If they read a poem that makes them flinch or feel uncomfortable, they can send it back with a form rejection slip thinking that they're being selective. Most of them probably don't bother to judge the work on its literary merit if their gut reaction is at all negative based on the subject matter. You heard her. She talked about science fiction as if it were unprintable garbage. *'I don't publish that stuff,'*" he said, capturing the inflection of disdain in the woman's voice.

"She has every right not to publish science fiction if she doesn't want to."

"Sure," he said. "But I wanted her to admit that her personal taste was the deciding factor."

"Are you satisfied?"

"I embarrassed you, didn't I?"

"A little," she admitted.

"Why?"

"I don't think you accomplished anything other than calling attention to yourself. They're still going to publish what they want to publish."

"I don't mind the attention."

"You like it!" she said.

He grinned. "It's better than being ignored."

"Aren't we going to your room to get your poems?" she said after she realized they had passed the path to Dickens.

"We'll get them later. Don't you want to walk after sitting all day?"

"It's too hot," she said, lifting her hair off her neck and shoulders.

"I'll take you to a place that's at least fifteen degrees cooler."

"The Inn isn't air conditioned. I haven't even seen a fan anywhere."

"This is better than air conditioning," he promised.

They walked around the circular driveway to the dirt-and-gravel road. "Where are we going?" she said.

"You'll see."

After they had walked close to a mile, he took her hand. "Come," he said, tilting his head toward the forest.

She looked at the dense vegetation bordering the road—Canada thistle, milkweed, and deeper in, bracken—and then at him, dubiously. "I can't walk through there in shorts."

"Sure you can. Follow close behind me."

He made a path for her, steering clear of the thistle. A wary expression remained on her face until they stepped past the bracken, which felt like green feathers brushing against her legs. Then she smiled. The forest was as cool as he had promised, dark and subtly fragrant, smelling of needles and decaying leaves. As they went deeper inside, scattered clumps of wood fern replaced the bracken until, finally, there was no vegetation except for infrequent sprays of oxalis and occasional exotically-colored mushrooms nesting between the bases of the trees. She pointed at the oxalis. "Do you know what that is?"

"Wood sorrel."

"Is it poisonous?"

"No."

"What were those plants we passed that had leaves like umbrellas?"

"May apples. The ones with double stems bear fruit."

She looked up at him, impressed. "Where did you learn this?"

"My grandfather was a naturalist. To him, a forest was sacred.

He'd get angry if he came upon any litter, even a gum wrapper, or if he saw carving on a tree. When I was a kid walking with him in the woods, I would look up at the canopy and feel as if I were in a place more sanctified than church."

He stretched out on the forest floor and patted the ground, motioning for her to join him. She sat down gingerly, as though she weren't sure what to expect. "It's soft," she said with surprise.

"I want to tell you about my grandfather," he said, "and my mother. I want you to know about them before you read my poems. They both had a problem with their body chemistry, a metabolic disorder. I have it, too. It's kind of like diabetes, only it's a salt deficiency instead of an insulin deficiency. Mine is controlled because doctors eventually discovered what the problem was. I take a pill after each meal and I'm fine. My mother and grandfather weren't as lucky. No one knew what was wrong with them and they both suffered horribly, especially my mother. It drove her to suicide."

"How awful!"

He shook his head at the enormity of what had happened. "Her life was a nightmare because the doctors she went to didn't diagnose the problem correctly. They did unspeakable things to her, they put her through torture."

Webb rolled onto his back and closed his eyes. She reached out and touched his face, tenderly communicating her sympathy. Then she was in his arms and they were making love under the green canopy, the trees towering and silent around them. She forgot her disappointment over her manuscript assignment; she forgot about the disappointing study group. Her body was singing.

***

Since Nettles' lecture on innovative fiction, Pierce had been consumed with his rebuttal. He had planned to read an essay on characterization for his lecture that he had written for the literary journal edited by Sara Newkirk, but Nettles' statement that plots could be eliminated because they were no longer necessary or relevant demanded the strongest answer possible, a direct refutation of every point the innovative fictionist had made. He had started writing the new lecture as soon as he could get to his laptop, his fingers moving furiously over the keys, pounding out words as if engaged in a deadly battle, each sentence a bullet shot at the enemy. Now he was trying to extricate himself from people who had been waiting to talk to him after his study group had ended.

The study group had met in Hackett Hall, and when it was over it had seemed to him that nearly a quarter of the people remained. He tried to be gracious, speaking to each person who had lined up to talk to him, but when a fellow whose hair was tied in a long black ponytail asked him if he wrote in long hand or used a computer, his patience evaporated. "A laptop," he said, "and that's where I should be now, pounding away at it. Thank you all for attending."

He left quickly, avoiding looking at the disappointed faces of the half-dozen-or-so people still waiting to speak to him, and on his way out stopped at his mailbox where he picked up three notes and Laura's manila envelope before heading to his room.

He read the notes as he walked; they were all from conference members asking him to read their work. Stuffing them into the pocket of his jeans, his mind returned to his rebuttal of Nettles, mentally weighing and discarding arguments. When he entered his room, he tossed the manila envelope on the bed and went immediately to his laptop.

He was typing rapidly when Leila came in. She happened to glance at the manila envelope on the bed, which irritated her; she felt as if she were constantly picking up after him. There were two uneven stacks of manila envelopes on the floor next to the desk, a short pile and a considerably taller one. She dropped the envelope on the shorter pile, which were manuscripts he had already read. He was too absorbed to notice.

***

At five o'clock the lower terrace was filled with people who had gathered for the cocktail party. Phyllis Baran, wearing a white skirt and a pink sleeveless sweater, moved uneasily through the crowd. Her eyes were defensive, her well-shaped mouth pinched with tension. The past twenty-four hours had been as miserable for her as any she had ever spent, almost as bad as the afternoon years ago in a lawyer's office when she had been offered the terms of her annulment. Since her lecture admitting the source of her fiction, she had been subtly avoided by her fellow staff members; too sophisticated to snub her outright, they had been distant and unapproachable, making no effort to include her in their conversations, acknowledging her with cool hellos and chillier smiles. When she had tried to join a conversation Marshall Stoddard and Andrew Cox were having in Clemens after lunch, both men had briefly tolerated her presence before excusing themselves. Aaron Green hadn't spoken a word to her when she had walked with him to the morning lecture, keeping her pace deliberately slow to accommodate the lame poet, except to give a begrudging response to her comment on the sparkling weather. But by far the worst snubs she had received had come from Sara Newkirk. Every time she had encountered Sara, the poet had flashed a smile resembling a grimace before turning her back to her. No backside was as broad or as formidable as Sara Newkirk's. The message couldn't have been clearer if it were written in a formal letter: she had been expelled from the club.

It was with relief and gratitude that she smiled at Talbot when he approached her. "Do you have a minute?" he said. "I need your help with a problem."

He led her to the grass beyond the terrace where they could speak without being overheard. "I'm in a tight spot," he said, putting his hand on his forehead to shield his eyes from the sun. "Ackerley is refusing to read on Sunday afternoon. He's claiming that as a practicing Baptist he can't read on the Sabbath. Frankly, I don't believe a word of it, but he won't budge. If he'd told me before we printed today's *BULLETIN*, I would have switched with him; now it's too late. I'm sorry to do this, Phyllis, really I am, but I have to put you in the afternoon spot."

The Sunday afternoon reading. Ignominy. She nodded, speechless, what little color she had leaving her face.

"Thanks," he said, patting her on the shoulder. "I knew you'd be a good sport about it."

She remained where she was standing after he left, unable to move. Finally, with as much dignity as she could muster, she started walking toward the terrace, shoulders squared, chin high, like an ailing actress determined to carry out her performance.

Diana and Webb were on the terrace near the bar, Diana fresh from a hurried shower after their intense lovemaking in the forest. Webb was attracting attention from Workshop members congratulating him for speaking out on editorial policy to the magazine editors on the panel. The crowd, the attention he was receiving, the noise of the conversations around him were acting as an elixir, boosting the speed of his already racing mind. He had forgotten to take a pill after lunch, and the three glasses of wine he'd consumed in rapid succession hadn't slowed his racing thoughts. "Shouldn't you take it easy?" Diana said after he told her he was going to the bar for another refill. "I don't think this is the place to get trashed."

Diana's roommate came up to them before he could respond. "Hi Marsha," Diana said, "I haven't seen you all day."

"I know," Marsha said pointedly. She looked up at Webb, her eyes bulging with curiosity.

Diana introduced them. "Are you a participant in fiction, too?" Marsha asked.

"In poetry."

"If you become famous, will you be the tallest poet in American history?"

"Maybe," Webb said. "Charles Olson was six-feet-eight-or-nine inches tall, depending upon which report you read. I'm six-nine-and-one-half."

"Who is Charles Olson?"

"He wrote *The Maximus Poems*. '*Off-shore, by islands hidden in the blood/jewels & miracles, I, Maximus/a metal hot from boiling water…*'" Webb recited.

"That's nice," Marsha said, interrupting the crowning work of Charles Olson's life as if it were a commercial for soap. "Who is criticizing your manuscript?"

"Aaron Greene," Webb said, raising his empty glass. He went to get a refill, leaving Diana with Marsha, who had temporarily run out of questions.

On the opposite side of the terrace, Agatha had just finished explaining Nettles' framework to Nan. "I bought his novel *Anagrams* yesterday after I learned that he'll be criticizing my manuscript, and I tried to read it last night. It's as impossible to understand as his lecture," Nan said. "I don't know why I was assigned to him. There is nothing about my novel that is experimental: it is a straight, conventional narrative. I have a feeling that our session is going to be catastrophic."

"Nettles has been teaching for years. I doubt that he expects all of his students to write as he does," Agatha said reassuringly. "As a teacher, I've always believed it's my responsibility to encourage each individual's voice, not to make every voice sound the same."

Jerry Hofstrand spotted Agatha and Nan and approached them. During the day he'd tried to discuss Nettles' lecture with people, specifically asking what the novelist had meant by the framework or structure necessary to write innovative fiction, and had gotten evasive responses; although they wouldn't admit it, he had the impression that the people he'd spoken with didn't understand the concept any better than he did. "Are you enjoying the programs?" he asked.

"They've been interesting," Nan said while Agatha nodded.

"Especially Nettles," he said. "I've been trying to find out what he meant by a framework, but no one I've spoken with seems to know."

Nan smiled. "We were just talking about that. Thank goodness Agatha explained it to me. You can talk about Nettles while I go to the bookstore to get another one of his books."

Agatha watched her disappear into the crowd, feeling abandoned. What would she say to him, she wondered.

"I hope you don't mind explaining Nettles' framework again," he said.

"N—not at all," Agatha said. "It's a literary device that binds the fiction together. The device could be anything—a train route, letters of correspondence between the characters, or puzzles such as anagrams. Whatever takes place in the fiction occurs within this frame of reference or relates to it in some way. I thought *Anagrams* was a difficult, disturbing book."

"I can relate to the difficulty," he said with a chuckle, "but why disturbing?"

Agatha felt his eyes on her, waiting expectantly for her reply. She could sense no repugnance in them; he was looking at her as if her face were quite ordinary. "I found the novel not quite human," she said, beginning to relax. "It was all surface, brilliantly done but devoid of emotion. My response was completely intellectual. I was impressed by his writing and at the same time uncomfortable because of its lack of feeling. I guess I'm old fashioned. I like to identify with characters, to live their lives while I'm reading about them."

"Most of us read for vicarious pleasure, although no one here will admit it," he said. "I see people going in for dinner. Will you join me? I'd like to talk more about Nettles' lecture."

"Shouldn't we wait for Nan?"

"She probably went in already," he said, surveying the terrace. "If we don't go soon, we'll be stuck at the end of the line for the buffet. It happened to me last night, and they started to close the dining room before I got my food."

"How dreadful," Agatha said, following him up the grassy slope. "What did you do?"

"Ate fast," he said, laughing.

Still on the terrace, Claire happened to look up and saw Agatha. Her mouth fell open as her eyes darted from her roommate to Hofstrand.

Claire's shock was brief. She hurried up the slope as fast as her legs could carry her, calling, "Agatha, Agatha."

Agatha stopped and turned, blinking with surprise. "Agatha," Claire said, rushing up to them breathlessly, her eyes fixed on Hofstrand, "I haven't seen you all day! Where have you been?"

Before Agatha could reply, Claire introduced herself to Hofstrand. She continued to talk nonstop through the buffet line and dinner, monopolizing the conversation with stories about her trips, her late husband (lingering on the word *late* whenever she mentioned him), and the students at the junior college where she taught, while Agatha sat withdrawn, as inconspicuous as a nesting bird.

***

The likeliest place to get decent cell phone reception at the Workshop was in the area around the Tabard Inn, which was situated on the highest point on the property. Laura excused herself before dessert was served so she could get a good spot, knowing there would be a rush of people looking for one when the meal was over.

The best reception she found was near the back entrance. Gretchen answered on the second ring. "How's it going?" she said.

"Michael Pierce said he would read a synopsis of my novel and get back to me."

"That's great!"

"I thought so too, until I found out that he's told other people the same thing. I put a few pages in with the synopsis, which I hope will hook him."

"Good thinking," Gretchen said. "Who else are you going to give it to?"

"Marshall Stoddard is my only other prospect. I won't go near Andrew Cox, I don't understand Eric Nettles' work, and people are so negative about Ackerley that I don't want to ask him. I tried to approach Phyllis Baran at the cocktail party this afternoon, but she looked so out of it—it sounds ridiculous, but she looked almost as if she were in a state of shock—that I backed away. There aren't the opportunities here that I expected."

"Maybe not, but you need only one writer to give you the help you're looking for," Gretchen said. "Just one."

"I'm beginning to wonder if that's a realistic expectation."

"Why wouldn't it be?"

"I've talked to some people here who have attended other writers' conferences, and none of them know of a staff member actually helping someone get published."

"That's hard to believe."

"I thought so at first, but now I'm not so sure," Laura said. "It's hard to judge. I don't know if the contributors here are good writers, and I have no idea of how willing the writers on the staff are to use their connections to help people get published. There is only one thing of which I am certain: I am one of many looking for the same opportunity, and not all of us are going to get the help we are hoping for."

People started trickling out of the Inn with cell phones in their hands. The two women talked for a few more minutes before Laura relinquished her spot to an older woman who gave her a grateful smile.

***

Talbot was determined not to let Ackerley's refusal to take the Sunday slot tarnish his evening. He read mainly from his unpublished book, selecting the best poems for the Workshop audience. Dressed in khaki slacks and a black knit shirt, he appeared poised and self-confident behind the lectern; only his eyes, occasionally rising above his reading glasses to gauge Eric Nettles' response to his poetry, gave a clue to his nervousness.

Listening intently in her usual seat, Dee Dee was enraptured not by the poems but by his sonorous voice, responding to his resonance as if it were a mating call. Her desire for him was exquisite, a gnawing, hollow ache that demanded satiation, stronger than any pang of hunger her over-padded body had ever expressed for food. It had to happen this summer, she thought. Maybe, maybe it would be tonight.

Several rows behind Dee Dee, Diana sat next to Webb, looking at her watch every few minutes. Webb's constant motion was making her increasingly edgy. He was shifting his weight from one side to another, re-crossing his legs, rubbing his hands, running his fingers through his hair. "Talbot's poetry stinks," he whispered to her midway through the reading. She put her index finger to her lips, gesturing him to be quiet. "It's junk," he whispered, ignoring her.

"Shhhhh," she whispered back, the expression on her face pleading with him to be silent. Admonishing glances from people sitting around them made her flush with embarrassment. He shifted in his seat yet again, put his arm around her and started rubbing her shoulder. She could feel his energy through his fingers, a force so powerful that she knew she could do nothing to check it.

Seated in the last row, Ackerley nodded to himself from time to time, his suspicion confirmed. Although he'd be the first to admit that he was no expert in poetry, he knew enough to recognize that Talbot's work was at best mediocre.

Talbot's voice deepened as he approached the last stanza of the final poem in his reading. Moved as much by his pride in the lines (he believed they were among the best he had ever written) as by their meaning, he read:

"My daughters raise their heads
To welcome me.
Their bright, open faces
Like tulips in the sun,
Are three blessings."

The audience applauded enthusiastically. Talbot removed his reading glasses, beaming his thanks. At the end of the first row, clapping wildly, Dee Dee was trying unsuccessfully to catch his eye. His attention, however, was fixed on Nettles. The burly novelist was applauding with the rest of the audience, but his face was impossible to read.

Webb and Diana were among the first out of the theater. The temperature had dropped drastically, and the cold air was jarring. "I should have learned from last night and brought a sweater," Diana said, shivering.

"Do you want to stop at the Shed for a hot drink?"

"No, thanks. I'd like to go back to my room, crawl into bed, and read your poems."

"You can read them tomorrow. It's my turn for the room."

She was exhausted, both from the day itself and the hour she had spent sitting next to him while he fidgeted. His energy enervated her. "Maybe you can switch with Hecker. Then we can have the room two nights in a row."

"He asked before dinner if he could have it and I refused. He acted like such a jerk about it that I told him off. I'm tired of agreeing to his rules, then having him change them on me. Can you imagine that guy drilling teeth? He must change drill bits every ten seconds trying to decide which one he wants to use while his patients watch him, squirming."

People around them were talking about the reading. "He read so well!" exclaimed a bespectacled matron to a group of women. "His poems are wonderful!"

Webb turned and looked at the woman. "You can't mean Talbot!" he said.

"Y—yes," she said, clearly taken aback.

"His poems are terrible! He…"

"Let's go," Diana said, interrupting him before he could tell the woman, and everyone else around them, what was wrong with Talbot's poetry.

Webb stood like a boulder. "In a minute."

She grabbed his hand and surreptitiously ran her finger across his palm. Distracted by the erotic gesture, he left the astonished woman and strode through the darkness with Diana to Dickens.

***

In Melville, Dee Dee lay in bed listening for the sound of footsteps in the hall. Every few minutes she checked the time, squinting myopically at the white-plastic alarm clock on her night stand, trying not to shiver. She was wearing her best nightgown, which was a deep pink, low cut and full with gathers that accentuated her breasts. The room was freezing. She thought of the heavy flannel nightshirt folded in the bottom drawer of the maple dresser, fighting the temptation to change and turn off the light. There was still time, it was only eleven thirty. He would have to notice that her light was on. Instead of stopping at Clemens after the reading, she had gone to her room, where she had showered and put on fresh make-up. Now she was anticipating his knock on her door, asking if she were awake. She would invite him in, her voice casual and friendly…

The stairs creaked. She heard the murmur of male voices, the dull thud of footsteps on the hall floor. She plumped her pillow and straightened the covers, arranging them so that her pink nylon-covered breasts were exposed. A door opened down the hall. More footsteps, these advancing toward her door. Her mouth was dry. She heard his doorknob click and, holding her breath, willed him to look in the direction of her room.

His door closed. Through the membrane-thin wall she heard him crossing his room, the squeak of a drawer opening, a hard object—probably his belt buckle—hitting the floor. Her lower lip trembled, her heart ached with impossible longing. When his toilet flushed, she buried her head in her pillow and sobbed.

***

At the opposite end of the hall, Andrew Cox was having sex with a woman who was astride him. Attracted to her because of her pendulous breasts and athletic body, he expected to have the kind of romp he enjoyed, where he was on top directing the action. He didn't have a chance with this woman. She was on top from the beginning, grasping him with her powerful thighs as if he were a horse, her breasts threatening to smother him while she rode her way to an orgasm. All he could do was hope that he would last. The next woman would be small, he thought, instead of a half-head taller with muscles bigger than his.

***

❧ WORKSHOP BULLETIN ❧

VOL. 74, NO.4   THE CLYMER WORKSHOP   AUGUST 14 2004

GOOD MORNING!

A perfect summer day is predicted, with sunshine and temperatures in the mid-eighties. To add to our riches, the evening will be comfortably cool.

MORNING PROGRAM

9:30 A.M. Fiction Lecture
(Michael Pierce)
10:30 A.M. Guest Lecture
(William Belden)

Michael Pierce will lecture on "The Necessity for Strong Plots and Strong Characterization."

AFTERNOON PROGRAM

2:00 P.M. Guest Lecture
(Sidney Deinhart)
3:00 P.M. Study Groups

EVENING READING

Eric Nettles, novelist and short story writer, will read from his fiction. The winner of a National Book Award, he has received fellowships from the Guggenheim and Rockefeller Foundations, the National Endowment for the Arts, and a grant from the American Academy of Arts and Letters. His books include *Lost In The City*, *Odes And Incantations*, *Memorabilia*, *The Drifting Banquet*, and *Anagrams*. He was a Visiting Lecturer at the Iowa Workshop and has taught at Swarthmore and Princeton. He currently holds the Griswold Chair of English at the University of Wisconsin and is the adviser/ consultant to the University of Wisconsin Press.

GUESTS

We are delighted to welcome William Belden on his first visit to the Clymer Workshop. Mr. Belden is a fiction editor for *Review Magazine*. He will discuss the current market for short fiction. Sidney Deinhart, who has graciously consented to visit the Workshop, will lecture on "Getting Published." Mr. Deinhart is a senior editor at Corydon Books. Before joining the world of hardcover publishing, he was the senior fiction editor for *Esquire*.

STUDY GROUPS

The locations for study groups are posted on the bulletin boards. Participants are to report to the study groups led by the staff members assigned to criticize their manuscripts. Observers may attend the groups of their choice.

REMINDER

Please check your mailboxes several times a day. If you have lost or forgotten the combination, you can obtain it at the Workshop office.

LIQUOR ORDERS

Liquor orders can be picked up in the sitting room after dinner.

SUNDAY SOFTBALL

Attention athletes, male and female: sign-up sheets for softball teams will be posted on the bulletin board outside the Workshop office. The game will be held at 10:30 tomorrow morning on the softball field. All equipment will be supplied. A baseball game isn't complete without cheering sections. Join the fun as a spectator and root for your favorite team if you don't trust your skill with a bat.

TIDBIT

"I'm sorry I don't remember you. I never forget a face, but I've met so many new people since I came here that my mind is saturated."

> *"...there is no technique that can be discovered and applied*
> *to make it possible for one to write."*
> Flannery O'Connor

Chapter IV

Claire Saxon's fingers trembled as she turned the tumbler to open her mailbox. She could see the folded white paper through the glass. It was, she was certain, a note officially making her a participant assigned to Michael Pierce. Setting the dial precisely on six, she heard a click before the lock sprung open.

She eagerly unfolded the note, but as she began to read, the excitement in her face turned into a dark scowl:

Dear Ms. Saxon:

We are happy to notify you that you have been changed from an observer to a participant. Your manuscript will be assigned to Merle Ackerley. All participants are required to pay an additional fee of $200 for the extra work and time involved in criticizing manuscripts. After we receive your payment (cash or check will be acceptable), we'll give Mr. Ackerley your manuscript for evaluation.

The note was signed *Roy Talbot*, with Dee Dee's initials following his name. Too livid to notice the tiny initials, Claire slammed the mailbox shut and marched to the Workshop office.

"I must speak to Mr. Talbot," she said, standing squarely in front of Dee Dee's desk, "now."

The note and Claire's tone of voice told Dee Dee more than she wanted to know. "He isn't here," she said as pleasantly as she could. Then, because Talbot had been furious with her for allowing the woman to barge into his office yesterday, she forced herself to add, "Perhaps I can help you."

"It's between me and Mr. Talbot. There's been a misunderstanding."

"Don't you want to be a participant?"

"How do you know about that?"

"I typed the note. I'm Mr. Talbot's assistant."

"You must have made a mistake, then," Claire said, thrusting the note under Dee Dee's nose. "According to this, I am to be assigned to Merle Ackerley."

"That's right."

"No, it isn't! I told Mr. Talbot yesterday that I wanted my manuscript criticized by Michael Pierce."

"Mr. Pierce's schedule is completely filled. He already has the maximum number of manuscripts."

"One more won't make a difference."

"Unfortunately, it would," Dee Dee said, briefly shutting her eyes as she summoned patience. "It would be unfair to you and the other participants assigned to him because he wouldn't be able to devote enough time to each manuscript. Everyone would be shortchanged."

"I don't mind."

"The others might," Dee Dee said, "and I know that Mr. Pierce would. He takes his responsibilities seriously."

"I'll ask him myself."

Dee Dee's response was quick. "He'll only direct you back here. All assignments have to come through this office."

"What about Eric Nettles? Can I be assigned to him or is his schedule filled, too?"

"We gave you the only opening in fiction. The decision is yours." Dee Dee placed her fingers on the computer keyboard. "I'm sorry," she said, "but I must get something done."

The tapping of the computer keys shut the lid on Claire's arsenal of arguments. She left the office in a huff. *It was a waste of time talking to that piddling assistant!* she thought. One never got anywhere with underlings. She would look for Mr. Talbot later this morning and speak to him directly. She would insist upon Michael Pierce. She was a published writer who probably had more credits than any participant at the Workshop. When Mr. Talbot became aware of that, he simply couldn't refuse her request!

***

The Circle Theater filled rapidly for the first lecture. There was no reluctance in the steps of the people who entered, no wistful glances back at the rolling landscape, which glistened in the morning sunlight as verdant as Eden, no last deep breaths taken of the fresh morning air they were forsaking to sit in a building where dampness clung to the wood walls and rafters. The ritual of the previous days, repeated before each lecture like grace before a meal, was repeated once again: chairs squeaked and scraped as they took their seats; pages fluttered in notebooks that were opened to clean, unmarked paper; ballpoint pens were in ready hands. The stale air, smelling faintly of dust and mildew, was thick with anticipation, with an intensity of desire stronger than sex. Perhaps today, this very morning, they would finally be told what they had come so far to learn: how to write poems and short stories, novels and non-fiction that agents would accept and editors would publish.

Pierce bounded up the steps to the platform and walked briskly to the lectern. Since Nettles' lecture on innovative fiction, he had been consumed with his rebuttal. The first draft was followed by a second, and then a third revised at dawn. A compulsive revisionist, he would have re-written the lecture again given the opportunity.

The conference members waited as if encapsulated in a bubble of expectation as they watched Pierce adjust the microphone, gazing at him as if he were a god who had descended to earth to speak to them, not a mortal with a head full of iron-gray curls who had circles under his eyes, a lean man of forty-three wearing jeans, a red-knit shirt and running sneakers. Even Leila, sitting in the second last seat in the front row next to Dee Dee, was briefly caught in the spell and forgot her irritation with her husband for waking her at dawn. Of the several hundred people in the theater, only Eric Nettles, four rows behind Leila, seemed immune to what was happening. He crossed his legs and leaned back; only his eyes, half-closed and serious, contradicted his relaxed appearance.

"This morning I am going to do something that no creative writer in his right mind would even consider," Pierce began, gripping the sides of the lectern. "I am going to tell you the plot for the next book I plan to write.

"Telling you the plot isn't as big a risk as it seems, because you are all witnesses to the fact that you heard the story from me first. But even if every one of you refused to testify on my behalf, I would tell the story anyway. I would give away the idea for a book—the key, the very heart of my vocation as a writer—if I knew that by doing so I could make you see the importance, the *absolute necessity,* for writing structured fiction. By structured, I mean stories that have beginnings, middles, and ends. Stories that have definite plots leading to a climax. Stories in which the action surges and ebbs as naturally as the tide. Stories in which a reader can lose all sense of time and place except for what is happening on the pages of the book that has captured his attention.

"The working title for the new book will be *Mr. McDermott and the Egg.* It is a children's story, which is the most difficult of all fiction to write. Children can't be fooled; nor can you talk down to them. They look at the world through unclouded eyes and understand more than you think they do. Most important, they will catch any mistake in the fiction, no matter how insignificant. They can't be hoodwinked like their parents, who will accept nonsense if it's given to them in an appealing package.

"Mr. McDermott, the protagonist in the story, is a retired mailman who is always looking for ways to improve things, which drives his wife nuts. One day while he's in the kitchen watching his wife put away groceries and unintentionally making her nervous by offering unwanted suggestions as to how to rearrange her cupboards so they would be more efficient, she drops a full carton of eggs. The eggs make an incredible mess; they break and splash all over the floor, the cupboards, and Mrs. McDermott's shoes. She's upset, but McDermott is excited. The accident has given him a wonderful idea: he will improve the egg. He will scientifically breed chickens to lay eggs that won't break when they're dropped.

"Mr. McDermott gets busy. He builds a chicken coop, fills it with chickens he selects from different farms, and buys grains that he mixes and measures, using a scale and various formulas he concocts. The chickens are terrific egg layers, but Mrs. McDermott still has to buy her eggs in the supermarket. She doesn't know that McDermott breaks the eggs he gathers, dropping them from a specific height into a special box he's designed to test the shells.

"It takes McDermott two years to accomplish what he's set out to do. On a sunny spring morning he goes out to the chicken coop and picks up an egg that has been laid by one of his favorite hens. Holding the egg over the test box, he lets it drop. The egg lands with a ping. Excited, McDermott grabs the egg and holds it up to the light, looking for cracks. The shell is as smooth as a piece of porcelain. He drops the egg again, this time from a greater height.

Again, the egg lands with a ping, the shell intact.

"Overjoyed, he runs to the house with the egg to show his wife. Mrs. McDermott watches him aghast as he drops the egg. The egg lands with a ping and rolls across the kitchen floor. She's amazed. He promises her that it will be as tasty as any egg she's ever eaten as he picks up the egg so she can cook it for breakfast.

"Mrs. McDermott puts a frying pan on the stove. Then she cracks the shell against the side of the pan to open the egg. The egg pings but it doesn't crack. She tries again, this time using more force. The egg won't crack; it's still as smooth as a piece of porcelain.

"By this time McDermott is becoming concerned. He tries to crack the egg with the side of a spoon, then with the side of a knife. The egg won't break. In desperation, he goes to the basement and returns with a hammer. Before his wife can stop him, he hits the egg with the hammer. The egg splatters all over the kitchen counter, making an inedible mess.

"McDermott's improvement is, in the end, a failure. Some things, he learns, are best left as they are."

Breaking the custom of waiting until the end of the lecture to show their appreciation, the audience applauded vigorously. Pierce smiled, then ran his fingers through his gray curls, impatient to continue. "The problem with much of what we call 'literature' that is being written today is that it is suffering from the same problem as McDermott's egg," he said when the clapping subsided. "In their effort to make something new, artists are creating work that is as alienating as a mixture of raw egg and crushed shell.

"Novelists whom critics categorize as *post modern*—a label heavy with both respect and implication—write books that are notable, among other things, for their absence of plot. We look in vain for characters with whom we can identify, for situations that make us nod our heads in recognition, for fiction that describes the world in which we live. Instead, we read paragraph after paragraph of words that are put together beautifully, words that are all surface, all texture, art as cold and glittering as a frozen lake under a winter sun. In their eagerness to make art new, the post-modernists have taken the soul out of it; or the fiction is so completely self-referential that we find ourselves trapped in a claustrophobic consciousness from which there is no escape.

"The reason for eliminating plots, post-modern novelists

explain in response to those who protest their absence, is that we have outgrown them; we have told every story there is to tell. I won't argue with that. There are no new stories. *But I will fight with anyone who says we have outgrown them.*

"We know from pictures on cave walls that stories have been told since the beginning of recorded time. It isn't difficult to imagine men sitting around a fire telling tales of hunts, of bravery and cowardice, of lust and greed. The lives of these men were, in every sense, as mundane as ours. There wasn't a great hunt every day, or a birth or a death or a monster to be slain; their existence was dreary, a day-to-day scraping for the rudiments of their survival. But when they were listening to a story they could forget their troubles while they vividly imagined heroes and heroines in situations that were familiar yet enthralling. They were transported to another place, vicariously participating in events they rarely experienced while learning truths about themselves that they might never have acknowledged or addressed.

"Man eventually abandoned caves for shelters of his own making, but he didn't abandon the stories on which he'd been raised. We have the greatest of these stories today—*Beowulf, The Odyssey*, the Greek plays. These archetypal stories are the foundation of our literature, the heart of all we know about ourselves as human beings. Their wisdom cannot be exhausted; only we, like well-meaning McDermotts, can abandon them in the name of progress.

"Our job as writers is not different from the storytellers who preceded us. We must re-create experience, making it intelligible. Fiction is a dream, a writer's vision of reality set down on paper. It has to be vivid. It has to be real. It has to not only create and sustain life, but be *better than life, more real than reality.*

Unable to listen any longer, Leila closed her eyes. It was painful for her to look at him, to see his passion for his art, a passion she was certain surmounted any feeling he'd ever had for her. The blaze of his eyes, the timbre of his voice, the forward thrust of his body, the strong gestures of his hands emphasizing each point he made—all spoke eloquently of his consuming love for an idealized fiction. He loved her, she knew, but he loved his art more; no woman could compete. *Fiction must be better than life.* To him it was better than life, more real than any reality he could have with her. She held back tears, wondering how she could prove to him that nothing, absolutely nothing, was better than life.

Every moment Talbot continued to listen was torture. His shoulders drooped as Pierce pointedly refuted every argument Nettles had made the day before. It was impossible to judge Nettles' reaction; the man was as impossible to read as his books. If Nettles held him responsible, he could forget about the publication of his poems.

Pierce looked gravely at the audience. "Our stories are our history. They are the chronicles of our experiences, the maps of our dreams. We must fashion the words we write into dreams as perfect as we can make them, vivid and real, with strong plots leading to strong climaxes. We must write novels that are adventures of the human heart! We cannot afford to do less."

People in the audience began to clap hesitantly at first, as if they were unsure their response was appropriate. After that brief faltering the clapping grew in intensity, louder and louder, until the plank walls vibrated. The applause continued long after Pierce left the platform.

Eric Nettles pressed his hands together without producing a sound. His motions were slow and automatic as his eyes swept over the excited faces of the people surrounding him. Pierce was clever, he thought, including these amateur writers in his broad use of the word "we," making them believe they were all on the same sacred mission when most couldn't write a decent paragraph, much less a piece of fiction worthy of publication. Pierce wasn't worth fighting; crusaders like him would come and go, but scholars would be reading books written by Eric Nettles for years. Still, he thought, focusing on Leila, a challenge was a challenge. She was a prize worthy of a brief skirmish. There was almost a week left, and having her in his bed would be a sweet reward.

Stoddard listened to the applause as if he were measuring its loudness in decibels. Stupendous, he thought, watching people engulf the slender novelist. If it weren't for him, Pierce might still be unknown. His review years ago had made Pierce, and the favor hadn't been returned, not to the extent it might have been. But Pierce didn't see it that way. Although it felt good at the time, confronting him about the review might have been a mistake. The new manuscript he brought for his reading was definitely unsalvageable. He'd have to read from *Places At The Table* again and hope that the good will of his colleagues would make them overlooking.

Talbot was in a foul mood when he left the theater. Barely out the door, he was confronted by Claire. "May I speak with you," she said, her jangling bracelets adding to her air of agitation.

Without waiting for his reply, she told him that she wanted her manuscript criticized by Michael Pierce. "I just can't accept Mr. Ackerley," she said.

"Then you'll have to remain an observer," he said curtly.

"You don't understand. I'm… I'm…" She wanted to tell him that she was a published writer. But then he would want to know where her stories had been published. The theater had emptied, and they were surrounded by observers and participants who sneered at *Redbook*, people who, if they had an inkling that she wrote and sold stories to the romances, would snicker at the sight of her.

"You're what?" he said impatiently, eyeing Nettles, who was talking to Leila.

"I believe my manuscript has merit," Claire offered tentatively.

"All writers feel that way about their manuscripts; it's characteristic of the disease," he said. "The decision is yours."

He turned and walked away. She looked around for someone she knew, anyone she could chat with so she wouldn't have to stand alone until they went in to hear the next speaker. Even homely Agatha would be better than no one, she thought, desperately scanning the crowd. People seemed to be either engrossed in conversations or deliberately wandering off by themselves. She was one of the first to re-enter the theater and took a chair in the last row. Her eyes bright with unshed tears, she watched the conference members file in; among them was Agatha, walking with a freckled woman and a stunning strawberry blond.

The sight of Agatha in the company of friends shifted the focus of Claire's frustration. If she had been given a halfway decent roommate, she might have had a pleasant time at this overrated, overpriced conference.

***

The guest lecturer, William Belden, a blond, fair-complexioned fellow in his late thirties who wore round metal glasses that made him look like a startled owl, was an editor for *Review Magazine*, a relatively new publication that was challenging *The New Yorker* for readers. After a brief, encouraging opening in which he told the conference members that *Review* wanted to help new writers and that they published manuscripts from the unsolicited pile whenever they could, his message was, at best, dismal.

"We receive between fifteen hundred and two thousand short story manuscripts a month," Belden said. "We publish approximately eighteen short stories a year. I'm sorry to have to give you these figures, but it would be unfair to mislead you."

During the question-and-answer period, Belden was asked to describe what the magazine wanted in a story. "We look for well-developed characters and distinctive language," he said. "In general, for well-crafted stories of high literary quality."

When he was pressed to be as specific as possible, he threw his hands in the air in a gesture of helplessness. "I know what you're asking, but there is no hard-and-fast rule governing the selection of the fiction we publish," he said apologetically. "If a story has something that grabs us for any reason, or for no particular reason at all, we might accept it or encourage the writer to submit more work."

Seated in the center of the theater, Webb nudged Diana with his elbow. "See," he whispered with satisfaction, "even in *Review*, what's published is a matter of taste."

Diana nodded her agreement, hoping he'd be sufficiently satisfied to remain quiet until the end of the session. Aside from being embarrassed by his uninhibited outbursts, she didn't want Belden sidetracked or angered. She was vitally interested in what he had to say because she had submitted several stories to the magazine, one of which had received a form rejection, the other rejected with an encouraging letter stating that they would be interested in seeing more of her work.

Laura saw Dynarski respond to what the editor said by squaring his broad shoulders as if he were getting ready for an argument. She didn't know that he had submitted over thirty stories to *Review Magazine*, each of which had been returned with a form rejection slip. She didn't know that stories written by some of the people who had been in his classes at Iowa had been published in the magazine, stories that were, in his opinion, no better than his. She didn't know that he was wondering if he could blow Belden's cool by asking him how many stories were accepted because the writers had pull, which he suspected though it was untrue. But she did know that Stan was attracted to her, and that he was profoundly frustrated and unhappy. He seemed to show up at her table at every meal, and if she hadn't been sitting with Nan and Agatha this morning, he would have taken the chair next to hers. She'd been discouraging him as much as she dared, yet at the same time she felt sorry for him; he seemed so utterly alone and so vulnerable.

As she listened to the editor and watched Dynarski, Laura realized that the novel she had written, for which she had felt such a triumphant sense of accomplishment at having completed, could lead her down a path paved with frustration and unhappiness like the one Stan was on if she weren't lucky. Maybe meeting Stan was a warning: if she invested too much hope in her book and couldn't find an agent and a publisher, she would end up like him, bitter and angry.

It would depend upon what happened at this conference, she decided. If she didn't get the help she had come here for, she would go home, put the manuscript in a closet, and get on with her life.

But she had put so much time and effort into the novel, and she believed as Gretchen did, that it was good. And Agatha's enthusiastic praise for the three additional chapters she had given her to read was unquestionably sincere. What if she couldn't let it go? The ten years she'd spent with Greg had ended in crushing disappointment, even though she'd known the danger of getting involved with him and had been warned many times.

Perhaps the best decision was no decision until she heard what Michael Pierce had to say.

***

Marsha walked down a musty corridor in the Tabard Inn to the room she shared with Diana, her lunch of a gray hamburger and sodden French fries weighing heavily in her stomach.

She doubted that Diana would be in their room. Diana was always with Doug Webb. It was just as well, she thought. If she had the room to herself she could have a good cry, although she had held tears back for so long they could be frozen inside her, crystals of ice impossible to shed. Asking every fiction writer on the staff to read one of her stories and being refused was more than she could take. Merle Ackerley's refusal had been the worst of all.

She didn't even value his opinion; she'd only asked him because there was no one left. He should have been grateful since everyone was avoiding him.

It wasn't as if she were asking them to expend an extraordinary effort for her. The story was only eleven double-spaced pages. Only eleven. It was her best one. She'd gone over and over it for almost two years, making each sentence as perfect as possible. Some of those sentences were masterpieces. Well, maybe not masterpieces, but close to it. And she'd been published. She once had a story in a little magazine. She'd told them that. Don't they have any sense of professional courtesy like doctors and lawyers? They'd told her that they were sorry. Then they'd had the audacity to suggest that she ask some participants to read her work, which was ridiculous. She was a published writer! What made them think she would value the opinion of an unpublished participant?

Diana was in the room. She was lying on her bed facing the wall, holding a sheaf of papers in which she was absorbed.

Marsha sat at the desk, slipped off her sandals, and then crossed her leg to look at her right heel, which had been bothering her all morning. The skin on the heel was an angry red except in the center, where a large white blister had blossomed. She stared at the blister as if it were an additional insult heaped on the many she had already accumulated.

"Do you have any band aids?" she said.

"What?" Diana said, startled. "Oh, Marsha, I didn't hear you come in."

"Do you have any band aids?" Marsha repeated in an injured voice.

"Sorry," Diana said, settling down again.

"What are you reading?"

"Poems."

"Whose?"

"Doug Webb's," Diana said impatiently. "This is the first chance I've had to read them."

"Did he ask you to read them or did you ask him?"

"I don't remember," she said, raising the papers as if they were a shield that would deflect further questions. "Please, I don't mean to be rude, but I just don't feel like talking. I'm trying to concentrate."

Marsha stepped into a pair of beige terrycloth slippers and raced out of the room and down the hall. When she was upset she had intestinal problems, and while Diana was talking she experienced sudden pain and pressure in her lower abdomen. Now bent over from its intensity, she hurried to the bathroom at the end of the corridor, praying that it was unoccupied.

The door was closed.

Frantic, she raced down an adjoining hallway where there were three bathrooms located midway in the corridor.

All three doors were closed.

Panicking, she started back down the hallway toward the stairs, thinking of the floor below where a bathroom might be free. She heard the sound of a door opening; it was to one of the bathrooms. She turned and raced past the previous occupant, tears spilling down her cheeks. Thank God, she thought, slamming the door shut.

***

Sidney Deinhart left Clemens in the company of his wife and Talbot to walk to the Circle Theater, his jowly face a moon of satisfaction. A senior editor at Corydon Books, this was Deinhart's third visit at the Workshop. He was vacationing at the Chautauqua Institution, where he and his wife stayed for two weeks every summer. He viewed his visit to the Workshop as a pleasant diversion; for the few hours he spent at the conference he was gazed upon worshipfully by aspiring writers as if he were a god in possession of privileged knowledge and unfathomable power, more than adequate compensation for his time.

This year the sixty-one-year-old editor arrived earlier than usual, motivated by a desire to make positive contact with Eric Nettles. Nettles did not have an agent; his books had all been published by the same house, his loyalty with an editor who had been a mentor early in his career, later a trusted friend. The editor had died in the spring. Therefore, Deinhart reasoned, Nettles could be persuaded to leave his publisher for Corydon, specifically for Sidney Deinhart.

His conversation with Nettles was promising. The innovative fictionist didn't make an outright commitment, but he was receptive, practically guaranteeing the editor a first look at his next completed manuscript. Deinhart made a mental note to write a follow-up letter, telling Nettles how much he had enjoyed their meeting. He'd write from Chautauqua, he decided. A handwritten letter would be the right touch, putting the relationship on a more personal basis.

Most of the chairs in the theater were filled when Talbot, the only staff member present, stepped behind the lectern to introduce his guest. The portly editor lumbered up the steps, his sharp-featured wife watching with pride. Talbot lowered the microphone, then left to find seats for himself and Mrs. Deinhart.

"Corydon publishes hardcover books," Deinhart began, thrusting his hands deep into the pockets of his tan slacks. "We publish over two hundred fifty original titles a year in fiction, poetry, history, the arts, biography, philosophy, science, and religion."

His small brown eyes gleaming as he warmed to his subject, Deinhart launched into an expansive, slanted account of the changes that had taken place in publishing during the past thirty years, repeatedly asserting that conglomerate-owned Corydon's standards had remained the same as when it was privately owned.

Sitting in the back of the theater next to Mrs. Deinhart, whose floral perfume was markedly noticeable in the warm air, Talbot was thinking of a letter he'd sent to Deinhart late in the fall concerning his third book of poems. The letter had been a risk. The editor's visits were valuable to the Workshop, and prevailing upon Deinhart's good will could put a strain on the relationship. But his manuscript had just been rejected by the publisher of his second book, who had once been a regular visitor at the conference; there was no one else to write, no other inside contact he could appeal to. Deinhart's reply was cordial: *By all means send your manuscript*, he wrote. *I'm sure John Ross, our poetry editor, will welcome a chance to read it.* John Ross kept the manuscript for six weeks, then sent it back with a polite note of rejection. There wasn't a word from Deinhart. When he wrote to the editor in the spring, expressing his hope that Deinhart would give another successful lecture on publishing at the Workshop this summer, he didn't mention his rejected manuscript. Deinhart's answer was friendly and affirmative, as was his manner today. To Talbot's relief, it was as if the manuscript had never been submitted.

Vaguely aware that Deinhart had been answering questions from people in the audience, Talbot remained immersed in his thoughts until he sensed Mrs. Deinhart stiffening beside him. Talbot immediately focused on the editor, who was standing red-faced behind the lectern, then at Webb, planted like a tower in the center of the theater. "How can you claim that Corydon is supportive of poetry after telling us that last year you published only two books of poems, which isn't even one percent of your total publication?" Webb said.

Deinhart glared at Webb as if willing him to disappear. Never, since he had been coming to the conference, had any Workshop member made him feel not only defensive, but responsible for decisions beyond his control. "As I explained," Deinhart said, struggling to keep his voice from rising, "books of poetry usually sell between one thousand and two thousand copies if we're lucky, not enough to pay for their publication. They are losses before they get into print. A number of houses have stopped publishing poetry altogether. It's a losing proposition."

"Maybe they're losing propositions because they aren't advertised," Webb said, his eyes blazing. "It's rare to see an ad for a book of poetry in *The New York Times Book Review*, yet you spend thousands of dollars advertising formula fiction and trendy nonfiction, aiming for the bestseller list. I bet if you gave poets the big advances you give to novelists, their books would sell. You'd make sure they sold. You'd put poets on the Today show and Good Morning America, and take out ads until their names were household words. You should be promoting these books instead of assuming that no one wants to read them. Years ago a fellow in advertising got the idea to sell stones. He put them in a fancy package, called them pet rocks, and sold thousands. If publishers feel any responsibility at all for our national literature, which is the soul of our society, if they have any conscience, if they have the vision to see beyond their yearly balance sheets, the very least they can do is back poets with the same ingenuity and enthusiasm that made people run to stores to buy ordinary rocks."

The people in the audience sat uncomfortably in their seats. A few faces registered astonishment and approval; most, however, were tight with embarrassment. The editor stood on the platform nearly apoplectic. Talbot was stunned. Although he had never thought of publishers' support of poetry in the way Webb had presented it and had reacted with grudging agreement to some of the young giant's statements, he could not and would not tolerate such behavior. Deinhart was an important guest and would be treated like one, with courtesy and respect, his opinions unchallenged.

Talbot looked at his watch. It was two thirty. Fifteen minutes left. He stood up, deciding to end the session immediately. "If there are no further questions, I would again like to thank Mr. Deinhart for joining us."

It was too late. In the front of the theater Jerry Hofstrand rose from his seat, solid and respectfully insistent. "I would like to question a statement Mr. Deinhart made earlier," he said.

Talbot sank into his chair with a groan.

"Mr. Deinhart," Hofstrand said, "you stated that agents aren't necessary. If that's true, why do almost all established writers use them? Isn't the purpose of an agent to negotiate the best possible contract for a writer? Wouldn't a writer who isn't familiar with the intricacies of publishing contracts be better off hiring someone knowledgeable who can protect his interests?"

"As I said before," Deinhart sputtered, "you aren't ahead if you use an agent because any additional money you might gain will be eaten up in the agent's commission. Further, any lawyer you take a contract to can read it as well, if not better, than an agent."

"Then why do the big-name writers use agents?" Hofstrand persisted. "It doesn't make sense that they'd give up a percentage of their earnings unless they were getting something in return. Also, aren't publishing contracts rather specialized? Wouldn't a lawyer have to be familiar with these contracts to be able to evaluate them properly?"

Deinhart had all he could do to maintain his composure. "Agents are a convenience," he snapped. "They're like secretaries—they send out your manuscripts and receive your rejections, keeping the bad news to themselves so your egos aren't hurt. Some writers like expensive coddling and are willing to pay for it."

Hofstrand nodded, though it was clear from the expression on his face that he was not satisfied with the editor's reply. After he sat down, Talbot stood and started clapping. The Workshop members rose from their seats as if they'd been cued, imitating the director. Deinhart accepted their applause with a relieved, half-hearted smile before shuffling across the platform and down the steps, exhausted. He would not, he thought, stop at the Workshop next year.

***

Ackerley watched the last of the people who attended his study group leave a small room in the cedar-shingle building known as the Studio. He pushed his wheat-colored hair off his forehead and rose from behind a battered table that had been placed in front of student desks, the expression on his gaunt face one of satisfaction. The session had gone well, he thought as he gathered up his books and papers. All nine of the people whose manuscripts had been assigned to him had been present, including the recalcitrant Gwen Eggleston. Her attitude had been so negative when she had attended the study group yesterday—she'd sat with a petulant expression, as though she were being punished—that he had been jarred by her open disdain and had made a point of getting her name. She was, after all, a participant whose work he was being paid to read. An attitude like hers could be infectious, souring the whole group. Even his fellow staff members with their constant snubs weren't that obvious in showing their feelings toward him, although since he'd had his reading switched they had been colder than he had believed possible. But today he had won her over; she had taken notes and had contributed to the discussion.

He hoisted his book bag over his shoulder and turned off the light, mentally replaying the high points that had occurred during study group. Description was always safe to teach, and using examples from his own work was the quickest, surest way to win their respect; published writing was irresistible to these people. Gwen Eggleston's conference should probably be one of the first, though it would be a tough one. Her manuscript was full of lyrical sentences that didn't say anything, just a lot of nice-sounding words going nowhere. There had to be some way to mollify her since she clearly had a high opinion of herself and her work. Maybe he could tell her that he would recommend an editor who might accept her manuscript and give her permission to use his name if she did a revision to his satisfaction before the Workshop ended, which was a safe promise to make because she couldn't accomplish it in less than a week. She'd probably never turn out a story worth reading, but it would keep her busy trying. Although leading her on this way might be considered questionable, it could do no harm. It could be looked upon as a gift of encouragement.

***

Laura waited in the Studio classroom where Stoddard had conducted his study group until everyone left. Less than a dozen people had attended, most of them individuals whose manuscripts had been assigned to him. In contrast to Pierce's stimulating study group yesterday, which she had enjoyed, Laura had found this one boring and offensive. Instead of teaching or attempting to lead a challenging discussion, Stoddard had used the time to promote his new book, *Places At The Table*. Not only did she feel that he was taking advantage of a captive audience, but his voice was grating, high-pitched and nasal. Still, he was a powerful critic, and he had eaten at her table for a number of meals. He would certainly recognize her and might be more inclined to look at her work because of her attendance.

He smiled when she approached him. "Do you have a minute?" she said.

"I always have time for a lovely lady," he said, stepping closer to her.

His breath smelled rancid. "I just finished writing a novel before coming here," she said, moving back. "If I had known it would be done, I would have applied as a participant instead of taking a last-minute opening to be an observer. I'm not asking or expecting you to give me detailed criticism, but if you would take a quick look at a chapter or two when you have time and tell me what you think, I would really appreciate it."

Ordinarily his response would have been an immediate refusal. Few things irritated him more than aspiring writers asking him to read their work. He had been, and still was, a well-known and respected critic paid to judge published books, and he wondered at people's audacity expecting him to read their unpublished, unproven manuscripts in his spare time. When he discussed this subject with his fellow writers, most of whom felt as he did, more burdened than flattered at having been asked, he often observed that the people who expected him to give hours of his time and attention to their writing with no compensation wouldn't dream of asking a surgeon to give them a free operation on their hernias on the doctor's day off. But she was exceptionally attractive, and he hadn't gotten laid in a long time. "Perhaps you can give me the synopsis and a chapter this evening after the reading," he said, his lascivious smile anything but subtle.

Laura swallowed hard. She looked at Stoddard's huge girth, at his shiny, shaved head and full beard (she detested beards), and was repulsed at the thought of him touching her. She absolutely could not have sex with him; she didn't even want to shake his hand. But she had the remainder of the afternoon to think of an excuse that would put him off. "I'll look for you," she said.

"Later then," he replied, his smile wider.

****

Phyllis Baran had gone to Clemens after her study group and was reading manuscripts mechanically, writing occasional comments in the margins with a pencil while sipping vodka, until she started to read Diana's manuscript. After she read the first few paragraphs, she sensed that the writer was gifted. And when her eyes rested on the last sentence, she knew Diana Rothenberg had the potential to be extraordinary.

Her discovery was exciting, one that she would have shared with her colleagues if she were feeling more comfortable with them, but by the time she finished reading the plot outline, her hands were shaking. It was difficult to put the manuscript back in the manila envelope; she couldn't return it quickly enough and her anxiety made the trembling in her hands worse. She slipped the envelope between the others she had with her and rushed out of the cottage.

She went directly to her room in Whitman, closed the door, dropped the manuscripts on her desk, and started to pace. Rubbing her hands together as if they itched, she told herself that she must be calm, that what she was thinking was unethical and immoral, the worst sin she could commit as a writer and a teacher. She must forget that the idea had ever occurred to her; even a trace of the thought was dangerous, and until it was gone she would have no peace.

Gradually her pacing slowed. When her hands were relaxed at her sides, she went to the desk to test herself. Minutes passed while she stared at the manila envelopes like an alcoholic confronted with a full bottle. She clenched her hands into fists. No, she thought, no. But the temptation was impossible to fight. Her hands trembling again, she shuffled through the envelopes until she found Diana's manuscript. Quickly, she reread Diana's plot synopsis:

Paul discovers that he cannot write on days that he doesn't see Gayle. He is convinced she is his flash-and-blood muse. Obsessed with her, he persuades her to move in with him.

Life with Gayle isn't what he expects. She both repels and attracts him. He is appalled by her lack of polish, her crude language and disregard for convention. Yet he can think of nothing but his book and possessing her. Gayle and his novel become intertwined in his mind.

He tries to correct her speech, attempts to teach her manners, lectures her on the arts. She laughs at what he says, mocks everything he believes in. She tells him he has been over-bred, like fancy, nervous dogs that have lost their instinct for survival. Then, as if to prove her point, she leaves him when he starts writing the last chapters of his book.

He finds himself incapable of functioning; he can neither write nor think. Desperate, he begins searching for Gayle and ends up in the impoverished town in West Virginia where she grew up. He knows nothing about these people or how to relate to them. His accent and imperious manner are alienating; they view him with suspicion and humiliate him whenever they have the opportunity. When Gayle finally comes to him, he is stripped of all the pretensions that have carried him through his life. Now, she tells him, we will begin.

Still holding the synopsis, Baran closed her eyes. She could write this book, she knew she could. The writer could be an architect or a sculptor working a commission. No one knew the hopeless struggle of being blocked better than she did. The impoverished town could easily be changed to a facsimile of Johnstown. How well she remembered the people in that town, their hard lives, defensiveness, and mistrust of outsiders. She could have been the girl, Gayle, if she hadn't escaped with a scholarship to Duke. She could model the character after her youngest sister whose language and manners were still coarse. It would be so simple to do, so incredibly simple! She could tell Diana Rothenberg that the novel wouldn't work, that no character possessing the intelligence of the protagonist, Paul, would allow himself to be degraded by a girl like Gayle. She could convince her that he lacked credibility and that the girl didn't have the brains or sophistication to know how to manipulate him to the breaking point. Diana might argue, but in the end she would probably accept whatever was said to her. But if she didn't...

"My God, what am I doing?" Baran whispered, looking around the room as if she expected to discover someone watching her. Then she covered her face with her hands and wept.

***

The Workshop members eating dinner in Hackett hall were more carefully dressed and groomed than they had been on previous nights. They could have been motivated by the fact that it was Saturday, or that Eric Nettles was scheduled to read; rumors had been circulating that outside guests would be attending the reading. Whatever the reason, their shirts, jeans, blouses and skirts were fresh; most of the women were wearing makeup, and the men's faces were cleanly shaven. A breeze coming in through the open leaded-glass windows stirred the aromas of perfumes, lotions, deodorants and after-shave lotions, blending them into a scent that was clean, pleasant and anticipatory, redolent of a desire to please.

Laura wasn't among the diners. After she ate a sandwich in the Shed, she went to her room and lightly applied a blue-green eye shadow under her eyes and powder to her face, just enough to give credibility to a claim of feeling unwell. Then she put the second chapter of her novel and a synopsis into a manila envelope and went downstairs, where she sat on a bench that gave her a clear view of Hackett Hall.

Dynarski, who was one of the first people out of the dining room, spotted her and came over. "I didn't see you at dinner," he said.

"I wasn't there," she said, rising. Then, anticipating his next question, she added, "I'm not going to the reading. I think I might be coming down with something and I want to beat it. I'll see you tomorrow."

"I have aspirin in my room. I was going to pick up my liquor before the lines get too long, but I'll get it for you now if you want it."

"Thanks for the offer," she said, feeling that she'd been too abrupt with him. "I think all I need is a good night's sleep. Maybe you'll tell me about the reading tomorrow."

"Sure," he said.

She watched him walk toward the sitting room where others were already heading, and wished that he'd find someone else to spend time with.

Stoddard emerged from the dining room dressed in khaki pants with an elasticized waist and a black knit shirt that didn't conceal layers of fat cascading from his chest to his belly. He smiled broadly when she approached him. "I was hoping to see you so I could tell you that I won't be going to the reading tonight," she said before launching into the same excuse she had given Dynarski. "I put my mail box number on the envelope. I really appreciate your doing this."

He accepted the manila envelope reluctantly, his disappointment clearly visible. "Nettles' reading is an event, you know."

"So I understand, and I regret that I have to miss it."

Instead of telling her that he hoped she would feel better soon, he lumbered away without a word. Not only was he physically repugnant, she thought, heading for the stairs, he was a jerk.

***

The sitting room was jammed with cartons and people waiting in line. After her foot was stepped on and someone's elbow accidentally jabbed her in the spine, Diana told Webb that she'd wait for him in the lobby. He came out carrying a carton which, by her rapid count, held nine bottles. "That isn't all yours?" she said.

"It's mostly wine," he said offhandedly. "Let's go to my room. I can get rid of this carton and we can open a bottle of wine."

After they left the Inn, she asked him a question that had been bothering her for hours. "Why did you give that editor such a difficult time this afternoon?"

"What is the point of coming to a writers' conference if you don't speak out? Are we supposed to sit like dummies, accepting everything they tell us? "

"He was a guest here and you attacked him."

"Deinhart had the audacity to present himself and his company as benefactors of the arts, as champions of literature, when Corydon publishes only two volumes of poetry out of over two hundred books a year. And even worse, he expected us to be grateful to them for doing it! Besides, I wasn't the only one who wouldn't accept what he said. What about that fellow who questioned his opinion of agents?"

"He wouldn't have challenged Deinhart if you hadn't."

"Which proves I was right to speak out! The fellow's questions were valid, and Deinhart handled them badly because he couldn't justify what he'd said."

"How was your study group?" she said, seeing the impossibility of restraining his outspokenness. "Was Aaron Greene any better today?"

"He was nastier. He read people's poems and then took them apart viciously, line by line."

"Did he read any of yours?"

"No, but he did say the manuscripts were all pretty hopeless except for one young man's poems, which showed potential but were too self-centered and self-pitying."

"Do you think you were the young man?"

Webb shrugged. "Probably," he said.

It was fortunate for Diana that he was far ahead of her after he bounded up the stairs in Thackeray. If she had been able to keep up with him, she would have been embarrassed walking in on Dan Hecker, who had just pulled off his jeans (he'd accidentally spilled wine on them). Webb stepped back into the hall and called to her to wait.

Hecker, standing in the middle of the room in his bikini briefs, snapped, "Could you close the door?"

Webb kicked the door shut and put the carton on the desk. "It's my turn to have the room tonight," Hecker said, peering into the carton.

"I know," Webb said. "It's yours after the reading."

"Technically, it's mine now."

"I'll cancel the agreement if you don't put your pants on and get the hell out of here."

Hecker went to the closet to get a fresh pair of jeans. As he was putting them on, he watched Webb open one of the wine bottles with the corkscrew from a penknife. "What are the pills you take?" Hecker asked.

"Vitamins," Webb said, reminded that he had forgotten to take an Eskalith. The bottle of pills from which he had removed the prescription label was on the desk; he popped a pill into his mouth and washed it down with a swallow of wine.

"What kind of vitamin?" Hecker persisted.

"Zip your fly," Webb said. "I'm opening the door."

Diana waited until Hecker left before she came in. He handed her a glass tumbler half-filled with red wine, then raised his glass to hers. "To William Carlos Williams," he said.

He put his glass down and bent to kiss her, his hand cradling one of her breasts. "Let's go to bed."

"We'll miss the reading."

"Not if it's a quickie," he said.

She didn't protest. Usually sensible, often cautious, she couldn't have explained to herself or anyone else why she found him so mesmerizing despite the warning signals that flashed so clearly in his poems. Excited by his impetuosity, the pressure of time, strange masculine footsteps in the hall outside his room, she was instantly moist. He surprised her by lifting her onto him when her jeans were off. For a moment she felt as if she were floating. Then she wrapped her legs and arms around his body and they came, laughing.

***

Laura waited until the Tabard Inn had emptied before she left her room to call Gretchen. In the fading light the hallway looked like a sepia photograph, the yellowed walls and old doors relics of another time. The stairs unexpectedly creaked when she descended them, which for no particular reason made her shiver. Walking unnecessarily fast, she left through the back entrance thinking of the thousands of unpublished writers who had inhabited the Inn before her. She wondered what had become of them, how many had actually gotten published, how many had kept writing without recognition, how many had simply lost hope.

Low hanging clouds blanketed the darkening sky. She tried a number of spots before she was finally able to get reception on her cell phone. Gretchen answered on the first ring. "I was hoping to hear from you," she said. "I have news: Greg called me this morning. He's been trying to reach you for a couple of days. He's separated from his wife; they're getting a divorce."

Her body wouldn't let her process the news calmly; her pulse quickened, perspiration formed above her upper lip. She thought of the messages he had left on her cell phone yesterday and today that she had deleted without listening to them.

"What he didn't tell me is even more interesting. After I talked to him, I called a friend of my aunt's who belongs to the same book club that his wife does. She told me that his wife knew he was having an affair—she didn't know who the woman was—and decided to retaliate by having an affair of her own. The affair turned into a full-fledged romance; she's planning to marry the man when her divorce from Greg is final."

"So I'm his back-up choice," Laura said, realizing too late that she sounded bitter.

"I don't know if I would put it that harshly. You know I've never been a fan of Greg's, but I believe he loves you. He said he's been miserable since you left him. He wants you back; he says he wants to marry you. I'm telling you this with misgivings because I think you can do a lot better than Greg Towbridge."

"A year ago I would have been thrilled…" Laura's voice trailed off.

"Exactly," Gretchen said, breaking the silence. "And you probably would have abandoned your book. Have you heard from Michael Pierce yet?"

"No."

"What about…"

Gretchen's voice broke up and the connection was gone. Unable to get a signal again, Laura walked back to the Inn thinking about Greg. Although their break up had been her decision, it didn't end her feelings for him; beneath her hurt and disappointment, she still cared. *If this had happened before she started writing her novel,* she thought, opening the door to the Inn, *if…*

But it didn't. She was here now, and she had to see this through.

* * *

The Circle Theater was filled for Eric Nettles' reading. Every seat was taken, and guests were leaning against the walls and sitting in the aisles. The guests had come from Jamestown, Olean, Axton, and the Chautauqua Institution; some had traveled from as far away as Buffalo. They were mostly teachers and writers, people who had a lifetime interest in the arts. This was Nettles' first reading in Western New York, a literary event not to be missed.

Unlike the other writers on the staff who had dressed casually for their readings, Nettles wore gray slacks, a navy blazer, white shirt, and a red paisley tie. People in the audience murmured their approval as he climbed the steps and walked across the platform to the lectern. Without uttering a word, he told them how he felt about the occasion—that reading was a privilege and that he respected them as an audience.

Nettles read his work well. The story he selected had a single character, a writer, debating whether he should write about the world ending in fire or in ice, while acknowledging that both endings were clichés. There were long, descriptive paragraphs which sang like poetry, particularly the ice passage that began: *Teardrops of ice clinging to faucets, milk in cartons bricks of white ice, cylinders of ice in glasses...*

The story closed as indecisively as it began, with the writer finally deciding to leave the selection of the ending up to his readers: they could pick fire or ice or imagine their own endings if they preferred, or they could abandon the idea altogether.

Talbot was one of the first to applaud. He rose from his seat clapping, happier and more relaxed than he had been in days. During the reading he had observed the people who had come from Axton College, gauging their reaction. It was obvious from the expressions of intense concentration on their faces that they were impressed. They knew he was responsible for bringing Nettles to the Workshop. The innovative fictionist's success was his.

Pierce also clapped, not as forcefully as Talbot or the others in the theater, but respectfully, acknowledging his colleague's skill. Although he abhorred Nettles' fiction, he could not deny that it was art and deserved recognition. *What a stupendous waste of a great gift!* he thought. Instead of writing shining books that would move men's souls, Nettles' art was mired in ambiguity, committed to no purpose other than self-reflective intellectual exercise.

Although Pierce left the theater with Leila, he was soon surrounded by people who wanted to speak to him. She slipped away unnoticed, preferring to stand under an ancient maple rather than to remain at his side feeling like an unnecessary appendage.

Her legs began to ache. She had walked for miles during the afternoon, trying to reconcile her new understanding of the man she had married with the hopes she had for their life together. Haunted by his statement that… *fiction had to be better than life*, she realized that she would have to make him see that creating human life was as vital as creating lives on paper, that a commitment to her and their marriage was as important as his commitment to his art. If she failed, if he still denied her a child, there would be no way to interpret his refusal except as a rejection of her. Then she would have to leave him.

Soon she was joined by Cheryl Hill, who was wearing navy slacks and a stunning summer sweater the color of lime sherbet. Leila immediately regretted not having made more of an effort to spend time with the striking African-American woman, realizing how uncomfortable it might be for Cheryl and her husband to be the only black people at the conference. "How do you stand it?" Cheryl said, glancing at the people surrounding her husband and Pierce.

Leila shrugged. "I've gotten used to it."

"At least you have males as well as females wanting his attention. This is worse than at Berkeley," Cheryl said. She didn't add that the women who were sending eager signals to her husband for sex were the same women who, when they saw a black man walking by while they were alone in their cars waiting for a traffic light, would lock their doors, *click. Click*, no matter what the man looked like. *Click.* There wasn't a black man in America who hadn't heard that *click.*

"Michael promised that this would be our last summer here, but he's said that before."

"I *know* this will be our only summer here!" Cheryl said with such conviction that they both laughed.

The two women chatted while they watched the people surrounding their husbands until Leila started to shiver. "It's getting chilly. I'm going to claim him now."

"That isn't going to be easy. There must be at least nine or ten people waiting to talk to him."

"I have my ways," Leila said.

She slipped through the group of people gathered around Pierce until she was at his side. "There you are," she said with a disarming smile, as though she'd lost him. "I'm sorry, we have to go now."

"Please excuse us," he said, leading her away.

It was a dance they had done so many times, they knew the steps perfectly.

They went directly to their room, avoiding any mention of Nettles' reading or the conviviality they could hear coming from Clemens as they passed the staff cottage. "Thanks for rescuing me," he said, putting his arms around her after their bedroom door was closed.

He kissed her neck, her cheek, working his way toward her mouth. "You smell delicious," he said.

They undressed each other slowly, taking time to enjoy each other. For Leila, their lovemaking would have been perfect if he hadn't slipped on a pre-lubricated condom before he entered her. But she didn't protest; nor did she show her disappointment. She raised her pelvis to welcome him, and when she was unable to come, she faked a convincing orgasm.

Afterward, he rolled onto his back with his eyes closed. "Can you go for a drive with me tomorrow?" she said, fingering the hair on his chest, which was turning gray.

"I'll try."

She withdrew her hand, wondering if the fight she had planned wasn't already lost.

***

✎ WORKSHOP BULLETIN ✎

VOL. 74, NO.5   THE CLYMER WORKSHOP   AUGUST 15 2004

GOOD MORNING!

Take out your slickers and umbrellas. Rain is forecast for most of the day. If the weather holds, the softball game will be played as scheduled.

AFTERNOON PROGRAM

2:00 P.M. Guest Lecture
(Nora Cushing)
3:30 P.M. Reading
(Phyllis Baran)
5:30 P.M. BYOB Mixer
in the Shed

Novelist and short story writer Phyllis Baran will read from her work. Her novels include *Lapses*, which received the Ernest Hemingway Award, and *Affair*. Many of the stories from her collection, *Revelations*, first appeared in *The New Yorker*. She was recently awarded a grant from the National Endowment for the Arts.

GUEST

It is our privilege to have Nora Cushing with us. Ms. Cushing heads the well-known Cushing Literary Agency. She will talk about the role of a literary agent.

EVENING READING

Aaron Greene will read his poetry. Mr. Greene is the author of *Crossing The Brooklyn Bridge*, *By The Lamplight*, *Dream Reader*, *The Packett Dump*, *Looking For Treasure*, and *Complete Poems*. He is on the board of the Academy of American Poets and is a member of the American Academy of Arts and Letters. He has twice received the Pulitzer Prize and has been the recipient of a National Book Award. Recently Mr. Greene was awarded the Bollington Prize in Poetry, honoring his lifetime career. Mr. Greene teaches at Stanford University in California.

REMINDER

Manuscript conferences begin tomorrow morning. Please check your mailboxes for messages.

WORKSHOPS

Materials for tomorrow's workshops will be placed on a table outside the office after dinner. There will be two sessions of workshops: Eric Nettles and Terence Hill will teach the first session; Andrew Cox and Aaron Greene will teach the second. Please take only the materials for the specific workshops you wish to attend.

BYOB MIXER

Bring your own bottles. Glasses, mixers and "nibbles" will be supplied.

EARLY MORNING EXERCISERS

Please be considerate of your sleeping neighbors. You are welcome to use the Shed for your calisthenics. It could be the beginning of the Clymer Health Club!

TIDBIT

"I don't know if I should get something to eat at the snack bar before dinner or after dinner."

"... people think poets are in touch with some mystical power and they endow us with qualities we do not possess and love us for words that we only wrote for ambition and not for love."
Anne Sexton, in a letter to Brother Dennis Farrell

Chapter V

Marsha Nudelman watched the luminous green numbers change on the face of her alarm clock. She was waiting until it was six o'clock. She had been waiting all night, watching the numbers change. In the bed opposite hers, Diana was sleeping. For hours the only sound in the room had been her roommate's even breathing. One unwelcome thought after another stirred in her head while she waited: she had been rejected by everyone she had met at the conference; she had felt as left out here as she did at home; at the age of thirty-six she had no dates, no prospects, nothing but a career teaching other people's children knowing she'd probably never have children of her own; the story that no one on the staff would read was her single, last hope and it was gone.

At five fifteen it started to rain. She tried to concentrate on the sound of the raindrops beating against the window so she wouldn't think. When she was a child she had loved listening to the patter of rain, especially in the dark; the sound had made her feel safe, warm, secure. But after five or ten minutes the steady rhythm of the water hitting the glass began to make her feel anxious. Now she wanted it to stop. She didn't want to drive back to Cleveland in the rain.

Finally, it was six o'clock.

Marsha swung her legs over the side of the bed and felt for her slippers. The light in the room was murky, the air chilly and damp. She needed more light to pack; if she raised the shade, there might be enough. She crossed the room, glancing at her roommate faintly silhouetted in the darkness. She wanted to be gone before Diana awakened.

There was slightly more light with the shade raised. It was gray outside, foggy and wet. She opened the dresser drawers slowly, hoping they wouldn't squeak. It was difficult to see anything in the closet; the clothes were blanketed in darkness. She removed as many as she could carry and walked to the window. Diana stirred. Marsha stood holding her breath. When Diana was still again, she picked out the clothing that was hers and returned Diana's things to the closet. Usually fastidious, she dumped her belongings into her suitcase without folding them, leaving out only the items she planned to wear. She made a second trip to the closet, then left the room to shower, closing the door silently behind her.

She returned dressed in jeans and a green sweater, carrying her robe, pajamas, slippers, and a plastic bag filled with toiletries. After she finished packing, she looked around the room to see if she had forgotten anything. The alarm clock. Diana didn't bring a clock. She'd have to get along without it, Marsha decided, putting the clock on top of her clothes. Diana woke as she was zippering the suitcase shut. "What time is it?" Diana asked groggily.

"Six thirty-five."

Diana raised her head off the pillow. "Isn't breakfast later this morning?" She looked at the suitcase and blinked, as if she weren't sure of what she was seeing. "What are you doing?"

"I'm leaving."

Diana sat up, fully awake. "Why?"

"You wouldn't understand," Marsha said, hoisting the suitcase off the bed. She grabbed her purse and started toward the door.

"Is it anything I did?"

"Not really."

"Are you upset because I was absorbed in Doug's poems yesterday and didn't want to talk?"

Marsha hesitated. She could say yes, she was upset, that it hurt to be ignored. Diana could have been kinder. Diana had youth and beauty and talent. Diana had so much and she had so little and Diana took it all for granted. The rain was coming down harder now; it was a long walk from the Inn to the parking lot. "Goodbye," Marsha said.

She hurried down the hall hoping no one would see her with her suitcase. The single mercy she wished for now was to slip away from this place unnoticed. She couldn't bear being embarrassed or hurt again. She had suffered more at this conference than she had ever suffered in her life. She would never be the same. Never. Having a story she had written published had been the one bright spot in her life and no one at the Workshop had cared. The disappointment she was feeling was so intense it frightened her.

She managed to get the suitcase down the stairs without making any noise. No one was in the lobby. She sighed. The only break she'd had at this place was escaping without being seen.

****

The rain, which had forced the cancellation of the baseball game, had put Talbot in a black mood. He had counted on the game to relieve some of the tensions in the Workshop atmosphere. People had been coming up to him with complaints: they complained that the lectures were too long, that they were too brief; they complained about the food, about the living conditions; they were unhappy with their roommates and with their manuscript assignments, which they wanted him to change; they wanted to hear less literary philosophizing and more concrete advice on how to improve their writing, how to sell their manuscripts. They delivered their complaints apologetically, as if they weren't sure they had the right to complain, as if they were afraid of some kind of retaliation, perhaps that the utterance of their unhappiness and disappointment would be a black mark against them, automatically labeling them as misfits, unsuitable for inclusion in the circle of published writers that they fervently hoped to join. Listening to them had pushed his patience to its limits. He had enough trouble satisfying the staff, and he had his own book of poems to worry about.

Talbot's lips were compressed into a line of anger when he entered the Workshop office. "Dee Dee," he said, marching to her desk. "I'd like you to explain this." He thrust a coffee-stained *WORKSHOP BULLETIN* at her, his index finger pointing at the last sentence on the back page: "*I don't know if I should get something to eat at the snack bar before dinner or after dinner.*"

"I overheard a woman say it yesterday and thought it was funny."

"Well, I don't! Putting that remark in was like pouring gasoline on a burning house."

Dee Dee shrugged. "Sorry."

Her easy dismissal infuriated him. "Don't you understand what you did?" he demanded.

In the past, she would have done her best to assuage his anger.

But for five nights she had slept in the room next to his and not once had he knocked on her door for anything but Workshop business. Last night was the worst night of all. Exhausted, she had stayed in Clemens struggling to keep her eyes open, waiting until he left so she could walk back to Melville with him. The cold night air had revived her. When they had reached their rooms at the end of the hallway, he'd said, "Good night," as if she were as sexless as the door he was opening. He'd given her nothing—not a gesture, not a word, not a crumb of hope. "I understand perfectly," she said, her eyes pools of hurt behind the lenses of her glasses. "The food has been horrible. Everyone has been complaining about it. I merely acknowledged what had to be acknowledged."

"You legitimized their complaints!"

"Their complaints are legitimate. They paid a lot of money to come here. They're entitled to decent food."

The telephone rang before he could reply. The caller was Howard Cruickshank, the president of Axton College, wanting to speak to Talbot.

"He's right here," Dee Dee said, handing Talbot the receiver. "It's Dr. Cruickshank."

"Good morning, Howard," Talbot said, the pleasant tone of his voice contrasting sharply with his angry glare at Dee Dee. She was supposed to screen calls!

"How are things going?" Cruickshank said. "How is the atmosphere there?"

"Intense, but no more so than usual," Talbot said, aware of what Cruickshank was really asking. During the long history of the Workshop there had been a number of attempted suicides, some successful, though none during his tenure. Due to the intensity of the conference the possibility was never far from his thoughts, particularly since the director who had preceded him had been fired after an unfortunate woman hanged herself in the barn. He and Cruickshank had agreed upon the code word *incident* to convey the occurrence of such a catastrophic event.

"Even with all the competition we have now, the Clymer Workshop is still considered one of the best writers' conferences in the country," Cruickshank said. "It has a pristine reputation, as does Axton College, and we want to keep it that way. We can't afford any incidents."

This wasn't the first time Talbot heard Cruickshank deliver this message and he resented it; an idiot would know that a suicide connected with the conference would bring an avalanche of negative publicity. "I'm well aware of that, Howard," Talbot said, managing to sound civil though he was bristling. "Did you hear about Eric Nettles' reading? It was a tremendous success, standing room only."

They talked about the reading, with Cruickshank mentioning that he and his wife planned to attend Pierce's reading. "He's always brilliant, better than an evening at the theater," Cruickshank said. "We look forward to his reading every summer. I can't imagine the Workshop without him. He's our biggest draw, he's what has kept us on top."

Talbot didn't need to be reminded of Pierce's importance to the Workshop. It was a relief to end the conversation. He always felt as if he were balancing on a tightrope when he was talking to Cruickshank, with the college president jerking the rope while he tried to maintain his balance.

***

Leila put down the book she was reading and went to the window. Rain was coming down steadily. She glanced at her watch and then at Michael, who was sitting at the desk reading manuscripts. There were three manila envelopes on the desk, manuscripts that he hadn't read; the other envelopes were stacked on the floor next to his chair. It was close to eleven. He wouldn't be finished until lunch at the earliest. "I'm going out," she said.

He looked up, startled. "What?"

"I'm going back to that farm, the one I told you about."

"The people might be in church."

"I'll take the chance."

She found the farm without difficulty. Set off the main road that was nearest to the Clymer property, the farmhouse and outbuildings were old but well-maintained. Leila parked behind a red pick-up truck, pulled up the hood of her yellow slicker, and trotted through the rain to the farmhouse.

There was no doorbell. She rapped on the frame of the screen door, which was painted black, as were the shutters. The white clapboard house had a covered porch that ran the full length of the front; on either side of the door there were wicker chairs that would sell for a small fortune in Connecticut antique shops. She eyed the chairs appreciatively, wondering if she dare make an offer to the people to buy them.

An ample, gray-haired woman in her early fifties who had a broad, pleasant face came to the door wiping her hands on a striped dishtowel. "Yes," she said, appraising Leila in an open manner that was curious, though not offensive.

"I'm Leila Pierce. I stopped here the other day and spoke with your grandson. I'm interested in finding out anything I can about Benjamin Clymer."

"That was my son, Gary. He told me you were here."

"Oh, I'm sorry," Leila said quickly. "I thought…"

The woman smiled. "It's all right. He was a late-in-life surprise. We tend to have them in our family. I'm Emily Thornton. Please come in."

Leila stepped inside and wiped the wet soles of her sneakers on a braid rug placed just inside the door. "Don't worry about messing the floor," Mrs. Thornton said. "I keep at it all the time."

The wood floor gleamed. "It smells marvelous in here," Leila said.

"Goodness, my chicken!"

Mrs. Thornton hurried down the narrow hallway with amazing speed. "Come along," she called, "I'll introduce you to Mother."

Leila watched Mrs. Thornton expertly remove golden pieces of chicken from an oversize cast-iron skillet. "Won't be but a minute," she said. "Have a seat."

Leila sat at the kitchen table, which was covered with food: freshly-made biscuits, two large peach pies, and a round relish dish holding pickles, celery, carrot sticks, and pickled cauliflower. Pots that she guessed held green beans and potatoes were sending up tufts of steam on the stove. "I hope I haven't come at the wrong time. I don't want to interfere with your dinner."

"No trouble," Mrs. Thornton said. "I have to help Mother to the table anyway. Her arthritis is terrible in this weather."

Mrs. Thornton disappeared into a room off the kitchen and returned with a woman whose body was bent over a cane she was grasping with a knobby hand. The woman's hair was pure white; the skin on her hands and arms was covered with large brown age spots that seemed to melt into each other. Despite the humidity, her legs beneath her loose-fitting blue cotton dress were encased in thick, flesh-colored elastic stockings. "We'll sit in the dining room so Mother won't have to get up again," Mrs. Thornton said, holding the old woman's arm to guide her along.

The dining room walls were papered in a large, old-fashioned floral print that had faded into pale grays and pinks. "What a beautiful table," Leila said.

"It was my grandfather's," Mrs. Thornton said, her broad face glowing with pride. "It's solid oak and all hand carved. I used to stare at the carving for hours when I was a little girl because it looked so real. I'm tempted to tell you who did it, but I'll leave that to Mother."

Mrs. Thornton helped the old woman onto a chair. "MOTHER," she said loudly, "TURN UP YOUR HEARING AID."

The old woman smiled guiltily, like an ancient child caught misbehaving, and turned up the dial.

"This is Leila Pierce," Mrs. Thornton said, her voice only slightly lower than before. "She's come from the Clymer place. She wants to know about Benjamin Clymer."

Leila extended her hand to the old woman. "Oh, sorry," Mrs. Thornton said. "My mother's name is Ashford. You'll have to speak up so she can hear you."

Mrs. Ashford reluctantly held out her hand. Leila looked at the swollen, twisted fingers and immediately understood. "Do you know anything about Benjamin Clymer?" she said, lightly touching the old woman's hand.

Mrs. Ashford smiled and nodded. "She didn't hear you. You'll have to speak up."

Leila repeated the question as loudly as she could without yelling. Mrs. Ashford's smile widened, revealing yellowed pegs of teeth. "You his kin?" she said. Her voice, high and rasping, lacked inflection, the near monotone of the hard-of-hearing.

"No," Leila said, not sure if the woman's reply was a statement or a question. "I'm staying at the Workshop, the place for writers that Mr. Clymer gave the money and land to build."

The woman's smile faded. "Oh, the college."

"I'll leave you two to talk," Mrs. Thornton said. "I have to see to my dinner."

Leila tried again. "Do you know anything about Benjamin Clymer?"

"It was his farm before the college took it over," Mrs. Ashford rasped, her watery eyes growing distant. She seemed to be focusing somewhere beyond Leila, beyond the room. "My grandfather knew him. Said he was a fine farmer, as good as any in the county before he left."

Leila blinked, astounded. Benjamin Clymer, a farmer! "Who were Garnet and John Clymer?" she asked, wondering if the old woman were senile or confusing Clymer with someone else.

"His wife and son. It was a tragedy, them both dying within days of each other." Mrs. Ashford shook her head. "People say his wife was carrying their second child."

"What did they die of?"

Mrs. Ashford's twisted fingers closed over the handle of her cane. "They took sick."

"Where did Benjamin Clymer go? What became of him?"

Mrs. Ashford didn't respond. She sat holding onto her cane; her eyes were closed as if she were praying or sleeping.

Mrs. Thornton returned carrying the relish dish and the biscuits, which she had heaped on a plate. "Did she tell you about the table yet?" she said.

"No," Leila said, concerned. "She doesn't seem to want to talk anymore. I hope I haven't upset her."

"Don't be concerned," Mrs. Thornton said. "Mother goes off sometimes, just closes her eyes and shuts the world out. She does it with her hearing aid all the time. Mostly it happens when the talk gets to sickness. I imagine she thinks about dying a lot. Her friends are all gone, and my father's been dead for twelve years. It gets lonely."

"But she lives with you."

"It's not the same as when it was her house. When a woman like my mother can't work in the kitchen or do any chores, some of the life goes out of her. It has to do with pride, I expect. Also, plain tiredness. And she never was a talker."

"She told me Benjamin Clymer was a farmer."

"That's true. But he was also a fine furniture maker and carver. This table is proof," Mrs. Thornton said, smiling. "Benjamin Clymer built every inch of it himself!"

Leila looked first at Mrs. Thornton, then at the table in disbelief. The heavy pedestal was perfectly turned, solid yet graceful, and the carving at the base—massive bird's claws, possibly an eagle's, that were powerfully rendered—was finer than any she had seen on furniture in exclusive antique shops. "Could there have been two Benjamin Clymers?"

"Not in these parts. The Benjamin Clymer who gave his land to the college and the man who built this table are one and the same," Mrs. Thornton said positively. "I can even tell you how we came to have it."

"Please."

"Well," she began, taking a chair opposite Leila, "my grandfather told me about him. He actually knew Benjamin Clymer. Said he was a good farmer and a good man. No one could understand the terrible luck he had, his wife and child both dying within days of each other. He stayed on the farm until the harvest was done, and then he went to all the neighbors, selling everything he owned for whatever they'd give him. It was unusual back then. People didn't up and leave places in those days like they do now. My grandfather took the table. Paid practically nothing for it, just what he could afford at the time. Benjamin Clymer didn't seem to care, my grandfather said. It bothered my grandfather some; he didn't feel right about profiting from another man's misfortune. But he wanted the table, and he knew that someone else would take it if he didn't. That's how we came to have it."

"What happened to Benjamin Clymer?"

"He left."

"Where did he go?"

"I can't rightly say. There are stories, but I've never paid much mind to them. He did come back, though. His body was shipped from Jamestown. He's buried beside his wife and child in the old church cemetery."

"Do you know anything else about him?" Leila asked excitedly.

Mrs. Thornton's face became contemplative, as if she were debating something. "Things have been mentioned over the years," she said finally. "Strange occurrences, you might call them. I really don't hold with such stuff, but the Indians believe it and so do some white people."

"What things?" Leila pressed when it became evident that Mrs. Thornton was reluctant to continue.

"Well, the Indians believe that the hills around here and everything on them—the trees, rocks, and so forth—have spirits, and that men have the spirits, too. They call the spirits a name that I can't recollect. Anyway, over the years people have claimed that they heard a man crying in the hills around the Clymer property, an awful weeping the likes of which they'd never heard before or since. The strange thing is that most said they heard it at the same time of year, in the summer. They believe like the Indians did, that Benjamin Clymer's spirit is up in those hills somewhere.

"I never heard it myself, so I can't really believe it. Sometimes the wind causes noises, creaking and moaning sounds when it whips through the trees. Maybe that's what they heard and they imagined it was something else. People will do that, you know, make up stories to give themselves something to talk about."

Leila heard a back door open and the sounds of men's voices and the thud of heavy boots on the floor. "I must be going," she said, rising. "Thank you for all the help you've given me."

Mrs. Thornton rose. "Would you stay for dinner? I've plenty of food, and it won't take but a minute to set another place."

"I'm sure I'll be missing a wonderful meal, but I really must get back."

Leila touched Mrs. Ashford's shoulder. The old woman had been sitting as if she were asleep, breathing shallowly, while Mrs. Thornton talked.

Mrs. Ashford's eyelids fluttered open. "Is it dinner yet?" she said, focusing hungrily on the biscuits.

"Soon," Mrs. Thornton promised.

While they were walking to the front door, Mrs. Thornton gave Leila directions to the cemetery where Benjamin Clymer was buried. "The church burned to the ground in the early sixties and all the records were destroyed, but you'll be able to see his headstone." Mrs. Thornton paused. "If you don't mind my asking, why are you interested in Benjamin Clymer?"

"No one at the Workshop knows anything about him, who he was or why he donated his land and money to build it. He's a mystery."

"Maybe he wanted to be a mystery. Some people don't like attention. They want to do their giving quietly, without a fuss."

There was a note of concern in Mrs. Thornton's voice, an unspoken warning of sorts. "Don't worry," Leila said, pressing her hand. "I'll respect his memory."

"That's good," Mrs. Thornton said with a nod. "The poor man had enough trouble in his life, more than most I'd say. He's deserving of his peace."

***

Pierce had lightly penciled numbers in the upper right hand corners of the manila envelopes that he had arranged in stacks on the floor. The numbers, one through three, were his code for grading the manuscripts. There were only two envelopes marked one, meaning that they showed promise. The envelopes in the tallest pile were marked three, which meant lacking potential; several of the threes had check marks next to them, his code for potentially difficult conferences requiring an extra measure of tact. He tried to find something positive to write in the margins on every manuscript, even if it was no more than praise for a sentence or a descriptive word that would cushion a writer's falling hopes.

Late for lunch, he paused before opening a slim envelope that seemed to have accidentally slipped in with the others. It wouldn't take long to read, he reasoned, and then he'd be done. He scanned Laura's note, unable to remember her, until he read the synopsis and recalled their meeting. Without expectation, he began to read the sample of manuscript she had enclosed:

Galen had no way to estimate how long they'd been traveling. There was no moon, there were no stars. The snow had stopped falling and the countryside was covered in a shroud of white. He held the horses on a loose rein, trusting them to follow faint tracks on the road. Betsy had stopped whimpering for Mama and had fallen into a fitful sleep, rocked by the movement of the buggy. No matter how hard he blinked, he couldn't stop seeing Mama, her lifeless body on the kitchen floor, O'Reilly standing over her. And on this silent night, on this silent white road, the sound of Mama's neck breaking under the force of O'Reilly's hands, the CRACK of bone shattering, echoed in his head.

When he thought he couldn't hold the reins in his frozen fingers much longer, the moon broke free from behind a cloud, shooting ribbons of light across the snow. An owl hooted. A hawk flew past, casting a shadow over them. And then he saw it: a ramshackle house that had one lit window and smoke coming out of the chimney. Warmth, he thought, maybe kind folks lived there who would let them stay the night.

It wasn't until they were perhaps thirty feet away that he saw her: an old woman with a crone's face wearing a battered black hat and men's galoshes, the woman they would come to call Crazy Gertie. She was sitting on the porch with a shotgun resting across her lap as if she were expecting them.

When Pierce finished reading the two pages of manuscript, he scanned her note again, trying to recall what she had said to him: that she had applied too late to be a participant? Or was that someone else? He'd been approached by so many people that it was impossible to remember. Whatever the case, he wanted to see as much of the novel as she brought with her. Laura Belmont was his reward for all the bad writing he'd had to slog through over the years. She would be his last conference.

He looked at his watch and rose quickly from his desk. He'd put a note in Laura's mailbox later. Now he wanted to get to the Inn so he could catch Sara and talk about his McDermott lecture.

***

Stoddard positioned himself outside the entrance of Hackett Hall before lunch was over so he could intercept Laura when she left the dining room. This morning he had begrudgingly started reading the chapter she had given him, still irritated and somewhat suspicious of her claim of ill health the previous evening. As he read, his resentment gave way to admiration: her prose was better than much of the fiction he was given to review, and he wanted to tell her so but in a most intimate way. If she responded as he hoped she would, he'd read her entire manuscript and offer his help if it proved worthy.

He had been standing for only a moment to two with a large black umbrella tucked under his arm and his clasped hands resting on his belly, just long enough to launch into a reverie involving Laura, when a graying middle-aged man approached him. "May I ask you about literary criticism?" the man said. "Can you tell me if there are specific rules you follow when you review a book?"

"The first rule is to read the entire book," Stoddard said, having been asked the question so many times that the answer came automatically. "And the second rule, which naturally follows the first, is don't give away the plot."

The man pulled his head back as though he'd been insulted. "Of course one should read the book! Maybe my question was too general. I'm an engineer, unaccustomed to all the talk I've heard around here about literature, so I'll rephrase it: how do you know whether or not a book is art?"

"It's like what Justice Potter Stewart said about pornography, '*I know it when I see it*,'" Stoddard replied, spotting Laura walking out of the dining room with Dynarski. "Excuse me, I must speak with someone."

Laura had reached the stairs when he caught up with her. "I see you're feeling better," he said. "I read the chapter you gave me, and I would like to talk to you about it. Do you have time now?"

"Sure," Laura said.

"Unfortunately, I don't have it with me; it's in my room. We can go there now, if you'd like. I have a nice wine that I think you will enjoy. There's nothing like wine to dispel the gloom of a rainy day."

"Could we talk in the sitting room instead of going out in the rain?"

"I like to have a manuscript in front of me when I'm discussing it," he said, the lechery in his smile unmistakable.

Laura hesitated. She had come so far to have her manuscript criticized, but not at his price. There had to be a way to manage this. "I'll get my slicker," she said finally.

"Oh, that isn't necessary. My umbrella is quite generous, large enough for both of us."

"The slicker is more for the dampness," she said. "I won't take long."

While she was getting her slicker, a green-plastic poncho that had a hood, she tried to think of how she could protect herself from him. It was clear to her that he wanted sex, and the thought of him so much as touching her was repugnant. But when she started down the stairs to meet him, she had come up with no plan to put him off, nothing other than the somewhat reassuring thought that other staff members might be in their rooms, and if the walls were as thin as they were everywhere else on the campus, someone would hear her if she called for help.

The rain had lightened to a steady drizzle. It was still dismal, the air sodden and the path that led to the staff houses slick with mud where water hadn't puddled. Stoddard held the umbrella above them while he talked about the chapter she had given him.

"Your writing is quite polished for a first novel," he said. "I am assuming this is your first novel."

"Yes," she said, frantically trying to think of a way out of this situation.

As they approached the bridge that crossed Barrier Creek, it seemed to Laura that every cell in her body was screaming *NO*. "I'm sorry… I don't think lunch agreed with me… I'm going to head back to the Inn."

"You can rest in my room. We're almost there."

"No, I can't," she said, stepping out from under the umbrella.

"This isn't how the game is played," he said.

Laura started backing away. "I'm not a player."

"You're making a big mistake. From the chapter I read, it's clear that you've written a mid-list book. No matter how good it may be, it won't go anywhere without help."

She stepped back further, wanting to put more distance between them. "What is a mid-list book?"

"Exactly what the term describes," he said. "It's a book that falls midway on a publisher's list. It's the place for books that aren't given big advances and big publicity budgets, the place for well-written books that aren't expected to have mass appeal. Publishers put a few of them on their lists so they won't be accused of being Philistines."

"What makes you so sure that my novel is a mid-list book?"

"It isn't a legal thriller; it doesn't fit the genres of crime, horror, or suspense. Your novel is about two orphans in a rural setting. You couldn't get more mid-list if you tried."

"Michael Pierce's novels aren't legal thrillers or crime stories, and they are very successful."

Stoddard's face turned livid at the mention of Pierce's name. "Michael Pierce would be spending his career in the darkness of obscurity if it were not for my spotlight. His first novel ended up on remainder tables, and his second book would have suffered the same fate if it hadn't been for my review calling attention to it. You can ask him if you don't believe me." He paused, his mouth twisting nastily. "Bad reviews can be equally powerful. A bad review that is prominently placed can practically ensure that a writer doesn't get another chance, particularly now that the publishing business has become so difficult.

"You have no idea how fortunate you are, an unpublished writer who has the opportunity to choose her novel's fate. There are people who would kill to be in your position."

The hood of her poncho had slipped, and rain was glazing her face. "Well, I'm not one of them," she said, pulling the hood on before she turned to walk back to the Inn.

"You'll regret this!" he called after her.

***

The Circle Theater was filled with people listening intently to Eleanor Cushing. Even the most unsophisticated of the aspiring writers had heard of the Cushing Literary Agency and of the lucrative contracts the agency negotiated for the famous writers it represented. Their thoughts were identical as they focused on the tall, attractive woman behind the lectern whose chin-length auburn hair was expertly colored and cut by one of the best stylists in Manhattan: they were wondering how they could get Eleanor Cushing to read their manuscripts and represent them.

Although this was the first writers' conference she had ever attended, Ms. Cushing had anticipated their thoughts. She had no intention of placing herself in the uncomfortable position of having to tell them that she was not interested in seeing their work. A successful litigation attorney before she happened, at the request of a friend, to negotiate a book contract, she was expert at selecting and controlling most circumstances that she voluntarily entered. Today she planned to speak for thirty minutes; there would be no question-and-answer period. It was pre-arranged that Talbot, who was seated in the front row, would thank her for her visit at precisely two thirty.

Ms. Cushing's purpose in traveling from New York City to Cattaraugus County wasn't to address aspiring writers. She had come to the conference to meet Eric Nettles, with the ultimate goal of representing him. And while she was at the Workshop, she also planned to make contact with Michael Pierce and the other writers on the staff; sometimes casual meetings had positive results.

Talbot found himself enjoying her speech, which was crisp and entertaining, a welcome respite from the complaints he had been fielding. He wasn't surprised at the collective grumble that rose from the audience when he walked to the platform and announced the end of the lecture. "I'm sorry," he said firmly, ignoring arms shooting up in protest, "we've run out of time."

He whisked her out of the theater before the audience finished applauding. "I told you we'd escape without a hassle," he said when they were outside. The sun had come out and lingering raindrops were glistening on the wet grass. "You were a great success. They were hanging onto every word you uttered. I know it's a year away, but I hope you'll consider coming next summer. I'd be delighted to have you back."

A plump woman rushed up to them, red-faced and panting, before the agent could reply. "Please… Ms. Cushing," she said, thrusting a tattered box into the agent's unwilling hands, "would you read my manuscript… I've written five novels… this is my fourth… I'll send you all… they're good… they really are… I've been writing for fifteen years… I just need a break… an agent… someone who will help me get published."

Out of breath, the woman gazed up at Eleanor Cushing, her expression full of hope. "I'm sorry," Cushing said gently, "but I don't read manuscripts from unpublished writers. I don't have the time, unfortunately. But I would be happy to read your work after it's published."

The woman's face crumpled. "I can't get published without an agent, and I can't get an agent to read my work unless it's published!"

"It is difficult," Cushing said sympathetically. She returned the manuscript to the distraught woman, adding over-brightly, "I wish you the best of luck."

"I feel awful," the agent said after they had walked a safe distance away.

"I'm sorry that happened," Talbot said. "But you handled the situation beautifully."

"She made a valid point: it is almost impossible to get anywhere without an agent. She's in a perfect Catch-22 situation. I can deal with her dilemma intellectually, but it will be hard to forget the way she looked at me, as if I were her only hope."

"You'll get used to it after you've been to more conferences. Everyone comes here with the same idea."

"How many of them are discovered?" she said, privately doubting that she would come back, the lure of an Eric Nettles not withstanding.

"None that I know of."

"How long have you been the director?"

"This is my sixth year."

"In that time, how many people have attended?"

"Over twelve hundred."

"And *none* have made a contact that has led to publication?" she said, her legal training compelling her to probe for as many facts as possible.

"Not that I'm aware of," Talbot said.

"Overall, if you had to guess, what would you say the odds are for an unpublished writer to make a contact at a writers' conference that would lead directly to publication?"

Talbot shook his head. "That's like asking me the number of jelly beans in a mason jar. Maybe one in twenty thousand might be discovered."

She turned to look at him. "You're not serious."

"Maybe it would be one in fifteen thousand. The chances are so remote that odds of five thousand more or less wouldn't make an appreciable difference."

"Do the people who come here have any idea of how high the odds are against them?"

"Probably not," he said. "But even if they knew, they'd still come."

"That's hard to believe."

"They want to be published. Any chance, no matter how slight, looks better to them than no chance at all."

They started up the puddle-strewn path to Clemens. "Tell me," she said, her curiosity having outgrown the borders of tact, "do you ever feel guilty taking their money?"

"Absolutely not!" Talbot said defensively. "We deliver exactly what we promise: we teach them about the craft of writing and criticize their manuscripts. Our responsibility ends there. What they get from the experience is up to them. If they are able and willing to learn, they can. If not, they've had a unique vacation."

And an expensive, potentially disappointing one, she thought, entering the staff cottage.

Her meeting with Eric Nettles wasn't successful. At first, the innovative fictionist seemed more interested in her as a female than as a professional. "So this is the famous Eleanor Cushing," he said, his yellow-green eyes sweeping over her after Talbot introduced them. "You are as attractive as you are successful."

Accustomed to such remarks after having had to continually prove herself in the legal profession, she was nonetheless taken aback, surprised that a writer of Nettles' stature and intellect would make a comment so patronizing. But when she reflected upon it afterward, she realized that the novelist was as human as any man, carrying a bundle of character traits and attitudes more commonplace than unique; only his accomplishments, his art, made him different.

Nettles listened attentively to what she had to say, but in the end he rejected her persuasive arguments. "If I let you represent me, I'd have to give up part of the pleasure of the game. I enjoy all of it, even the aggravation," he said with a smile that reminded her of an aging king reaffirming his absolute rule. "It keeps my blood circulating."

She gave him her card, aware as she handed it to him that he would more than likely discard it later.

***

Phyllis Baran sat woodenly at the far end of the front row in the Circle Theater, only subliminally aware of people arriving to hear her read. She had been up most of the night, trying to forget that she had ever thought of stealing Diana Rothenberg's novel. The harder she struggled, the more the idea became fixed in her mind. When she did finally drift into a fitful sleep, she dreamed that her reading was a disaster; the audience had snickered at her, their snickers turning into waves of laughter that grew louder and louder until Talbot escorted her from the platform. She had awakened sobbing, her nightgown pasted to her body with cold sweat. Now she was hollow-eyed; her forehead was creased and the blush she had applied sat on her cheekbones like twin bruises.

At three o'clock she rose and walked to the platform. She placed her manuscript—a story she had spent months unsuccessfully reworking—on the lectern, and stood stiffly before the audience. The same thoughts were circling over and over in her head: she should have chosen a published story to read instead of taking a risk with unproven material… but she had read published work last year and the year before that. In attempting to confirm her on-going creativity, she would, in the next hour, be giving evidence of its non-existence.

The first few minutes were excruciating. She read too rapidly and stumbled, her voice cracking over words like shattered glass. Talbot, seated in the center front row, lowered his eyes. Damn that Ackerley, he thought, embarrassed for her. She looked terrible, probably felt humiliated. He wouldn't have taken the evening slot if he'd known Ackerley was going to pull that Sabbath business. Her lecture had been a mistake, more like a confession than anything. He'd better concentrate on her reading; the story was new. Maybe he'd misjudged her.

Midway through the reading the people in the audience began to shift uneasily in their seats. Not only was the story wandering aimlessly, but the sentences were dotted with clichés that most novice writers knew to avoid. The tops of Talbot's ears turned pink when he heard Baran read, "The thought came to her like a breath of fresh air." And his ears were crimson when she said, "Her hopes sank like a lead balloon." He had to force himself to continue listening; never had he wanted a reading to end as quickly as this one.

Most of the staff members' reactions were similar to Talbot's, except perhaps to the degree of their discomfort. What was happening to Phyllis Baran could happen to them. They were witnessing the realization of one of their deepest fears: that they might someday lose their creative powers and critical judgment and stand before an audience reading work that would tarnish their names and reputations. The nightmare was being played before them, vivid and real, and they could not help but internalize it. Beads of perspiration rose on Marshall Stoddard's bald scalp; Terence Hill's handsome features were set in grim sympathy; Andrew Cox slid down in his chair as if he were trying to disappear beneath the seat in front of him; and Merle Ackerley, who had come into the theater feeling vindicated, sat hunched in his chair as if he were somehow to blame for what was happening. Only Sara Newkirk seemed unaffected; she listened intently, massive and expressionless except for her eyes, which were constantly in motion, registering everything she observed.

The reading ended with polite applause that lasted longer than usual; it was uncertain rather than enthusiastic, an award given for effort and sustained by the feeling that it might not be sufficient. Before anyone could get to her, Talbot rose from his seat and met Baran as she descended the platform steps. He put his arm around her and maneuvered her toward the double doors.

"It was awful, wasn't it?" she said when they were outside. She looked upset beyond tears.

"The story needs work," Talbot said. Her shoulder felt fragile beneath his hand. "But before you do anything with it, take out the clichés, especially that one about her hopes sinking like a lead balloon."

She grimaced as if he'd struck her.

"Slip-ups like that can happen to anyone," he said. "When you write thousands of words, it's bound to occur. You just have to be vigilant and catch them."

She nodded, then stood with her eyes downcast as if waiting for dismissal.

"Let's go to Clemens," he said. "We could use a drink."

"Thanks, but I'll pass if you don't mind," she said, aching for the privacy of her room where she could drink alone.

***

Leila entered Clemens and went directly to the trestle table, where she mixed a gin and tonic with quick, angry motions. She hadn't had an opportunity to speak privately with Michael since she had returned from the farm. She had come into the dining room just before they had stopped serving lunch, and seats at the table where he was sitting were all taken. Before she was finished eating, he left Hackett Hall with Sara Newkirk; she didn't see him again until they met at the Circle Theater before Phyllis Baran's reading. At that point her initial excitement over the discovery she had made about Benjamin Clymer had been replaced with resentment. Michael had time for Sara but not for her. His explanation—that they had been discussing revisions of his McDermott lecture to make it suitable for publication in the journal Sara edited—only increased her annoyance. Writing. All he talked about, all he was interested in, was writing. He didn't give a damn about anything else. Except for his damn running, which was what he was doing now.

Every chair in the cottage was taken. Bits of conversations drifted over to her, commonplace talk about cars, about houses, about cities and restaurants, about anything except what was really on their minds: Phyllis Baran's reading. It wasn't that they were above gossiping or that they wanted to protect their colleague.

Rather, their avoidance of discussing the pathetic story she read was a matter of taste, of not wanting to feel or appear harsh, although Baran's relationship with them would never be the same unless, at some time in the future, she would write a book so dazzling that they could reflect upon what had happened as an insignificant stumble in her path to grace.

Nettles crossed the room to the table. "We have a full house," he said, refreshing his drink. "I'm surprised your husband isn't here."

"He's running," Leila said.

"In the mud? He must be dedicated."

"He is."

"You're welcome to my chair."

"Thanks," she said, "but I think I'll sit on the porch."

"Would you mind company?"

Although she would have preferred sitting alone, there wasn't a tactful way she could refuse him.

They sat on the front steps. "This conference must be rather tedious for you," he said.

"At times," she admitted.

"Then why did you come?"

"I'm here for the same reason that Cheryl Hill is here: to stand between my husband and his packs of female admirers. If our husbands were insurance salesmen, we'd be home," she said. "Are you married?"

"Yes."

"Your wife must be a trusting woman, either that or she has more self-confidence than the rest of us."

"We've been married for twenty-eight years, so she's a veteran at being a writer's wife. It isn't always easy, but we have an understanding."

"She sounds remarkable."

"She's overlooking, and she knows I'll always come back to her. I'd be the same if the situation were reversed. It's a matter of being aware of temptations and acknowledging how hard it is to deny them. Novelists like your husband do it all the time in their books."

She wasn't sure if his remark about *novelists like her husband* was a casual statement or a deliberate reminder of the argument between the two men. "I hope Michael's lecture yesterday didn't upset you," she said hesitantly. "I'm sure you understand his passion for what he does."

"Passion," Nettles said, as if savoring the word. "It comes from the Latin *passus*, I believe, which literally translated means suffer or endure. But when I think of passion, I think of strong desire and compelling emotion. You, Leila, are a perfect object of passion—exotically beautiful, sensuous, intelligent. If I were your husband, I'd probably be doing what you're doing here: I'd be keeping a watchful eye on your admirers."

She drank what was left of her gin and tonic. "I thought you had a liberal attitude toward temptations."

"I understand them," he said, leaning toward her. "But that doesn't mean I would always be liberal. You, for example, are too much of a prize to risk."

She wanted to end the conversation gracefully, yet at the same time she was conscious of the closeness of his body, which hinted both power and sex. There was something undeniably attractive about him, and dangerous. She started to rise and glimpsed Michael crossing the bridge over Barrier Creek. At the pace he was running he'd see her with Eric. "There is Michael now," she said, wondering why she felt guilty. She had done nothing wrong.

Pierce's sneakers were spattered with mud; his T-shirt and headband were soaked with perspiration. "Enjoy yourself?" Leila said, meeting him where the path and the road joined.

"Was I hallucinating or were you drinking with him?" he said, jogging in place. He tilted his head in Nettles' direction.

"We talked for a few minutes."

"I thought you had better taste."

"I couldn't be rude," she said. "I'll go back to the room with you."

"Don't bother," he said, taking off in the direction of Hawthorne.

For a moment she stood motionless on the path, holding her empty glass. She didn't want to go back to Clemens; nor could she return to their room. Her eyes stung. Blinking, she forced herself to walk up the road toward the bridge. She didn't look back; if she had, she would have seen Nettles standing on the porch, smiling to himself.

Stoddard was the next person to leave Clemens. He'd had two drinks, which he knew would play havoc with his glucose levels, but Baran's reading had shaken him. He could see himself repeating her performance, reading work that should have been thrown in the wastebasket, and knew from gauging his colleagues' reactions to what they had witnessed that he would lose the respect it had taken him years to earn if he read either from the hopeless manuscript he had brought to the conference or read again from *Places At The Table*. Baran's predicament would be his if he didn't come up with a solution. His mistake had been to let his gonads do his thinking instead of his brain; there was also the fear that his diabetes might make him impotent, although it was too soon to know. He was taking four shots a day here, double the injections he took at home. It was the irresistible free liquor that was making his blood sugar harder to control, certainly not the food, which had been vile.

The first thing Stoddard did when he got to his room was hurry to the bathroom, where he opened an alcohol swab and lifted his shirt top, revealing a massive, hairy abdomen, pale as the underbelly of a fish. After swabbing a spot between his navel and his side, he gave himself an injection in clear skin, avoiding a freckle. It was at that moment the idea came to him: he knew how he could get out of his reading, but he would have to be very, very careful.

***

Agatha entered the Shed with some misgivings, unsure of her decision to go to the mixer alone. Conscious of her nose, which still looked like a red beak from the sunburn she'd gotten on Friday, she felt what little self-confidence she possessed faltering. She would have felt more at ease if either Laura or Nan was accompanying her, but both women had decided not to attend.

The barn-like building was filled close to bursting. Every sofa and chair was taken, and people were clustered around an extra-long table that held plastic glasses, basins of ice cubes, and a variety of non-alcoholic beverages. There was also a crowd around a smaller table, where bowls of pretzels and potato chips were rapidly emptying.

After she waited to get a drink, she made her way to the smaller table. She didn't particularly care for snack food, but nibbling on a few pretzels would at least give her something to do. "What are you drinking?" someone behind her asked.

It was Jerry Hofstrand. "Ginger ale," she said.

"Would you prefer wine?" he asked, holding up a bottle.

"No, thank you."

"Are you sure?"

"Really, I'm fine," she replied, wishing she could think of something else to say.

"I was hoping I'd get a chance to talk to you," he said. "You're the most knowledgeable person I've met here, and I'd like your opinion of the story Phyllis Baran read."

She thought the story was a dismal effort and was embarrassed for the writer; more than that, the reading had raised doubts in her mind as to Baran's competence and critical judgment. Still, she didn't want to be unkind. "I was a little disappointed," she said.

"Only a little?" Hofstrand said. "I thought the story was terrible, really bad. It made me angry."

"Why angry?"

"I came here assuming that the writers on the staff were competent. I wasn't so naive as to think they all had equal ability, but I expected them to be solid in their field."

"They're human," Agatha offered.

"So they are," he said, looking at her shrewdly. "Tell me the truth: you didn't think any more of that story than I did, did you?"

"No, I didn't."

"Then why were you afraid to say so?"

"I wasn't afraid, exactly. I just didn't… I guess I feel sorry for her. It's going to be uncomfortable for her facing everyone here. Until Andrew Cox's reading, I had never thought about what it must be like to be a writer. It always seemed so wonderful to me, such a special gift to be able to write stories and poems that others would read and praise. But now I see a darker side. I see how exposed writers are: their failures, as well as their successes, are public. Once they present their work, they're judged for what they've done. They can't take it back."

"I hadn't thought about it quite that way, although I suppose I should since I'm trying to enter the arena."

"You'll do fine," Agatha said, feeling that this solid man could do no less than write solid books. Then, so relaxed that she no longer felt self-conscious, she added, "If the offer is still open, I think I might enjoy some wine after all."

***

Feeling a need to escape from the conference, Laura took a walk on the tree-lined gravel road that led away from the Inn, relieved to be alone after spending days in the company of others. Although she didn't regret rejecting Stoddard, even with his implied threat of retaliation, she wanted to think about what he said regarding her novel being a mid-list book, particularly since she researched bestsellers on her laptop immediately after she left him. What she found confirmed what he said: most of the novels on best-seller lists were legal thrillers, crime and suspense books, and mysteries. Novels like hers were near strangers to the lists; no more than one or two at a time found a place there, if that. Going back two years, then three years, didn't change the picture; year after year, thrillers and mysteries triumphed.

With each step she took she became more convinced that she had been unrealistic in her expectations for her novel. Despite Gretchen's enthusiasm, she doubted that it had a chance at becoming a bestseller. Common sense should have told her that people wouldn't be wildly interested in a book about two orphaned children. But she didn't write the novel with the hope that it would become a bestseller. She recalled how the idea for the story had come to her in an inspired moment, and that she had pursued it because she had promised herself in college that someday she would try to write a novel. She started writing because it was a challenge, because she found the story compelling, because she liked the feeling that she was using her time creatively instead of filling empty evenings with television and rented movies. Now she needed to adjust her expectations. If she had learned anything at this conference, it was that her hope for a career as a novelist was unrealistic. She had met too many people who had written multiple unpublished novels. And even if by some miracle her novel were accepted for publication, she wouldn't be paid much because it was a mid-list book. The thrill of being published would have to be her reward. She had to be able to support herself, an immediate concern since she had quit her job.

It had taken her years to realistically adjust her expectations and end her relationship with Greg; at least with her novel, she would have an idea of what to expect in less than a week.

When she got back to the Inn, she checked her mailbox for a note from Michael Pierce. The box was empty, as it had been for days. Although she had steeled herself for it, the disappointment still cut.

She assumed that Gwen would be at the mixer, but she was in the room. "My conference with Ackerley is tomorrow. I'm one of the first ones," Gwen said importantly.

"Good for you."

"Has anyone on the staff looked at your work yet?"

"Marshall Stoddard."

Gwen's mouth gapped open in surprise. "Really? He's been refusing to look at anyone's work other than the manuscripts that have been assigned to him. What did he say?"

"He told me that my writing is polished."

"Did he say he would help you get published?"

"I rejected him."

Gwen looked at her, incredulous. "You gave up a chance at getting help from Marshall Stoddard?"

"He wanted me to go to his room," Laura said, pausing to make sure they had direct eye contact. She felt compelled to ask, though she believed she knew Gwen's answer. "What would you have done?"

Gwen averted her head. "I… uh… I'm married."

Laura didn't push her, satisfied that she'd gotten the answer.

***

Pierce left the mixer before it was over; he disliked attending these gatherings, which were mandatory for the staff. It was easier with Leila at his side. He wasn't approached by as many women and people weren't as long-winded, sometimes telling him their entire life histories, including not only their unsuccessful attempts at getting published but intimate details of their lives that they should have saved for their psychiatrists.

He took a deep breath, which made him realize how smothered he'd felt, and started walking briskly toward Hawthorne where he hoped he'd find Leila, forgetting the note he had in his pocket that he had planned to drop in Laura's mailbox. He wouldn't let himself think about the possibility that Leila might not be in their room as he reflected on how stupid he'd been to lose his temper because she'd been talking to Nettles. He had nothing against the guy personally; his argument—a battle now—was about art. He had taken out his frustration over the manuscripts on her. He always lashed out at the person closest to him, a habit he'd never been able to break. Maybe she was still resentful about not going to that escarpment. She'd been sensitive since she'd started the baby business again. Although she hadn't said anything in a while, he knew she hadn't given up. She'd have to get over it somehow. It was hard, but it would be worse if she knew the reason for his refusal. There hadn't been a day in years when he hadn't thought about the time he had left.

To his relief, she was in their room. "Let's go out to dinner and get some decent food," he suggested.

She put down the book she'd been reading. "You might want to take a sweater," he said. "It's getting chilly."

They said little to each other during their ride to Jamestown. Too proud to apologize for his earlier behavior, he tried several times to start a conversation, but she was unresponsive. He drove to a restaurant just outside of town that they had enjoyed the previous year. It wasn't until he broached the subject of Eric Nettles after a waitress took their order that Leila was willing to talk. "I overreacted this afternoon," he said. "I guess I didn't separate Nettles from his fiction. I've been fighting him so hard that I lost perspective."

"He's a charming man."

"I don't doubt it. But I have a legitimate argument with him. He's spreading poison with that innovative nonsense."

"It isn't nonsense to him," she said. "He's respected and highly successful."

Pierce pushed his beer aside and leaned across the table. "You don't agree with him?"

"You know I don't, but he has every right to preach what he believes. The same right that you have."

"No, he doesn't, not in a place like the Workshop!"

"You're raising your voice, Michael."

"He has no right to tell beginning writers that plots aren't necessary," he said, his voice lower, "or he'll have them believing they can put down anything that they want—a string of his so-called episodes—and call it art. Before Picasso made abstract paintings, he worked at becoming a skilled draftsman, and he was superb. Nettles is no Picasso, no matter what the critics say!"

"You don't have to convince me." She put her hand over his. "I just wish you wouldn't get so worked up. Most of the people at the conference won't become writers anyway. You're aggravating yourself unnecessarily. It simply isn't worth it."

Their dinner arrived before he could argue further. They had both ordered chicken, which the waitress set before them with a warning that the plates were hot.

Leila told him about her visit to the farmhouse while they ate. "What a terrific beginning!" he said. "Where are you going to go next?"

"I'm not sure. I'll visit the cemetery, of course, but I don't think I'll learn anything there."

"Clymer's will has to be on file."

"Where? In Jamestown?"

"Call a local lawyer tomorrow," he said, checking his watch. "We'd better go or we'll be late for Aaron's reading."

He paid the check and left a generous tip. When they were outside, Leila said, "Doesn't Aaron's attitude ever bother you?"

"What do you mean?"

She waited until they were in the car before replying. "Aaron has such obvious disdain for the participants. He's been unconscionably cruel, yet he's never criticized; everyone seems to overlook it."

"Aaron has the right to conduct himself as he chooses."

"No one has the right to crush people in the manner in which he does. Think about it: the people whose work he criticizes all want to become poets. They are trying to master an art form that isn't widely read or appreciated. They know they'll never become rich writing poems; the most they can hope for is recognition, if they are lucky enough to get published. The fact that they come to the Workshop seeking help should be respected. They are entitled to constructive criticism."

"Aaron probably has his reasons."

"Are you saying that you approve of his cruelty?"

"No, I think it's wrong, but it's not my responsibility."

"Then whose responsibility is it?"

"Roy's."

"Roy overlooks Aaron's behavior because of his name. You and Aaron are the biggest draws for the Workshop."

"The Workshop is a business. I'm not defending Roy—he's a

jerk, and he's been toadying to Aaron for years—but he has to fill the conference, and Aaron is insurance. People who want to become poets grab at a chance to study with Aaron Greene."

"I don't understand you," she said. "You'd battle Eric Nettles until you dropped, but for years you've been ignoring Aaron's meanness. He's a nasty drunk and you know it."

"I can't change the man or his drinking habits. My fight with Nettles is one of philosophy. I'm a novelist, not a poet."

"But you're also a teacher at the conference, and by overlooking Aaron's brutality, you're condoning it. You, who always try to be tactful no matter what you think of a manuscript you're criticizing. Even in your workshops, you won't allow negativism."

"I told you, I can't change Aaron Greene," he said. "He is what he is. Besides, the conference is brief, not even two weeks, and there is enough intensity without adding to it by promoting trouble among the staff."

"For some people it's a lifetime," she said under her breath.

They drove in silence until they passed through Randolph. Fog was beginning to settle, and swirls of mist played in the twin beams cast by the headlights. She sat uneasily on the black leather seat, regretting having talked about Aaron Greene. She had made him feel defensive about a situation that he was unwilling, and probably unable, to change. If they were going to argue, she thought, it should be over something important: their marriage, their priorities. Having a baby. "I'm sorry," she said. "I shouldn't have pushed so hard about Aaron."

"Don't apologize when you're right."

"Aren't you angry?"

"Guilty," he said. "I've overlooked Aaron's behavior because it was easier that way. I guess I rationalized it by thinking that he was doing most of them a favor because they don't have talent."

They turned into the circular driveway. Ahead, rambling and medieval, the Tabard Inn was shrouded in mist.

***

Copies of the manuscripts that were going to be used for the workshops were stacked on a long table outside the office. Without hesitation Nan picked up materials for the Nettles and Cox workshops. Agatha couldn't decide between Nettles' workshop or Terence Hill's. "I can tell you about Nettles' workshop and give you the manuscript to read," Nan offered. "It won't be the same as attending, but at least you'll get the flavor of it."

"That settles it," Agatha said, picking up the materials for the two poetry workshops. "Thank you."

They were early and chose seats in the center front of the theater. "Why don't you read this now," Nan said, handing Agatha the manuscript for Nettles' workshop. "I'll read the material for Cox's and then we can switch."

Agatha was shocked at the quality of the work she was reading. The manuscript for Nettles' workshop was so egregiously poor that the writing wasn't up to the level of the fiction the students wrote in her high school honors classes. Laura's novel was captivating. The two chapters she'd read of Nan's novel were absorbing and well-written. The prose (if it could be called that) in this handout had run-on sentences, grammatical errors, stilted dialogue… so many problems that it was an insult to contributors who wrote well.

Completely absorbed, she didn't notice Aaron Greene enter the theater. He limped up the steps to the platform, leaning heavily on his carved cane. Tucked under his free arm was a book in which perhaps a dozen manuscript papers were caught between the pages. He set the book on the lectern and gazed indifferently at the people in the packed theater, his body tilted at an angle despite the elevated shoe he was wearing. Beneath his heavy lids, his brown eyes were glazed with alcohol and pain. His lame leg was severely arthritic, and the cumulative effect of the rain and the penetrating dampness of the cool night air had caused a constant, throbbing ache in the stunted limb that the scotch he had been drinking since morning hadn't touched. The leg felt like a huge, festering boil, radiating pain all over his body. To most of the people in the audience, however, the angle at which the poet stood, his impassive, heavy-lidded expression, his full head of white hair, the elegant cane propped against the lectern, all contributed to his aura as an elder statesman of American letters—brilliant, accomplished, a man worthy not only of respect but awe.

Greene opened the thick volume of his collected poems. There were no markers stuck between the pages, nothing to indicate which poems he planned to read; nor was there a list with page numbers and first lines among the loose papers he had brought with him. He had done no advance preparation. If anyone in the Circle Theater had dared to ask him how he could stand before a filled auditorium to read his poems without some sort of plan, a sequence that would make the reading enjoyable for his listeners, he probably would have said that he knew his poetry so well that a plan wasn't necessary. But the truth was that he didn't give a damn. He was seventy-two years old and tired of singing for his supper. There wasn't one person among the more than two hundred people waiting whose opinion mattered to him. He knew the worth of what he had accomplished and nothing could take it away from him. He did not owe them any more than he chose to give.

"I might as well start here," he said, randomly picking a page. "It's as good a place as any to begin this business."

The tenor of the reading was set.

Greene selected the poems he read by flipping through the pages in his book, stopping at whatever happened to catch his interest. Several times he paused and stared at a page, as if he were reading silently to himself or making a decision, while the audience waited. A number of the poems were so well known to some conference members that they applauded before he read past the first line. Greene acknowledged this flattery with a grimace of irritation at the interruption. His occasional remarks prefacing poems were either tinged with condescension or were outrageous to the point of silliness.

Agatha was at first surprised, then stunned by Greene's behavior. She had committed many of his poems to memory. It was impossible to reconcile this indifferent, imperious man with the lines of poetry he had written, which were sensitive, humorous, and down-to-earth in their repeated message that men make too much of themselves, yet the people around her with the exception of Nan, whose furrowed brow expressed her disapproval, did not seem at all disturbed by what was happening; they were clearly enjoying his performance, as if unaware that they were being insulted. Feeling that his behavior was inexcusable, she decided to close her eyes for the remainder of the reading. This was definitely an occasion when listening was preferable to seeing. He did, after all, read his poems exceptionally well.

Greene concluded with a whimsical new poem about a young

boy who follows a man selling popcorn. The people in the audience applauded while he gathered up his papers and tucked them into his book. Ready to leave the platform, he picked up his cane, but the applause grew louder. A dark expression came over his face, as if he were annoyed at being detained. Then, in a mocking gesture, he lifted his cane and waved it above his head in circles. The waving cane drew more applause. They were still clapping when he descended the steps and limped through the double doors.

Talbot left the theater immediately after Greene's departure, debating whether to say something to the poet about his behavior. The Workshop needed Greene, but that performance was over-the-top. He hesitated just long enough for a woman to catch up with him. "Please, Mr. Talbot," she said, "may I speak with you privately for a moment?"

It was difficult to see in the darkness, but he guessed that she was somewhere in her thirties; she was of average height and had shoulder-length blond hair. "Could it wait until tomorrow?"

"No," she said firmly. "I'm leaving early tomorrow morning and I want you to know why."

"Follow me," he said, walking off the path toward one of the larger maples.

"It's hard to say this… Late Thursday night Andrew Cox came into my room… He must have been following me… I hadn't turned the light on yet… He was drunk… He tried to…"

She started to weep. "Somehow I managed to get him off me before he… Then he realized…"

She took a tissue out of her jacket pocket and wiped her eyes. "He was looking for someone else. He called her a bitch for standing him up. I don't know if he found her, poor woman. I didn't report this before because I'd come so far—all the way from Colorado—to have my manuscript criticized. I never thought something like this would happen to me here. I requested my conference early. I had it late this afternoon so I can leave."

"Are you sure it was Andrew Cox?"

"Positive," she said. "I saw his face from the light in the hall. He's violent, just like his books."

"Are you planning on pressing charges?"

"No, I just want to leave, but I do think you should speak to him about it. The woman he mistook me for is probably still here. She could be in danger."

"What is your name?"

"Mary Carthage."

"I appreciate your telling me, Mary, and I'm truly sorry about what happened. We haven't had an unfortunate incident like this before, and I'll do my best to ensure that it never occurs again."

He walked with her to the Tabard Inn and wished her a safe trip home. Then he headed toward Clemens, where he knew he'd find Andrew Cox. Despite the chilly night air, his shirt was soaked with sweat beneath his suede jacket.

Cox wasn't in Clemens. He was in his room with a woman who wasn't particularly attractive—her hips were too wide, her face too long and rectangular—but she promised him he'd have the best sex of his life with her, and she was peeling off his jeans while Talbot was looking for him.

The woman kept her promise. She did tricks with her tongue and her hands, an amazing performance like nothing he had ever experienced. He moaned when he ejaculated, his body flooded with ecstasy.

There was nothing better in the world than being a best-selling novelist, he thought.

***

❧ WORKSHOP BULLETIN ❧

VOL. 74, NO.6   THE CLYMER WORKSHOP   AUGUST 16 2004

GOOD MORNING!

It will be rainy and humid in the morning, with a possible thunderstorm. This afternoon should be clear and sunny. Bundle up tonight: a cold front will be coming, bringing cool winds.

MORNING PROGRAM

9:15 A.M. Fiction Lecture
(Andrew Cox)
10:15 A.M. Panel on Writing for Children
(Michael Pierce, Sara Newkirk, Merle Ackerley)
11:15 A.M. Manuscript Conferences

Mr. Cox will talk about "The Story That Won't Go Away."

AFTERNOON PROGRAM

2:00 P.M. Workshops
(Eric Nettles, Terence Hill)
3:00 P.M. Workshops (Aaron Greene, Andrew Cox)
4:00 P.M. Manuscript Conferences

EVENING READING

Novelist Merle Ackerley will read from his fiction. His novels include *Possum Tree*, *The Arising of Jimmy Pye*, *Sleeper*, and *The Purdy Feud*. He is also the author of a children's story, *The Wishing Well*. Mr. Ackerley teaches at Tulane University.

WORKSHOPS

Materials for tomorrow's workshops will be available after dinner outside the Workshop office. Please take materials only for the workshops you plan to attend.

ATTENTION

All six copies of the Sunday *New York Times Book Review* have disappeared, as have the sports sections. It would be appreciated if the papers were returned to the sitting room so that others might enjoy them.

LOST

Woman's gold bracelet, in the vicinity of the Shed. If found, please bring to the Workshop office for a reward.

WARNING!

Watch out for and avoid healthy vines that have shiny green leaflets growing in threes, which could be either poison ivy or poison oak.

*"If I had to give young writers advice, I would say don't listen
to writers talk about writing or themselves."*
Lillian Hellman

Chapter VI

Wrapped in a lavender terrycloth bathrobe, her gold bracelets jangling (she wouldn't take them off even to shower, fearing that they'd be stolen), Claire Saxon walked down the hall to the room she shared with Agatha. Her skin was pale and porous without make-up; her puffy cheeks sagged with unhappiness. Nothing at this conference had worked in her favor, she thought. Nothing. Her room was dingy and claustrophobic; her roommate was homely, a person with whom she didn't want to associate; the rest of the people were all snobs and pseudo-intellectuals; all the men that she would have considered prospects, of which there weren't many, had rejected her for others; and if that weren't enough, she was a published writer and she couldn't tell anyone!

The first thing she saw when she stepped into the room made her bristle: Agatha, already dressed in a light blue blouse and navy slacks, was standing in front of the mirror over the dresser. "Are you almost finished?" she snapped. "I have to put my make-up on."

Agatha stepped away as if responding to an order. "Whatever happened to your face?" Claire said, staring.

Translucent patches of skin were peeling off Agatha's face like large, irregular polka dots; on the areas that had already peeled, her skin was a glossy, tender pink. "My sunburn…" Agatha started to explain, clearly distressed.

"You aren't planning to go downstairs looking like that," Claire interrupted.

"I have no choice."

"If it were me, I wouldn't leave this room," Claire said, unzipping her bulging cosmetic bag.

Agatha's hands fluttered to her face. "Is it that bad?"

"Frankly," Claire said, smearing foundation on her nose and cheeks, "you look like you have a disease."

Agatha made her bed, debating what to do. If she stayed in the room, she'd miss the lectures and the workshops. She was supposed to meet Nan for breakfast; she'd better find her now to explain.

She hurried down the hall, keeping her head bent. Nan was alone in the room, tying her sneakers. Averting her face, Agatha said. "I won't be going to breakfast."

"Aren't you feeling well?" Nan asked with concern.

Reluctantly. Agatha turned. "I can't be seen looking like this."

"That's not so bad. Sit at the desk and I'll have you fixed up in no time."

While Nan was working on her, removing loose skin, then applying a soothing moisturizer and make-up, Agatha told her what Claire had said. "My roommate has had her moments, but compared to Claire, she's a peach," Nan said, furious. "You have to ignore people like her."

"I'll try," Agatha said, still so upset that she didn't ask why Nan was putting something on her eyelids, which weren't peeling. She sat with her eyes closed, perfectly still, until Nan handed her a mascara wand. "You'd better put this on yourself," Nan said, giving her a small mirror. "It's new, just out of the package. You can keep it. I have another one."

Agatha gazed into the mirror, astonished. Except for a few dry patches, her face was pink and glowing. But more than that, her eyes appeared larger and rounder, her nose less beaked. She was, she thought, almost… presentable. "What did you do to my eyes?"

"I put some liner on."

"I must learn!" Agatha said with delight.

***

Talbot took a *WORKSHOP BULLETIN* off a pile stacked on the mahogany table outside Hackett Hall and walked into the dining room for breakfast, reading. When he reached the center of the dining hall, he stopped and looked around. Dee Dee wasn't sitting at any of the tables. He turned abruptly and strode out of the room, his jaw set, his cheek muscles contracting with anger.

He saw her as she was coming into the back entrance of the Inn and waited until she reached him, his jaw and cheek muscles working furiously. "I can't believe you did this!" he said, thrusting the *BULLETIN* under her nose.

Conscious of interested glances from people walking past them to the dining room, Dee Dee reached for the *BULLETIN,* the gesture defensive rather than aggressive. Talbot wouldn't release it, and the paper ripped. "I'll be happy to discuss it with you," she said, staring at the fragment in her hand, "privately."

They walked in silence to the Workshop office, Dee Dee taking two steps to his one. After he unlocked the door, she rushed behind her desk as though anxious to put the massive, scarred piece of furniture between them.

"There's nothing here but the day's schedule and whining about missing sections of the *Times.* Anyone reading this," he said, crumpling the section he had in his hand and tossing it across the room to a metal wastebasket (he missed), "would think we were running a military school instead of a writers' conference."

"Yesterday you complained about the tidbit, so I omitted it today."

"I had a legitimate reason to complain! That remark about the food was disastrous! The *BULLETIN* has to be lively. It's a record of what we're doing here, so it should be positive, a reflection of a stimulating, exciting experience."

"I don't write fiction," she said stiffly.

Talbot grimaced as if he'd bitten into something terribly sweet. "That's cute."

"I'd like to go for breakfast now."

"Is that all you have to say?"

"It's almost eight thirty. They'll stop serving soon."

"What about the *BULLETIN*?" he demanded, so angry that he had to restrain himself from adding that, with her figure, she'd be doing herself a favor by skipping breakfast.

"I've run out of ideas, and I don't have time to dream up new ones. I've been stuck in the office all day. I don't see or hear anything that's entertaining. I field complaints. If you want the *BULLETIN* to be entertaining, write pieces for me to put in."

"I don't have time," he said. "Besides, it's your job."

She started to cry.

Damn, he thought. She'd written a lousy *BULLETIN* and now, because she was crying, he'd have to apologize. What was the matter with her anyway? "I guess I overreacted a little," he said.

She opened a desk drawer and pulled a tissue out of a box she kept there. He waited while she wiped her tears and blew her nose, hoping that she would stop crying, but she didn't. After she reached for a third tissue, he suggested that they go to breakfast. "Go without me," she sobbed.

He left feeling both relieved and resentful; her crying had made him uncomfortable. It was unfair of her to react that way, he thought, hurrying down the corridor. Writing the *BULLETIN* was her responsibility, not his. She'd been acting peculiarly for days. Maybe she was having female problems, PMS or something.

When he entered Hackett Hall, he spotted a table with an empty seat opposite Eric Nettles. Forgetting about Dee Dee, Talbot crossed the dining room, his thoughts swinging to his unpublished manuscript.

Alone in the office, Dee Dee locked the door, then returned to her desk, weeping. What a fool she had been, what an idiotic fool! All these years she had pined for him, had worshiped him, had done everything she could to show how she felt about him, and he had humiliated her in public! He cared more about the damn *BULLETIN* than he did about her feelings!

She reached into her desk drawer and pulled out a handful of tissues. Five years of devotion meant nothing to him! Neither did she! They had slept in rooms next to each other for days, and he hadn't made an overture to her, not one.

The thought of the thin wall that separated them started a new flood of tears. He treated her as if she were useful for nothing but work. Dee Dee the drudge, that was all she meant to him. She could see it clearly now and she knew what to do: at the close of the Workshop, she would give notice.

***

Andrew Cox stood before the Workshop members with a calm, serious demeanor. There were four people in the audience whom he wanted to impress: Michael Pierce, Eric Nettles, Marshall Stoddard, and Sara Newkirk. They were the contacts he had come to the Workshop to cultivate; they all had influence, they were all masters of literary politics. Even with his best-selling books, he was still an outsider. If he ever wanted a grant or a fellowship or a job at one of the better universities, their friendship would be invaluable.

"Some writers start their fiction with an idea," he began. "I am not one of them. I start with a story, a story so strong I feel my head will explode if I don't write it."

He went on to discuss how he wrote his first book, the mistakes he had made and the lessons he had learned. He described instances in which he had become mired in language, his difficulties writing dialogue and description, the trouble he had with revision. "There were many times when I thought of revision as my penance for having the audacity to think I was a writer in the first place," he said. "Now I know that revision is a necessary and vital stage in the long process of making fiction work. It kills me to cut out sentences that I labored over for hours—it feels like I'm cutting off my fingers one by one—but I do it because the story comes first."

Sitting at the end of a row near the double doors, Talbot nodded to himself. Although he wouldn't have chosen the amputation of fingers as a metaphor for revision, he approved of the message: be a servant to the story.

Talbot had a reason for choosing a seat near the doors: he had been unable to find Cox last night, and a telephone call he had received this morning made talking to the novelist imperative.

Cox didn't make it easy. Talbot approached him as he was leaving the theater with a petite blond. "Excuse me," Talbot said. "Andrew, I'd like a word with you privately."

"Let's make it later," Cox said, his confidence restored with the positive response his lecture had received.

"No, it will be now."

Cox didn't move.

"Andrew and I are going to take a walk," Talbot said to the blond. "He'll see you later."

"What's so important that it can't wait?" Cox said, seething.

"I'll tell you when we can't be overheard."

The sky, which had been a murky gray since dawn, was charcoal as Talbot walked around the theater to a road that led to the back of the campus. A flash of lightening followed by tremendous clap of thunder made the air vibrate. "Where are we going?" Cox said, eyeing the black sky uneasily.

"To the barn," Talbot said, quickening his pace.

The oversize garage had weathered vertical siding, two sets of double doors that were fastened shut with crude wooden latches, and a green tin roof. The two men entered the building through a service door just seconds before they would have been pelted with rain.

Inside, there was a tractor with an attachment for bush-hogging, a blade for snow plowing, riding lawnmowers, a long workbench, shovels, garden forks, rakes, a wheelbarrow—almost any tool or machine needed for property maintenance. Rain, coming down heavily now, was making a machine-gun racket on the roof. "I didn't know this building was here. Is it the proverbial woodshed?" Cox said caustically.

"I looked for you last night after a woman told me that you tried to rape her Thursday evening. She said you were drunk and that you were looking for someone else who'd stood you up," Talbot said, watching the effect of his words.

Cox's skin took on a sickly greenish cast, the color of a lima bean. "It was a mistake," he said quickly, his arrogance gone, "a mistake. I was drunk, I wasn't thinking clearly. It won't happen again."

"So you decided to rape her and by mistake you nearly raped someone else," Talbot said, making no effort to hide his contempt.

"Like I said, it was a mistake. It won't happen again."

"That isn't all that won't happen again," Talbot said, his voice level and cold. "I got a call after breakfast this morning from a local farmer whose daughter is a waitress here. He told me that you've been making passes at her."

"There's no harm in a little flirting."

"*No harm*?" Talbot repeated, his tone even icier. "The girl is sixteen. The age of consent in New York is seventeen. Her father told me that if you so much as speak to her again, he'll take care of you. Believe me, you don't want that to happen, though you deserve it."

Talbot's eyes bored into Cox. "The Workshop is over on Friday. From now until it ends you are to keep your pants zipped and your flirting impulses on hold. Is that clear?"

"I got the message," Cox said. "About that incident with the woman on Thursday night. Did she mention telling anyone else?"

Talbot took his time to respond. "She said something about leaving the conference early. You might get lucky," he said, "or maybe not."

The drumming of the rain on the tin roof had eased to a light patter. Talbot walked to the workbench where there was a box of large plastic garbage bags, and pulled one out. "I'm going back now," he said, noting with satisfaction that Cox looked thoroughly chastened.

Talbot didn't wait for the novelist. He left through the service door and headed toward the road holding the garbage bag over his head as a shield from the rain.

***

Webb walked down the hall on the second floor of the Tabard Inn, the wet soles of his sneakers squeaking against the wood floor, looking for Diana. She hadn't been at breakfast; nor did he see her at the lecture. A door to a bathroom opened as he turned into the hallway connecting the two wings. She emerged carrying a towel and a quilted toiletry case; her hair, wet and shining like black ribbon, hung almost to the waist of her white terrycloth robe. "Diana," he called, breaking into a trot.

She jumped. "What are you doing here?"

"I was concerned when you weren't at breakfast or the lecture," he said, pulling her to him.

She wriggled out of his arms, unaware that the top of her robe had opened, exposing her breasts. "You're wet and you're not supposed to be up here."

"I got caught in the rain. Where is your room? I'll dry off there," he said, his eyes fixed on her breasts.

"No," she said, closing her robe. The longer she could postpone his finding out that Marsha had left, the better. "The women will be back soon and you won't be able to leave inconspicuously."

"No one will give a damn as long as I have my clothes on."

"But I do," she said.

"Why are you always so uptight? You're afraid to let anyone see me coming out of your room; you don't want to ask Talbot to switch you from Baran to Pierce; you…"

"Please, Doug," she interrupted, pointing her finger in the direction of the staircase. "GO."

"All right," he said. "I'll meet you downstairs in half an hour."

She waited until she heard him descend the stairs and then walked to her room, smiling. He was incorrigible, she thought. But he was right about Phyllis Baran. She had to ask Talbot to switch her, especially after that awful story Baran read yesterday. She also had to do something about getting up in the morning. With Marsha gone, there was no alarm clock in the room. She'd have to ask the women in the room next to hers to wake her up.

Webb was waiting when she came downstairs. He had changed into dry clothes and was pacing the reception area. "Let's go for a walk," he said, unable to stand still.

"I'd like to stop at the Workshop office first," she said, falling into step with him.

"Are you going to ask Talbot to switch you?"

"Yes."

"Good," he said. "Let's go."

"It's my problem. I have to handle it myself."

"He's going to give you a hard time. What if he refuses?"

Webb's agitation was starting to draw stares from people coming into the Inn. "Give me five minutes," she said.

He was leaning against the wall opposite the Workshop office when she came out. Her face was grim. "Talbot refused?" Webb said, more as a statement than a question.

"Let's get out of here," she said. "Let's go for a drive."

She didn't speak again until they were inside his Volkswagen. "What did he say to you?" Webb asked, turning on the ignition.

"He said it was impossible to reassign me; it was too late and Pierce already had the maximum number of manuscripts. He tried to dismiss me quickly, but I wouldn't leave. I told him that Phyllis Baran couldn't teach and that the story she read yesterday was terrible. He looked at me as though I had colossal nerve and demanded to know on what basis I was making such strong judgments. He was really cutting, almost nasty."

"Then you left?"

"No," she said. Her chin quivered, but she was too angry to cry. "I told him that I have an MFA from Brown, so I've been in enough writing seminars to know whether or not an instructor is competent. Then he made a snide remark about unpublished writers having the audacity to judge published writers. His attitude changed when I told him that one of my short stories is going to be published in the *Georgia Review*. He congratulated me and got friendly, like he was thinking of making a pass. He was disgusting."

"Did he touch you? I'll beat the shit out of him!"

"I left. On my way out, I told him that I was going to collect all the manuscript samples from the workshops and send them to Brown so the people I studied with would know the quality of the work he was accepting."

Webb grinned. "That's great idea! We should collect everything—prose and poetry—and send copies to Iowa, Stanford, Columbia…"

"You can," she said. "I'm going to hound Michael Pierce until he agrees to read my manuscript."

They drove past a small development of one-story houses set back off the road; a pair of Indian boys, perhaps nine or ten years old, were playing catch in one of the gravel driveways. A few minutes later the road made a sudden, sharp right into the hills. Webb shifted gears for the steep climb. "Stop," Diana said, pointing.

Webb pulled the car off the road and they got out, the Workshop forgotten. They walked to the edge of the escarpment Leila had found and gazed in wonder. Below, holding tiny islands that looked as if they had been chipped off the green hills and scattered on the water, the Alleghany River glistened like a dark mirror, silent and powerful. Webb took a deep breath. "I have to make love to you here," he said urgently, "now."

Before she could reply he went back to the car and removed a blanket from the trunk. Then, taking her hand, he led her to a recessed ledge that wasn't visible from the road.

The waters of the Alleghany swept past the tiny islands, moving, moving.

***

In one of the drab classrooms in the Studio, Jerry Hofstrand was seated opposite Pierce on an ancient, oversize student desk that was tight for his large frame. Hofstrand was listening intently, holding a pen over a yellow legal pad. He hadn't taken a note since the manuscript conference started; nearly a quarter of the conference time had lapsed and he was still trying to comprehend what the novelist was telling him. "I'm sorry," he said finally. His eyes met Pierce's, steady and direct. "This is embarrassing, but I don't quite understand what you mean by having the characters tell the story."

Frowning, Pierce flipped through the pages of the manuscript. The furrows in his forehead disappeared when he found what he was looking for. He held out the page for Hofstrand to see, pointing toward the bottom. "In this paragraph you tell the reader that your character, Ned Piper, called a woman to arrange for her to sleep with one of the Pentagon brass. You also say that she agreed, after which Piper left his hotel room to go out for dinner with friends."

"That's right," Hofstrand said.

"No," Pierce said, "that's wrong! You don't *tell* the reader that Piper called the woman, you *show* him calling. You have him find her telephone number, dial, and talk. The most effective fiction shows, not tells. You must dramatize the story in the reader's mind. First you see Piper calling and then you render the scene for the reader, giving enough details so the reader can see what you're seeing. What you want to do is transfer the dream that's in your mind to the reader's mind."

Hofstrand nodded, writing rapidly. "What kind of details do I give?"

"It depends on what you're trying to show, the mood and overtones that you want to evoke. In this case, Piper is in a hotel room calling a woman who has sex for money. He's pimping and she's prostituting, yet neither character fits into a stereotyped image—they aren't low-life, street-corner types. You could briefly describe the room, perhaps a piece of furniture, which could be a plastic imitation of a classic style, or have the carpet plush and red like a bordello. There are all kinds of possibilities, and that's just the beginning!"

Pierce opened his hands and gestured widely. "Then you go beyond the call itself. You've created an opportunity here which you can't let pass. The reader knows that your character is under a lot of pressure. Piper is trying to get a multi-million dollar contract from the Pentagon. He's a member of an elite group of salesmen who are practically stationed in Washington because they're competing for the most lucrative business in the world. Their jobs, their companies, their lives depend on the contracts they win. In your novel, Piper essentially represents the whole crew. You've already shown him wining-and-dining the military brass. Here you have him actually pimping for them, and then you let it pass as if it's standard procedure."

Hofstrand squared his shoulders. "Unfortunately, it is standard procedure."

"*You* know that," Pierce said, pointing at him, "but you haven't let your readers know. How many times has Piper done this? How does *he feel* about procuring women? The guy has a wife and kids in the suburbs; he goes to church every Sunday. And he pimps for the Pentagon brass to make a living! That's strong stuff!"

"How should I handle it then?"

"Get into the guy's mind, but not with a lot of philosophical garbage. Maybe have him flash back to the first time he procured a woman to get a contract. Or you could have him show how he feels about what he's doing. Have him put the receiver down with disgust, perhaps wash his hands or shower afterward. Or, if he doesn't have any moral qualms about what he's doing, have him congratulate himself, maybe pour himself a drink."

Hofstrand's face brightened. "You want me to show the incidents and then go beyond them."

Pierce grinned. "Exactly!"

They continued talking about specific scenes, Pierce giving so many suggestions the Hofstrand's pen didn't stop moving over the yellow pad. When the session was almost over, Pierce placed his chin in his hand, studying the older man. "Your idea for this novel is along the lines of a thriller, isn't it?"

"I know thrillers aren't considered serious fiction," Hofstrand said apologetically. "My roommate talks about them like they're junk—throw-away books. But I think I have a good story to tell, and I'm familiar with the subject matter."

"It's what you do with your material that matters. You have the beginning of a book that could be strong fiction if you handle it properly."

"How do I do that?"

"For the purposes of your novel, the Pentagon has to become the world."

"What do you mean?"

"Everything that happens in the novel relates in some way to the Pentagon. Therefore, the Pentagon is the core of the book, the foundation upon which the action takes place. The good or evil that occurs happens within its boundaries or frame of reference. As a result, the world the reader sees is not only defined by the Pentagon, but *is* the Pentagon. Anything else in the novel becomes intrusive."

"Then in a sense, it's like a metaphor."

"Exactly," Pierce said, leaning back. "Now I'd like to know, just for myself, how much you intend to reveal."

"Nothing classified." Hofstrand shifted uncomfortably on the wood seat. "I've been having some problems, though, even with the stuff that isn't classified," he confessed. "There's a lot I could tell that I don't feel right about. I was a career officer; I spent my life in the Air Force. I don't know what it is—loyalty, patriotism— but I find myself holding back, glossing over material that could make the novel stronger. Maybe I'm afraid the men I worked with will shun me if I tell the truth. I don't know if I'm making sense, but I worry about betraying them and betraying my profession."

Pierce nodded. "I understand. But if you want to write this book, you're going to have to forget about your friends. If you don't tell the truth as you see it, if you aren't as honest as you can possibly be, you'll be betraying the story and yourself. Your fiction won't be worth a damn."

"That sounds so absolute."

"It is absolute. You can't hold anything back. You have to be as honest as the Pope making his confession."

"No matter what the cost? Isn't that a little idealistic?"

Pierce smiled. "That's the irony," he said. "Fiction is an elaborate lie, a fabrication, a dream. Yet within these long, intricate fabrications the creator of the lie, the writer, must always tell the truth. If he's dishonest, the fiction fails, the dream is broken."

Hofstrand shook his head as if he'd been given a task that he wasn't sure he could accomplish.

The novelist checked his watch; the conference had run over the allotted time. He rose and extended his hand. "You have the makings of a fine book."

Hofstrand eased himself out of the desk and grasped Pierce's hand firmly. "Thank you," he said.

***

As Agatha and Laura were crossing Hackett Hall, Laura happened to glance at the plates on a table that had just been served. Her stomach immediately recoiled at the sight of a thick, rust-colored gravy that had a greasy sheen which was smothering flat noodles. "Agatha, let's have lunch in the Shed, my treat," she said, looking pointedly at the plates.

"Good idea," Agatha said, "but you don't have to treat."

"Yes, I do. We'll call it a celebration," Laura said. "I'll explain on the way."

It had stopped raining, and the sky had begun to clear. "I got a note from Michael Pierce," Laura said. "He wants to read my manuscript, and he said he'd meet with me at five o'clock on Thursday afternoon."

Agatha put her arm around Laura and gave her a half-hug. "That's wonderful! I just knew he would!"

"Maybe you did, but I had just about given up. I was checking my mailbox constantly. I was starting to feel that I'd caught what I've begun to think of as *desperation disease*. There's an epidemic of it here, people so uptight that they look like they've lost the ability to swallow."

"You've described it perfectly," Agatha said with a sigh. "I've never been in a situation as intense as this conference, so many people seeking answers, all of them desperately wanting their work to be published. I don't mean you, of course."

Laura laughed. "I'm anxious but not desperate," she said, deciding to tell about her experience with Stoddard.

Agatha listened with growing astonishment as Laura related what had happened. "He actually intimated that he could give your novel an ugly review and ruin your chances to get another book published?"

"He could make me or break me, both literally and figuratively."

"That's… that's despicable! It's unethical!"

"It stinks," Laura agreed, "but it's probably what really goes on in the realm of arts and letters instead of the lofty world of literature that they present here. All the talk I've heard since we arrived has been about art. When I was in college, I could philosophize for hours; it made me feel intellectual and important. But I'm beyond the point in my life where I want to listen to debates about art for art's sake. During Michael Pierce's lecture, I waited for him to tell us *how* to construct a strong plot, *how* to make characters vivid. I enjoyed the lecture because he's so dynamic, but I couldn't help feeling cheated at the end. I'm now at the point where I'm wondering if writing can be taught at all."

There was already a line of people at the snack bar waiting to place their orders when they entered the Shed. "Could you find us a table while I get our sandwiches?" Laura said. "I'm going to have a BLT and lemonade. What would you like?"

"I'll have the same," Agatha said, opening her tote bag.

"It's my treat," Laura reminded her, pointing to one of the few remaining empty tables.

She was back soon, carrying their sandwiches and drinks on a tray. "It seems we got here just in time," Agatha said. "The line for the snack bar is almost to the door."

After they started eating, Laura looked at Agatha critically. "There is something different about you today. You look as though this country air really agrees with you."

"It's make up," Agatha said with a chuckle. "Nan put in on me because my face was peeling. Thank you for noticing."

Laura told Agatha what Stoddard had said about mid-list books. "Mid-list novels may be harder to get published, but they are the books that matter. Thrillers are ultimately forgotten unless they are most unusual; books like *To Kill a Mockingbird* last forever," Agatha said. She reached across the table for Laura's hand. "You are gifted, truly gifted. I wouldn't say it if I didn't mean it. I know how discouraging it must be for you to see all the desperation here, but you can't succumb to it. You must have faith in yourself and your novel. I hope you're not considering giving up on your book, or on writing."

"I don't want to end up like some of the people I've met."

Agatha shook her head. "I'm not unrealistic. I've read wonderful, deeply moving novels that have disappeared before reaching an audience. Until now I didn't realize how much a writer's fate depends on luck. I have no idea of how much luck you will have, but if you give up, you'll never know."

"I don't want to become bitter like Stan. Right now he's probably tracking down his roommate, who had his conference with Michael Pierce this morning."

"What is his roommate's name?"

"Jerry, I think. Stan is furious that his conference was first since he's writing a thriller." Laura paused. "Though if his book is a thriller, he certainly has the right genre."

Agatha wasn't thinking about genres. She was wondering if the

Jerry was Jerry Hofstrand.

***

Talbot left the Inn looking as though he were suffering from a bad case of indigestion. The day had been nothing but aggravation: first the skimpy *BULLETIN;* then his fight with Dee Dee, who was getting more impossible by the minute; then having to discipline Cox; and finally Diana Rothenberg threatening to send copies of participants' manuscripts to Brown. He'd handled Rothenberg badly; she deserved to be assigned to Pierce and she knew it. She was striking-looking and had a spectacular rack. That was one pair he'd never get his hands on. His handling of the cook was even worse. The guy was probably throwing pots against the kitchen walls now. He could have been more tactful, but that lunch today was inexcusable, even with the tight budget for food. An hour or so in Clemens would be a welcome break; the booze wouldn't hurt either.

Someone called his name as he was about to step onto the bridge over Barrier Creek. "Mr. Talbot, Mr. Talbot."

Shit, he thought, turning to see who it was.

She ran up to him breathing heavily, a woman of about forty. Her short hair was a light auburn, her skin creamy, her figure full but not overweight. Her skin and hair had a rosy glow in the sunlight that reminded him of a ripe piece of fruit. The thick folder she was carrying, however, told him a different story, as did the pencil that she had stuck behind her ear. He braced himself for more trouble.

"I'm Joanne Howe," she said. "I had my conference with Marshall Stoddard this morning, and it was a waste of time. He seemed to be in a hurry. All he did was line edit my manuscript! I didn't lay out hundreds of dollars to come here to have my sentences proofread. An editor in New York is interested in my book and wants to see the first three chapters; he already has the outline and likes it."

"You can't expect Mr. Stoddard to write the chapters for you."

"I didn't," she said, patches of color erupting on her face and neck. "Nor did I expect him to make a cutting remark about the title and subject matter of the book, as if it were far too commercial for him to be wasting his time on. There's so much of that snobbery here! If you want literary manuscripts, you should state that plainly in your brochures. I came here for help and instead I was insulted!"

"I'll speak to Mr. Stoddard. Meanwhile, I want you to tell me about your book. But let's get out of the sun. We can sit over there," he said, gesturing toward a stand of trees between Tabard II and the creek.

She walked slightly ahead of him, Talbot eyeing her swaying hips. With all the problems he'd had since the Workshop had started, he hadn't had the time or opportunity for extra-curricular activities. Joanne Howe could be a gift.

"Tell me about yourself first," he said after they settled under an oak.

"I was a stockbroker for eighteen years. Last year I finally had enough money to quit."

"Then you didn't enjoy being a stockbroker?"

"Oh, I liked it," she said. "It was a challenge, and I had some great clients. But there were some aspects that I didn't like. Eventually the balance tipped, so I worked to get out."

"What didn't you like?"

"Every morning at a meeting before the market opened, we were told by management what stocks and bonds to push. More often than not, I wasn't enthusiastic about their choices and didn't feel comfortable pushing them."

"Isn't that somewhat dishonest—on the part of the brokerage house, I mean?"

Joanne shrugged. "It's a common practice. They all do it. Vacations were a problem, too. It's an exceptionally competitive business. I couldn't take off for more than three or four days without worrying about losing clients to another broker. And although it's better now than it was in the past, advancement is still tilted toward men over women.

"After I quit, I took a long vacation and thought about what to do next. For years I'd wanted to be a writer, and I got the idea for a book. The tentative title is *For Women Only: Making Money in the Stock Market*."

Talbot looked at her quizzically. "How can you make the stock market gender specific?"

"You can't," Joanne said with a husky laugh. "I think it's a great title that I hope will catch the interest of men as well. It's provocative. No one wants to be left out when it comes to learning about how to make money."

"You mean stock tips?"

"Oh, no," she said. "It's nothing like that. In fact, one of the chapters will be about stock tips and why you shouldn't listen to them. The book is really about empowerment, educating people to make sound investment decisions. Women control over fifty per cent of the money in this country, yet they defer to men when it comes to investments. I hope my book will change that."

"I'm sure it will," Talbot said.

He found her smart and sexy, and the fact that she'd been successful in a world dominated by men added to her appeal. As they continued to talk, he was delighted to hear that she was presently unattached (she was divorced). Before they parted, they made discreet plans to meet late in the afternoon.

***

Agatha and Nan had arranged to meet in the Shed after the workshops. "I'm thirsty," Nan said. "Let's get something to drink."

They took their place at the end of one of two long lines that snaked around the tables. "I'd like to own the concession here," Nan remarked.

"So would I," said Jerry Hofstrand, who took a place in line behind them.

"How were your workshops?" Nan said.

"Terence Hill's was excellent," Agatha said.

"And Aaron Greene's?"

Agatha hesitated. "He didn't have one positive thing to say. He was mean, truly caustic."

"He has a lot in common with Eric Nettles," Nan said. "Nettles tore a young woman's manuscript apart. Everyone knew who she was because he didn't have the decency to remove her name from it. He was unconscionably cruel. The poor thing had all she could do not to burst into tears."

"That bothered me, too," Hofstrand said. "You'd think that a man as intelligent as Nettles would have enough sense to keep people's names off their manuscripts when he knows in advance that he's not going to treat them well."

Nan excused herself after they'd gotten their drinks. "I'm still slogging through Nettles' novel," she said.

"Your friend seems a bit uptight," Hofstrand commented after she left.

"She's anxious about her conference," Agatha explained, wondering if she should have gone with Nan. She didn't want him to feel as though he was stuck with her.

"I had mine this morning. I should have told her not to worry, that the worst part is the anticipation."

"Then it went well?"

"I think so. Let's go outside and find a place to sit, and I'll tell you about it."

By the time they found lawn chairs near a large oak, Agatha was relaxed. She was, she kept reassuring herself, just having iced tea with a friend.

He told her about the conference, quoting Pierce practically verbatim at Agatha's urging. "Congratulations!" she said when he was finished. "I just knew you'd be successful."

Hofstrand smiled. "I have to finish writing the book first."

"Oh, you will!" she said. Then she hesitated. "Would you mind if I jotted down some of the pointers he gave you? I'd like to share them with my students."

"Not at all." He studied her for a moment. "You're really dedicated, aren't you?"

"Teaching is my life. I try to give whatever I can to my students."

"They're lucky kids. I wish my two daughters had had teachers like you. We moved so much when they were young because of my career that their education was uneven until we finally settled in Washington. Then we enrolled them in private schools, and they had to work twice as hard as the other kids to catch up."

It was the first time he had mentioned his family to her. "Moving frequently can be a hardship," she said, chiding herself for having thought there was any possibility that a man as attractive as Jerry would be unattached.

He nodded. "It was hardest on my wife. She…"

Agatha waited for him to continue, but he didn't. Instead, he looked at the green hills rolling across the horizon, his eyes half-closed as if he were struggling to control sadness or pain. "The hills are beautiful," she finally offered. "I've never been anywhere as lovely. It makes you forget that there is a world outside this place."

"I never realized how much forgetting could be a blessing," he said, almost to himself. "My wife passed away in December from cirrhosis of the liver. I've been blaming myself for so many years that I wasn't aware of how heavy the guilt was until a few minutes ago. I haven't thought about her in hours, maybe even a day. My mind's been on my manuscript and everything else going on around here."

Agatha looked at him with compassion. Never had she seen such visible guilt. Slouched forward in his chair, his shoulders were sagging forward toward his knees. She would have liked to pat his arm comfortingly, but her reserve wouldn't allow her to touch him. "You shouldn't blame yourself," she said consolingly.

"Alcoholism is common among military wives. The explanations are fairly cut-and-dried: husbands' absences, constant moving to new places where the wives don't have friends or family, the pressure of taking care of children alone. It all boils down to loneliness, marriages that aren't marriages because the husbands aren't there. I have no excuse. I wanted my career and she paid for it."

"But didn't you pay? Weren't you lonely, too?"

"Yes," he said, "but I had my work."

"She had your daughters. Children can be wonderful company; they're so full of energy and interest in everything around them that I imagine she was kept as busy as you were with your work," Agatha said, her secret, never-to-be-fulfilled wish for a child of her own giving her words a poignant earnestness. "I can understand why you feel responsible, but perhaps you're blaming yourself too much."

"I never thought of it that way before," he said, straightening his shoulders. "You know, Agatha, you really are a remarkable person."

"Oh… my," she stammered, astonished at the compliment.

Later, when she went to her room, she studied her reflection in the mirror. The makeup Nan had applied that morning still looked fine. All day she'd felt different, more confident, more like everyone else. Over and over again she'd wondered why she hadn't tried to learn about makeup on her own, why she hadn't even thought of it, until she realized that she'd accepted her homeliness as something that couldn't be changed. She'd also thought about her life, of the comfort she'd found in teaching and a few close friends, never venturing past the boundaries she'd imposed upon herself until she'd finally ventured out to attend this conference. She couldn't complain. She'd had a nice life, a quiet life. A sheltered life. A life she'd created to protect herself from the unkindness of others. A life so circumscribed that, with a pang, she realized how much she had missed.

Maybe it wasn't too late. While the people here were learning how to improve their writing, she could think about how to improve her life. One of the first things she was going to do when she got home was go to the best department store in Lincoln and learn how to apply make up from a cosmetician.

***

Merle Ackerley had begun his conference with Gwen by praising some of her sentences. "You seem to have a feel for language," he said, "and a good eye for detail."

"Then you think my novel is good?" Gwen said, her happiness so evident that it was difficult for him to look at her.

They were in a classroom in the Studio, Ackerley struggling to find a tactful way to tell her that the fiction she submitted to him to be criticized, three chapters of a novel about a woman whose four-year-old son had died, simply didn't work. "I wish I could say that her actions in response to her child's death, particularly her affair just weeks after his death, makes sense, but I can't," he said finally.

The happiness vanished from Gwen's face. "I don't agree with you. I think it's perfectly logical for the heroine to have an affair six weeks after her son's death. She's so numb with grief, so hollowed out by it, that she needs to connect."

"Sex with a stranger is *connecting*?"

"He wasn't a stranger," Gwen said defensively. "She knew the man from the bereavement meetings she attended."

"You don't have her speaking to anyone at those meetings. You don't show her having any interaction with the man. And she isn't interested in sex with her husband."

"Because she's so numb with grief," Gwen said, as if it were all perfectly logical.

Her expression was dark now, as contemptuous as it had been in his study groups. "The loss of a child is a tragedy from which some people never recover," he said. "I want you to think of other ways to convey the depth of the woman's grief and how she copes with it. If you can revise your manuscript before the Workshop ends to where I think it could be publishable, perhaps I could recommend an editor."

Despite his dislike for her, her response was so ecstatic that he felt a twinge of guilt for having given her a challenge he knew she was incapable of fulfilling. But he had his workshops to consider, and he wouldn't have them spoiled by her negative attitude if he could prevent it.

Gwen hurried to her room, her stride reflecting her rushing thoughts. She had practically no time at all… less than three days to revise her manuscript… it was almost impossible… she could do it if she skipped the workshops and lectures and stayed in her room and worked… maybe not all of it but enough so that he would recommend her book to an editor… she'd have to do a lot of cutting, which would wreck the plot… but the story wasn't about plot anyway… it was about grief… she would need absolute quiet… Laura would have to understand, though Laura rejected Stoddard so she might not get it… Stoddard was gross… but if Laura had been smart, if she'd really wanted a chance at getting published, she would have found a way to get Stoddard to help her… all it took was brains and desire…

Laura was in the room sitting at the desk. "I'm going to need a favor from you," Gwen said, nearly breathless. "I just had my conference. I'm going to need the desk…"

"You need to look at the note that's on your bed," Laura interrupted. "The woman from the office was here. Your husband has been trying to get in touch with you all day."

Gwen grabbed the paper and quickly unfolded it. *Please call home as soon as possible. There has been a family emergency.*

"OHMYGOD." She reached into her purse for her cell phone and ran out of the room.

She didn't turn her phone on until she left the Inn through the massive front door; there were at least ten messages, all from her husband. He answered on the first ring. "Don't you ever check your messages or have you completely forgotten about us?" he said, the frustration in his voice unmistakable.

"I told you… I'm at workshops and lectures all day… I just had my conference."

"Justin has a broken leg. It happened this morning at camp."

"How?"

"He was playing soccer. A kid in front of him tripped, which caused him to fall. He landed badly, and there was a pile-up on top of him."

She tried to picture Justin, her oldest child, energetic and irrepressible, with a cast on. "Oh, Tom…" she started to say.

"There's more. Jess came home from camp with the chicken pox, and Sasha quit as soon as she saw her. 'I'm outta here,' she said."

Justin, Jess, and Sasha. It was too much to take in at once.

"If you leave at around seven tomorrow morning, you should be home before five."

"Leave? I can't leave! I had my conference this afternoon with Merle Ackerley. He told me that if I revised my book to his satisfaction before the end of the Workshop, he'd recommend me to an editor. This is my opportunity! It's what I came here for!"

"Be realistic, Gwen. There's no way you can revise your manuscript in a couple of days. Tell the fellow why you have to leave. If he's sincere, you can mail the manuscript to him and get the recommendation then."

"What if he doesn't agree?"

"Then he doesn't agree. Your family needs you, or don't we count anymore?" he said in a tone of measured anger. "I have an important trial starting on Wednesday, which means I'll have to prepare at home tomorrow while I take care of the kids. I'll expect you before dinner."

There was no one she could ask to help so she could stay. Her mother worked full time, and Tom's mother was weak from chemotherapy; her friendships weren't as close as they had been since she had been devoting all of her spare time to her writing.

When she went back inside, her eyes red-rimmed from weeping, people were starting to enter Hackett Hall for dinner. She picked an inconspicuous spot in an alcove where she could see the entrance to the dining room so she wouldn't miss Ackerley. She didn't have to wait long. "May I speak with you," she said, approaching him. He was dressed for his reading in pressed khakis, a long-sleeved green shirt, and a black string tie.

He listened sympathetically while she explained why she had to leave the Workshop. "Your husband has his hands full."

"Please, since I must leave, could I send you the revised manuscript?"

"I'm sorry, but this brief window is the only time I have to consider your work. I must prepare for the fall semester when the conference ends, and the galleys for my new novel will be coming any day now," he said. "I wish you luck."

"But…"

He was already in the dining room, moving as swiftly as his long legs could carry him.

***

Leila parked the Maserati and climbed wearily out of the car. She had spent the afternoon in the County Clerk's office in the town of Little Valley looking through docket books to find the estate of Benjamin Clymer. A clerk helped her fill out a form that required the estate number, and now she had photocopies of the will and the deed to the Workshop property in her purse. But the hours she had spent didn't yield much: with the exception of learning that Benjamin Clymer's private collection of books was donated to the Workshop to be used as the nucleus for a library, the will contained nothing about him that she didn't already know.

Pierce returned from his manuscript conference as she was putting on a pair of jeans. "We're going out to dinner with Sara," he said.

Damn, she thought, visualizing the next few hours: he and Sara would talk, and she would sit at the table like an extra place setting. "Could we skip it?"

"No one is going to Ackerley's reading. I don't feel right about what they're doing, but since I can't change the decision, I want to get out of here soon."

She gasped. "How awful! What he did was wrong, but what you're doing is worse. Not one of you has made an effort to be civil to him. Maybe, if you'd treated him decently, he wouldn't have demanded to have his reading switched."

"It's too late for maybes now. Besides, Sara got a fix on him the day he arrived. She said he was so full of himself that he expected everyone to welcome him as if he were William Faulkner."

"And you believe her?"

"I trust Sara's judgment."

"You're wrong and you know it!"

"Please," he said, "we have to go. I don't want to be late. Sara's probably downstairs now, waiting for us."

We can't keep the queen waiting, she thought, walking to the maple dresser. She jerked open a drawer, pulled out a sweater, and then slammed the drawer shut. The banging of the wood triggered a new thought: boycotting Ackerley's reading was Sara's idea. All these years she'd never understood Sara's hold over the writers. Sara, the undisputed leader of the group, the one they always listened to and whose favor they cultivated. Sara picked on Ackerley because he was an easy target. Phyllis Baran was another victim. Sara built her power on weakness. "Michael," she said, feeling vulnerable, "please don't tell Sara where I was today."

"Did you find anything?"

"I have a copy of the will and the deed to the property, but there's nothing new in them."

"Don't be too sure. Sometimes a detail that seems insignificant is a key to everything you want to know. We'll look at it together when we get back."

Sara was waiting for them on the front porch. Round as a tree trunk in the shapeless brown dress she had worn for her lecture, she greeted them with a warm smile that concealed any annoyance she might have felt at being kept waiting. But her eyes, buried in her fleshy face like slivers of onyx, glinted imperceptibly at Leila. It was a glint that in a man might have been interpreted as lust or passion, in a woman as envy. In Sara Newkirk's eyes, however, it was impossible to tell.

***

Merle Ackerley sat in the front row of the Circle Theater, color creeping up his skinny neck like mercury rising in a thermometer. He loosened his string tie and unbuttoned the collar of his shirt. It was one minute before eight o'clock, and with the exception of Roy Talbot, there wasn't a writer on the staff in sight. He couldn't believe it! He had endured their insider chumminess, their coldness, their outright rudeness, but this was outrageous! No matter what they thought of him, attending his reading was a courtesy that writers extend to each other. To single him out like this with no provocation went beyond the bounds of decency!

He rose to walk to the platform with his chin high and his spine straight. He would give the best damned reading of his life!

Sitting in a back row next to Joanne Howe, Talbot was so upset that he didn't hear Ackerley's opening sentences. He stared at the novelist's bobbing Adam's apple as if he were hypnotized. Not one writer on the staff was in the theater! And worse, he'd had no inkling of what had to be a preconceived plan. Even Dee Dee wasn't there; nor had she told him that this was going to happen. Maybe he should have gone to Clemens or to their rooms to look for them. But then what would he have done? Order them to attend the reading? Demand it? He had every right as the director. He had hired them. But how could he order men like Aaron Greene, Michael Pierce, and Eric Nettles to do anything?

As the reading continued, Talbot slid down further and further in his chair, as though the floor were being slowly removed from beneath him.

The staff member whose scheduled reading Ackerley had usurped was unaware of what was happening. No one had told her about the boycott, and now she was beyond caring. She was sprawled on her bed, too drunk to know anything. Somehow she had managed to get herself through her manuscript conference before she went to her room and closed the door. The last coherent thought she'd had was of Diana Rothenberg's novel: she could write that book and it would save her.

***

Ackerley's reading was an impressive failure. His selection of a novella was a mistake; the piece was too long to be heard in one sitting. Although he read superbly, capturing the speech inflections of his entertaining Appalachian characters, people began to fidget after an hour and a half had elapsed. The outside temperature had dropped to the mid-fifties, and the air in the unheated theater was becoming increasingly damp and chilly. People started to shiver; their noses turned red, their fingertips puckered with cold. After two hours had passed, their initial enjoyment turned to icy resentment. When the reading ended at ten forty-five, they clapped perfunctorily and filed stiffly out of the theater.

Talbot maneuvered himself into the center of a group leaving the building, wanting to be enveloped by the crowd to avoid Ackerley. He couldn't look the man in the eye, let alone congratulate him. Outside, he waited in the darkness for Joanne Howe. Then they ran to Melville.

"I thought your room would be heated," she said, rubbing her arms. "I'm wearing two sweaters and I'm freezing."

"I'll take care of that," Talbot promised.

He warmed his hands with his breath before he embraced her. But when he reached under her sweaters to undo her bra, she squealed at the touch of his cold fingers. "We'll be warm in a minute,' he said, cupping her breasts in his palms; her nipples were erect, either from excitement or cold, or both.

Through the thin wall, Dee Dee heard Joanne's squeal. She lay rigid in her bed, tears trickling down her face, listening to the sounds of their lovemaking. She could hear the rustling of their clothes as they disrobed, every squeak of the mattress, the low murmurs they made like purring. When she heard his breath quicken and a grunting sound come from deep in his throat, she pulled her pillow over her head and held it with her fists clenched to muffle her sobs. "Damn you, Roy Talbot," she cried silently, "damn you to hell!"

***

In Hawthorne, Leila undressed in the darkness and slipped a red flannel nightgown over her head. Her movements were quick and cautious so as not to awaken her sleeping husband. Then she tiptoed across the cold floor to the bathroom, closed the door, and switched on the light.

She stood on the icy tile, staring into the mirror as if she were dreaming. She raised her hand to her lips and traced them with her fingers. It couldn't have happened; Eric Nettles couldn't have kissed her. But he did. He kissed her and she responded. It seemed like an accident now, like an innocent mistake that is worse after it happens than when it occurs.

She turned on the faucet, letting the water run until it was hot. It would be stupid to make anything of it, she thought, washing her face. Eric had walked her back from Clemens and had kissed her good night. No one had seen them, not that it would make a difference. The kiss was impetuous. She had been surprised more than anything, and flattered. That she had responded was simply a matter of circumstance. Michael and Sara had talked throughout dinner, excluding her. Then Michael had refused to go to Clemens for a nightcap, claiming he had a headache; he'd forgotten about the will that she had spent hours searching for. The only time during the day that she'd had the pleasure of someone's company in relaxed conversation was with Eric in Clemens.

Brushing her teeth harder than necessary, her defensiveness hardened into anger. It was Michael's fault. If he hadn't insisted that they go out to dinner with Sara, if he had gone with her to Clemens, if he had looked over the will with her instead of going to bed…

She tiptoed back into the bedroom. Michael was sleeping on his stomach; she could barely see the outline of his head, a mass of tousled curls. Again, she put her fingers to her mouth. If that kiss were an impulse (which she was sure it was), it was a strong one.

She shivered in the darkness, either from remembered enjoyment or from the feel of the chilly sheets.

***

Agatha was having trouble falling asleep, but the cause wasn't the cold or Claire's window-rattling snores. She had never had such a perfect evening. First sitting with Jerry at the reading, then going out with him for hot chocolate. It had almost been like a date, even though it had happened by accident. If there had been three seats together instead of two, Nan would have sat with them. But Nan had excused herself after spotting a seat several rows back. Did Nan do it deliberately? And Nan had refused to go to the Shed with them, which had to be intentional. Still, Jerry hadn't acted as though he felt he was stuck with her. They had talked and laughed and she hadn't been uneasy or self-conscious. She'd felt like other women must feel, relaxed and comfortable and so incredibly happy.

Then ever after in this cold existence/I was always a little outside life. There were no lines of poetry that described her life better, and they had been written by a woman like herself, tall and ungainly. She looked enough like Edith Sitwell to be her sister. But Sitwell could wear elaborate headdresses and medieval clothes that made men want to paint and photograph her because she was gifted. A middle-aged English teacher from Lincoln, Nebraska wearing a costume would look like a fool. Tonight she hadn't felt the need to be gifted, to be special, to be anything but herself.

It was hard to believe how much her life had changed in a day. Now she had make up, she had the experience of this evening, she had possibilities that she had never dared hope for.

***

❧ WORKSHOP BULLETIN ❧

VOL. 74, NO.7   THE CLYMER WORKSHOP   AUGUST 17 2004

GOOD MORNING!

Sweater weather is promised. It will be cloudy and cool, with the temperature dropping in the evening.

MORNING PROGRAM

9:15 A.M. Poetry Lecture
(Aaron Greene)
10:15 A.M. Nonfiction Lecture
(Marshall Stoddard)
11:15 A.M. Manuscript
Conferences

Aaron Greene will discuss "The Aims of the Poet." Marshall Stoddard will speak on "Research: Too Many Facts Can Be Paralyzing."

AFTERNOON PROGRAM

2:00 P.M. Workshops
(Phyllis Baran, Aaron Greene)
3:00 P.M. Workshops
(Sara Newkirk, Michael Pierce)
4:00 P.M. Manuscript
Conferences
5:00 P.M. Mixer in the Shed

EVENING PROGRAM

Sara Newkirk will read her poetry. A winner of the Lenore Marshall/*Nation* Poetry Prize, she has received fellowships from the Guggenheim Foundation and the National Endowment for the Arts. Her books of poetry include *Hidden In The Shadows*, *The Skylark Sings*, *The Last Fortune Teller*, and *Placing The Stone*. She is also the author of a children's book, *A Buttercup Under Your Chin*. Ms. Newkirk has taught at Sarah Lawrence and Vassar, and is presently teaching at Wellesley. Last year she was named editor of the *Literary Review*.

WORKSHOPS

Materials for tomorrow's workshops will be available after dinner outside the Workshop office.

BLANKETS

Extra blankets can be obtained at the front desk in the Inn. All blankets must be signed for and returned when they are no longer needed.

MARK TWAIN

Contrary to rumor, the ghost of the celebrated author is not in residence in Clemens, inebriated or sober.

be picked up in the office.

FOUND

A variety of garments, male and female, have been found in wooded areas. These items, some of which have been placed in envelopes for discretion, can

TIDBIT

"I haven't watched the news in so long that I've stopped worrying about how the world is doing."

> *"It is better not to touch our idols:*
> *the gilt comes off on our hands."*
> Gustav Flaubert in *Madam Bovary*

Chapter VII

Nettles awakened with an erection. He tried to recall as much as he could about the dream he'd had: Leila was in his bed leaning over him, one of her breasts brushing against his belly as she took his penis into her mouth. Smiling, he vividly replayed the scene in his mind, imagining every detail of her long graceful body. His thoughts reinforced his engorged organ, which began to throb, demanding attention.

A fastidious man, and one unaccustomed to sexual deprivation, he got out of bed and crossed the wood floor to the bathroom, where he spent his passion into the toilet. Afterward he showered, then dried himself briskly, his thoughts moving to the workshop he had conducted yesterday and the young woman who had been his unwitting accomplice. Normally he avoided discussing inferior work, preferring when he could to focus on the positive, but the woman had given him an opportunity he couldn't refuse. By using her manuscript he was able to show the novice writers in a most dramatic way that innovative fiction was not a bunch of run-on, meaningless sentences but rather the highest art, on a plane far above Pierce's structured stories. Now they knew, or at least they were beginning to understand, that the primary subject of a modern novel was the writing of the novel. Next he would hammer Pierce's plots until he shattered them into hopeless pieces so he could present them for what they were: irrelevancies. As for the woman, it was a shame but she would recover; she was young, resilient, and totally lacking talent; she would meet a man and have babies, which was the most a person of her ability was capable of creating.

Thrusting his arms through the sleeves of a heavy, cream-colored hand-knit sweater, he was reminded of his wife. Peg had survived their moves from university to university, his affairs with other women, his preoccupations. She had been there, always.

Now she was waiting for the momentary birth of their first grandchild as if the baby were a bona fide miracle. He wasn't as enthusiastic, but the continuum of his genes was pleasing. It was too bad Peg wasn't here to enjoy this little skirmish with Pierce; she would catch nuances that everyone else would miss. But she would also be aware of Leila. On second thought, it was better that she was at home knitting for the baby. Even the strongest union could be strained beyond repair by the likes of Leila Pierce.

***

Despite the chilly morning, the Circle Theater was filled with people waiting to hear Aaron Greene's lecture. They were dressed in summer sweaters having expected steamy August weather. The buzz of their conversations was interrupted with sniffles, sneezes, and syrupy coughs; noses were red; some shivered in lightweight jackets; others rubbed their hands together, trying unsuccessfully to warm them. Still, they sat patiently, their notebooks open, their pens ready in icy fingers to record the wisdom of the revered poet.

Each step Aaron Greene took to the lectern reinforced his misery. Thermal underwear, aspirin, and scotch were ineffective protection against damp, cold weather. He had spent an agonizing night, his arthritis making sleep impossible. It had been an ordeal to get dressed, to put a sock and shoe on the foot of his lame leg. Finally at his destination, he opened a folder which contained an essay he had written the previous month in his office at Stanford. The essay was the first of a dozen he planned to write on poetics; together the essays would complete a book for which he had already received a nice advance from his publisher. But standing before the Workshop audience, his immediate goal was to get through the next forty-five minutes so he could go back to his cabin and his bottle. He raised his heavy-lidded eyes and looked at the people waiting to hear him speak. Idiots, he thought, he was wasting his energy on idiots.

"Poetry," he began, "is a verbal art. It is a form of literature specifically written to be read aloud, a fact often ignored or forgotten…"

Sprawled on an aisle seat in the middle of the theater, Webb listened intently until midway through the lecture when Greene spoke of poems that were self-pitying, poems that were cries for sympathy, poems that were litanies of personal horrors. "The poet's private terrors should be kept private," Greene asserted. "Poems should not be regurgitations of life; nor are they vehicles for self indulgence."

He's wrong! Webb thought, thrashing his legs. A poet's life belongs in his poems; it's the only valid experience he's had and it can't be compromised. Greene was just like the editors who rejected his poems, claiming they were too shocking.

While Webb was mentally defending his poetry, Diana, sitting next to him, was rehearsing her appeal to Pierce to criticize her manuscript. She couldn't find the novelist last night, but he was in the theater this morning. She'd have to be the first to catch him during the break between the lectures, she thought, glad that she'd had the foresight to bring two copies of her manuscript to the conference. She had once heard about an editor who would continue reading a manuscript until he found a mistake. There were no mistakes on the first page that she was aware of, nor on the second and third pages; the first three chapters were better than the story the *Georgia Review* had accepted. If he would just read what she'd written, she'd have a chance at convincing him.

Diana left her seat at the end of the lecture while the audience was still clapping. She walked toward the back of the theater and stood against the wall opposite the row in which Pierce and Leila were sitting. Then, her pulse quickening, she waited for the novelist to leave.

"Excuse me," she said when he stepped into the aisle, "I know it's an imposition, but I'd really appreciate it if you'd read this. It's a few paragraphs. It'll only take a minute," she said, thrusting a single page of manuscript into his hand.

"I… suppose," he said, looking at the paper. "The light is better outside."

She waited until Leila was also in the aisle, then followed the couple out the double doors. Despite her nervousness, she had noticed a flicker of annoyance pass over Leila's face and didn't want to antagonize her further.

The wind that had been forecast the previous day had arrived sometime during the lecture. Pierce started to read as soon as he was outside, holding the fluttering paper with both hands. After his eyes swept down the page, he looked at Diana with interest. "Do you have more with you?"

She took the paper and pulled several additional pages from a manila envelope, conscious of glances from people who were gathering on the lawn around them. "May I?" Leila said, reaching for the page he'd read.

"Sure," Diana replied with what she hoped would be accepted as a friendly smile.

The Pierces continued to read until the Workshop members started going back inside for the next lecture. Phyllis Baran walked past, her head fuzzy from her night of drinking. If she noticed them, it didn't register. Even if her head were clear, she knew Diana only by the name on her manuscript. There was no way she could associate the young woman whose long black hair was whipping in the wind with the novel that she was now resolved to steal.

When nearly everyone had gone inside, Diana said, "I came here hoping you would criticize my novel. I requested you, but I was assigned to someone else."

"Who?" Pierce said, still reading.

"Phyllis Baran."

He stopped reading. "How much of this do you have?"

Diana heard a distinct note of anger in his voice. "Three chapters and an outline," she said.

"Give them to me," he said. "I'll get back to you."

Webb, who had been watching at a distance, rushed up to her after the Pierces went inside. In one sweeping motion he picked her up and swung her in a circle as if she were the size of a three-year-old.

"You ox!" she cried, pounding on his shoulders, "Put me down!"

He set her down, grinning broadly. "You did it!"

She nodded, suddenly so overcome with relief that she couldn't speak.

Webb, however, had enough words and energy for both of them. They skipped Ackerley's lecture and went to the Shed for coffee to celebrate. Webb talked nonstop. He was exuberant, charming, funny; he was so entertaining that she laughed harder than she had ever laughed in her life.

* * *

A lack of new material to present at his reading wasn't Stoddard's only problem in regard to what was expected of him at the Workshop. He was also to have prepared a stimulating lecture on the writing of nonfiction, an unwelcome duty which he had postponed until the night before he was to deliver it. Now caught by his own negligence, he had nothing more than the title that he had given Dee Dee at the beginning of the conference. Unlike most of the other staff members, he was not a part of the academic world; he hadn't written any scholarly articles that he could use for the lecture. He felt that he had said all he had to say about the writing of non-fiction in previous years, yet he didn't want to repeat himself. After hours of struggle during which he sat at his desk plucking at his beard, as though tugging at the hair would somehow pull an idea out of his head, he managed to cobble together a lecture that outlined an orderly approach to researching non-fiction. Perhaps it was the sight of people listening attentively and taking notes that inspired him to make a statement which caused them to look up in bewilderment. "There is a point where you can do too much research," he said, his high-pitched voice more nasal than usual for emphasis, "so you must know when to stop." The audience waited in anticipation for him to explain or describe this crucial moment, but he did neither; instead, he concluded by observing that too many facts can be paralyzing.

His observation could have been well applied to the people in the theater. They sat motionless, as if paralyzed by unfulfilled expectation, until they finally gave him measured applause.

Pierce applauded with them, though he had only marginally listened to Stoddard. His thoughts had been on the envelope that held Diana's manuscript. If Baran got this one, what did Nettles get? What did Talbot give them while he was handed barely literate work? Roy Talbot owed him! For years he'd been the main draw in fiction at this conference. Never again would he save that bastard's ass!

Oblivious to the reaction he'd caused, Stoddard was interested in only one person's evaluation of his performance: Sara Newkirk's. He lingered near the door of the theater while people filed out. When Sara emerged, talking animatedly to Nettles, she paused long enough to flash the writer a crooked half-smile. Stoddard accepted his reward with a nod of thanks, as if it were a medal, reassured to have a confirmation that he was still a member of the club.

***

Talbot steeled himself before he entered the kitchen to check on what was going to be served for lunch. After recalling with revulsion the lunch that had been served yesterday, he was certain today's noon meal would be better.

The cook, a tattooed fellow in his fifties who looked like an aging biker, had just started ladling a viscous, light-mustard-colored gravy in which unidentifiable lumps were swimming over pieces of toasted bread on plates that were lined up in rows on a long stainless steel counter top.

"What is that?" Talbot said, staring at the plates. It looked like vomit on toast.

The cook eyed him warily, still resenting the verbal lashing he'd received after yesterday's lunch. "It's… uh… It's kind of a take-off on chicken-a-la-king, with tofu instead of chicken in a light curry sauce. The curry will give it some taste."

"It looks like vomit! All that's missing is the stink."

"Like I told you yesterday, it's next to impossible to serve decent meals on the budget you've given me for food. I should quit!"

"No," Talbot said, putting his hands up as if to block the thought. "You're doing the best you can."

"Damn right, I am!" said the cook, dipping the ladle into the steaming pot with an air of justification.

Talbot went out the back door of the kitchen. As he walked to the Shed for a hamburger, he experienced a surge of resentment for the position he'd been placed in. The cook couldn't be entirely blamed for the unappetizing food that had been served since the conference had started, although he had been hired because he was cheap. The meals were the direct result of the budget he'd been given. Howard Cruickshank and the Board of Trustees had told him before he planned this year's conference that they wanted bigger names—"brighter stars"--as they put it. But when he requested a ten percent increase in the budget to pay for the big names, all they gave him was a four percent increase. Only four percent! They got their stars, but he couldn't get them for nothing. Nettles demanded double what he offered; Cox used his bestseller to justify his price. Even Marshall Stoddard, whose new book was headed straight for the remainder table, wanted a ten-percent increase. Then there was Aaron Greene, who insisted upon being given first class, round-trip airplane tickets from California, plus a raise over last year, and Greene drinks a quart of good scotch every day; his wife drinks a quart of gin, and she demands Beefeaters.

The Workshop was Axton's cash cow, milked since the day it was established, but it would be impossible to either explain or justify that to the people who had complained about the food. They had every right to complain: they had paid an ample price to attend, more than enough to entitle them to decent meals. He hadn't enjoyed eating the garbage that had been served any more than they had. But there was no alternative; even a magician couldn't make this work on the budget he'd been given.

He ordered a hamburger to go, deciding that it wouldn't look right to be seen eating in the Shed. When it was ready, he set off for Clemens hoping to have the cottage to himself. To his surprise, he found Stoddard there; writers on the staff were supposed to eat in Hackett Hall. Although Stoddard had often articulated his feelings about this rule, he was no exception.

Stoddard had planned to leave before lunch was over. Aware that his visits to Clemens had been too frequent and too lengthy, he had been unable to deny himself the indulgence; he'd been a constant presence there, soothing his disappointment in the sales of his book and his ego in his failure to score with even one female at the conference with as much vodka as he dared to drink without embarrassing himself or endangering his glucose levels. Now that the chore of his lecture was over, he had decided to come to the cottage at less-frequented hours, sensing that his fellow writers had begun to view him with diminished respect.

"I see that you're drinking your lunch," Talbot said, regretting the words as soon as he uttered them.

Stoddard straightened, shifting his girth on the wicker chair. "I'll wager it's better than the food that's being served."

"You got me on that one," Talbot said, putting the paper bag that contained his lunch on the trestle table. As long as he had Stoddard alone, he should talk to him about Joanne Howe.

"This might be a good time to discuss a conference you had yesterday with a woman named Joanne Howe. She complained to me that all you did was line-edit her manuscript. She said that you seemed to be in a hurry and that you didn't give her constructive suggestions on how she could improve her book."

"Really, what can one say about a book that's focused on the subject of making money? Money is even in the title! It's a supermarket book."

"Marshall, you've taught at this conference for years, and you've never made an effort to hide your disdain for the people who come here; no matter what you think of them privately, they're entitled to your respect and the criticism they've paid for. Joanne Howe is a smart woman. She has an editor who is interested in her book, and she'll probably make a lot of money on it. But the issue beyond what you did to her is the potential damage you've done to the conference. You can be sure she'll talk, and the talk will spread. If you can't make an effort give people's manuscripts constructive criticism, no matter what you think of the subject matter, then perhaps you shouldn't teach here."

What followed was a stony silence. Then Stoddard gulped the remainder of his vodka and rose to leave, fuming. Talbot wouldn't have dared chastise Greene or Nettles for their treatment of participants' work! *The hell with Talbot!* There were other writers' conferences, dozens of them, that would welcome him and probably pay him more than he was getting here.

Talbot busied himself with unwrapping his lunch while Stoddard left. Although he hadn't planned on going quite as far as he did, he had no regrets. He had never liked Stoddard. He considered the man to be a glutton, a snob, and an ineffective teacher. But he had continued to invite him back to teach year after year because of his reputation as a critic and his close ties to Sara Newkirk and Michael Pierce. Losing Marshall wouldn't be a problem. There were plenty of nonfiction writers who would rush at the chance to be on the staff of the Clymer Workshop.

***

When Nan didn't appear in Hackett Hall for lunch, Agatha went to her friend's room and found her sitting on her bed, scowling at a piece of paper. "Here," she said, "read this."

The novel would be more interesting if the baby remained in the mother's womb, reacting to the parents' thoughts, conversations, activities, etc. until its birth.

"Do you believe it?" Nan said in response to Agatha's puzzled expression. The deep worry lines that had been between her eyes for days were gone; her forehead was smooth, her skin was glowing with anger. "Instead of giving me suggestions on how to fix the end of my novel, Nettles wants me to completely rewrite it, making the unborn baby the third major character! The whole point of the book is the effect that the birth of the baby has on the parents' lives—the infant turns their neat world upside down."

"Did you tell him that?"

"Of course," Nan said, "but he didn't care. He thought the concept of the unborn baby would be more challenging. *Innovative* is what he really meant. When I disagreed, he told me that the novel as it is would probably be a commercial success. He said *commercial* as if it were a dirty word. I've been getting that message since I came here: if a book is a commercial success, then it's a failure as art. If a book makes you laugh or cry or simply entertains you, then it can't be good. Is that right? You have a doctorate."

Nan's question raised an issue which Agatha had been pondering for years. She had once tried to teach Henry James' novel *Washington Square*, and her students had responded apathetically, to the point where they'd had nothing to say during class discussions no matter what she did to challenge them. One of the brightest students in the honors class, a vivacious girl of seventeen, finally confessed that every time she tried to read the novel she fell asleep; then, in all seriousness, she suggested that people who take sleeping pills should read *Washington Square* instead. "There isn't an easy answer," Agatha replied thoughtfully. "Some books are important even though they aren't enjoyable; they break new ground in some way, either stylistically or imaginatively or by showing us something about the human condition that we haven't seen in fiction before. But there is no reason why a book can't be both entertaining and art. Hemingway considered *The Adventures of Huckleberry Finn* our greatest American novel, and it's as entertaining as any book ever written. I enjoy it more with each reading."

"And it's still in print!" Nan said enthusiastically. "It wouldn't hurt Nettles and the others to think about Mark Twain while they're drinking in Clemens. I'd leave today if it weren't too expensive."

"Because of Nettles?"

"Nettles, the literary snobbery, this awful unheated room," Nan said, waving her hands in the air. "Nettles was nice, even encouraging, but on his terms. I want to write my fiction, not his. What makes me angry is that I know he could have helped me, but he didn't because he wasn't interested in improving what I've done. The conference was really over after the first ten minutes. It was ridiculous! We argued politely for another twenty minutes and that was it.

"I was so upset that I called the airline to see if I could get a flight out of Jamestown, which was more bad news. If I changed my super-saver ticket, it would cost a fortune. At that point I didn't care, so I went to the office to ask if they could arrange for transportation for me to the airport. The woman I talked to told me that I'd have to hire a private limousine, which would cost one hundred dollars. In cash! Fortunately, I hadn't changed my ticket because I wasn't sure I could get to the airport."

Agatha's shoulders sagged. Hard as she tried, she couldn't think of anything comforting to say. "I'm sorry," she offered finally.

Nan grasped her hand. "You of all people shouldn't apologize for what's happened. You've been so supportive, the best friend I've made here. You're the brightest spot in this experience.

"You know," she said reflectively, "I never truly realized how lucky I am until I tried to call my husband. When I couldn't reach him, I came back to this dreary room and thought about him and our boys. In spite of their grumbling, they've been proud of my writing. I think I lost my perspective for a while. My novel became so important to me that I didn't focus on what is really important, my family and the wonderful life we've built together."

"Oh, yes," Agatha said, blinking.

Later, while they were walking to the Shed so Nan could get something to eat before the workshops started, Agatha reached unobtrusively under her glasses and wiped a tear from her eye. She liked Nan too much to feel the slightest bit of envy, but oh how she wished that she had a family, even one person to love who would love her in return.

***

At Aaron Greene's request, the tables in Hackett Hall had been moved so that the center of the enormous, high-ceilinged room could accommodate over one hundred chairs arranged in a circle, two chairs deep. The moving and arranging had been done by grumbling waitresses, who were nowhere in sight when people started to arrive for the poetry workshop. Gathered around a long butcher-block table in the kitchen, the young women were neither interested in nor impressed by the famous poet. Greene meant nothing but extra work for them: three times a day they took turns carrying trays of food to his cottage, a bothersome chore which they unanimously disliked. While the circle was filling with Workshop members, they were finishing lunches they had brought from home—thick sandwiches on fresh bread, homemade cookies, and fresh fruit and raw vegetables prepared in farm kitchens. Not one of them would eat the food they served everyday, though meals were included with their jobs.

Greene limped into the center of the circle at five minutes after two; he requested a chair, which a bearded fellow leaped to fetch. The poet thanked him with a nod, then swallowed the remains of a breath mint he'd been sucking on to cover the odor of scotch. He pulled a folded wad of papers out of a pocket of his tan windbreaker, put on a pair of tortoise-shell glasses, and began to read the poem on the top page.

Greene read stanza after stanza with exaggerated drama; his voice was mockingly rapt, brimming with disdain. When he finished, he took off his glasses and, leaning back in his chair, cast a heavy-lidded gaze around the circle as though he were looking for something which he was positive he wouldn't find. No one moved. Caught in a net of embarrassment, they waited for a cue from the poet to release them. "Does anyone have a comment?" he said.

His question was the most positive remark Greene made during the time that followed. Agatha listened with dismay to the most deliberately destructive criticism she had ever heard. The poem wasn't a masterpiece, she thought, but it wasn't bad, certainly not as awful as he was making it out to be. The most effective teaching was positive, not negative. What could he hope to accomplish by encouraging cruelty, she wondered, noticing a thin, acne-scarred young man sitting in the outer circle who was nervously chewing on a Bic pen. The young man bit further and further down on the plastic as if he were preparing to swallow the pen whole. When the discussion was finished, with almost everyone seeming to agree that the poem was trite and shouldn't have been written in the first place, the pen was completely mutilated; twisted, bent, and chewed, only the point was recognizable.

Another poem was read and discussed, then a third. At Greene's urging they tore apart each one, probing for flaws like birds pecking for worms. Greene was merciless. He pointed out examples of mixing high and low speech, strained metaphors, and impossible occurrences. "No one can become one with a tree," he said, waving the papers in the air as if he were looking for a garbage can in which he could toss them. As he lowered his arm, he glanced at his watch. There was twenty minutes remaining before the workshop was over. "Have you had enough or must we go on with this?" he said, as if he'd already worked too long at an odious chore.

It was suddenly quiet. Then Webb stood up, his great height commanding their attention. Although he had spoken only once since the workshop had started, he had not listened indifferently. Greene's attitude, the biting comments of the people who had contributed, everything that had occurred had added to his growing agitation. On an upward mood swing for days and beyond the point where the minimal amount of medication he was taking would stop or even control his increasing manic high, he was afraid of nothing. He could say what he pleased and it would be right, proper, perfectly justified. "I think we should continue," he said, his eyes darting around the circle, "but with a different attitude. So far this has been more like a massacre than a workshop; almost everything that's been said has been destructive. Instead of going for a kill, we should aim for balanced criticism."

Several people in the circle gasped; some cringed; others sat stone-faced with shock. Greene's hand tightened around his cane. "Since it is apparent that you believe you know how to teach," he said acidly, "perhaps you will share your expertise with us and conduct the remainder of the workshop."

"I didn't say that I know how to teach. The point I'm making is that these poems were written with honest intentions. No matter how good or bad they are, they deserve respect."

"An 'A' for effort?" Greene snapped.

"Fair treatment," Webb snapped back.

Greene raised his heavy eyelids and glared at Webb. Decades of students had been immobilized by that glare, had been rendered speechless or worse. It was a look full of loathing and contempt, a weapon that had made men forget their names, their birth dates, their desire to become poets.

Someone in the circle swallowed audibly. Eyes traveled between the two men, back and forth as if they were players in a tennis match. "We're wasting time," Webb said. "We have another ten minutes that we could use profitably."

"Since you're the only one who has voiced a complaint, I believe the decision should be made by the group. Will those who wish to continue please raise their hands?"

The fury in Aaron Greene's voice could have burned a hole through cloth. Not a hand was raised. "The decision, it appears, is contrary to your wishes," Greene said. He rose stiffly and walked out of the dining room, his limp more pronounced than usual.

The circle emptied quickly, everyone avoiding Webb. The three poets whose work had been destroyed, those who had contributed to the destruction, and the rest who had listened without comment all raced out the arched doorway like people fleeing from an earthquake. Even Agatha, who agreed with Webb's assessment and who might, under different circumstances, have stopped to tell him so, scurried with the others, carried by their momentum.

***

Unaware of what had transpired in Aaron Greene's workshop, Pierce was surprised when he entered the Circle Theater and saw three-quarters of the people attending the conference waiting for him. Instead of being flattered, his immediate reaction was that of concern. The heavy attendance meant that Sara's workshop was sparsely filled, which would not sit well with her. There had to be an explanation, he thought, one that she would accept so she wouldn't take it personally.

Rather than stand behind the lectern, he hoisted himself over the edge of the platform so he could sit facing them. Although his workshops usually consisted of a brief lecture followed by a group writing assignment, today he had a different agenda. "You all know my opinion of innovative fiction," he said, pushing up the sleeves of his gray sweatshirt. "I respect Eric Nettles; he's an intelligent, capable writer. I do not, however, share his enthusiasm for fiction that reflects on itself. He has told you that the subject of a modern novel should be the writing of the novel. What this means, essentially, is that you, as authors, must interrupt the scenes you create to comment upon them. For example, if you've labored hard and succeeded in writing a moving death scene, one that brings tears to a reader's eyes, and you then tell the reader that the character really hasn't died or that the death was but one possibility and you are now going to present other possibilities, the reader might react by throwing the book down in disgust. You've played games with him, you've manipulated him, you've made him feel like a fool for crying.

"You've broken the dream that you created."

Pierce paused, confident that he had them now. "As fiction writers, you want to create a world in which the reader becomes so immersed that actual life is briefly suspended. The reader's focus is so concentrated on the narrative that it would take a significant disruption—a ringing doorbell, the whistling of a teakettle, the loud buzzer of an appliance—to break the dream that you and the reader share. To achieve this, you have to master the basic tools of your craft.

"I want you to imagine someone: it can be a person you know or someone you've never seen. Close your eyes and block everything out of your mind except for that person's image. Concentrate until the image is as sharp and clear as a life-sized poster."

Pierce waited, his legs dangling over the edge of the platform, while they followed his instructions. The exercise was one he used often in workshops, yet each time he was fascinated by the expressions on people's faces, the varying degrees of their concentration visible in frowns, faint smiles, pursed lips, open mouths, eyelids tightly shut or passively closed, all clues to their personalities, which he would briefly expand for his own mental exercise.

"You may open your eyes," he said, reluctantly getting back to work. "Now I want you to write a scene in which you are on a bus and the character you have imagined boards. Describe the character so that we can see him as you see him. You may use dialogue if you wish, but I want you to concentrate on physical details, which might include how the person moves, for example. Try to avoid stereotypes, like a smelly bum wearing ragged clothes. You will have ten minutes. Then volunteers will have an opportunity to read aloud what they have written."

Everyone in the theater except for Dynarski began writing. Dynarski watched them, his upper lip curled with disdain. An exercise for beginners, he thought, a waste of time. He might as well forget about the workshops; he wouldn't get anything out of them. He wasn't here to learn how to write anyway. If he'd had a break, he'd be on the staff instead of waiting for an audience with Pierce. They were all so eager, even Laura, writing with intense concentration like the rest of them, which was surprising considering the quality of her work. She'd been looking at his hands. He'd better make up a story about a construction job that she'd believe, driving a bulldozer or operating a crane, something that wouldn't give him calluses. She was better company than anyone else he'd met here; too bad she wasn't interested in being anything more than friends. This place was like all the others— middle-class, middle-aged people wanting to be writers, hustling like clowns. Some of them, like Hofstrand, didn't have a clue. The guy probably misinterpreted everything Pierce said at his conference. A thriller. Trash! It would blow Hofstrand's neat military mind if he knew that he was sharing a room with an arsonist. Laura's too, although it shouldn't. It wasn't as if he were killing people or even harming anyone. He wouldn't touch an inhabited building, only decaying wrecks. Someone would do it, so it might as well be him; he did a thorough job and no one was ever hurt. There was no reason for him to break his back when he could get ten percent of the insurance for a few hours of work. A couple of big jobs a year and he had no worries about money.

When people around him started raising their hands, volunteering to read what they had written, Dynarski decided to skip Pierce's next workshop. With so many people attending, he wouldn't be missed.

***

Leila crossed the Axton College common, an oval, grassy area bordered by stately red-brick Georgian buildings, and climbed the tiered stairs to the library. After explaining her purpose to a clerk at the front desk, then to an assistant librarian, she was finally taken to the office of Mrs. Evelyn Lang, the head librarian. "How can I help you?" Mrs. Lang asked. She was a slight, gray-haired woman whose inquisitive brown eyes were assessing Leila with polite curiosity.

"I'm looking for information about a collection of books that were once kept at the Clymer Workshop," Leila said. "The books were donated by Benjamin Clymer. I believe they were from his private library."

"Oh, yes!" Mrs. Lang said excitedly. "It was a wonderful collection, wonderful! There was a first edition of Fitzgerald's *This Side of Paradise*, also *The Great Gatsby*. Fitzgerald is one of my favorites. I could go on and on. Mr. Clymer must have had a sixth sense: I don't believe there was an important book published between 1900 and 1928 that wasn't in that collection!"

"Where are the books?"

Mrs. Lang shook her head as though she'd been reminded of the death of a friend. "They were all sold, every last one, to a private collector. I was so upset at the time. I argued with the trustees, I even begged, but they wouldn't listen. That collection meant so much to this library! It was unique, a treasure that would have grown in value every year. I'm not talking about money. I mean the books themselves, the range of the collection, its value to scholars and students. But the trustees couldn't see it. They robbed this college of a great legacy."

"When did this happen?"

"In 1998," said Mrs. Lang, sighing.

Leila frowned. "Are you sure?"

"Positive! I'll never forget it! I made such a fuss that I nearly lost my job. Why do you ask?"

"I spent most of this afternoon trying to contact trustees. I managed to reach several who might have been on the board then, but they spoke as though they knew nothing about the books."

"They're embarrassed," said Mrs. Lang, her voice ringing with vindication. "They know what they did was wrong, so they're trying to bury it." She paused. "Now it's my turn for a question. Why do you want to know about the books?"

"I'm looking for information about Benjamin Clymer."

"For a paper? A book?"

"Curiosity," Leila said. "My husband teaches at the Workshop."

Mrs. Lang smiled. "I don't know your name."

"I'm sorry, I should have introduced myself. I'm Leila Pierce."

"Michael Pierce's wife! This is exciting! Please tell your husband how much I have enjoyed his books. I wish there were more writers like him."

"I will," Leila said. "Thank you for your help."

"It wasn't much, I'm afraid. Do you have any other leads? I'd like to know something about Benjamin Clymer myself."

"You were my last hope. I have a copy of his will, but I can't find any leads in it."

"May I see it?"

Leila took a folded copy of the will out of her purse while Mrs. Lang put on a pair of reading glasses that were hanging from a chain around her neck. The librarian read rapidly, flipping through the pages with practiced skill that comes from decades of tracking information. When she reached the last page, she held her chin in her hand, staring at the signatures. "I don't know how much help this will be, but I believe that the son of the lawyer who wrote the will is practicing law in Jamestown. His name is John Gustafson. His father, Charles Gustafson, was the most respected lawyer in Chautauqua County. I was born and raised in Jamestown, and people came from all over to see him."

"Do you think his son would know anything about Benjamin Clymer?"

"He may have his father's old files. It's certainly worth a try."

Again, Leila thanked her. "It's my job," Mrs. Lang said. "Now you be sure to tell your husband how much I admire his work."

For once Leila didn't mind being given a message to carry to her famous husband. She walked purposely through the library and out the building thinking about John Gustafson.

***

Talbot would have been unaware of the sheriff's arrival if he hadn't happened to glance out his office window as the white Ford Explorer with SHERIFF boldly printed in yellow and black on the sides of the vehicle came to a stop in front of the Inn. He leaped out from behind his desk and hurried to the front door, arriving just as Sheriff Tony Coniglio was entering the building. "I'm Roy

236

Talbot, the director of the Workshop," he said. "Is there something I can help you with? Is there a problem?"

Coniglio was an observant man, a trait that had helped him keep his job for eighteen years. He noted that Talbot was nearly out of breath, and from the anxious expression on his face that he was overly concerned about the visit. "It depends on what you consider a problem. A woman named Gwen Eggleston who was attending your conference died in a single-vehicle accident today. I'm here to do a follow-up investigation."

"That's tragic," Talbot said. "But if it was a single-vehicle accident, why are you investigating?"

"All vehicular deaths are investigated. Her car hit a concrete bridge abutment just outside Albany; no other vehicles were involved."

The sheriff was armed and was in full uniform. Standing at five feet ten inches and weighing one hundred eighty pounds, Coniglio wasn't an unusually large man, but he wasn't inconspicuous, either. Conscious of people's curious glances as they streamed into Hackett Hall for dinner, Talbot wanted to get him out of their sight as quickly as possible; he also wanted the Explorer parked where it couldn't be seen through the dining room windows. "Why don't you park your SUV beyond the circle so emergency vehicles can get through, and then we'll talk about your investigation in my office. I'll wait for you here."

Talbot's lack of subtlety made Coniglio take his time re-parking the Explorer so he could mentally review bits of information he had collected about the Workshop over the years. People who lived in the county didn't think much of the place, their views based on stories told over decades by farm girls who had worked at the conference as waitresses, tales mainly about sex and bizarre behavior; locals also bristled at the attitudes of a series of directors who made it very clear that the Workshop property was exclusive, that people who lived in the county weren't welcome to hunt or fish there. The fees the conference charged were a subject of local discussion, the general consensus being that people who were willing to pay such outrageous prices to talk to writers about writing would be better off spending their money getting their heads examined. There had been three suicides during the years he was sheriff—a fellow who asphyxiated himself in a pick-up truck, a woman who took an overdose of sleeping pills, and a woman who hung herself; there were also a number of suicide attempts that the Workshop had covered up. In the vehicular death today there were no mitigating circumstances: the weather was clear and there were no other cars involved. When the state police called him to investigate, he wasn't surprised when they told him that she'd been attending The Clymer Workshop.

When Coniglio returned, Talbot hustled him to his office. "What exactly are you looking for in regard to Gwen Eggleston's accident? I'll answer any questions you might have," he said, gesturing for the sheriff to sit.

Coniglio ignored the gesture and remained standing. "Were you aware that Mrs. Eggleston had left your conference?"

Talbot shook his head. "The people who come here are all adults. We prefer it when they let us know, but we don't make it mandatory."

"Who might have known? Did she have a roommate?"

"I'll have to check on that. Are there any other questions?"

"Just see if she had a roommate and find a fellow named Merle Ackerley. Her husband mentioned his name to the state troopers."

Talbot started to perspire. "Dinner will be over soon. I can wait outside the dining room and catch Ackerley when he is leaving."

"I want to talk to her roommate first."

"But even if I get her name—assuming that Gwen Eggleston had a roommate—I don't know what she looks like. There are over two hundred guests here."

"Since everyone is eating now, that shouldn't be a problem," Coniglio said. "Simply announce her name and ask her to come here when she's done eating."

"It's highly unusual for an individual's name to be announced at a meal. If I do what you're suggesting, it will call attention to her; people will ask her questions later," Talbot said. "I'll look up her name—again, if Gwen Eggleston had a roommate—and leave a note for her to come see me in her mailbox."

At the age of fifty-six, Coniglio had seen dozens of people in situations they were trying to control; experience had taught him that if he was absolutely firm and perfectly clear at the onset of an investigation, it generally went smoothly. He looked at Talbot, who was practically dancing with nervousness, and tried (not too successfully) to hide his irritation. "We'll do it my way," he said. "Get me the name."

Talbot went to a file drawer in the front office, debating whether to give the roommate's name or to tell the sheriff that she didn't have a roommate, which would keep the death quiet. No one would know except for Ackerley, and handling him wouldn't be a problem. But what if impeding an investigation was a criminal offense? The potential cost to cover this up was too high for him to pay personally, he decided, pulling out a file that contained room assignments. "Her roommate's name is Laura Belmont."

"Let's go," the sheriff said.

"You can wait here."

"I'll be outside the dining room while you make the announcement," Coniglio said firmly.

***

Laura didn't stay to have dessert after Talbot made a brief announcement requesting that she come to the Workshop office after dinner. "Do you want me to go with you?" Dynarski asked as she rose to leave.

"No," she said. "Finish your dinner. I'm sure it's probably nothing."

But she wasn't sure; nor were the people whose eyes followed her as she left Hackett Hall. When she saw the sheriff, she tried unsuccessfully to squelch a feeling that something was seriously wrong. "What's happened?" she said.

"The sheriff is here with some tragic news," Talbot said.

Laura's eyes widened in alarm.

"That's it!" Coniglio said. "Miss Belmont and I are going into your office to talk. While we're in there, I want you to find that Ackerley fellow and bring him here. You can wait with him until we're done."

"But…" Talbot started to say.

"Now!" Coniglio ordered.

Coniglio told her about Gwen's accident after they were seated on the chairs in front of Talbot's desk. "Oh, no," Laura said, clearly distressed. "How did it happen?"

"It was a single-car accident; her car hit a concrete bridge abutment head-on. When was the last time you saw her?"

"I heard her leave very early this morning. I was trying to sleep. She had been up most of the night crying."

239

"Do you know why?"

"She didn't want to leave. She kept insisting that she could revise her novel in a couple of days. I tried to reason with her, I really tried. I told her it was impossible, that even Michael Pierce couldn't revise a novel in two days. But she was so fixed on it; she kept saying it was her chance to get published. She was distraught.

"I don't know why Merle Ackerley made that offer to her in the first place. He knew it was impossible. And when she asked him if she could send him the revised manuscript because she had to leave, he told her he wouldn't have time to look at it." Laura paused as unexpected tears welled in her eyes. "You said it was a single-car accident. She had a husband and three children. You don't think it was deliberate, do you?"

"We don't know."

"Once when I was driving, I sneezed four times in a row. I almost went off the road. Your eyes close when you sneeze. I never thought about it until that happened. Maybe she sneezed a number of times. Or maybe she fell asleep because she'd been up all night."

"Maybe," he said.

"But you don't think so?"

"No one will ever know for sure," he said.

Seeing how upset she was, he was glad he hadn't told her that the report he'd received stated that the accident victim's eyes were red and swollen from crying at the time of death.

Ackerley and Talbot were in the outer office when Laura emerged with the sheriff. "I'll see you now, Mr. Ackerley," Coniglio said, noting how pale the writer was.

Talbot started to follow Ackerley into the inner office when Coniglio's arm shot out, blocking the entrance. "I have every right to be in there," Talbot said. "It's my office!"

"Not while I'm using it," Coniglio said, closing the door.

Ackerley started talking as soon as they were seated. "Roy told me about Gwen's accident. It's a tragedy."

"Yes," Coniglio said, "especially for her husband and three young children. Tell me, Mr. Ackerley, how well did you know Gwen Eggleston?"

"Her manuscript was assigned to me to criticize. I had my conference with her yesterday."

"And how did that go?"

"I told her that her novel needed work, but I put it in a positive way."

"Did you tell her that you'd help her get it published if she fixed it?"

"There's no harm in giving starting writers encouragement. She was happy after I made her the offer."

"It's my understanding that you gave her a deadline of a few days to re-write her book, which I've been told is impossible. Is that true?"

Ackerley shifted his lanky frame uncomfortably in his chair. "It was the encouragement that mattered."

"Then why did you refuse to let her send the book to you when she told you she had to leave?"

Ackerley was unable to conceal his surprise at the unexpected question. "I was hired to criticize manuscripts while I'm here. That's what I'm paid for. I'm under no obligation to continue working with people after the conference is over."

Coniglio rubbed his chin thoughtfully. "Let's see if I've got this right: You made her an offer that she couldn't possibly fulfill, and when she came to you to ask if she could send you the manuscript because she had to leave, you refused because you had no obligation."

Ackerley took a while to answer. "I regret what happened to her, but I don't think that I'm responsible."

The sheriff rose to indicate that their session was over. "I imagine you must sleep well at night."

"Why do you say that?"

"You don't seem to have much of a conscience," Coniglio said as he headed out the door, feeling that he'd had more than enough of this place.

***

The public request that Laura report to the office was so unusual that her friends gathered in the lobby to wait for her. Agatha, Nan, Dynarski, Diana, and Webb all wanted to be there to give her support if she had been the recipient of bad news. When she came out of the office and saw them looking concerned, she was so touched her eyes welled with tears again.

Dynarski was the first to speak after she told them about Gwen and repeated what she'd said to the sheriff. "I was at another writers' conference where something similar happened," he said. "They'll try to cover-up her death. They'll attribute the accident to exhaustion and tell everyone to be careful driving home when they leave."

"What about Ackerley?" Webb said. "What he did was inexcusable!"

"It was morally wrong, but I doubt that he broke any laws," Nan said.

"Laura, do you think Gwen might have taken her own life?" Agatha asked.

"Maybe she got distracted, maybe she fell asleep. No other cars were involved," Laura said. "I guess we'll never know."

Talbot approached the group. It was probably too late to do much damage control here, he thought, but he still had to know what she'd told the sheriff. "Sorry to interrupt," he said. "Laura, I'd like to speak with you for a moment."

He walked her away from the group, and at his request she repeated what she had told Coniglio yet again. Talbot's expression darkened as he listened. "Are you sure Mr. Ackerley refused to let Gwen send him her manuscript?"

"Positive," Laura said.

"I'm sorry you had to go over it again. I'm sure this has been upsetting for you."

"Yes, it has."

"Do you want to see the nurse?"

"No," she said, "unless she has a pill that can change what has happened."

He patted her awkwardly on her arm before going back to his office. Ackerley hadn't mentioned his refusal to let Gwen send him the manuscript; nor had he said that he made the offer to recommend her work to a publisher on the condition that the novel be revised in two days. Ackerley's omissions were the same as lies!

The novelist was still in his office. "I have the whole story now, everything you neglected to tell me," Talbot said. "From what I can see, you may very well have contributed to Gwen Eggleston's death."

"I don't believe I did, but I imagine it could be looked at that way," Ackerley said. "I was waiting to ask what legal help you could offer me if I should need it."

"As far as I'm concerned, you're on your own. This is my sixth year as the director of The Clymer Workshop, and to my knowledge no writer on the staff has ever made an offer to a participant as empty—maybe heartless is a better word—as the one you made to Gwen Eggleston. That kind of thing isn't done here, it just isn't done."

"Gwen had an attitude that was close to being outright insulting. I'm no fool. I know everyone here wants Michael Pierce to criticize their manuscripts, but most folks have the good sense or decency or whatever you want to call it not to show their disappointment. Except Gwen Eggleston. She sat in my study group like she was being punished, so I made a point of giving her one of the first conferences, thinking that if I found anything promising in her manuscript I might turn her around. But her manuscript was worthless; she was way out of her depth, which made me wonder why she was accepted here. This is supposed to be one of the best writers' conferences in the country. If you deserve even a fraction of your lofty reputation, you should have refused her admission. The other manuscripts I was assigned aren't much better than Gwen's. I realize that the other writers on the staff were probably given better manuscripts than I was, but the issue here is a matter of quality. If your reputation is to be believed, she shouldn't have been accepted in the first place.

"I think you need to adjust your perspective," Ackerley said, rising. "For some reason I was singled out to be the staff scapegoat from the day I arrived. I don't know why, and at this point I don't give a damn. I accepted your contract and I've honored it. But I want to make this clear: if I go down, y'all are going down with me."

After Ackerley left, Talbot poured himself a generous drink and sat for a while, thinking. When the glass was half empty, he called Howard Cruickshank and briefly related what had occurred from the time of Sheriff Coniglio's arrival to Ackerley's threat. "Jesus," Cruickshank said. "Who is this Ackerley anyway?"

"A Southern Appalachian writer. He teaches at Tulane."

"Why did you hire him?"

"Someone on the Board of Trustees got the idea to invite regional writers to be on the staff to broaden our demographic, and you all went along with it," Talbot reminded him, bristling. "What he did was indefensible, but I've thought about it, and I doubt that he could be charged with anything. I'm not sure it could be proven that her death was a suicide; it could have been a tragic accident. I don't think anyone will ever know for certain. What I believe we need to do now is have Axton's lawyers research the situation so we know where we stand in terms of any liability."

"I've already made a note to call one of them tonight. Will you be available?"

"I have to go to Sara Newkirk's reading. It's starting soon."

"Can't you skip it? This is more important."

"Sara's powerful. No one, not even Aaron Greene, would skip her reading."

"I suppose I could give them the facts," Cruickshank said. "How are you planning to handle this?"

"Her tragic accident will be reported in tomorrow's *BULLETIN* with no details; there will also be a brief commentary about the necessity of getting enough rest while at the conference, which will imply exhaustion as the cause."

"How is the atmosphere there?"

"The same as always, intense but manageable."

"As long as Jean and I are planning to attend the reading tomorrow night, we might as well come early and have dinner in Hackett Hall. I feel a need to gauge the intensity level myself."

The Cruickshanks having dinner in Hackett Hall! What could he say to discourage him? What? "The meals… uh… haven't been particularly appetizing."

"Then tell the cook to put more effort into it," Cruickshank said before he hung up.

While Talbot finished his drink, he wrote a note to Dee Dee that he placed on her desk. Then he went to find the cook.

The accommodation for the cook was an ancient Air Stream trailer nestled near a stand of trees away from the central area of the campus; the rounded aluminum body of the trailer gleamed dully, catching the fading light. As he approached he saw the cook, who was sitting and smoking on a lawn chair that had broken webbing. But it was the odor, musty and pungent, that made Talbot suddenly alert. Inhaling deeply, he experienced a surge of unfettered envy. Weed. For a moment he forgot the reason for his visit. All he wanted was to sit in the woods smoking a joint.

The cook looked up at him quizzically. "To what do I owe the honor?" he said.

"There has to be a change in the menu," Talbot said. "The menu for the farewell dinner has to be served tomorrow night."

"Can't do it."

"Get it done and there's a two hundred dollar bonus in it for you."

"Double the bonus and you got a deal."

Talbot didn't know where he'd get the money, but he'd find it somehow. "You won't forget," he said.

"I ain't that stoned," the cook said.

There wasn't enough time to get something to eat before Sara's reading, so he went directly to the Circle Theater, where he saw that approximately a quarter of the seats were empty. It could have been worse considering the chilly weather, he thought, aware that Sara would never win a popularity contest with the people who paid to attend the conference. But she was a draw for the staff, which put the balance in her favor.

Dee Dee was sitting in her usual seat in the first row wearing a bulky down vest over a gray sweatshirt. He motioned to her from the door, beckoning her outside, where he told her about Gwen. "I wrote something for you to print so we could attach it to the BULLETIN in the morning, but I've changed my mind. I'll make an announcement at breakfast instead."

"I talked to her husband yesterday; the poor man was having a hard time then. I hate to think of what he's going through now."

"It's a tragedy," Talbot said. His stomach growled loudly. "Sorry, I haven't had dinner."

"Why don't you go to the Shed and get something to eat?"

"Sara wouldn't understand," he said. "We'd better go in. I'll get something after the reading."

Before he sat down next to Dee Dee, his eyes happened to meet Joanne Howe's. She was sitting several rows behind them. He nodded and smiled, mouthing the word *later*.

Joanne was waiting for him outside the entrance after the reading. "I have to get something to eat," he said, rubbing his hands together. His fingers were numb with cold. "Come to the Shed with me."

"A hot chocolate might help thaw me out," she said as they fell in step together.

"That's my job."

"Would you mind if I shower in your room tonight so I don't have to stand in line at the Inn tomorrow morning? "

"I'll help dry you off."

She held up a large quilted tote bag. "I came prepared," she said.

Dee Dee had been standing inside the theater watching them. At least she knew who the woman was now, not that it made any difference.

***

Guided by the wide beam from a lantern flashlight, the Pierces crossed the bridge over Barrier Creek, arm in arm. Below them, chilly water gurgled as it swept past stones in the rocky creek bed. "Let's stop at Clemens for a drink," Leila said.

"I'd rather not."

She withdrew her arm from his. "Are you going to work?"

"I don't know," he said, unwilling to admit that he'd been avoiding Stoddard, who was ever-present in Clemens, since Stoddard had blamed him for the slow sales of his book.

"We haven't stopped for a drink together after a reading since we got here. Don't you think Sara would want you to celebrate with her?"

"She won't miss me. Besides, she knows I've felt pressured with this new book."

I just spent the past half-hour waiting in the cold for you to escape your fans, she wanted to say. *I did it because I love you. Can't you do the same for me?* But then he would accuse her of trying to manipulate him with guilt. They would argue and the result would be the same: he'd still refuse. "I'll see you later," she said when they reached the path to Clemens. All she could see of him when she looked back from the porch steps was the beam from his flashlight, a barely discernable spark in the fog.

It took a moment for her eyes to adjust to the brightly-lighted cottage. The Hills were talking to Sara, who was nodding at what they were saying. Cox was chatting with Eric Nettles. Stoddard, who looked distracted, rose to leave as she went to the trestle table.

Nettles excused himself and walked up to her. "It's too bad they don't have the fixings for Irish coffee," he said, watching her mix a gin and tonic. "It's the perfect drink for a cold night."

"Yes," she agreed, wondering where she would sit so that it wouldn't look like she was encouraging him. His kiss last night was an accident that she didn't want repeated.

He made the choice for her. "Let's sit over there," he said, tilting his head toward a pair of wicker chairs beneath a window.

She followed him, again aware of his sensuality, hypnotic and compelling. Soon, however, she was relaxed, laughing at anecdotes which he told as masterfully as the best traditional storytellers whom he criticized. Across the room Sara sat with the Hills, wide and inscrutable, observing them as though they were actors performing for her benefit.

"I'd better go," Leila said after almost an hour had lapsed.

"You don't have a flashlight. I'll walk you back."

Fog enveloped them as they started down the path. "I want to talk to you about what happened last night," he said.

"Forget it," she said, glad that he couldn't see her face. "It was impulsive, a mistake."

He put his arm around her. "You don't believe that."

"Of course I do," she said, firmly removing his arm. "I'm happily married."

"What does that mean?"

"That I don't take sex casually, that I have no desire for extra-curricular activities."

"You responded."

"Not really," she said, increasing her pace.

"Then why are you running away?"

She slowed down. "It's cold."

In the darkness, his green eyes flickered like a cat's. "Don't lie to yourself. You were running for every reason but the cold. You're afraid to acknowledge what you felt."

"There's nothing to be afraid of."

He grasped her shoulders and pulled her to him. Before she could protest his mouth was on hers, his tongue parting her lips. She tried to resist but then responded as if her body were no longer under her control. "You're as attracted to me as I am to you," he said after he released her, "so why deny it?"

"Because it's wrong."

"Leila," he said patiently, "life is not plotted like the novels your husband writes, each action leading to a significant consequence. What we could give each other would have no effect on our lives whatsoever, except to bring us brief, extraordinary pleasure."

"I love Michael. I couldn't... I can't betray him. Our relationship would never be the same."

"Would he be as faithful if the situation were reversed?"

"Yes," she said too quickly, as if she couldn't allow even a second of doubt.

They walked in silence to the steps of Hawthorne. "I am as obsessed with you as your husband is with his fiction," he said, brushing his hand against her cheek. "I won't give up."

"Forget about it."

"I can't," he said, his face inches from hers, "no more than you can order him to stop writing."

After she went inside, he turned off his flashlight and stood leaning against a post on the porch for a while, reflecting that when he'd decided to come to the conference, he'd had no expectations other than spending hours of his time teaching people of little or no ability on whom his efforts would be wasted. There was nothing that either he or anyone else could tell an individual which would transform that person into a writer. Instruction was as wasted on those of great talent as it was on those who had none. The talented would learn on their own; nothing would help the others. He was here to pick up a few extra dollars, which was what the place was all about—making money. If he hadn't accepted the job, it would have gone to someone else. He certainly hadn't expected to be challenged by Michael Pierce, especially after pursuing an idea in his art until he had fulfilled his goal with his last book. No other modern writer had come as close as he had to completely eradicating himself from his fiction. He had accomplished the impossible. Pierce, by comparison, was nothing but a diversion, a contest of little consequence. It was the challenge that mattered. Leila was not only beautiful and entertaining but intelligent, a prize he hadn't expected. If he were younger and weren't married, he'd pursue her with serious intent. Like most crusaders, Pierce was a fool. If the fellow had any common sense, he'd watch his wife and stay within the confines of his antiquated fictions, playing contentedly instead of wandering off to pontificate. Leila had responded to him; soon she would be warming his bed.

Thinking of Leila and challenges triggered the memory of the reason he had embarked on the path of innovative fiction. As he stepped off the porch to go to his room, he recalled the first important review he was asked to write. It was an assignment from *The New York Times Book Review* to review a novel written by a fellow named Neal Gilroy entitled *Lost*. He'd been profoundly moved by Gilroy's book, and he'd written a review giving it unreserved praise, expecting that it would be a huge success. Instead, the book didn't go anywhere. As he witnessed its downward spiral into oblivion, he was incredulous that such an outstanding work could suffer this ignominious fate. At the time he was working on his second novel, a traditional narrative. His first novel had been sparsely but critically well-received, and his hopes were high for this second book. After seeing what happened to Gilroy's book, he abandoned the novel he was working on, reasoning that if a novel as good as Gilroy's could simply vanish, he was wasting his time. He would create a new fiction, one that was demanding, a fiction so innovative that it would not only command attention but inclusion in college syllabi. His books would live long after he was gone.

Only once had he regretted his choice, and then just briefly. It was a memory he had successfully repressed for years, but for some reason it surfaced now:

A well-dressed woman of approximately his age whom he mentally classified with some disdain as a 'suburban matron' approached him after a reading he had given. "I came here tonight because I want to ask you a question," she said. "Years ago I read your first novel and I was so moved that I literally wept when the little girl died so senselessly. You made me feel her parents' loss as if it were my own. A book hadn't moved me to tears since I was thirteen and I cried over Melanie's death in Gone With The Wind. *You have a great gift, the power to touch people's souls. Why aren't you writing novels like your first book that could change the world?"*

"I appreciate your faith in my ability, but I don't believe it is possible for a book to change the world," he said with a smile that had a tinge of condescension.

"Uncle Tom's Cabin did," she replied, "and Harriet Beecher Stowe didn't have even half your talent."

She walked away leaving him with a sudden, profound feeling of emptiness, that he had used his gifts to pursue glitter rather than substance, that there was nothing in the shiny box of his career but a lump of coal. The feeling passed almost as quickly as it had come. He was, after all, Eric Nettles, the master of an innovative fiction in which no one was his peer.

***

Laura didn't go to the reading. After she called Gretchen to tell her about Gwen, she went to bed. Hours later she was still awake despite the lack of sleep she'd had the previous night. From the moment the sheriff told her how Gwen's death had occurred, she had been unable to get the image out of her mind: she kept seeing Gwen in her car, Gwen weeping as the car hit the concrete bridge abutment.

"It may very well have been an accident," Gretchen had said. "You tried your best to help her; there was nothing more you could have done. You weren't responsible for her life or her choices."

No, she wasn't responsible. The truth was that Gwen was selfish and self-centered. But she was also a wife and a mother; her loss would be devastating to her husband and children. Maybe her death was an accident. But if it wasn't, what had she died for? A chance at getting an editor to read her manuscript? It was senseless. It was stupid. And yet in some twisted, perverted way, it was entirely plausible in the context of The Clymer Workshop.

The room was freezing. She got up to put on socks and another sweater, then slid back under the covers. Sleep, she had to get some sleep. Finally she did fall into a restless slumber in which she was unable to escape from Gwen…

… the small airplane was on the tarmac… she was standing at the gate with her boarding pass in one hand, her laptop in the other… Gwen was at the bottom of the stairs calling to her… "Laura, hurry up, the plane is going to take off"… she hesitated, unsure of what she wanted to do… then she started walking, not toward the plane but back to the terminal, still debating her decision, so lost in thought that she didn't notice the open-sided truck loaded with baggage coming toward her… she didn't see it until she was directly in front of it, too late to get out of the way…

❧ WORKSHOP BULLETIN ❧

VOL. 74, NO.8   THE CLYMER WORKSHOP   AUGUST 18 2004

GOOD MORNING!

It will be overcast and cool again. The weather, like writers, could benefit from the exercise of imagination!

MORNING PROGRAM

9:15 A.M. Fiction Lecture
(Merle Ackerley)
10:15 A.M. Informal Gathering
(John Baty)
11:15 A.M. Manuscript
Conferences

Merle Ackerley will talk about "Beginnings." John Baty is a Boston-based literary agent who has recently established his own agency. He will conduct an informal question- and- answer session in the Shed, and will meet with those who are interested afterward.

AFTERNOON PROGRAM

2:00 P.M. Workshops
(Roy Talbot, Marshall Stoddard)
3:00 P.M. Workshops
(Terence Hill, Merle Ackerley)
4:00 P.M. Manuscript
Conferences

EVENING PROGRAM

Michael Pierce will read his prose. A Pulitzer Prize-winning novelist, his works of fiction include *Prime Land*, *Coming Into The Light*, *Blue De Soto*, *Blessing's Last Will*, and *The Wanderers*. He is the author of three children's books: *Cora and the Incredible Hat*, *Chief Thundercloud Rides Again*, and *Fish Story*. The recipient of a Guggenheim fellowship, he has also had awards from the National Endowment for the Arts and the American Academy of Arts and Letters. He has been writer-in-residence at numerous universities, including Harvard, Duke, and Northwestern. He recently returned from England, where he was a visiting writer at Cambridge University.

WORKSHOPS

Materials for tomorrow's workshops will be available after dinner outside the Workshop office.

BACK BY POPULAR REQUEST

Liquor orders will be taken again in the sitting room after lunch. Cash must accompany each order. Cheers!

SALE!

Starting today, all books, notions and sundries in the bookstore will be discounted twenty percent. Come early to get an armful of bargains!

TIPS

Before you spend all your money at the bookstore, please think of the waitresses who have cheerfully served you. A contribution of fifty dollars per person would not be excessive for the many meals you have had in Hackett Hall. Cash or personal checks should be put in an envelope and deposited in the specially-labeled box in the Workshop office.

FOR THE AMBITIOUS

Announcing a Limerick Contest. All entries have to be in the Workshop office by 5:30 P.M. The limericks will be read tomorrow night at our farewell dinner, so keep them tasteful, please. The winning limerick is guaranteed publication in the final edition of the *BULLETIN*.

TIDBIT

"I've been thinking about getting a degree in business administration."

"No one can make you feel inferior without your consent."
- Eleanor Roosevelt

Chapter VIII

Pierce woke to the beeping of his PDA, which he had placed under his pillow so it wouldn't disturb Leila. Always a bit edgy on the day he was to give a reading, he wanted to make sure he had plenty of time for his run. He dressed quickly and slipped out of the room.

It was overcast and crisp, ideal for jogging. Absorbed in the consideration of a plot turn that had occurred to him during the night, he ran further than he had planned; his stomach was growling when he got back to the campus. Rather than shower first, he decided to have breakfast and continued on to the Shed.

Shapeless in a black sweater and a green shift dress similar in style to the one she had worn for her lecture, Sara Newkirk was sitting at a round table in the snack area eating a powdered-sugar donut that was oozing red jelly filling. He ordered a large glass of orange juice and a bowl of granola and milk, which he brought to the table. "Ah, a friend to play hooky with," she said, licking jelly off a dimpled finger.

"The food's been so vile that Roy's probably too embarrassed to enforce his rule about staff eating in the dining room."

"Where were you last night?"

"Working," he said.

"You're more compulsive than ever."

He smiled guiltily. "I'm a prisoner after the first fifty pages."

She took a greedy sip of hot chocolate, her eyes narrowing above the steaming paper cup. "I've noticed that Leila hasn't been around much during the day."

"She's keeping busy."

He would have overlooked Sara's remark if she hadn't frowned, as though Leila's absence were cause for concern. "There's nothing for her to do here. She has a project now, which has been keeping her occupied."

Sara's frown deepened. "That's good," she said, the creases in her forehead contradicting her words. "I've noticed that she's been coming into Clemens alone after the readings. It doesn't seem to bother her, though. A woman as beautiful as Leila will never lack for attention. I've been wondering about you, whether you're giving up on your friends."

"I'm at the point in the novel where I have to work every chance I get," he said defensively.

She gazed at him shrewdly. "That business with Marshall has kept you away also."

Wondering how much she knew about his altercation with Stoddard, he pushed the cereal bowl aside and leaned across the table. "He's been behaving like a jerk!"

"He helped you once."

"And I repaid him in full!"

"You were good friends," she reminded him. "No matter how justified you feel, you should think about it: Marshall's hurting, which is understandable. He'll get over his disappointment eventually, but he never forgets."

Sara didn't have to say more. He knew exactly what she meant: Marshall had developed powerful connections as a critic; he could be as harmful as an enemy as he had once been helpful as an ally. He shook his head with disgust. "There's no way to escape that shit, is there?" he said, more to himself than to her.

"It's part of the business," she said. "You can't fight politics any more than you can stop falling rain."

Her reference to politics reminded him that her workshop had been sparsely attended. "I heard Aaron scared them silly yesterday afternoon. It's a shame you weren't scheduled first."

"These things happen," she said, as though it weren't important. But his acknowledgment was and she smiled, pleased.

When he rose to leave, he gave her a pat on the back, a man-to-man gesture of friendship which she accepted with a nod of satisfaction.

Leila was taking her keys out of her purse when he returned to their room. She was wearing black linen slacks, a white blouse, and a black linen jacket that had flowers embroidered on it in white, the clothes he knew she planned to wear for his reading. "Where are you going?" he asked.

"Jamestown," she said. "I'm going to try to see that lawyer."

"What lawyer?"

"I told you last night: the lawyer whose father wrote the Clymer will."

"Can't you call him from here?"

"I'd rather see him in person, if that's possible," she said, giving him a dry peck on the cheek before starting out the door.

***

Talbot had a choice: he could either make the announcement regarding Gwen's death at breakfast or he could wait until the conference members had gathered in the Circle Theater for Ackerley's lecture. He preferred the Circle Theater, but he was concerned that making the announcement immediately before Ackerley's lecture might be interpreted as being accusatory. Although he privately believed that Ackerley bore a good share of the responsibility for the woman's death, to protect the Workshop he couldn't imply publicly that the novelist had any connection with it.

The first meal of the day had become increasingly quiet since the conference had started. People straggled into Hackett Hall exhausted from days of regimented activity, from restless sleeps on sagging mattresses, from submerging their deepest hopes in the perpetual smiles of the anxious. Caught in a net of intensity from which they couldn't escape, they sat bleary-eyed, cradling their first cups of coffee as if gathering strength for yet another day identical to the ones that had passed. Still, hope was mingled with the steam that rose from the cups they were holding. Perhaps today they would get what they had come here for—a word of encouragement, a promise of help, a chance to see their names in print—and they would be ready to grasp the most slender thread of opportunity, anything that would put them closer to their dreams.

Talbot walked to the center of the room and stood quietly until he felt he had a sufficient amount of attention. "I have a sad and difficult announcement to make," he said after clearing his throat. "A conference member, Gwen Eggleston, perished in a tragic automobile accident yesterday. She had to leave because she had a family emergency.

"Participating in the Workshop can be tiring. I urge you all, particularly those who traveled here by car, to make an effort to get sufficient rest before the conference ends on Friday so that you are rested for your drive home."

An immediate buzz of conversation rose in the room as Talbot went to take a seat at one of the tables, people who knew Gwen and those who were trying to identify her suddenly awake with the news. Dynarski, who had waited outside the dining room for Laura so he could have breakfast with her, leaned toward her, pressing his shoulder against hers. "See," he said. "Just like I told you last night—they're blaming her death on exhaustion."

Before Laura could respond, a woman sitting opposite them who had overheard him started asking questions. Dynarski was bitterly expansive. He talked and they listened, and then they talked and others listened. It is an unpleasant aspect of human nature that people converge on accident scenes to gawk, and that they probe to find out whatever details they can about personal tragedies that don't involve them. There wasn't a sleepy pair of eyes in the dining room; they were all awake now and talking, wanting as much information as they could get about Gwen and the circumstances surrounding her death. When Laura left her unfinished breakfast and rose to leave, they talked about that, too.

Talbot was surprised when he entered the Circle Theater to attend Ackerley's lecture and saw no more than twenty people there, not counting the staff, who were all present. Although he wasn't sure of the reason for the empty theater, he felt that if anyone deserved public condemnation, certainly Ackerley did.

Ackerley grasped the podium with both hands as he gazed at the vacant seats, looking as if he couldn't believe what he was seeing. Normally self-confident and often cocky, he forced himself to read the lecture he had prepared, which was as competent and thorough a discussion of beginnings in fiction as any member of the staff could deliver (with the exceptions of Pierce and Nettles, who were, despite the novelist's self-pride, his betters). The conference members who expressed their opinion of his treatment of Gwen by their absence missed an opportunity to learn how to improve their writing, while the man giving the lecture had to will himself to deliver it to the end.

While Ackerley was explaining that the beginning of a story sets the tone for the fiction and tells which characters to watch, Laura and Agatha were finishing their breakfast. Agatha had seen Laura leaving Hackett Hall; noting the distress on her friend's face, she had excused herself from another table to follow in long, purposeful strides. Insisting that today was her treat, they went to the Shed where they had muffins and coffee. "I have a feeling that this will be the best part of my day," Laura said, finishing the last of a buttery cherry-almond muffin. "When I got up this morning, I was determined not to think about Gwen. Now people will be asking me questions about her because Stan couldn't keep his mouth shut; he was practically crowing about getting it right after the director made his announcement. I've done everything I can to discourage him without being unkind, but he's attached himself to me and he won't let go."

"Then Nan and I will attach ourselves to you. I doubt that he's interested in us for company."

"Well, I'm interested in you for company, and it might work. Thank you," Laura said with a smile that disappeared as a middle-aged woman whose hair was colored a brassy red walked by.

"Is something wrong?" Agatha said.

"Did you notice the redhead who just walked past us?"

Agatha nodded.

"Her name is Marge. Yesterday she was walking to the Inn with me and we saw Nettles talking to the young woman whose manuscript he eviscerated in his workshop. 'Oh, look at how nice he is to take time to talk to her,' she said.

"I was so shocked at her statement that I told her it was the least he could do after humiliating the woman in public by leaving her name on her manuscript and then tearing it to pieces. I asked her how she would have felt if it were her manuscript."

"What did she say?"

"She told me that it wouldn't happen to her because her manuscript was far superior, so I asked her who was criticizing it," Laura said. "She wouldn't tell me. She won't even look at me now. I bet she's assigned to Ackerley."

"I've been troubled by Aaron Greene's workshops. He had such disdain for contributors' poems, and he permitted attacks on them that were vicious. It was almost as if he were enjoying their nastiness," Agatha said. "I was uncomfortable witnessing it. No one learned anything in those workshops of any value, which is what they came here for. Maybe it bothered me more than most people because I went to college to learn how to teach, and I'm still learning after so many years. I realize that the writers here are artists, but it wouldn't hurt them to get some teacher training."

"No, it wouldn't," Laura agreed, "but I doubt that will ever happen. I can't even imagine anyone as arrogant as Aaron Greene being willing to learn how to teach."

"Neither can I," said Agatha sadly.

****

Early for her conference with Diana, Phyllis Baran entered a Studio classroom wan and puffy-eyed, a woman who had aged years in less than a week. She was, however, remarkably calm despite her appearance. During a long, sleepless night she had mentally rehearsed for the next hour, proposing and rejecting arguments until she knew precisely what she would say to secure Diana's novel for herself. Nothing could possibly happen that she wasn't prepared for; she was so certain that she had driven to Olean to photocopy the manuscript and now had it locked in her suitcase. No one on the staff was familiar with Rothenberg's manuscript except Talbot, and he read so many manuscripts that he wouldn't remember it. She could easily change the settings, the characters' names, and the opening scenes so that her first three chapters would bear no resemblance to Rothenberg's. It was the kernel of the story that mattered and it would be hers, deliverance from the nightmare of having nothing to put on paper. Diana Rothenberg was exceptionally gifted; she could write another book.

Familiar only with the name on the manuscript, her eyes flickered with recognition when Diana came into the room; she vaguely remembered Diana from her study groups and workshop. "So you're Diana Rothenberg," she said, extending her hand. "You're a talented young woman."

Diana accepted her hand with a smile. "Thank you."

Baran moved a student desk so they could sit opposite each other, then withdrew Diana's manuscript from a manila envelope. "I didn't write on your manuscript or use a separate comment sheet for several reasons," she said. "First, as I told you, I believe you are exceptionally talented. You have already overcome the most difficult hurdle: you have found your voice, and it is confident and distinctive. Further, you have a gift for language and a novelist's eye for detail. I didn't find any slips or mistakes in craft. You definitely have the ability to sustain an extended work of fiction."

Diana's fair skin glowed in perfect response to Baran's plan. "The only problem you have that I'm aware of is with this particular novel," Baran said with a regretful smile. "The more I've thought about it, the more I'm convinced that it simply won't work. Your characters are too extreme—the famous, erudite novelist and the raw, unmannered girl/woman. A man as cultivated as your protagonist would be repelled by someone like her; she's the antithesis of everything he is comfortable with."

"But that's the point!" Diana said. "He's fascinated with her precisely because she represents everything that is outside his life."

Another regretful smile. Her plan couldn't be working better. "Above all, fiction must be plausible. There has to be an underlying basis for belief, a justification for what occurs."

During the next half hour, Diana's arguments were met over and over again with sighs and regretful smiles. "I'm sorry," Baran said finally, putting the manuscript back into the envelope. "The more I think about it, the more convinced I am that your plot is implausible. The best advice I can give you is to abandon this novel. You're much too talented to waste your effort on a flawed premise."

She rose and handed the envelope to Diana. "Good luck," she said as she was leaving.

Diana remained at the student desk looking stunned, as if she'd just been told that her best friend had died. After a while she pulled her manuscript from the envelope and started reading, her brow furrowed, trying to understand where she had gone wrong.

***

Leila put down an old *TIME* magazine she'd been reading and looked at her watch, debating whether to stay or leave. It was twelve o'clock. She had been sitting in John Gustafson's sparely furnished reception room for over an hour. His secretary, an older woman who had a drooping lower jaw like a bulldog's, told her that Mr. Gustafson was trying a case and would be in court all day. "I can give you an appointment with him next week," she'd said.

When Leila explained the reason she wanted to see the lawyer, the secretary's expression softened when the name Clymer was mentioned. "He usually pops in on the lunch break to check his messages. You're welcome to wait."

At twelve thirty, just as Leila had decided to leave, Gustafson arrived. A trim man of medium height with a full head of silver-gray hair, he walked purposefully to the secretary's desk without so much as a glance in Leila's direction. "What do you have for me, Edith?" he said.

She gave him his messages, which were written on pink slips of paper, then nodded in Leila's direction. "She's been waiting a long while to speak to you. She says it's about Benjamin Clymer and his will."

Leila rose as he turned to look at her. "My name is Leila Pierce," she said, walking toward him. "My husband teaches at the Clymer Workshop. I have a copy of Benjamin Clymer's will that your father wrote. I'd like to ask you some questions if you have time."

"Actually, I don't have time, but you're welcome to come into my office and talk while I go through these messages."

His office was completely different from the reception area: the walls were painted in a subtle shade of eggshell and there was a handsome, hand-woven rug in rusts and browns on the floor. But the focal point of the room was an exquisitely-carved Sheraton desk as beautiful as any she had seen in fine arts museums. "What a magnificent desk," she said.

"It might interest you to know that it was carved by Benjamin Clymer," Gustafson said. "My father gave it to me when he retired; he wanted it to be used. It's the only piece of furniture he owned that he cared about."

Leila's eyes widened. "Benjamin Clymer?" she said in disbelief.

Her reaction made the lawyer smile. "My father never discussed his clients; he considered it a breach of ethics. The one exception was Benjamin Clymer. Whenever he talked about integrity and decency, he'd mention Clymer, as if the man were the standard by which he measured all others. Years ago, children were raised on tales by Hans Christian Anderson; my sister and I were raised on the story of Benjamin Clymer.

"I'm sorry I can't give you more time, but I have to go through these messages and get back to court," he said, re-focusing his attention.

Determined not to be dismissed after coming so close to the answers she sought, Leila withdrew the will from her purse. "Since you hold Benjamin Clymer in such esteem, you might be interested in knowing that the terms of his will were broken by the trustees of Axton College. They sold all his books in 1998. A librarian at the college told me that the collection was unique, full of valuable first editions. I highlighted the clause in the will that specifically states that the books were to be kept together and used by writers at the conference," she said, handing him the will.

As Gustafson read, his expression darkened.

"We're leaving Friday morning," she said. "I've been trying to learn about Benjamin Clymer for a week and a half, since the conference started and the caretaker put up a plaque he'd found that had been lost for years. The plaque said the Clymer Workshop was the gift of Benjamin Clymer in memory of Garnet and John Clymer. A woman whose farm is near the Workshop told me that Garnet and John were Benjamin Clymer's wife and son; he abandoned the land after they died. But she really didn't know what happened to him after he left or why he gave money to establish the conference. He's a mystery."

"I usually don't come to the office on Fridays during the summer. This Friday morning I have an early round of golf," he said. "Could you come here at eleven thirty?"

She knew Michael would want to leave for Connecticut early Friday morning, but she had accompanied him to the conference for years. He owed her this much. "I'll be here," she said.

"Before you leave, please ask my secretary to make a copy of the will so that I can read it in its entirety. After hearing my father talk about it for so many years, it may be illuminating for me as well."

***

Polly Talbot turned her green Subaru into the narrow road that led to the Workshop. Although it was midday, the gray sky and dense forest shrouded the road in darkness. She'd made excellent time from Axton, she thought, turning the headlights on. Surprising Roy was a wonderful idea; spontaneity was what their marriage needed. They'd each been so tied to their routines that their relationship had fallen into a pattern of habit, which had affected her more than him. Instead of spending time on herself, she'd given all her energy to the girls and the house. But no more.

She'd already lost four pounds, and the exercise class she'd joined would get her toned while she lost another twenty. He probably wouldn't notice the weight loss, but he'd see the difference her new haircut made. Wearing her hair long for years had been a mistake, proof really of how she'd neglected herself. This smart, short style made her look so much younger. Even her hair color seemed different, more auburn than brown. For the first time in ages she was feeling good about herself. Jean Cruickshank had noticed the change when she met her this morning in the supermarket. It was Jean who had given her the idea to come to the Workshop. "We try not to miss Michael Pierce's readings," Jean said. "We're going early for dinner. You should come so you and Roy can join us. It will be a great evening."

After she parked in the circular driveway, she glanced in the rearview mirror and smiled. The new haircut was such a drastic, positive change that she still wasn't used to it. If she weren't careful, she'd start primping as often as her daughters.

She went directly to the office. At first, Dee Dee didn't recognize her. "You look terrific."

"Thanks," Polly beamed. "Do you know where Roy is?"

"I haven't seen him since breakfast."

"I'd better re-park the car and take my suitcase to his room."

"He's in Melville, the second floor, the second-last room on the left of the staircase," Dee Dee said as crisply as if she were giving directions to Jamestown.

Polly didn't knock before she entered his room. She'd been married to Roy Talbot for nineteen years and had seen him in the most intimate of conditions. She was not, however, prepared to see Joanne Howe, who was standing next to the unmade bed wearing nothing but a black thong. Polly noticed that the woman's buttocks were smooth and high, not dimpled and sagging like her own. "What do you want?" Joanne demanded, grabbing a pillow to cover herself.

A maroon sweater she had given him on Valentine's Day was draped over the desk chair; she recognized his sneakers, a pair of Nikes worn at the little toes, which were on the floor at the foot of the bed. This was definitely his room. Too shocked to speak, she stared at Joanne, vaguely aware that the shower was running in the bathroom. "You're in the wrong room," Joanne said with unconcealed irritation.

Polly heard the shower turn off; her hand tightened around the handle of her suitcase. "Would you please leave," Joanne said impatiently.

"What did you say?" Talbot called from behind the bathroom door.

"There's a woman in here and she won't leave," Joanne said, glaring at Polly.

"A what?" The bathroom door opened and Talbot emerged dripping, a bath towel wrapped around his waist. He froze when he saw Polly, his face a deathly white.

Joanne looked first at one, then the other. "Oh, my God!" she gasped, dropping the pillow.

Both Talbots studied the ceiling in silence while Joanne hurriedly dressed. She pulled on her jeans, stuck her arms through a blouse which she didn't bother to button, stepped into a pair of leather moccasins, and gathered up as many of her belongings as she could—her purse, a notebook, an aqua nightgown, a mocha-colored sweater—and rushed out of the room, forgetting, among other things, the pencil that was perpetually stuck behind her ear as if it were growing out of her head.

They didn't speak to each other until Joanne reached the bottom of the stairs. "You look wonderful, Pol," he said with a tentative smile. "That haircut is really becoming."

The haircut. Polly's chin trembled. She started for the door that Joanne, in her haste, had neglected to close.

In his rush to intercept her, the towel Talbot was wearing slipped off. "I'm sorry, Pol," he said, pushing the door shut. "Believe me, she means nothing… I was lonely and the pressures here have been incredible… constant aggravation… I needed some diversion… that's all she was… just a hop in the sack to release tension… You are and always have been the only woman who's ever mattered to me."

Polly reached for the doorknob with her free hand, her hazel eyes traveling from his face to his narrow shoulders down to his exposed genitals, which had shriveled close to his body and hung as sexless as dried fruit. "You might have done pushups," she said.

She swung the suitcase, forcing him to step aside, opened the door and left.

He put on a pair of jeans and ran out of the room barefoot. He reached the front porch as the Subaru sped past, spewing a stream of gravel and dirt.

***

Few things excited Pierce more than finding a new writer of exceptional talent. He could feel physically—a tingling in his skin—the potential for creation, for worlds yet to be conceived in the artist's mind. And no one knew better than he the difficulty of beginning: the doubts, the faltering confidence, the hunger to succeed at what often seemed impossible. He had never wavered from his decision to become a novelist; it wasn't so much a choice as an imperative, the only thing he wanted to do with his life. He struggled because he had to struggle, and his successes didn't make it easier. Each book was harder to write than the one before: he set higher standards for himself, more difficult challenges, more impossible goals. He was his own taskmaster, driven by an elusive ideal of perfection always beyond his grasp. Yet he would have it no other way. And when he came upon someone whom he believed had the gift, he was generous. He thought of himself as a temporary guide, a traveler on a treacherous path, aware that even with his advice the individual would journey alone. But his generosity wasn't entirely selfless. If the impression he made was strong, if the lessons he taught were lasting, the kind of fiction he had committed his life to writing would be perpetuated. Strong plots and strong characters would continue to grapple with serious questions long after he ceased to exist; not only his life but all human life would be affirmed.

So when he entered the Shed early in the afternoon and saw Diana, it was to be expected that he would approach her to ask about her manuscript conference. "I had it this morning," she said in the monotone of someone trying to suppress emotion. "I was told that the plot is implausible."

He had intended to get something to eat that he could take to his room so he could work on his novel. Unwilling to sit at a table in Hackett Hall without Leila at his side directing the conversation so he wouldn't be badgered with questions throughout the meal, he had skipped lunch because she wasn't back from Jamestown. "What?" he said in disbelief.

"She told me to abandon the book."

He calculated the time it would take him to eat and go back to his room to get her manuscript. "Can you meet me here at two o'clock?"

"Yes," she said.

She was waiting for him outside the Shed when he returned. "Let's go inside," he said.

After they were settled in the lounge area on worn, overstuffed chairs, he asked her to tell him exactly what Phyllis Baran said "She told me that a literate man of the protagonist's sensitivity would be repelled by a woman as crude as Gayle. She said that Gayle's speech alone would make it impossible for Paul to tolerate her company, much less fall in love with her."

"What else?" he said.

"Nothing really. She told me that I was talented and that I should abandon the novel because I'd be wasting my effort."

"And you believed her?"

Pierce's gaze was so strong that Diana squirmed as though she were being shot with pins. "Y… yes," she said.

"Why?"

"Because she's a published writer. Because she's on the staff."

"Because she's paid to criticize manuscripts doesn't mean that what she says is right! Being a published writer has gotten her a job and that's all it has done! It hasn't made her judgment infallible. Did you argue?"

"Yes, but I couldn't convince her."

"Do you think you can complete the novel successfully?"

Diana's fingers curled protectively around her manuscript. "I've gone over and over it and I still think it will work."

Pierce leaned back and looked at her challengingly. "Tell me why."

"Gayle is crude, but she's also street smart. Maybe intuitive is a better word. She sees through conventions in society because she's never accepted them, has never been a part of them; things that are important to Paul are nonsense to her. He, on the other hand, has reduced his life to his work. His novels are all that matter to him until he meets her. Their relationship is based on more than a clash of wills. While he's trying to civilize her, she's teaching him the value of life. He can't finish his novel—the best work he's ever done—after she leaves him. Only when he eventually finds her after he's been ridiculed and humiliated by her people does he understand that she's not his muse, that the life in his book came from what she forced him to feel."

Pierce, who had been listening intently, nodded; his expression was grave, but his eyes were kind. "Never, *never* take anyone's advice, no matter who it's from, unless you're absolutely convinced that it's right! Be open to criticism, but trust your own instincts. Don't change a word, not a comma, unless you're positive that it should be changed!"

"But how will I know?"

"You must question and question until you can't question anymore."

"I've been so upset," she said, visibly relaxing. "I was sure the novel would work, and when she told me that it wouldn't, I started doubting everything I've done. Why did she do that to me?"

Pierce shrugged. He had a good guess, but he wasn't willing to share it. "When you read my comment on Gayle's language, you'll see that my reaction is the same as Baran's. In trying to set up the situation, you went too far. You were afraid to trust the intelligence of your readers. It's a common mistake and easily correctable."

He rose and extended his hand. "I'm looking forward to reading books with strong plots and memorable characters written by Diana Rothenberg," he said. "I expect wonderful novels from you."

"I'll try my best," Diana said gratefully.

Pierce studied her for a moment, looking deep into her wide-set eyes. "You'll make it," he said. "You'll succeed."

Diana stayed in the classroom after he left, hungrily reading the notes he had scrawled in the margins of her manuscript.

***

Leila was lying on the bed reading when Pierce returned to their room. She had changed into jeans and a black turtleneck sweater. "I thought I'd find you pounding away on your laptop," she said.

"I'm going to work now," he said. "I met with Diana Rothenberg. I'll tell you about it later."

He has no time to go with me to the escarpment, but he has time to meet with Diana Rothenberg. With that thought, she swung her legs over the side of the bed, grabbed a denim jacket and left.

There was no place for her to go but Clemens. In contrast to the dismal day, the drab staff cottage seemed almost festive with all the lights on. Phyllis Baran was sitting in a corner reading a manuscript, a drink in her hand; Sara Newkirk was chatting with Michelle Hill; and Nettles was talking about literary magazines with a respectful Andrew Cox, who had arrived just minutes earlier. Both men watched Leila make a gin and tonic. "She's magnificent," Cox said under his breath.

"My drink needs refreshing," Nettles said, excusing himself.

When Leila thought about it later, she rationalized her willingness to go out on the porch with him: she wanted to be distracted; she was bored and he was entertaining; she wanted to punish Michael. But the most compelling reason, which she did not acknowledge, was that Eric Nettles made her feel desirable in a way that her husband didn't. The yellow flecks in Nettles' green eyes danced when he looked at her, and when she spoke, he tilted his head in complete absorption, as though every word she uttered was worthy of his interest. He was self-assured and accomplished, as successful as Michael, yet he told her by every gesture and nuance that it was a privilege to be in her company.

But it was impossible to rationalize going with him to his room. She could have refused and didn't.

His meticulousness surprised her. The bed was sharply made, items on the desktop were precisely arranged, and there was no clothing in evidence. His neatness made her think of Michael, who left his clothes wherever he dropped them and whose desk was always in disarray, a jumble of notes and files under which pens, pencils, and paper clips were buried. "This is a mistake," she said, starting for the door.

Nettles slipped in front of her as smoothly as a cat. "On the contrary, it would be a mistake to leave. We may not have this opportunity again, and it's something we both want."

He wasn't touching her, but she could feel his power drawing her to him. "It's wrong," she said. "I explained before… I told you… I love Michael."

"Of course," he said, "but your love has nothing to do with this moment. Your desire is as strong as mine. It's foolish to deny it, to walk away from an experience in which the only consequence will be extraordinary pleasure."

He placed his hands on her face and kissed her. When his tongue parted her lips, she tore herself away and ran from him.

She stood outside for a moment as though she were lost, her limbs weak, her heart pounding. Then she slowly walked to Melville, the taste of him still in her mouth. No one was around, she thought with nervous relief, no one had seen her.

But minutes earlier, in Clemens, Sara had watched them leave together. And Sara had smiled as though she'd been treated to a delectable platter of her favorite food.

***

Agatha had started taking showers in the afternoon during the time the manuscript conferences were scheduled. Unlike the morning, it was quiet then so she could relax without being conscious of people waiting outside the bathroom door. She was standing in front of the mirror in her bedroom trying to apply just the right amount of blush that she had bought in the bookstore when Claire, who had also decided to shower late in the day, entered the room wrapped in her lavender bathrobe. "I need to use the mirror," she said, jostling Agatha's arm as she set her bulging cosmetic bag on the dresser top.

Fortunately, Agatha didn't have the brush on her face or it would have left a clown spot on her cheek. "I'll be done in a few minutes," she said.

Claire looked at Agatha critically. "I don't know why you even bother."

There is a limit to how much unpleasantness even the most reticent people can take, a threshold that when overstepped one time too many breaks the bonds of tolerance, unleashing a well-deserved push back. Agatha spun around. "That insult was uncalled for," she said. "I have gone out of my way to accommodate you and have received nothing but nastiness in return. I don't know if you work at it or if your unpleasantness and lack of consideration comes naturally, but I have had quite enough. I won't accept this kind of treatment anymore. There is a vacant bed two rooms away, on the right. I saw the woman, Liddy Carson, leave this morning. Since you are obviously unhappy sharing a room with me, I suggest that you go there now and ask Liddy's roommate if you can move in."

Claire's skin turned a mottled pink, then red. "Move? You want me to move?"

"Yes," Agatha said firmly. "Look at your side of the room: clothes, shoes, papers strewn all over. It's unsightly, an obstacle course. I have never lived with such a mess, and I don't choose to tolerate it another minute."

"But moving… it would be so hard…."

"Go down the hall and ask if you can move in," Agatha said firmly.

Although she appeared outwardly calm, Agatha was truly shaken. She had never spoken to anyone that forcefully and without tempering her words to spare their feelings. As she watched Claire leave, she thought of poor Liddy Carson, whom she had happened to see in the hallway before lunch. She knew that Liddy, a pleasant, friendly woman who was a contributor in poetry, had had a morning manuscript conference scheduled. Liddy was pulling a suitcase and looked deathly, as though she'd just been told she had a terminal illness. Agatha would have liked to give her a comforting hug, but the woman appeared so devastated that rather than intrude on her misery, she hurried away to give her privacy.

Claire was back within minutes. "She told me I can't move in. She wants the room to herself."

Agatha wasn't surprised. As far as she knew, Claire hadn't made any friends at the conference; she had developed a reputation for being haughty and difficult. "Then you have two choices: either behave civilly and clean up your side of the room, or go to the office and ask them to find you a different room."

Wordlessly, Claire started picking up shoes and gathering up clothes.

***

Dee Dee knew there was trouble when Talbot came into the office. He stopped at her desk, his expression dark. "Did you know that Polly was coming today?" he said.

"No," she said, immediately guessing what the problem was: either Polly caught him with the redhead or found some of her belongings in his room. If things were all right between them, they would be in Clemens together. Polly knew most of the people on the staff and would want to see them.

He scowled as though he suspected she was lying, started to say something, then shook his head and went into his office, slamming the door behind him.

Dee Dee looked at his closed door and sighed. If her guess was right, he was getting what he deserved, but she didn't feel vindicated or even pleased. She'd had a twinge of guilt when she'd given Polly directions to his room, although she shouldn't have. Protecting him wasn't her responsibility. Polly had asked and she had answered. It was as simple as that. Besides, why shouldn't Polly know what she'd known for years? Polly was his wife. But Polly seemed so happy. *Damn Roy Talbot!* she thought, yanking open a desk drawer.

Talbot sat at his desk, staring at the telephone. He had left immediately after teaching his workshop, an assignment he looked forward to every year, elevating himself to the level of the staff even though he wasn't their peer in accomplishment. Instead of enjoying himself, he could barely concentrate; his thoughts kept drifting to Polly. The session was a waste of everyone's time.

He picked up the receiver, thinking that he would apologize again, that he would try to talk to her reasonably. He would discuss the girls, the wonderful family they had, the work they had done together on the house, all the experiences they had shared. Somehow he would make her understand that he had made a stupid mistake, nothing more.

His youngest daughter, Meredith, the child who resembled him most, answered the phone. "Hi, honey," he said. "What have you been doing?"

"Mom said she wouldn't call to check up on us until tonight," Meredith complained. "She promised!"

A film of sweat glazed his forehead. If Polly wasn't home, where was she? "I'm not calling to check up on you. I just want to know how you are."

"Me and Emily made brownies. We're going to have pizza for dinner."

"That's nice," he said, half-listening as she went on with her plans.

After he hung up, he looked at his watch: it was five o'clock. Polly should have been home by now. He'd call again later. The more time she had to cool off, the better.

He rubbed his eyes, trying to forget the expression on her face when he came out of the bathroom, the look of betrayal, the indescribable hurt. This wasn't going to be easy.

He waited in his office until he saw the Cruickshanks' black Lexus pull into the circular driveway; then went to the lobby to greet them. Howard Cruickshank entered Inn with his head thrust forward, as if he were fighting a strong headwind. A short, tightly-built man, he had thick wavy gray hair and a squat, misaligned nose, broken years ago in a college boxing match, which gave his face a distinctly pugnacious appearance that aptly fit his personality. Jean Cruickshank was taller than her husband. She was a strong tennis player and a low-handicap golfer and had the toned body of an athlete; her sun-streaked hair and large hazel eyes set off a disarming smile that had been known to take some of the edge off her husband's abrasiveness. They were both dressed for the chilly weather in slacks and sweaters. Talbot shook hands with Howard and hugged Jean. "Where's Polly?" she asked as they started walking to the dining room. "When I saw her this morning at the supermarket, it didn't take much coaxing on my part to convince her to come to the reading. She was really enthusiastic."

"Something came up at the last minute. She didn't want to miss it, but it couldn't be helped," Talbot said after a slight hesitation. "I picked a table for us by the windows."

The dinner that was served wasn't exactly the one that had been planned for the last night of the conference—chicken breasts with a mushroom sauce had been substituted for Cornish hens—but the accompanying fresh salad, rice pilaf, green beans and chocolate mousse were the same. The cook had delivered as he had promised, ensuring his bonus. "This is quite good," Cruickshank said, spearing a piece of chicken. "It's amazing with the budget you have this year. Your cook must be a miracle worker."

"It's the best meal we've had since the Workshop started," Talbot commented, deciding it would be best not to say more. There would be time for that when the conference was over.

Pierce had just started eating his chocolate mousse when he saw Phyllis Baran leaving the dining room. "Excuse me," he said, getting up from the table. He touched Leila lightly on the shoulder. "I'll see you later."

He caught up with Phyllis as she was leaving through the back door. "Let's take a walk," he said.

It was the first overture a fellow staff member had made to her since her reading. "We can go to Clemens," she suggested brightly.

"We need to talk privately," he said. "I had a conversation with Diana Rothenberg this afternoon. She told me that you advised her to abandon her novel. I want to know why."

Phyllis' mouth opened in a silent gasp; she felt her body flush with perspiration despite the cool air. "The plot is implausible," she managed to say. "Rothenberg is trying to build a relationship between two characters who are such opposites that the whole concept is strained from the beginning. If you'd read the manuscript, you would agree."

"I did read it."

Phyllis' hands trembled; her mouth was dry. "When?"

"Yesterday," he said. "I wanted her to have her conference with you first, as a courtesy."

"How did you get it?"

"She gave me the first page, then fed me a few more. After that I was hooked. I was also angry. It's one of the best manuscripts this conference has had in years, and I was given junk! Why did you try to kill it?"

"What did you tell her?" she said, desperately wanting a drink.

"You know what I told her." His voice was hard and uncompromising. "Now answer my question."

They weren't far from the road that led to Clemens and the staff lodgings. It took every bit of self-control she possessed not to run from him, to flee to the safety of her room. But she knew, even if she did run, that he would follow her; he would press until he had an answer. "I don't think the novel will work. It's as simple as that."

"The truth, Phyllis," he demanded, grasping her shoulders.

"What right to do you to interrogate me like this?" she said, trying to twist away.

"I've spent my life writing and teaching. If I didn't believe there is honor in what I do, and trust, it would all be a sham."

"You sound like one of King Arthur's knights," she said caustically.

"Maybe," he conceded, "but that's how I feel and I refuse to apologize or be embarrassed. I'm asking again: why did you do it? You were given a remarkable manuscript, and you tried to destroy it and the writer."

"That's not true! I told her she was talented."

"And then you undermined her confidence until she lost faith in her judgment!"

"I gave her encouragement. Apparently she couldn't separate my criticism of her novel with my assessment of her ability. All she must have heard was the negative. In fact, I didn't even write on her manuscript."

She regretted the admission as soon as it was uttered. He stopped walking. They were close to the bridge over Barrier Creek; she could hear the water rushing over the stones. "You didn't write on the manuscript?" he said.

"It… it wasn't necessary. It… it would have been a waste of effort. I told you, I don't think the novel will work."

Pierce's face had the grim determination of a man refusing to accept a stalemate. "Diana Rothenberg is going to write that novel, and it will be terrific. It's hers, and I'm going to read everything you publish to make sure that it remains hers."

"How dare you imply…" She couldn't finish. It was impossible to say.

Her hesitation told him what he needed to know. "That isn't all I'm going to do. If I hear you are teaching creative writing anywhere, I'm going to write a discreet letter."

She began to shake. "You can't do this… I have to support myself...… I have to live."

Pierce winced as though he were the one being punished. "You've given me no alternative. What you were contemplating and your treatment of Rothenberg was heinous. I could never be sure it wouldn't happen again."

She was shaking uncontrollably. "Please, Michael…"

"I'm sorry," he said, "there is no other way."

Somehow she managed to get to her room and fill a glass with vodka. The liquor burned as it went down. She poured another glass and took it into the bathroom, where she opened the medicine cabinet and reached for a prescription container of Ambien. There were three pills in the plastic container. A low moan of hopelessness escaped from her throat as the container slipped out of her hands onto the tile floor.

The second glass of vodka calmed her. She went back into the bedroom and sat on the bed. Her whole life, everything she wanted and had worked for was lost. There was nothing now, she thought with an alcoholic grimace as she visualized herself sitting in front of a computer struggling for ideas that wouldn't come. The writing courses she'd taught the past few years at Temple had saved her, but they were gone, too. Emptiness. There was nothing left but emptiness.

She poured another drink, set it on the nightstand, then took off her clothes and went back into the bathroom. She stepped into the stall shower and let hot water run over her body. After she dried herself, she picked up her cosmetic case. The only razor she had was disposable, the narrow twin blades set at an angle in pink plastic. She tried to pry out a blade and cut her finger. She watched the blood well and drip onto the floor and started to laugh hysterically when the thought struck her that a cheap disposable razor had saved Roy Talbot the aggravation of trying to cover up a staff suicide. He didn't deserve his luck, the bastard.

She wrapped her finger in a wad of toilet paper, walked unsteadily into the bedroom, put on a bathrobe, and pulled her luggage out of the closet. It was a while before she unlocked the suitcase, where inside lay Diana Rothenberg's manuscript in an innocent manila envelope. Finally, between sips of vodka, she buried the envelope under clothes she removed from the closet and dresser. When the suitcase was full and the drawers empty, she looked around the room, nodding drunkenly to herself. There was nothing left to do but wait for dawn to drive to Philadelphia. On the second shelf in the medicine cabinet in her apartment there was a full container of Ambien. She would burn the manuscript first.

***

Atmospheric conditions had made cell phone communication erratic all day. When Nan found a message in her mailbox to call her husband, she told Agatha and Laura to go to the theater without her. "It's going to fill up fast," she said. "If you can, please save me a seat."

Although it was a weekday night and unseasonably cold, they had to move quickly to find three adjoining seats; Agatha put her tote bag on the seat next to her to save it for Nan. There were many unfamiliar faces in the unheated theater, people from all over Western New York who had come to hear the acclaimed novelist read. As she was glancing around, she heard someone say, "I hope that seat's for me."

It was Jerry Hofstrand. "It is," Agatha said, rising. She picked up the tote bag and set it on an empty seat behind them in the next row.

"I see you're dressed for the weather," he said.

She was wearing a white turtleneck and a burgundy sweatshirt that had the Axton College logo imprinted in white. The clothes softened her boniness and made her appear younger.

"Turtlenecks and sweatshirts suddenly appeared in the bookstore this afternoon," she said, unaware that the clothing, which had been reduced at the close of the spring semester to half-price at the Axton College bookstore, had been re-ticketed at full price and sent to the Workshop. "And they were a bargain: twenty percent off!"

"I think they look great on her," Laura said.

"So do I," he said.

Nan arrived several minutes before the reading was scheduled to begin. Agatha, who had been watching for her, stood and motioned toward the seat she'd saved. Nan inched past the people in the row. She was breathless; her color was high, her eyes sparkling. "My novel was accepted! My agent called this afternoon. I can't believe it!"

People around them turned to look at her. There was envy in their eyes, and awe, as if she'd announced that she'd just flown to the moon and back. Agatha clasped her hands. "Oh, how wonderful, how wonderful!" she exclaimed.

Laura and Hofstrand rose from their seats. "That's fabulous!" Laura said as Hofstrand offered his hand in congratulations.

Sitting five rows back Claire watched them, nearly overcome with jealousy and unhappiness.

The theater quieted as Pierce, carrying a cream-colored folder, climbed the stairs to the platform. Conversations ceased as every eye focused on the slender man wearing sharply-pressed khaki slacks, a red turtleneck sweater, and a navy blazer. Despite his gray curls and the lines around his mouth and between his eyes, he appeared almost boyish, a young man with a bounce in his step dressed for a cool summer evening on which he would be the focus of attention. It had been a risk to confront Phyllis before he was to read, but as difficult as it had been, he was relieved he had done it rather than let it nag at him as it had all afternoon. The worry over what she planned to do was gone; he was rid of it, his mind was clear.

After he set the folder on the lectern and adjusted the microphone, he reached into the pocket of his blazer and surreptitiously removed a stub of pencil which he concealed in his palm. He would use the pencil while he read, marking passages or phrases that sounded awkward to his ear with a magician's sleight of hand; no one in the audience would be aware of what he was doing. Later he would find each mark, then revise and revise, reading the sentences to himself until he could live with them. Never truly satisfied, he wouldn't read his books after they were published; on every page he would find a word or a sentence or a paragraph he wished he had written differently. When he finally relinquished galleys to his editor, he considered a book abandoned rather than completed. No work of fiction, he believed, was ever really finished.

He was as eager to begin as his audience was to hear him. Although readings are, in every sense, performances, and he did not enjoy performing, he wanted to observe their reaction: to see, hear and feel their response to his work. It was for them that he labored and he would observe the results, his successes and his failures, in their faces. They would give as much to him, perhaps more, than he was giving to them.

"I shall read from a new novel, which is still untitled," he said. "When I start with a title, I always change it later, so this may be an omen of some kind. Whatever it means, I don't think a title is necessary for what you will hear tonight."

He took a sip from a glass of water which had been placed on the lectern and began…

"He said his name was William Caine. He came into town on foot the third Monday in September, a steamy, overcast day more like mid-August. He had no money, no identification. He claimed he'd been beaten and robbed while he was camping out at Noah's Ridge. It was hard to guess his age. Tall, rangy and full-bearded, he could have been anywhere from his late twenties to his mid-thirties. A diagonal gash across his cheek and a nasty bruise on his forehead testified to his claim that he'd been beaten. But he also said he'd never been in this part of Pennsylvania before. A stranger wouldn't know the name of the land folks around here call Noah's Ridge, which is a good distance from the highway and ends jutting out twenty feet above the river like a wedge of pie.

"There were three of us getting gas at Phil Stanfield's Sunoco station that morning. It was early, and as I mentioned before, hot. Caine asked if we knew of a place where he could find work before we thought much about Noah's Ridge. He said he'd do just about anything but he preferred to be outside."

Nettles leaned back in his chair, his eyes gleaming as though he'd stumbled onto treasure. The old-stranger-in-town story, he thought, smiling to himself. The most traditional of beginnings—worn, tired, used for centuries. There was nothing Pierce could do with that story that hadn't been done before.

Nettles' smugness was short-lived. As Pierce continued to read, the people in the theater were drawn deeper and deeper into his story. They sat entranced, like children listening to a fairy tale; nothing short of fire could have forced them from their seats. Not only was the fiction packed with the elements that have captivated listeners since man learned to tell a tale—strong characterization, vivid description, drama, and an intriguing plot promising a satisfying resolution—but Pierce read his work exceptionally well, using his bass voice as a skilled musician plays an instrument, conscious of phrasing and rhythm and, above all, the melody, the story he had to tell. When he was finished an hour and fifteen minutes later, the audience rose, applauding wildly. Despite their discomfort from the cold, they would have gladly sat longer listening to the man to whom they were giving a standing ovation.

"I'm definitely going to buy his book when it comes out," Hofstrand said.

Laura smiled. "I think we all are."

Nan was surrounded by people congratulating her and asking her questions. "Are you going to stay?" Hofstrand asked.

Agatha shook her head. "It's Nan's moment in the spotlight."

"Then let's go to the Shed for some hot chocolate, my treat."

"Thanks, but go without me," Laura said. "I'm going to try to get some sleep."

As they were leaving the theater, Agatha noticed Leila sitting alone, waiting for Pierce who was engulfed by well-wishers. She seemed shut out of his triumph, Agatha thought, just another bystander waiting her turn.

After they finished their hot chocolate, Hofstrand walked Agatha to Tabard II. "I hope you don't mind if I ask you a question," he said, focusing his flashlight on the path ahead of them.

"Not at all."

"You seem so knowledgeable that I'm curious: how many degrees do you have?"

"Four," Agatha said reluctantly. "After I got my Masters in education, I decided to get one in English just for my enjoyment. Going for the last degree seemed to follow naturally."

"That's impressive. You should be proud of what you've accomplished, yet you seem to be embarrassed."

"Maybe I've known too many people with doctorate degrees who use the title *Doctor* in front of their names to tell the world how smart they are. I'm not saying all of them are self-important, but a fair number of them are. To me, all any college degree means is that an individual has attended a college and completed the required work; it doesn't necessarily mean that that person is bright. The smartest person I've known in my life was my uncle, and all he had was a high school education. But he was highly skilled—a tool-and-die-maker—and tremendously creative and sensitive to the world around him. He was my mother's sister's husband. My mother used to lord it over my aunt because my father wore a suit and tie to work, but it was my uncle, not my father or my mother, who saw how difficult my childhood was and who made me feel that he saw something special in me. When I was young, I thought that his understanding came from the fact that he had an unpopular, old-fashioned name—his name was Horace—like I did. But as I got older, I realized how quick his mind was, how keen his powers of observation were. I was the only one in the family who wasn't surprised when federal agents came to his house because he had drawn plans for a primitive nuclear reactor that he had sent to some government agency, trying to be helpful. It happened years and years ago. They had a hard time believing that a man with a high school education had done it."

Hofstrand turned off the flashlight, the lights shining from Tabard II making it unnecessary. "Agatha, you're truly special," he said, leaning forward to kiss her.

It was a tentative kiss, a tender kiss, a kiss of hope and promise. It was Agatha's first kiss and she was nearly breathless with happiness.

***

Alone in his office, Talbot gulped down the last of the scotch in his glass. Twice he had reached for the telephone and hadn't been able to pick up the receiver; the hesitations had cost him what little courage he had left. The awful expression on Polly's face had been with him all evening while he was hosting the Cruickshanks and other outsiders who had come to hear Pierce read. Not once during the nineteen years of their marriage had he considered the possibility that she might discover one of his infidelities—he had always been so careful, so circumspect; nor had he ever contemplated the possibility that she might leave him. She was the one constant in his life: steady, reliable, always there when he needed her. Happy memories of her and the girls at birthday parties and picnics flashed through his mind, each one making his eyes mist as he was reminded of what he could lose. He couldn't argue away what had happened. The only advantage he had, he believed, was that he knew Polly well, better than she knew herself; she needed the security of their marriage as much as he did. If he emphasized the strengths of their relationship instead of dwelling on his mistake, she would forgive him.

Be positive, he told himself as his hand encircled the receiver. But his finger moved uncertainly over the buttons, as if engaging each number required great effort, more than he was capable of giving.

Polly answered on the second ring.

"Pol," he said, "I tried to call you late this afternoon."

"Meredith told me."

Polly's voice was calm, a good sign, he thought. "Where were you? I was worried that you might have had an accident."

"I stopped to see Parker."

Talbot gulped. Parker Kenley was their friend; he was also their attorney. "How is Parker?" he asked with forced cheerfulness.

"He's sending you a letter. You should get it tomorrow morning, Federal Express."

The receiver jumped in Talbot's hand. "A letter? What kind of letter?"

"I'm filing for a separation. Parker's letter will explain everything."

"I don't want a separation!" Talbot's voice rose hysterically. "We have the girls, the house!"

"The girls and the house aren't a marriage."

"I'm sorry, I said it all wrong. I'm too upset to think clearly. I love you, Pol. You're my wife. We've been married for nineteen years, *nineteen years*. How can you even contemplate destroying everything we've built together?"

The receiver crackled in his ear while he waited for her reply. "I'm not the one who destroyed it."

She hung up. The click was distinct, a final, unarguable ripple of sound. "It was a mistake," he shouted into the dead instrument, "a mistake."

He wiped tears off his face with the back of his hand. She can't do this, he thought, she can't. He'd call Parker now. No, he'd wait for the letter, then call and tell him what he could do with it! Damn that Parker! How could he have considered that bastard his friend!

Sniffling, he picked up the bottle of scotch, then put it down. He'd force Polly to be reasonable. He wouldn't allow her to file for a separation; he'd fight every step she took. But now he had to be calm. The conference was almost over. Tomorrow night he would give his manuscript to Nettles. He had to be cool and self-assured, in control. If there were the slightest hint of desperation about him, Nettles would sense it. He couldn't let anything affect him, not even Polly, that would jeopardize the publication of his poems.

***

Webb's roommate, Dan Hecker, had left early in the morning. "I've had enough lousy food and freezing my ass off," he'd said after he'd finished packing. "You need help. I don't know what those pills are that you take, but they're not working."

Hecker's departure on the day of Pierce's reading was confirmation to Webb that his assessment of the dentist had been on target from the beginning. As for Hecker's medical advice, it was unwelcome and rejected. Webb was glad to see him leave.

After the reading, he and Diana went to his room. They had sex twice within the hour, and he was again aroused. "No," Diana said when he tried to ease himself between her thighs.

He kissed her while trying to separate her legs with his hand, but her knees were clamped shut. "You're spoiling the celebration," he said.

"I'm tired," she said, "and you should be saving your energy for your conference."

"I have more than enough energy!"

"I know," she sighed wearily. "But you should go over your manuscript so you'll be as prepared as possible. I've been hearing about Greene's conferences; he's supposed to be merciless. People have left because of what he's said to them."

"They allowed him to intimidate them, like you let Baran try to destroy your novel. He can't do that to me because I won't let him! I can defend every line I've written. I also have a good idea of what he thinks of my work: it offends his delicate sensibilities. He's the worst kind of hypocrite, mean as hell, but he doesn't let his meanness come out in his poetry. He's like a cat hiding its claws. Frost was the same type—just as mean and also petty—but in his poems he was a simple country boy, a real pussycat. I write about life as I know it. I don't leave anything out!"

"Then why did you come here to have Greene read your work?"

"He's brilliant and one of the best craftsmen around, maybe the best. I have some questions that he can answer."

He reached for her breast. "We still have time," he coaxed.

Diana had other things on her mind; for days she'd wanted to ask him about Yale. "The poem you wrote about the professor flying through the window," she said. "Did that really happen?"

He didn't reply right away. "Yes," he said finally.

"Is that why you left Yale?"

He leapt off the bed. "I wasn't taking medication then. I had the problem I told you about but I didn't know it. The guy was an unbelievable asshole! He had no business teaching anything! He wouldn't have been hurt if the window had been open. He landed in the bushes; the room was on the first floor."

"Did you try to get readmitted?"

"They wouldn't take me back, and they put it on my record so I couldn't apply anywhere else. I went there a year later with a letter from a doctor, but they refused to read it! At the time I was on so much medication that I accepted what they said without a peep. I just put the letter back in my pocket and went home. For a while I didn't write at all. I couldn't. The pills had killed everything!"

"What did you do?"

"What I'm doing now," he said, pacing up and down the room.

"I started cutting lawns to earn some money and it grew into a small landscaping business. In the winter I plow driveways. The work isn't bad. It's honest, I'm outside, and I can limit my customers so I have time to write."

He stopped pacing and looked at her excitedly. "I could expand the business, hire people, buy another truck!"

Diana knew what he was thinking. "Don't," she said, reaching for her clothes. "You shouldn't be concentrating on anything but your poetry."

"It wouldn't take much effort. I could support us easily. We could write in separate rooms. It would be great! Think of the feedback, the…"

She gently put her fingers on his mouth. "Thank you for what you're suggesting, but I need to be alone for the next few years to finish my novel."

"You'd be alone all day."

"I need to be completely alone, to be by myself with my characters."

"That's ridiculous! All writers have lives outside their work. Wallace Stevens was an insurance company executive; William Carlos Williams was a doctor…"

She gazed up at him, only half-listening to his persuasive arguments. He was extraordinary, exciting and gifted. She had never known anyone like him and was sure that she wouldn't again. But she couldn't live with him. His explosive energy would enervate her until she had nothing left to give to her fiction. "I'll probably regret this for the rest of my life," she said, her eyes filling with tears, "but I have to say no."

She dressed quickly, Webb still trying to persuade her to live with him. He'd marry her, if that's what she wanted. Her face was streaked with tears when she ran out of the room.

He started to pick up his jeans, then dropped them and went after her. Two men coming in the front door intercepted him. Webb tossed them aside as if they were pillows. "You can't run around here bare-assed," one called after him. "You should be locked up."

The threat forced him back. He didn't give a damn about propriety. He wanted Diana. But he also wanted his conference with Aaron Greene.

There were unopened bottles of wine on the dresser. He

uncorked one and drained the bottle as if it were water. Then he reached for another bottle, accidentally knocking his medication onto the floor. The pills rattled in the plastic container as it rolled under his bed; he didn't check to see where it finally landed. He hadn't taken an Eskalith since Tuesday, or maybe Monday. He couldn't remember and didn't give a damn.

***

Pierce walked into Clemens looking for Leila; he had already looked in the Shed and she wasn't there. His nose was red from the cold and his face was lined with exhaustion. He went up to Sara, who was sitting with Stoddard. "You were great tonight," Sara said. "You've got a winner."

"Thanks," he said. "Have you seen Leila?"

Sara shook her head. "Make yourself a drink and pull up a chair."

If Stoddard hadn't been there, he would have asked if she had seen Nettles, whose absence in the cottage was conspicuous. "Another time," he said.

Sara's eyes glinted at the refusal of her invitation. "I don't ever remember Clemens being as empty as it is this year. It seems *everyone* is busy, even Leila. She was here this afternoon, but she only stayed a few minutes, then left with Eric."

He reacted to Sara's remark as though it were a general, passing observation. But when he was outside he broke into a run, and when he stepped onto the porch at Hawthorne, he lurched forward as a searing pain shot across his chest. No, he thought, terrified. It can't happen now. He had a book to finish, work to do. He needed another ten years. Even eight, he'd take eight. Or seven.

The pain left as quickly as it had come. He stood under the porch light checking for numbness in his left arm. There was none. He breathed cautiously, as if the shallow movement of his lungs would fatally jostle his heart. It must have been heartburn, he thought, or a freak muscle spasm. But he climbed the stairs to his room slowly, his legs stiff with fear, his skin pasty.

Wearing one of his sweatshirts over her nightgown, Leila was in bed reading. "I couldn't wait for you any longer," she said. "I was freezing. Didn't you see me trying to get to you through the crowd?"

"Later," he said, going into the bathroom to take his pulse.

The light was out when he came back into the bedroom; he undressed in the darkness and crawled between the freezing sheets. His pulse was elevated, he thought, but within a normal range. He'd have to be more careful, avoid any stress. That business with Phyllis was harder on him than he'd realized. Worrying about Leila and Nettles hadn't helped. Maybe he should start meditating, eliminate every pressure in his life and concentrate on his work and achieving a state of tranquility in which nothing would bother him. That had to be the key. His father's heart attack had hit at a time of stress. Tonight was a warning. He had to have another ten years…

***

❧ WORKSHOP BULLETIN ❧

VOL. 74, NO.9   THE CLYMER WORKSHOP   AUGUST 19 2004

GOOD MORNING!

Finally the sun will shine on us again in what promises to be a beautiful day.

MORNING PROGRAM

9:15 A.M. Workshops
(Aaron Greene, Merle Ackerley)
10:15 A.M. Panel on Character
Development
(Michael Pierce, Andrew Cox,
Marshall Stoddard)
11:15 A.M. Manuscript
Conferences

AFTERNOON PROGRAM

2:00 P.M. Workshops
(Sara Newkirk, Phyllis Baran)
3:00 P.M. Manuscript
Conferences
4:00 P.M. Manuscript
Conferences
6:00 P.M. Cocktail party on the
terrace

EVENING PROGRAM

Marshall Stoddard will read. His most recent book is *Places At The Table, A Memoir*. He is also the author of *Sport of Kings*, a history of the sport of horse racing, and a novel, *Old Flames*. A well-known critic, he is the book editor for *Sir Magazine*.

YOU'RE INVITED!

Relax this afternoon so you'll be rested and ready for the farewell cocktail party, which will begin at 6:00 P.M. on the terrace.

BOOKSTORE BONANZA

Everything in the bookstore will be discounted at fifty percent off. The sale will run as long as the merchandise lasts, so hurry in for fabulous bargains!

TIPS

Please don't forget the waitresses who have graciously served you. Your contribution should be placed in an envelope and deposited in the specially-labeled box in the Workshop office. A contribution of fifty dollars is suggested, though anything additional would naturally be welcome. The donations will be divided equally among the young women.

FOUND

There are a number of miscellaneous articles which have been waiting to be claimed in the Workshop office. This is your last chance to retrieve any items you have been missing.

CHECKS

We regret that we will no longer be able to cash personal checks.

DEPARTURES

Van service to the airport will be running every hour from early Friday morning to mid-afternoon. The times are posted on the bulletin board outside the Workshop office. Since the vans have limited space, please sign up today for the time you wish to leave so that you will be assured of transportation. Allow an hour of traveling time from the Workshop to the airport. The transportation charge will depend upon the number of people in the van; money should be paid to the driver upon arrival.

FRIDAY MEAL SCHEDULE

Juice, donuts, coffee and tea will be available in Hackett Hall from 6:45 A.M. until 10:30 A.M. A full lunch will be served at noon, after which the kitchen will be closed. The snack bar in the Shed will be open until 2:00 P.M.

TIDBIT

"I've decided to write all my poems about poems. It's the only subject that's left."

*"I'd rather learn from one bird how to sing
than teach ten thousand stars how not to dance"*
ee cummings

Chapter IX

Leila didn't get out of bed until nine thirty. She'd heard the alarm go off and Michael wash, dress, and leave for breakfast, but there was no point in getting up. There was nothing for her to do, nowhere to go and no one with whom she could spend the day. Michael would be on a panel, have his conferences, jog and write; his hours would be as full as hers would be empty. All she had to look forward to was her visit with John Gustafson tomorrow. She thought about last night, how Michael had left dinner without an explanation; she'd come back to the room and waited for him, but when he returned and she'd asked him about it, he'd said, "Later." And after his reading he didn't so much as glance in her direction. He had more than earned his triumph, but she'd felt like a faithful dog left waiting until its master was ready to leave. She gave him what he wanted and needed because she loved him, but she too had needs and desires. She wanted a baby and she would have to make him understand that having a child meant as much to her as his writing meant to him. If he still refused, their marriage was over; she couldn't live in the house in Connecticut and see the empty rooms everyday without her resentment turning into hate.

After she showered and dressed, she walked to the Shed for breakfast ignoring the bright sun and cloudless sky. Eric Nettles was sitting at a round table near the snack bar eating a bagel spread thick with cream cheese. "Good morning," he said cheerfully. "I've been hoping for company."

She couldn't avoid joining him after she got her coffee and toast. Charming as ever, Nettles lightened her mood and she was smiling when Michael saw them.

He had come to the Shed for orange juice before going to the theater to lead the panel on character development. If Leila and Nettles hadn't been sitting at the table where he had sat with Sara the previous morning, his reaction might have been different. But they were sitting at the exact table, and his highly-developed visual memory, a gift which served him as a novelist, went immediately to work. Seeing them triggered an image of Sara's deep frown after her observation that Leila was keeping busy. *A woman as beautiful as Leila will never lack for attention.* The sight of them, the image flashing into his mind, Sara's words, all took no more than a second or two. He turned and left.

Leila, who was listening intently to Nettles amusingly describe a disastrous reading, didn't see him and started to laugh.

***

Holding an envelope that had just been delivered by Federal Express, Dee Dee knocked on Talbot's closed office door. Although she was curious about the envelope's contents, she wished someone else could give it to him. He'd been in a foul mood all morning, and since she was now counting the hours until she resigned, she had neither the patience nor the desire to cope with his behavior. In fact, since Polly's departure yesterday, she'd had to force herself to be civil to him. It was almost as if Polly's discovery were hers as well; in her manner and attitude she was much like a betrayed wife who had long suffered through an unsatisfying marriage.

Talbot accepted the letter wordlessly, his face as expressionless as if she were handing him an advertising circular. But after she left he tore the envelope open. Inside there was a second, cream-colored vellum envelope with the return address of Parker Henderson, Attorney at Law, printed in the upper left hand corner. His hands were trembling when he finally unfolded the letter.

She can't do this! he thought, leaping out of his chair when he finished reading. The house was as much his as it was hers! He'd put hours of backbreaking labor into making it the finest Victorian in Axton. There wasn't a wall he hadn't papered or painted; he'd spent hours refinishing the woodwork and floors. He wasn't a tenant she could evict! And she had no right to separate him from his children! They needed a father as much as a mother.

He stopped pacing and picked up the telephone. That bastard Parker was going to have every word of his letter thrown back at him!

Parker Henderson was with a client. Talbot barked at the

secretary to interrupt him. She refused. He slammed the receiver down and called back fifteen minutes later, unable to restrain himself a second longer. The secretary put his call through.

"How are you, Roy?" Parker said.

"I just got your fucking letter! There's no way you're going to keep me out of my home or away from my children!"

"I can understand your being upset," Parker said calmly, "but I think you'd better consider this situation more reasonably. I'm speaking now as a friend."

"Some friend!" Talbot interrupted.

"Look, Roy, as Polly's attorney I really shouldn't be speaking to you at all. As long as I am, it's in your best interest to listen to what I have to say."

"Like hell it is! You want to evict me from my house, separate me from my kids, saddle me with all their expenses so I won't have a nickel left to live on, and you have the gall to tell me to listen to you!"

"You have two choices," Parker said crisply. "If you return to the house, Polly will go to court to get an order which will force you to leave, and you will have antagonized her to the point where reconciliation will be close to impossible. Your best alternative is to stay away for a while until she cools off. Then you might have a chance at working things out."

"It's my home!" Talbot yelled. "My children! She has no right to do this! I won't let her!"

"Get an attorney," Parker said. "Maybe he'll be able to help you see this clearly. Goodbye."

The receiver clicked hard against his ear. Enraged, Talbot threw the dead instrument against the wall.

Startled by the crashing sound, Dee Dee, who was working on the computer, jumped. She thought of the letter, the contents of which were now easy to guess. Polly wanted a divorce. She smiled bitterly, forgetting the years she had waited for this to happen. He's getting what he deserves, she thought, feeling strangely empty.

***

Talbot stood outside the arched entrance to Hackett Hall waiting for the Pierces to arrive for lunch, his narrow shoulders hunched with tension. A woman who was scheduled to have her conference with Phyllis Baran at eleven fifteen had come into the Workshop office a few minutes before noon, complaining that Baran hadn't showed. He'd sent Dee Dee to the novelist's room, where she had found the dresser drawers and closet empty. Baran was gone. Now he had to find a replacement for the afternoon workshop. There were also three conferences that would be impossible to reschedule; no one would be willing to take them on such short notice. He'd have to refund the money, which he would take out of Baran's check. He'd also deduct a healthy amount for the workshop, and he'd enclose a letter telling her exactly what he thought of her irresponsible behavior. She would not be invited back! First Parker's letter, then this, he thought, forcing himself to smile at people greeting him as they walked into the dining room. He should stand somewhere else, but he couldn't chance missing Pierce.

The Pierces were among the last to arrive. "Michael,' Talbot said, intercepting them. "I'm sorry to do this but I have to ask a favor: could you take Phyllis' workshop this afternoon? She left without giving notice."

"Sorry," Pierce said, accepting the news without a flicker of emotion.

"Then you'll do it?" Talbot said, not sure if Pierce's *sorry* was for Baran's behavior or a refusal.

"Get someone else. I headed the panel this morning."

Talbot's face reddened. "After all these years, I thought I could count on you. I have to announce a replacement before lunch is over."

"You'll find someone," Pierce said, following Leila into the dining room.

Talbot grabbed his arm. "I'll remember this next year."

Pierce shook his arm free. "There isn't going to be a next year, Roy. I'm not coming back."

Three pieces of calamitous news in one morning. Swaying as if he were ill, he stepped into Hackett Hall. The odor of onion turned his stomach. He scanned the room, his eyes settling on Andrew Cox. He went to Cox's table, bent down, and spoke briefly to the novelist. Cox nodded.

Talbot walked to the center of the dining room and raised his arms. "There has been a change in the afternoon program," he announced. "I regret that Ms. Baran had to leave unexpectedly. Mr. Cox will be taking her workshop. Those of you who were scheduled to have manuscript conferences with Ms. Baran should report to the Workshop office after lunch."

He ignored a few raised hands and went directly to his office, where he poured a full glass of scotch. He'd have Dee Dee write refund checks for the manuscript conferences. As for Pierce, he had plenty of time to replace him, the ungrateful bastard. He wouldn't think about Polly until tomorrow. What he needed now was a breather. He'd take the afternoon off, relax and rest, maybe read some Coleridge; nothing could occur that Dee Dee couldn't handle. Tonight was the staff party and he would give Nettles his manuscript. He was almost there, so close he could smell the new binding on his book.

He raised the glass to his lips and took a deep drink. The liquor went down with a pleasant burn.

***

Stoddard was aggrieved that he was forced to put himself in a position in which he would have to literally risk his life to protect his reputation. All morning he'd thought about lucky people who were born with gifts, people who were given beauty, talent, brilliance, creativity, athletic grace. Others, like himself, had to work hard to earn whatever they achieved, with no help outside of their own perseverance. He was smart, not brilliant, and what he lacked in talent he compensated for with tenacity and a calculated shrewdness, using his position as a critic to pick unknown writers who would become winners under his spotlight, a gift tied with a string of obligation. His life, his career, all he had was his hard-earned reputation, which was in jeopardy unless he went through with his plan, which was to put himself near death. He wasn't a fool: he was aware that it was dangerous, but in moments when his courage faltered, he thought of the public embarrassment of Phyllis Baran's reading and felt that he had no alternative.

The timing was critical. He'd had a shot of insulin early in the morning and had taken a double dose at noon; to ensure that the plan would work he had skipped breakfast and lunch. He had barely participated in the panel on character development, letting Pierce and Cox carry the program while nodding his head occasionally in agreement with what they were saying. When he entered Clemens at one thirty, he was lightheaded and sweating. There was no one in the cottage! He collapsed in a wicker chair near the door, panicking. Too late he realized that he hadn't considered that it was the last full day of the Workshop and that his colleagues might be too busy with final manuscript conferences and packing to spend time in Clemens. He had counted on people being there after lunch… someone… anyone… who would call the nurse. She might administer something to help him, but he would insist upon her calling an ambulance to take him to the hospital. But the cottage was empty!

He was so lightheaded it was hard to think about what to do next… tired, he was so tired… the light seemed to be fading, going in and out like a badly focused camera… he had to get up, he had to try to get up… to get up…

When Ackerley walked into Clemens forty-five minutes later for some fortification before his conferences, he found Stoddard face down on the floor unconscious and was unable to rouse him. He ran to the back of Tabard II where an addition was attached to the building like an afterthought; above the door there was a white sign with INFIRMARY printed in red letters. The nurse, Cynthia Randall, a plain woman whose long brown hair was held with a clip at the nape of her neck, listened to his description of Stoddard skeptically. She'd been a nurse for thirty-three years, fifteen of them in an emergency room, and had never been in a place where there were so many uptight people; for almost two weeks she had heard unending complaints from rashes to headaches to constipation described as though the sufferers were critically ill. Still, seeing the urgency in Ackerley's face, she rushed with him to the staff cottage.

Stoddard's pulse was dangerously rapid and weak. She noted his bulk and the clamminess of his skin. "Do you know if he's a diabetic?" she said.

Ackerley shrugged and shook his head.

"I don't see a medic-alert bracelet, but he may have a chain around his neck. Help me turn him over."

Sara Newkirk walked in carrying the materials for her conferences as they were trying to move him. It took the three of them, pushing and grunting, to roll Stoddard's body onto his side. They found a stainless steel chain, which had been buried in a deep fold in his neck. "He's in a diabetic coma," Randall said after reading the medallion on the chain. "I thought he was a diabetic from his symptoms and the size of him. We need an ambulance right away. He has to be treated with intravenous glucose for hypoglycemia as soon as possible."

Neither Sara nor Ackerley had cell phones with them. "Neither do I," she said. "Go to the office and have someone call. Stress that this is a dire medical emergency."

"How dire?" said Ackerley.

"This is no time for questions," she snapped. "He could die before the ambulance gets here, or he could survive with permanent brain damage. Hurry!"

Ackerley wasn't a man given to self-doubt, but as he rushed to the office he thought of Gwen and the unaccustomed feelings of guilt he'd been carrying since her death despite trying to convince himself that he didn't have a significant role in what had happened to her. Although he disliked Stoddard, who had openly snubbed him since the conference had started, he was doing his best to help the fellow. After he entered the office and told Dee Dee, he watched incredulous as she called Talbot to report what had happened before calling the ambulance. "I know," she said after Talbot told her to make sure to instruct the ambulance driver to turn off the siren when he entered the road to the Workshop.

Concerned that he could be blamed for Stoddard's problem if something were to go wrong, Ackerley was livid. "The man could die! Why in the hell did you call Roy instead of an ambulance?"

"It's the procedure here," she said. "I'm calling the ambulance now."

"Your fucking procedure might have killed him!" he said, storming out of the office.

He didn't have much time to get the material for his three o'clock conference, but he stopped at Clemens first. Sara was still there. "The woman in the office called the director before she called the ambulance," he said pointedly. "Is he going to be okay?"

"He's barely hanging on."

"Sorry I can't stay with you. I have a conference."

"You've done all you can," the nurse said. "Thanks."

Sara left with him. "I don't doubt you, but it's astonishing that Dee Dee called Roy before she called the ambulance."

"Astonishing isn't the word I'd choose, but that's what

happened. I was standing there listening when she made the call," he said. "If you have any doubts, you can check with her. She'll tell you what she told me, that it's the procedure. All I can say is God help anyone who needs critical emergency treatment here."

It took four men—Talbot, the ambulance driver and two attendants—to place Stoddard on the collapsible gurney. Ackerley, who had cut his conference short, arrived as they were putting him in the ambulance. Sara arrived after he was inside. "How is he?" she asked.

One of the attendants picked up Stoddard's wrist to take his pulse; frowning, he used a stethoscope to check his heart. "He's gone," the fellow said, removing the needle that was feeding him glucose so he could put a sheet over the body.

For once Sara's inscrutable expression vanished; her fleshy features seemed to melt together in shock. Ackerley turned to Talbot. "This shouldn't have happened. The ambulance might have been here in time if the call had been made right away."

"A few minutes wouldn't have made a difference."

"Sometimes just a few seconds does," Ackerley said, leaving for his next conference.

***

While Ackerley and the nurse were struggling to roll Stoddard over, Leila had been trudging up the stairs in Hawthorne, her legs tired from the walk she had taken. Usually she enjoyed walking, but even the bright summer day didn't lift her mood. She felt as if the decision she'd made had forced her to a place from which there was no turning back, that by insisting upon what she wanted— what she knew was right—she might destroy her marriage to the only man she'd ever loved. When she'd passed Clemens, she'd hesitated and then continued on, afraid that Eric would be there; she'd resisted him yesterday but didn't trust herself to resist him today.

Pierce was sitting at the desk, staring at his laptop. He had started working after lunch, and he hadn't written a single sentence worth saving; since he had experienced the searing pain in his chest he had been able to think of little else, with the exception of Leila and Nettles. Instead of seeing his characters, visualizing them in his mind alive and fully-fleshed, as real and familiar to him as his own hands, he could see nothing but Leila and Nettles sitting together at the round table in the snack bar, Nettles cocky and self-assured, Leila laughing. His effort to remain calm had yielded a consciousness of his beating heart and visions of his wife with the man whose fiction he detested.

She sat on the bed and took off her sneakers. "I think we should talk."

He turned and looked at her sharply. "About what?"

"You left dinner abruptly last night and you've hardly spoken to me since. Where were you?"

"I could ask you the same question: where were you last night?"

"And I'll answer it! I was waiting for you outside the theater, freezing."

"I was with Phyllis," he said reluctantly. "I had a hunch she was planning to steal Diana Rothenberg's novel, and I was right. I looked for you in Clemens after the reading, but you weren't there. Neither was Nettles."

Leila stiffened. "I came back here and got into bed."

He shrugged and turned back toward his laptop.

"If you start typing, I'll leave!" she said. "I'll pack and be out of here in ten minutes! Then you can write without interruption. You can hire someone to do your errands and take your calls and you can have sex with one of your groupies when you're in the mood!"

He shot up, knocking the desk chair over. "That's unfair!"

"You have no right to talk to me about fairness. We don't do anything unless you want to do it. Our lives revolve around your desires!"

"Tell me about your desires," he said. "You can start with Nettles."

"I've spent time with him," she admitted, coloring. "He's charming and entertaining. He's also anxious to sleep with me, but he hasn't succeeded."

Pierce rubbed his chest. "I shouldn't have said anything. Let's drop it."

She watched him pick up the chair and sit down. He started to type. Shaking, she went to the desk and closed the laptop. "You don't believe me."

"There's been talk," he said, unable to look at her.

"Sara?"

He nodded.

"What did she say?"

"That you've been spending time with him. I saw you together in the Shed this morning. You were laughing, enjoying yourself."

"I went for breakfast and he was there, so I ate with him. It would have been rude to sit at a different table. If I was laughing, it's because he's good company," she said, her eyes flashing. "He treats me as though I'm a human being."

"What's that supposed to mean?"

"You have time for everything that's important to you—your work, running, teaching. I get whatever's left, which is next to nothing. You don't even talk to me: the proof of it is that I didn't know about Phyllis. You didn't say a word about your suspicion."

"There wasn't time and I wanted to be sure before I said anything."

"You had time to talk to Sara, who is a manipulative bitch! She plays all of you against each other to her advantage. If she can't find trouble, she makes it to get everyone to rally around her. She did her nasty business to Merle Ackerley and then to Phyllis, and she still wasn't satisfied, so she started working on me."

"That's not true! Sara is a good friend."

"A good friend doesn't make a husband doubt his wife!"

He knew she was right, but the suspicion that had been eating away at him made it impossible to acknowledge. They glared at each other, stunned by the longest and most bitter fight they'd ever had. Both proud and stubborn, neither was willing to apologize. Then Leila spoke. She knew that it was the wrong time and that he would become even angrier, but she didn't care. It had to be said, and like it or not he would listen. "I want to have a baby, Michael. I know I agreed not to have children…"

"You're incredible!" he interrupted. "A few minutes ago you admitted that you've been enjoying another man's company, and then you bring up a subject that you promised never to mention again!"

"I enjoyed being with Eric and I explained why: I was lonely and he was there. As for breaking my promise, I realize now that I shouldn't have made it. We weren't married then. I didn't know what my life would be like."

"Are you telling me that you haven't been happy?"

"I love you and I'll always love you, but that isn't enough," she said, tears welling in her eyes. "You have your work, which comes before everything else; nothing is more important to you. It hurts to know that I come second, but I understand. What I want is for you to understand me. I need something for myself."

"You've managed to keep busy."

"Yes," she said bitterly, "I've managed. I put almost as much energy into fighting boredom as you put into your books."

"Boredom is no reason to have a baby!"

"I want to hold and love and raise our child. That is what I was meant to do with my life. I'm a nurturer. I've nurtured you since we've been together."

"No!" he said emphatically.

"Why?" she demanded. "You must have a reason!"

Because he'd be dead before the child's tenth birthday, he wanted to say. Because if the child were a male and inherited his genes, he'd be giving him a death warrant for a legacy. Because last night he'd had a pain in his chest which had told him in no uncertain terms how close the end was. But he could say nothing.

"Why don't you answer me?" she sobbed.

He took three thick manila envelopes off the desk. "I have conferences to go to," he said.

He walked toward the Studio, misery deepening the lines around his mouth. It was too late to promise to be a better husband, to spend more time with her, to make her feel included in his work. She wouldn't believe him if he told her that the years they had been together had been the most secure and productive of his life because of the love and comfort she had given. The novel he was writing now, which had been going well until he saw her with Nettles, was already in trouble; suspicion had made him drop the thread, and if she left him, he could lose the book. Even a day lost was more than he could spare. A divorce would upset his balance completely.

The classroom where he was to meet Dynarski was at the far end of the narrow hallway in the weathered shingle building. He had scheduled his two most difficult conferences—Dynarski's and another with a woman to whom he would have to explain that her manuscript, a cliché-ridden family saga filled with poverty, illness, and occasional, preposterous strokes of luck, was contrived and frankly not worth further effort—before meeting with Laura. He sat on a student desk and removed two short stories and three chapters of a novel from one of the envelopes. Frowning, he flipped through the pages of the short stories, refreshing his memory by reading comments he had written in the margins. This was going to be a rough conference, he thought, knowing the writer's history without having met him. Each sentence had the stamp of an MFA program on it. The writer had been through an academic mill, maybe more than one, and had the anonymous voice that issued from those places—short, punchy sentences, psychic distance, no narrative thrust. Dynarski's stories were first-person pieces told in the present tense, ambiguous fragments of angst-filled prose which were neither whole nor satisfying; they weren't even interesting as fragments.

Pierce was skimming the first chapter of the novel with irritation (there were no commas or semi-colons) when Dynarski entered the room. Dynarski's broad jaw was tight, his gray eyes eager behind the thick lenses of his glasses. "Have a seat," Pierce said, vaguely recognizing him for standing out in the groups he'd taught for some reason that he couldn't recall.

Dynarski chose a student desk opposite the novelist's and hunched forward, indicating that he was more than ready.

"You have a degree in creative writing," Pierce said, more as a statement than a question.

"Yes, an MFA," Dynarski said. "I've also been to Bread Loaf and Bennington."

Pierce nodded to himself. "How long have you been writing?"

"Eleven years."

"Do you still have any of your early stories, the ones you wrote before you enrolled in a writing program?"

Startled, Dynarski sat up. "I threw them out after my first semester," he said. "Why?"

Pierce rubbed his chin. "I wish there was an easy way to say this, but there isn't. You've put a tremendous amount of effort into the material you've given me and it shows, which is one of your problems."

"What do you mean?" Dynarski interrupted.

"Your work is too polished. *Style* is stamped on every sentence. The shame of it is that I don't think these sentences are your style, your unique, individual form of expression. Instead of hearing your voice, I'm hearing some teacher telling you how to write."

Dynarski's jaw shot forward. "What's wrong with my sentences?"

"They're all short, they're tight, they don't breathe. If you talked the way you write, you'd speak all the time in groups of four to eight words, which is unnatural."

"The editors of *The New Yorker* and *The Atlantic Monthly* don't object to short sentences."

"Short sentences are effective when they flow naturally from a writer, which isn't the case here. What you're doing is writing with a formula. You went through an academic factory and came out with its imprint on you. The two stories you gave me have *creative writing program* written all over them—no plots, unresolved endings, poignancy interspersed with banality, and the requisite moments of epiphany, one to each story."

Dynarski stared at the novelist, his jaw muscles working furiously.

"It's a shame you threw out your early stuff because comparing it with what you're doing now might help you. I've written comments on your manuscripts which repeat what I've just said. I'm sorry, but I can't do much with what you've given me."

"You don't understand! I've worked my ass off! I see stories published all the time that aren't as good as mine—stories without plots, stories that have unresolved endings. They're published every day. I know you push plots, but that doesn't mean what I'm doing is wrong. There is a market for my work. I don't want your criticism! I need you to get my stories to an editor. That's why I came here—for a break. I want my chance and you can give it to me."

"You don't honestly believe that I can get your stories published!"

"You're damn right I do!"

"Well, you're wrong! I have no influence over editors' decisions. If I did, I still wouldn't be getting letters of rejection."

Dynarski's jaw dropped. "I don't believe you!"

"My agent has been trying to place one of my short stories for four months. It's a strong story and she hasn't found an editor who will take it."

"Your novels are accepted!"

"Yes, I've been lucky; however, others on the staff haven't been as fortunate. I know for a fact that one writer has had difficulty placing each of his books."

"Who?"

As much as he disliked Stoddard for hassling him over the review he had written of Stoddard's book, Pierce wouldn't break a trust. "The writer told me in confidence. I can't betray that."

"All I'm asking for is a chance." Dynarski's voice broke; he blinked hard and swallowed. "I've worked for eleven years. I have no pull, no connections. A few phone calls or a letter from you will make them look at my work."

"Connections won't get you published. The best advice I can give you now is to stop writing for a while. Put your energy into whatever it is that you do to support yourself."

He handed the manila envelope to Dynarski and started walking toward the door.

"Wait!" Dynarski said. "You don't understand!"

Pierce turned. "I do understand," he said. "However, you must understand that you'll have to change your attitude and forget the formula you're using, neither of which you seem willing to do. Even if you were willing, I'm not sure that it's possible."

"I don't want to do anything but be a writer."

You and thousands of others, Pierce thought, you all want to be writers regardless of whether or not you have a grain of talent. "I gave you my honest opinion," he said. "I can't do anything more."

Dynarski clenched his powerful hands, but he didn't stir from his seat until Pierce was gone. Then he got up and slammed the door shut so hard that the thin-walled building shook. Tears were streaming down his cheeks but not a sound issued from his mouth. He started to pace up and down the room, moving back and forth across the groaning floorboards. His face was contorted with rage, with misery, with the bitterness of defeat. He had done all the right things, gone to all the right places, he thought, as Pierce's words played over and over in his head.

The room was stifling. He went to the window to raise it and glimpsed the Circle Theater sitting placidly in the sunlight; beyond he could see the dark, heavy timbers of the Tabard Inn. *Put your energy into whatever it is that you do to support yourself.* His mouth twisted vindictively.

Dynarski's eyes were dry and his face was composed when he left the Studio. He stopped on the path before he reached the road and looked back at the cedar-shingle building as if he were contemplating buying it. Again, his mouth twisted. He continued on until he could see the barn-like Shed, the clapboard building that housed the laundry, the oddly-shaped theater, the looming Inn and its namesake, Tabard II. This place would go up like a tinder box, every damn board in every damn building, he thought, the lenses of his glasses reflecting the sunlight like mirrors.

***

Aaron Greene limped across the porch to his cottage and sat down after descending two steps, easing his arthritic body onto the warped porch floor. He placed his carved cane beside him, put on a pair of reading glasses, and opened a folder which contained Webb's poems as casually as if he had just awakened refreshed from a long afternoon nap. His movements were calm and deliberate, giving no indication that he had, within the past hour, told a man who had traveled from England to attend the Workshop that his poems weren't worth the effort of consideration. He had spent less than twenty minutes with the fellow, making no effort to hide his disdain, before he limped away leaving the man too stunned to protest the ill treatment he had received.

The pages in the folder fluttered in the warm breeze. Greene had read Webb's poems several times; lines were marked with penciled slashes and arrows, words were crossed out, comments were meticulously written in the wide margins. After finding and quickly scanning the closing stanzas of Webb's longest poem, *Asylum*, Greene closed his heavy-lidded eyes, remembering his meeting with Spencer Holcomb, an editor who had befriended him many years ago. He recalled his fury at the spare, bespectacled man who had told him that his poems were self-pitying, that he would not succeed as a poet until he stopped whining. Never had he been so angry! But Holcomb had been right: poetry was not the place to nurse private wounds. Today he planned to say to Webb what had been said to him. Webb had the gift, a dazzling potential which would not be realized until he expunged every trace of self-pity from his poems. He would make Webb furious and then direct that anger like a laser, burning the whine out of the young poet's voice as if it were a tumor. There was no other way. The time would come when Douglas Webb would be as grateful to him as he was to Spencer Holcomb.

Greene didn't consider the possibility that he might not be able to handle Webb's anger. Familiar with Webb's poems, he was well aware of the young man's turbulent history, which did not impress him as being of consequence. Eager poets had been coming to him for better than forty years, and he had never had the slightest difficulty bending them to his will, no matter how upset they became, if he felt it was necessary. Webb had a rare talent worth shaping. This was the only conference he had scheduled that he had looked forward to; he had deliberately waited until today, saving the best for last as a reward for having had to work through the others.

Greene nodded at the giant striding up the path to his front porch as if he were seeing a younger, larger, strong-limbed version of himself.

Webb's eyes were burning with manic intensity. He hadn't taken his medication for better than forty-eight hours. Excited and agitated for days, he had been functioning on two hours or less of sleep a night. Last night, after Diana had refused to marry him, he had been unable to sleep at all. Instead, he had tossed on the lumpy mattress, devising wild arguments to make her change her mind. Running three miles at dawn hadn't diminished his energy. He had been more restless than usual during the morning programs, and at lunch he would have thrown a heavy trestle table at a man with whom he was arguing if Diana hadn't stopped him. The argument had been about William Carlos Williams' poetry, although Webb couldn't remember an hour later what the man had said that had infuriated him. His mind was racing at incredible speed: thoughts, images, ideas were coming to him in rapid succession, all with the brilliance of fireworks. Oblivious of the effect of his behavior on others, it seemed to him that everything he said, everything he did was justified. Perfect. *Exquisitely appropriate.* Never in his life had he felt better or more sure of himself. He was not only omnipotent but invulnerable.

Greene gestured for Webb to sit down beside him on the porch. Webb, however, wasn't taking suggestions; there was another matter he intended to discuss before his poetry. "You cheated those people in the workshop this morning," he said, towering over the elderly poet. "They paid to have you teach them and you didn't even attempt to fulfill your obligation!"

"They were given my opinion of their potential as poets, which was full payment as far as I'm concerned," Greene said dryly. "They wouldn't have benefited from anything more."

"How can you make that judgment when you aren't familiar with everyone's work?" Webb demanded, his voice rising. "There could have been people in that workshop with tremendous potential. Even if there were only one or two, they were entitled to your help!"

"They were given an excellent lesson: they were shown by example not to waste their time on drivel," Greene said, giving Webb the legendary glare that had made generations of novice poets shrink. "You have two choices: you can either calm down and sit here so we can discuss your poetry, or you can take your manuscript and leave."

Amanda Greene, who had been dozing in a chair inside the cottage, was awakened by their angry voices. She got up, a frail woman whose skin was jaundiced from years of heavy drinking, and walked slowly to the screen door to see what was happening. She watched the tall young man reluctantly sit beside her husband on the front porch. Usually she ignored Aaron's conferences, but she decided to listen. There was nothing else to do and it would keep her occupied so she wouldn't be tempted to have a drink; she'd already had a stiff one after lunch and didn't want to have another until dinner. She'd had three drinks yesterday, and if she could limit herself to two drinks today, she'd be ready for her visit with her sister in Buffalo tomorrow. Two drinks (maybe three) a day while she was in Buffalo would keep her steady until they went back to California next week.

"I have some questions," Webb said, unaware of the elderly woman watching him from behind the screen door.

"Later," Greene said. "First, you're going to listen. You're a gifted young man, but you'll never amount to anything as a poet until you stop whining. Lick whatever wounds you have privately. Don't use your poetry to shock people, to frighten them. And don't ever write lines like *My skin is soaked in the sweat of terror*, which is a blatant cry for sympathy. Or worse, *My mind teeters over the edge of an abyss*, which is sheer melodrama."

"Those lines are honest! That's what I felt!"

"You aren't the first person who has suffered; nor will you be the last. Poetry isn't the place to put on a private horror show."

"Poetry is about life! I won't compromise what I've experienced!"

Greene sighed. "No one cares what you have experienced."

"I care!" Webb exploded. "It's my poetry and I won't let anyone tell me what I can or can't write about! You said in your lecture that poetry depicts experience. I write about my experiences as honestly as I can, without compromising!"

Greene raised his eyes as though his patience were being tried unnecessarily. "I also said in my lecture that the experience must be carefully chosen. A poet must be selective. You urinate and defecate. You have vomited. Do you intend to put those *experiences*, as you call them, in your poems or are you going to keep them in the toilet where they belong?"

Webb grabbed Greene's shirt. "You're the one who craps on people, not me! You're arrogant and cruel! You don't give a damn about people's feelings! You sit on your high perch and shit for enjoyment on anyone who comes near you!"

Amanda Greene, who had been gazing at the hills debating whether she should have her drink before or after dinner (she didn't think she could last until after dinner, but here was the long evening to consider), hadn't been listening to what they were saying. Webb's shouting drew her attention. She looked down and saw the young man holding her husband by his shirt, shaking him. Aaron's head was bobbing back and forth as if it were going to snap off. Alarmed, she grabbed the nearest object she could use as a weapon to defend him, a nearly fully bottle of gin, which was on a table near the door.

Webb, still shouting, didn't hear the screen door open; nor did he sense her standing behind him, raising the bottle. But when Greene called out to her to stop, she paused as Webb turned and shot up. The bottle flew out of her hands with a resounding CRACK, smashing across Webb's temple. Amanda fell backward, landing in a pool of gin and glass.

It happened so quickly that the Greens sat motionless for a moment, Amanda afraid that the crack she'd heard meant that her hip was broken so she wouldn't be able to go to Buffalo, Aaron waiting for the giant sprawled over the porch steps to rise so he could give him the tongue lashing he deserved. But Webb didn't get up. He lay with his head at an angle, his temple washed in blood from above his ear to his eye.

Greene picked up his cane and rose stiffly, feeling the effects of the shaking he'd been given. He stepped around Webb and, leaning on his cane, offered Amanda his hand. She got up gingerly, as if she weren't sure her bones would support her, and stood trembling in her floral-printed housecoat. She reeked of gin. "Are you all right?" he asked.

"I don't know," she said, her voice quavering. "I thought I might have broken my hip, but I can stand." She held out her arms to examine them. A jagged piece of glass was caught in the parchment skin below her right elbow. Wincing, she plucked out the glass. "What a nasty young man! The least he can do is clean up this mess before he leaves."

Greene poked Webb in the ribs with his cane, but Webb didn't stir. He poked him again, harder. "Why doesn't he get up?" Amanda said, her pale blue eyes happening to focus on the label sticking to the broken bottle. "That was my gin!"

She babbled about her gin while Greene stooped to take Webb's pulse. "I have to get help," he said, releasing Webb's wrist.

"What about my gin?" she cried.

Greene looked at her with unconcealed disgust. "Get yourself cleaned up," he said.

When Greene limped into the infirmary, Cynthia Randall was writing up what had happened to Stoddard, which she planned to include in her final report. "There has been an accident," Greene said. "A fellow is out cold on my porch. His head is bleeding."

This time Randall didn't take any chances. After she grabbed her emergency kit, she dropped her cell phone into her shirt pocket and they left.

"How did the accident happen?" she asked.

"My wife came out on the porch to offer him a drink. He didn't see her behind him and stood up, knocking her down. His head hit the bottle she was holding."

The nurse's feet itched to move quickly. Greene's pace was so frustratingly slow that by the time they approached Barrier Creek her patience was gone. "I think I'd better go on ahead. Where exactly did the accident happen?" she asked.

"At the cottage just past the first curve, the one with the red-shingle roof."

She was finishing taking Webb's vital signs when Amanda, fortified with a generous shot of her husband's liquor, came out of the cottage wearing a clean housecoat. "Are you the nurse?" she said, holding a folded scarf against the arm she was cradling. "I can't get this cut to stop bleeding. It's been bleeding since I took the glass out. I fell, you know, I landed hard but I didn't break anything, nothing that I am aware of. That fellow was shaking Aaron; he was shaking him so hard that Aaron's head was bobbing. Awful fellow. That's why I came out with the bottle. It was the first thing I could grab."

"What were you planning to do with the bottle?" Randall said, unaware that Greene had come up behind her. She raised Webb's eyelids to look at his pupils.

"She was going to offer him a drink like I told you," he said, glaring at his wife. "Get in the house, Amanda. The nurse will take care of your cut later."

Randall was only half-listening. Webb's pupils were both dilated, and one was larger than the other. He definitely had a concussion. She took the cell phone out of her shirt pocket, called 911, and told them to send an ambulance as quickly as possible. When she was finished she looked for Greene, but he had followed his wife into the house and had shut the door firmly behind him.

Diana was in the Shed when she heard the siren; she'd been waiting for Webb and he was late. Instantly, she sensed that whoever the ambulance had come for, he was involved. She ran, ignoring the unspoken rule that participants weren't welcome on the other side of Barrier Creek unless they were in the company of someone on the staff.

Two husky attendants were strapping Webb onto a gurney when Diana arrived at Greene's cottage. Talbot, who had been in his office, also ran, arriving within seconds after she did. "What happened?" Diana said, looking first at Webb, then at the nurse and the blood and the broken glass.

"I'm sorry, but I can't permit you to stay here," Talbot said, furious that the nurse hadn't followed the emergency procedures she'd been given. She'd been told when she was hired that any calls for emergency vehicles must be placed through the Workshop office. He put his hand on the shoulder of one of the attendants. "I want you to take him to Colden Hospital."

"I'm going with him," Diana said.

Talbot stepped forward. "That's impossible."

"If you try to stop me, you'll have two people on stretchers," she said, climbing into the ambulance.

She moved aside to give the attendants room to place the gurney. Webb's eyes were closed; his skin was a lifeless white.

"How far is the hospital?" she said.

"About seventy-five miles," said the taller of the two attendants. "It's a private hospital outside Axton."

She gasped. "Why so far?"

He tipped his head toward Talbot. "That's what the man ordered."

Diana looked at the gauze covering Webb's temple. "How is he?"

"Not good," the attendant said.

***

Waiting for her conference had made the day seem endless to Laura. Early for her meeting with Pierce, she sat in an empty room in the Studio thinking about Agatha's last words to her: *Believe in yourself as much as I believe in you*. After spending so many days at the Workshop, it was hard to know what to believe other than that it was impossibly difficult to get published. Greg was still calling every day, and answering his call had become tempting; it would be so much easier to say yes to him than to struggle to find an agent, to hunt for a new job, to establish a new career. She remembered the vow she had made before she came here that she would never again allow herself to feel like a loser. She thought about Gwen and all of the disappointed people she'd met. A woman she talked to today had been trying to get an agent for three years and had spent most of her vacation money coming here instead of going on a cruise with her husband; her conference had been with Michael Pierce and he wasn't encouraging. It was as if she were getting a message, repeated over and over again: it is a risk to hope, if you hope you will be crushed.

Pierce was on time. "Would you like to go to the Shed and get something cool to drink? We could relax in comfortable chairs," he said. "It should be fairly empty; most people will be getting ready for the cocktail party."

They heard an ambulance siren as they entered the Shed, which was empty as he predicted. "I don't believe I've ever heard a siren here before," he commented. "It must be serious."

"It's the second ambulance today."

"I didn't hear another one, and sound really travels here."

"The siren wasn't on," Laura said. "I happened to see it as it was leaving. It was for Marshall Stoddard. I heard that he died. Apparently he'd been in a diabetic coma."

Marshall, dead. It didn't seem possible. Again, as he had last night, Pierce became painfully conscious of his own mortality. "I didn't know," he said hollowly.

They settled into overstuffed chairs with glasses of lemonade. After taking a long drink, Pierce put his lemonade on a low table in front of them and removed her manuscript from the manila envelope. "What you've given me is remarkable. You drew me into the story right away, and your voice gets stronger with each page," he said, studying her. "How long have you been writing?"

"Three years," she said. "That's how long it took me to write the novel."

"From the outline you gave me, you've written a moving book about good and evil. It's especially moving because the main characters are orphaned children who are struggling to stay together and survive. What gave you the idea for the story?"

"Both my parents were dead by the time I was eighteen. I was an only child, which made losing them even more devastating. Although I had some distant relatives, I truly felt as if I were alone in the world. I was lucky because my best friend's family kind of adopted me, but there were still moments when I was almost overwhelmed by the loss and felt sorry for myself. I didn't want to be a self-pitying person, so when those moments occurred I would think of all the advantages I had—friends, an adopted family, enough money to get an education—and how much worse my life would be without them. That kind of thinking became a habit, and I suppose the novel somehow took seed from it."

Pierce nodded. "You have a strong imagination. Your sentences are solid and well-crafted, but I'd like to see you push yourself. In your next book, write full paragraphs that are one long sentence; write a full page, maybe two pages, that is one paragraph."

"I'm not sure there will be a next book."

He sat forward in the chair. "You're not serious!"

"Writing the novel was a personal challenge: I wanted to see if I could do it, and I'm proud of what I've done. At first I was practically euphoric, but what I've learned since that time has almost made me regret that I ever had the idea for the story.

"It's almost impossible to get an agent, and without an agent it's even harder to get an editor to read my manuscript. Yesterday morning an agent came here, and he was so mobbed by people that the poor fellow looked like he wanted to run. But even if by some miracle I was able to get an agent and my novel was accepted, I was told that it's a mid-list book; and without a powerful champion, mid-list books usually don't go anywhere, they simply disappear. If that happened, I doubt I'd get a chance at another."

"Who told you that?" Pierce asked sharply.

Laura hesitated. She remembered Pierce's review of Stoddard's book, and how Stoddard had taken the credit for Pierce's success, but there was no way she could avoid answering. "Marshall Stoddard," she said finally. "He told me that I'd regret it when I rejected him, not that it makes any difference now."

"And I imagine he told you that his review was responsible for my success," Pierce said, continuing without waiting for her reply. "There's no question that his review of my second novel gave it a substantial boost, but other reviews contributed as well. Unfortunately, Marshall didn't think of it that way; he had an exaggerated sense of his own importance.

"I can't tell you that mid-list books have a great chance of success, but for you to simply walk away without trying would be a tremendous waste."

He reached for a pencil that someone had left on the table and wrote on the manila envelope before handing it to her. "There's my agent's name, address and telephone number. I'll be talking to her early next week, and I'll tell her about you. I won't forget, I promise."

She took the envelope from him, her face lit with gratitude and excitement. "Thank you!" she said.

"I forgot to ask: what is the title of your book?"

"I don't have one yet," she said. "Nothing I've thought of so far seems right."

"Make sure you have one, even if you aren't in love with it, before you submit the manuscript, so that an agent or an editor doesn't pick it for you."

They left the Shed together, Pierce sensing that despite referring her to his agent and talking about submitting her manuscript he still hadn't completely convinced her. Then he thought of Stoddard and the idea came to him. "Marshall was supposed to read tonight," he said. "How would you feel about taking his place? You could give a brief synopsis of your first chapter and then read the second and third chapters."

His proposal was so unexpected that Laura's emotions swung from hope to fear. "I… I don't think I'm ready to read. Besides, I'm only an observer."

"That means nothing," he said. "It's just a label. You came here because you wanted to be a writer. Has that changed?"

She thought about all the anxious, unhappy people she'd met and her fear of becoming like them. But after the encouragement he had given her, she had to answer, "No."

"Then let's go to the cocktail party and find Roy. Unless he has someone else lined up, it will be almost impossible for him to refuse if you're with me."

Talbot was waiting to have his glass filled at the table where waitresses were serving wine. He knew his alcohol intake for the day was broaching the point of excess, but he was able to rationalize it because of the calamitous day he'd had—first Parker's letter, then Baran, Pierce, Stoddard, and Webb. Nothing was working for him, not even the old superstition that bad news usually comes in threes. So when Pierce and Laura approached him, he braced himself. "I heard about Marshall," Pierce said. "Do you have someone to read tonight?"

Talbot looked at him suspiciously. "Are you offering?"

"This is Laura Belmont," he said. "I'm offering to introduce her tonight. I've read the first three chapters of her novel, and they're outstanding. I have them here if you want to read them."

"Laura and I have already met," Talbot said, nodding to her. He looked at the envelope and saw the agent's name, address, and telephone number that Pierce had written; to his knowledge, the novelist hadn't recommended even one participant to his agent or editor in all the years he'd been coming to the Workshop. "I'm sure it is outstanding, but a participant has never had an evening reading."

"She's an observer, not a participant, and having her read would go a long way toward ending the Workshop on a positive note, which it sorely needs."

"I'll make the announcement at dinner," the director said, leaving them without taking the manuscript.

"I'm not sure I'm ready for this," Laura said.

"Once you start to read, you'll be fine," Pierce assured her. "You'll be in familiar territory, reading sentences that you've read countless times."

He raised his glass to her after a waitress served them wine. "To Laura, who is going to have a long career writing moving books that have strong plots and strong characters."

"Thank you," she said, feeling as though she had stepped into a dream.

***

A need to fill the evening program wasn't the only reason Talbot was willing to let Laura read; in past years the last reading hadn't been well attended. Some people were getting together with friends, others were packing, some went to bed early to be rested for a long drive home. So Talbot was surprised when he entered the Circle Theater and saw that it was filled. If Stoddard had been reading, at least a quarter of the seats would have been empty.

Laura, dressed in the black linen slacks and white sweater she had worn when she went out to dinner with Dynarski, was sitting in the front row between Agatha and Nan. Her pulse was racing and her mouth was dry. It was insane to have agreed to do this, she thought. What if she read too fast? Too slow? What if her voice didn't carry well? What if the conference members didn't like her work?

As if aware of her thoughts, Agatha, who was wearing the nicest summer outfit she'd brought to the conference, a simply-cut linen skirt and matching blouse in robin's egg blue, patted Laura's arm. "Trust me, you'll do just fine," she said. "I know you will."

Promptly at eight, Pierce walked up the platform steps to the lectern. "Tonight it is my pleasure to introduce Laura Belmont to you. Laura is here as an observer. Although I haven't had the privilege of reading her entire manuscript, I have read an outline and three chapters of what I believe is a compelling novel. Her book addresses the twin themes of good and evil that have occupied serious writers for centuries. What makes her novel particularly moving is that her main characters are orphans who are thrown into a world where they are at the mercy of strangers. But I have probably said too much already. Please welcome Laura," he said, extending his hand to her.

She rose stiffly and tried to force a smile that wouldn't come. By the time she was standing behind the lectern, she was wishing that she hadn't written the novel. After Pierce adjusted the microphone, he put his arm around her. "Relax and breathe," he whispered in her ear. "Give the introduction that we talked about and then pretend you're reading aloud for your own pleasure. It works every time."

"My novel doesn't have a title yet," she began, her strawberry-blond hair gleaming under the lights. "It takes place in a mostly rural area outside Chicago at the beginning of the twentieth century. The novel begins when a fourteen-year-old boy, Galen Riordan, wakes with an earache. He goes into the hallway and hears voices, so he stands at the top of the stairs to listen and hears his mother arguing with Duff O'Reilly about money from his father's livery business. O'Reilly and his father had been partners. After his father's death, O'Reilly said he would buy out his father's share of the business, but he has stopped making payments.

"Galen knows his mother is worried about money. He also knows that she's afraid of Duff O'Reilly, a big, fierce-looking man who has the florid complexion of a hard drinker. When Galen reaches the doorway to the kitchen, he sees O'Reilly holding his mother by the neck with one hand. With his other hand, he pushes her head back. There is a horrible cracking sound. O'Reilly lets go of her and she slides to the floor.

"He sees that O'Reilly has killed her and he runs from him, grabbing coats off hooks to throw in O'Reilly's path. O'Reilly stumbles and crashes to the floor, out cold. Galen moves fast. He hurries upstairs, gets dressed, and then rushes to his little sister's room. His sister's name is Betsy and she's seven years old. He gets her up, wraps her in a comforter, and carries her out of the house. He knows O'Reilly will find him if he stays in town so he must leave. He has no close relatives and no idea of where he should go.

"O'Reilly had come with a horse and an open two-seat buggy that belonged to the livery. Galen brushes snow off the seat. He tells Betsy that they're going for a ride, and they head off into the bitter winter night."

Laura paused to take a sip of water. "Their journey begins with the second chapter," she said, "when they come upon Crazy Gertie."

Just articulating the name—Crazy Gertie—evoked an image in Laura's mind of the old woman sitting on her porch in the dark with a shotgun resting across her lap. By the time she finished reading the first sentence—"*Galen had no way to estimate how long they'd been traveling*"—she had settled into her story.

***

Diana walked determinedly to the nurses' station on the second floor in Bradford Hospital, which was located a few miles northeast of Axton. A stocky, middle-aged nurse who was writing on a chart glanced up. "Visiting hours are over," she said briskly.

"I came here in an ambulance hours ago with Douglas Webb, and I would like to speak to his doctor."

"Were you injured?"

"No," Diana said. "I want to know Mr. Webb's condition, and I want to see him."

The nurse found Webb's chart and scanned it. "His doctor won't be in until tomorrow morning."

"Then I want to speak with a resident," Diana insisted. "I haven't been able to speak to anyone about him."

"Mr. Webb's condition hasn't changed since he was admitted. The best thing for you would be to go home and come back tomorrow morning."

"I'm staying at the Clymer Workshop," Diana said with frustration. "I have no way of getting back there. I'm the only person within hundreds of miles of this hospital who gives a damn about Douglas Webb. Please let me see him."

The nurse looked at Diana with new interest. "Are you a writer?"

Diana nodded. "Please help me."

"When I get a chance, I'll talk to the resident."

Diana thanked her and went back to the waiting room, a cheerless alcove at the end of the corridor furnished with vinyl-upholstered chairs in dreary shades of yellow and green. The resident arrived a half hour later. He was of medium height and build and badly in need of a haircut. "You wanted to speak to me about Mr. Webb?"

"What is wrong with him?"

"He has a concussion."

"Will he be all right?"

"It's too early to tell. The blow was severe."

"I want to see him," she said.

Webb's head was swathed in gauze, and he was being fed intravenously. Above him, a gray machine that looked like a small television was displaying a zigzag green line; wires connected to the machine were taped to his chest. "What is that?" Diana asked anxiously, pointing to the machine.

"A cardiac monitor."

"Is something wrong with his heart?"

The resident looked at the green line. "His heart's okay."

Diana noticed a lounge chair in a corner of the room. "I'd like to stay with him."

"Sorry, it's against the rules."

"I came from the Clymer Workshop. I have nowhere else to go."

She stood by the bed in the semi-darkness after the resident left, watching the steady movement of the iridescent line on the screen of the cardiac monitor. She had never seen him so still. It was as if the machine were taking the life out of him, using his energy to keep the green line going. She took his hand in hers. "It's Diana," she said. "I'm here. I'm going to stay with you. If you can't open your eyes or talk, just squeeze my hand. Please try, please."

There was no response from the hand cradled in hers.

***

A table in Clemens had been set up to hold a platter of jumbo shrimp with cocktail sauce, a tray of imported cheeses, a basket filled with an assortment of crackers, and a hollowed watermelon filled with fresh fruit. Afraid that he would appear insensitive in light of Stoddard's death, Talbot repeatedly explained to everyone who entered the staff cottage that the food had been ordered several days ago for a farewell staff party and had already been delivered when Stoddard died.

Although he had been a constant presence in Clemens, no one was talking about Stoddard or sharing stories about him as people usually do when a friend or colleague dies; not even a brief reminiscence was spoken that would pay a small tribute to his life. Instead, everyone with the exception of Dee Dee, who was attacking the shrimp, and Sara Newkirk, who was cutting a generous chunk of Brie, was standing around the bar talking about

Laura's reading. When Cox congratulated Talbot for using her as a substitute, Pierce looked at the director sharply. "It was Michael's idea," he said with more graciousness than he felt.

Talbot didn't touch the food at the buffet table. He decided to stay close to the bar, reasoning that after Nettles had something to eat he would eventually want to refresh his drink. The moment finally came. "Could we speak outside for a few minutes," he said after Nettles replenished his glass with ice and a generous splash of vodka.

The warm ground meeting the cool night air caused a mist which was fragrant with the scents of spruce and pine. Nettles stood on the porch, inhaling deeply. "I'm going to miss this invigorating country air," he said. "It's like a tonic, great for sleeping."

"Yes," Talbot agreed, breathing shallowly. After planning and scheming for months to reach this moment, his courage was faltering. He rubbed his damp palms together in an effort to appear nonchalant. "I've just completed a poetry manuscript, my third. Normally I'd submit it to my last publisher, Wren Press, but they're so disorganized that less than a dozen copies of my book were sent out for review. After having been burned, I want to be cautious this time around."

"That's understandable. Poetry is never easy, and without effort on the part of the publisher, it's impossible."

The novelist's response gave Talbot a boost of self-assurance. "I couldn't decide what to do until this morning, when I recalled that you are the adviser to the University of Wisconsin Press. I don't know why I didn't think of it before," he said with well-rehearsed ease. "I hate to impose, but if you could take the manuscript back with you tomorrow for consideration, I'd sleep easier knowing it was in safe hands."

Nettles' eyes shone like sharp yellow lights in the darkness; his face was inscrutable. "I resigned as adviser to the Press two years ago over a difference of opinion on editorial policy. I've had nothing to do with it since."

Resigned. Talbot tried to laugh at his blunder, but what came out were high-pitched bleats.

"I sent an old background sheet for your brochure. It was carelessness on my part, although that position really had no bearing on what you hired me for."

"No, no it didn't," Talbot managed to say. "You've done a fine job this summer, excellent. I hope you'll consider coming back next year."

"I promised my wife we'd spend the summer in France," Nettles said. "It's getting chilly. Are you going back in?"

"I will soon," Talbot said, not trusting his legs.

Nettles paused before he stepped inside. "Good luck with that manuscript."

Talbot's throat was too constricted to reply.

***

The Pierces were among the first to leave Clemens. "Why didn't you let me read Laura Belmont's manuscript?" Leila said after they were out of earshot from the cottage.

"I didn't finish reading it until this morning before the panel," he said, his memory of the bitter fight they'd had early in the afternoon still fresh.

This was the first night in a while that the temperature in their room was pleasant. "I'd like to get out early tomorrow morning," he said, starting to get undressed.

"I have an appointment with John Gustafson tomorrow at eleven thirty in Jamestown."

"Who is John Gustafson?"

"The son of the lawyer who wrote Benjamin Clymer's will. You encouraged me to find out what I could about Clymer, remember?"

"I'm sorry," he said. He crossed the room and put his arms around her. He rubbed her back, then her shoulders, but her body was unyielding. "I've had other things on my mind. The past few weeks have been difficult. Let's put what's happened behind us so we can enjoy the drive home."

"And everything will be the way it was: Michael and Leila Pierce will live happily ever after in their house in Connecticut."

"There's no reason why it can't be that way."

"Your fairy tale will have one of two endings," she said. "In one ending, Michael and Leila will go back to Connecticut and have a baby. In the other ending, Michael will live in the house alone, writing his books. Since you're the novelist, you decide. Which will it be?"

Despite her ultimatum, her voice was so naked with hurt and longing that he released her. "Leila," he said gently, "thousands of married couples choose not to have children."

She took a deep breath and held it for as long as she could. She would not cry. "That's true," she said finally. "But it's not my choice, and I can't live with yours. Maybe I could if you gave me a reason I could accept, but you won't even do that."

She turned away from him. He reached out to touch her, then let his arm fall.

***

Too excited to sleep, Laura was in bed mentally replaying the most exciting evening of her life, the huge ovation she'd been given, people rising and applauding as enthusiastically as they did for the staff writers, Pierce's broad smile and waving arm telling her that she was a success, conference members surrounding her afterwards, offering congratulations and promising to look for her novel when it was published, and Agatha, especially Agatha, whose eyes were brimming with tears of joy. Although she and Agatha had been friends for less than two weeks, she felt closer to the gentle schoolteacher than she did to people she had known for years. The intensity of the conference magnified everything, including friendship. She was fortunate to have met Agatha, who was so decent and intelligent, a truly remarkable woman.

Even Stan was happy for her. He told her that Pierce wasn't going to help him get published, and he didn't seem at all upset. He said he should have realized that Pierce wouldn't do anything for him because his emphasis was on mood rather than plot. Stan was relaxed and pleasant, completely different from the frustrated, bitter fellow she'd seen for days. His transformation reminded her of the eye of a hurricane, the calm center in a sea of turbulence. Stan's calmness was as absolute. Apparently she had really misjudged him.

She remembered what Agatha had said to her. "I know how hard it has been for you here, but I've never stopped believing in you and your talent, not once. I'm just so sure of it, and now you must be sure of it, too. You're going be one of the lucky ones to have a long career writing wonderful books. You must promise me that you won't quit."

She had given Agatha a qualified promise, that she would give it her best effort: she would try until either she succeeded or common sense told her to stop. At this moment, however, for the first time since her parents died, she was feeling truly lucky.

***

It was after midnight when Talbot wearily climbed the stairs in Melville. His face was haggard. When he reached his room, he paused and looked at Dee Dee's closed door. He could talk to her a while, not about anything in particular, just talk in general. Dee Dee had always worshiped him, which is what he needed now.

He raised his hand to rap on her door. At this hour she'd expect to have sex, he thought, hesitating. She'd been pining for him for years. Maybe if he kept his eyes closed and pretended she was someone else. No, he couldn't even then. He would just keep his distance; after all these years he shouldn't have any trouble handling her.

Dee Dee wasn't asleep. She'd been in bed mentally rehearsing her resignation speech. She also had a formal letter in the top drawer of her desk that she planned to give Talbot in the morning, but there were things she wanted to say to him that didn't belong in a letter. As she rehearsed, each grievance reminded her of another and another and another, insults and insensitivities which she had overlooked, hoping that one day he would return her love. The more she rehearsed, the angrier she became. She was feeling like a fool and thinking of Talbot as a bastard when she heard his knock on her door.

She put on a pink bathrobe she had bought months earlier after gazing into a dressing room mirror, wistfully imagining the moment he would see her in the confection that cost more than she could afford. But now the robe was another reminder of her stupidity, and when she opened the door she was shaking with anger.

"I'd like to talk," he said, thinking that she looked like a ball of cotton candy. He detested cotton candy.

"So would I."

He walked across the room, carefully avoiding the bed, and started to remove a plastic bag filled with dirty laundry which was on the desk chair so he could sit down. "Leave that," she said. "I was going to wait until tomorrow to tell you, but I've changed my mind. I'm quitting. My letter of resignation will be on your desk in the morning."

Talbot's eyes popped. "You're not serious. Heh, heh, you're joking."

"I assure you, I'm not joking! I'm tired of doing your dirty work. I'm tired of running and fetching for you. I'm…"

"Dee Dee," he interrupted, "I know you're tired. It has been a rough conference, the worst we've had. You need a vacation. Take next week off, go somewhere and rest. You can even take two weeks."

"I'm entitled to one week, which is the notice I'm giving, and I expect to be paid. It's the vacation I have coming!"

Talbot's mind reeled. If he still had the job as director, he couldn't run the Workshop without her… he couldn't even train someone to take her place… he wouldn't know where to begin. He half-listened to her recount an incident in which he had made an error for which she had taken the blame. From that incident, she went to another. He tried in interrupt her, but she was going on like a tape recorder that didn't have an *off* button. There was only one thing left for him to do, he thought, fighting revulsion.

The pressure of his arms around her made her stop in mid-sentence. He felt her sway. But then she looked up at him; his eyes were closed, his thin lips were compressed into a line of determination. "Get out of here!" she said, pushing him away.

"Please, Dee Dee, I need you."

She marched to the door and yanked it open. "Dee Dee," he tried again, half-hoping, half-dreading that she might reconsider.

"If I had a gun, I'd shoot you," she said.

***

Marian D. Schwartz

❧ Workshop Bulletin ❦

VOL. 74, NO.10   THE CLYMER WORKSHOP   AUGUST 20 2004

GOOD MORNING!

The weather forecast promises a warm, sunny day for traveling.

WINNER

Congratulations to Carol Harrison, the author of the following limerick, which was judged the best among many fine entries in yesterday's contest.

There was a young poet from Philly,
Who thought superstition was silly,
So he dressed like a cat,
And he hissed and he spat,
'Til they took him away willy-nilly.

MAIL

All first class mail will be forwarded.

NOTICE

Items left in the rooms will be combined with unclaimed belongings in the lost-and-found carton in the Workshop office to be sold at the annual Axton College lawn sale. Check before you leave.

TIPS FOR THE WAITRESSES

Please don't forget them!

PARTING WORDS

Thank you for your participation in the seventy-fifth Clymer Work-shop. We know that you will never forget the days that you spent here; nor will we forget you. We intend to keep in touch* and we are already looking forward to your letters. You are the Workshop, the reason for its existence and its continued success. Our best wishes go with you in all your endeavors.

* Every holiday season all observers and participants will receive an appeal for money to fund building maintenance and scholar-ships; each spring they will be sent a brochure and application. Only when a mailing is returned *undeliverable* is a name stricken from the master list.

The spirits of hills and rocks and trees and men are called oran-tas. When a man dies, his oran-ta and the oran-ta of the hill he
is connected to look the same.
Ancient belief of the Seneca Indians

Chapter X

Agatha was getting dressed when Laura knocked on the door to her room before seven o'clock. "The time of my flight was changed, and I couldn't leave without saying goodbye and thanking you for helping me get through these past ten days," she said, looking tired but happy. "I don't want to lose touch with you, *ever*. Your friendship has meant so much to me."

Agatha's eyes misted as she recalled Laura's acceptance of her from the moment they met. "I should be saying that to you."

At that moment Nan entered the room. "Saying what?" she wanted to know.

"We were talking about friendship," Laura said. "I'll miss you both."

"This place does foster strong bonds," Nan said with a chuckle. "I have an idea: we can have our own annual reunion! Can you come to Denver next summer and stay with us? We have plenty of room."

"I'm looking forward to it already!" Agatha said.

A strong sun had taken the chill out of the air when Agatha walked out of Tabard II to get breakfast. She was wearing a fresh white blouse and the same blue jumper she had worn when she traveled to the conference, but she looked entirely different in the clothes. It could have been her carriage, her shoulders no longer pitched slightly forward in reticence but set back in confidence; or it might have been the lightly yet skillfully applied makeup she had on; or perhaps it was the way she held her head, chin up, eyes meeting the world instead of cast down, hiding from it. She didn't expect to see Hofstrand rise up from a wood lawn chair to meet her. He was dressed in khakis and dark blue sport shirt. "Good morning," he said. "I was hoping you'd come out soon so we could have a quick breakfast together in the Shed. I signed up for the next van; it leaves in an hour, so we don't have much time."

"I'd enjoy that," she said.

He brought their breakfast to the table on a tray—juice, bagels and cream cheese, and coffee. "With all the excitement around Laura's reading last night, I didn't get a chance to talk to you. This isn't the atmosphere I would have picked for what I have to say, but it's too important to let slip.

"You know I was kind of shell-shocked after my wife's death, probably as much from feeling guilty as from the trauma of it, but I'm all right now. I'm looking forward to a new start, and I'd like it to include you. I can't remember when I've enjoyed a woman's company as much as yours. Unless I've badly misjudged, I sense that you feel the same."

Agatha nodded, smiling, too overjoyed to speak.

"I don't want you to feel rushed. We have plenty of time to get to know each other better. I know how committed you are to your job, so I can travel to see you. In fact, my sister who lives in Omaha invited me to come for Thanksgiving, and Lincoln isn't far from Omaha."

"There is a relatively new Strategic Air and Space Museum between the two cities that you must see!"

They talked about Thanksgiving and made tentative plans for Agatha to spend Christmas in Washington. The time passed too quickly. He walked Agatha back to Tabard II, where he kissed her goodbye. "I'll call you tomorrow," he said.

Agatha stood in a daze of happiness long after he was gone.

***

It was nearly eight o'clock when Talbot climbed the steps to Bradford Hospital. Sleeplessness and worry had carved dark hollows around his eyes. He had been up most of the night, tossing over his broken marriage, his crushed hopes for his manuscript, Stoddard's death, Webb's accident, and the resignations of Dee Dee and Pierce. He was less than five miles away from Axton, and his proximity to his home and family made Polly's legal action painfully real. He felt as if the scaffolding upon which he had built his life had collapsed, leaving him buried in the rubble, homeless and alone.

As he approached the reception desk in the small, tiled lobby, he saw Fred Hamilton coming out of the elevator. Hamilton was his personal doctor, as well as a neighbor and friend. Several times over the years he had discussed the possibility of a medical emergency at the Workshop with Hamilton and was confident that the doctor would cooperate. "Fred," he called, hurrying to speak with him.

Hamilton, a well-built man whose features were spare except for a rather wide, fleshy mouth, extended his hand. "I just left Douglas Webb."

"How is he?"

"Still unconscious," Hamilton said. "We're watching him closely. I've asked a neurologist to come in on the case, Peter Grant. You met him at our New Year's eve party last year."

Talbot didn't remember the neurologist. "Why hasn't Webb regained consciousness?"

"We don't know. If he doesn't come around by early this evening, we'll be dealing with a coma. The blow was severe. How did it happen?"

"It was a bizarre accident," Talbot said, his left eyelid twitching. "An old woman—the wife of a poet on the staff—was standing behind him holding a bottle. He didn't know she was there, stood up and met the bottle."

Hamilton frowned skeptically. "That is bizarre."

"The truth usually is," Talbot said with a nervous laugh.

"We haven't heard from any members of his family, which could present a problem. The young woman who stayed overnight in his room isn't a relative. Hospital policy frowns on that, you know."

"I'm taking her back to the Workshop."

"Then you aren't stopping at home?"

"No," Talbot said.

Diana was standing beside Webb's bed when Talbot came into the room. Her eyelids were swollen, her face drawn. "I've come to take you back to the Workshop," he said, jarred by the sight of the tubes and wires connected to the unconscious man. Webb was deathly still.

"I want to stay."

"I'm sorry, but the decision isn't yours to make. I just spoke with Dr. Hamilton. You broke a hospital rule by staying overnight;

it won't be permitted again."

The loathing in Diana's eyes made him step back. He saw himself as she was seeing him and experienced a surge of self-disgust. But then he thought of the trouble she could cause and his moment of self-revelation passed as swiftly as it had come. "He's getting the best medical care possible," Talbot said, thinking of the release Webb had signed absolving the Workshop of any responsibility for his welfare. "There is nothing you can do here to help him that isn't being done by professionals."

"I can talk to him. Talking is supposed to bring people out of comas."

"He isn't in a coma; he's unconscious," Talbot said firmly. "The strain you're putting yourself under has made you imagine that his condition is worse than it actually is. You must want to shower and change. You should also consider that the Workshop officially ends today after lunch; all the buildings will be closed by six o'clock. I don't know what your plans are for traveling home, but I won't be able to come back here for you. If you don't leave with me now, you're on your own."

She had left the Workshop with less than five dollars in the pocket of her jeans, which she had spent on candy bars and coffee. Her head bowed with defeat, she took Webb's hand in hers and squeezed it before reluctantly following Talbot out of the room.

They drove back to the Workshop in silence, Talbot keeping his eyes on the road. Diana sat stiffly in the passenger seat of the beige Camry, hating herself for leaving Webb and detesting Talbot for allowing her no alternative. She didn't trust herself to speak without screaming until they were driving on the road that led to the campus; the trees looming on either side of them felt oppressive, suffocating. "How was Doug hurt?" she said.

"It was an accident," Talbot said, prefacing his explanation.

Diana listened with growing disbelief until he was finished. "She deliberately hit him with the bottle."

"No, she didn't!" Talbot said emphatically. "Mrs. Greene is an old woman; she can't weigh more than one hundred pounds. It would be physically impossible for her to inflict that hard a blow, particularly to someone the size of your friend. If you doubt me, I'll introduce you to her."

"Please."

They went directly to the Greene's cottage after Talbot parked the car behind Melville. Amanda Greene came to the door dressed in a faded purple housecoat, her arms and legs sticking out of the voluminous garment like sticks. Diana shook the elderly woman's dry, trembling hand and apologized for disturbing her.

***

Leila checked the drawers and closet, making sure that everything was packed except for the clutter on Michael's desk and the clothes he would wear after he showered. He was running now, and she didn't want to be in the room when he came back. She had slept little, and restlessly; the walls of her throat were thick with unshed tears. She felt that if she allowed herself to cry, she wouldn't be able to stop. Not only was her marriage over, but Michael didn't care enough for her to offer any explanation whatsoever. He meticulously justified the actions of the characters he created, yet he wouldn't give her the barest of reasons for his refusal to have a baby.

As she heaved the suitcases off the bed, she realized that she had no plans. What would she do when they got back to Connecticut? Where would she go? Rejecting ideas as quickly as they came to her, she rushed out of the bedroom.

Habit steered her in the direction of the Shed, and once she was there she decided to go in for a cup of coffee. Nettles was standing at the snack bar paying for his breakfast. He greeted her with a broad smile and waited while she ordered. "Do you want anything else?" he said, putting a ten-dollar bill on the counter.

Leila shook her head and thanked him.

They sat at one of the round tables, Nettles savoring his scrambled eggs and corn muffin as if he were eating caviar and crepes. His enjoyment was so obvious that Leila was distracted from her troubles. "Do you always eat with such relish?" she said, half-expecting him to purr with satisfaction.

"Eating is one of life's greatest pleasures, as is sex. I'm an unashamed, unapologetic sensualist. The problem with most people is that they deny themselves enjoyment of sensual experiences because religion and society have trained them to suppress their instincts; they're trapped in straitjackets of guilt. They plod through their lives trying to adhere to arbitrary standards of goodness and decorum, and wonder why they feel miserable and cheated."

The corners of Leila's mouth lifted. "You think I'm one of those people."

He returned her smile. "You did surprise me. I thought we were alike, you and I, able to seize a moment for no other reason than it can give us pleasure."

"Pleasure is transitory."

"So is life," he said. "The older I get, the more convinced I become that nothing takes more talent than living. And that includes writing books. I don't want to die burdened with regrets." He smiled apologetically. "But you're much younger. You have years ahead of you, plenty of time before you begin thinking of such things."

Despite his reference to his age, she could feel physically his power and masculinity, sex as potent as a devil's brew. She wasn't a moralist; she had lived with Michael for two years before they were married. And now there wasn't a marriage to respect, or protect. Her mouth quivered with what could have been interpreted as indecision.

"Fortunately, life sometimes offers more than one opportunity," he said suggestively. "We still have time."

She had been thinking that nothing would hurt Michael more than to have sex with this man and to let him know what she had done. But her throat was still full of unshed tears, and beneath the almost unbearable hurt she was feeling she loved her husband too deeply to want revenge. "We're leaving soon. We have an appointment in Jamestown."

"Well, then, this is goodbye. I truly enjoyed the time I spent with you."

"I'm flattered," she said, rising. "I'll probably always wonder about what might have happened if circumstances had been different."

He stood and reached across the table for her hand. "You're a remarkable woman, Leila. I wish you a happy life with as few regrets as possible."

The tears she had been holding back sprung into her eyes. She pulled her hand away and left, hoping that he hadn't noticed.

***

Pierce came out of Hawthorne carrying his manuscript and files in a cardboard carton. The luggage and his laptop were in trunk of the Maserati, which was parked behind the building; Leila was waiting in the passenger seat. As he descended the front steps, he heard his name called and saw Nettles hurrying toward him. Pierce ground his teeth. He hadn't spoken with Nettles since the opening reception and had no desire to do so again. He could not, however, be rude.

"I'm glad I caught you before you left," Nettles said. "I want to thank you for making this conference interesting for me. I doubt that anything either one of us said will have an appreciable effect, but a few people might have learned something. Whatever the case, it's been a challenge."

"I can't argue with that," Pierce said, unwilling to be any less gracious than his adversary.

Nettles glanced at the box. "Your new novel?"

"Yes."

"Someday you may rethink your position and come over to my side of the fence."

"Never!" Pierce said. "I'll continue to write stories with plots, as will others after me. That will never change."

"It has already changed and will continue to do so regardless of your arguments. You can't stop a flood with your fingers."

"What you call a flood is a trickle, a stream in which critics and academics amuse themselves by splashing water on each other. Nothing has or will change basic human pleasure in a well-told story."

The two men glared at each other. Pierce shifted the carton under his arm; Nettles' burly chest rose and fell as he took angry breaths. Finally, the innovative fictionist spoke. "Our only point of agreement, it seems, is your wife."

Pierce's eyes flashed. "What about my wife?"

"Leila is an extraordinary woman."

"I'm aware of that! I've also been aware of your interest in her!"

"Call it your factor of human pleasure. Leila is beautiful and intelligent. She is also neglected, which is a circumstance you are responsible for." Nettles tilted his head toward the carton. "It seems you have a penchant for misdirecting your effort and your energy."

The innovative fictionist turned sharply and walked away, leaving Pierce holding the carton like an errand boy whose package has been refused.

***

When the Pierces entered John Gustafson's office, what impressed the attorney most was the couple's obvious unhappiness. From the uneasy distance they maintained from each other to the misery in their faces they were telling him that they were having marital problems. If their appointment had been for a regular office visit, he would have assumed they were there to inquire about a divorce. But they had come to learn about Benjamin Clymer, and Gustafson, whose work demanded professional impassivity, greeted them as if he were unaware of the message they were sending.

There was an extra chair at the side of the beautifully-carved Sheraton desk from which a slender, even-featured woman rose; she had fair skin and shoulder-length hair that was dark blond touched with gray. "This is my sister, Ingrid Widmark," the lawyer said after he shook hands with the Pierces. "My father lived with her the last few years of his life, and he occasionally mentioned Benjamin Clymer. Also, though I don't like to admit it, she may have a better memory regarding Clymer than I do. She's always been partial to stories, especially that one."

"I'm particularly partial to novels," Ingrid said, her hazel eyes sparkling. "It's exciting for me to meet you, Mr. Pierce. I've read your books and have enjoyed every one of them."

"Thank you," Pierce said.

After they were seated, Gustafson picked up his copy of the will. "My father met Benjamin Clymer in the spring of 1927," he said. "He came to his office after he'd finished work, a plain-spoken man dressed in laborer's clothes. My father noticed that Mr. Clymer was quite taken with his desk. When he commented on his interest, Mr. Clymer explained that he had done the carving on it and didn't often get to see pieces he had worked on after they left the factory—only once before, also a desk but one that wasn't particularly to his liking. Later my father learned that he was considered the best carver in Jamestown, which was no small achievement. With the exception of the Kittinger Company in

Buffalo, some of the finest furniture in America was made here.

"My father was surprised when Mr. Clymer told him that he wanted a will drawn leaving his estate to Axton College to be used to establish a working place for writers. He had visited Axton College over the weekend and thought it was a wonderful place. His visit happened to fall on graduation weekend, and he had met the president of the college, Otis Hackett, at a reception. Hackett, as my father described him, was impressive: about six feet four or five and over three hundred pounds. My father said Hackett was a mountain of flesh, as smooth as a snake and as slippery. To a man with Clymer's background, Hackett must have seemed nearly god-like.

"Clymer's estate was substantial for a man of his position. He owned land in Cattaraugus County and had better than twenty thousand dollars in cash, which was a considerable sum in those days, his life savings. He spent little on himself; he lived in a rooming house and had his meals there. His only indulgence was his books, each one carefully chosen."

Ingrid Widmark leaned forward. "My father told us that Benjamin Clymer had a reverence for education that he had observed in few men. He often wondered if his attitude was the result of his years of illiteracy. His wife taught him to read. He told my father that when he read, he felt as if she were still with him, that he could feel her presence in the pages of his books. Although she'd been dead for over thirty years, his books remained his link to her, as well as his only luxury. So it was especially meaningful to him that his library would be used by writers, for whom he had the greatest respect."

Pierce, who had been listening intently, sat up sharply. "What books?" he interrupted.

"I told you about the books the other day," Leila said. "They were supposed to be at the Workshop. Instead, they were kept in the Axton College library until they were sold."

"After Benjamin Clymer died, my father went to the house where he boarded," Ingrid said. "Every wall in his room from floor to ceiling was covered with shelves of books, even the closet. He'd read each one, and they were all in perfect condition."

The lawyer nodded his agreement. "Benjamin Clymer would never have suspected that his wishes wouldn't be honored. My father believed the man was incapable of deceit. After the will was drawn, Mr. Clymer objected to a standard clause stipulating that, should Axton College fail to agree in writing and fail thereafter to carry out the terms of the gift within one year of its receipt, all property would revert to the estate.

"He was against the clause; he felt it was insulting. Although he had met Otis Hackett only once, Hackett had impressed him as a man of integrity, which, as far as he was concerned, was sufficient.

"My father said he had never met a man as decent as Benjamin Clymer. The fellow was too well-read to be naive, yet his trust was absolute. He couldn't conceive of the possibility that Hackett would be less than honorable. He was determined to give the gift in good faith, believing that Hackett's word was as good as his own.

"When my father explained to him that, in his experience, a man's word wasn't adequate protection where money was involved, Clymer told him that he was being unkind. My father said that he felt as if he'd been accused of being overly suspicious and mistrustful, of having a flawed character.

"Finally, they compromised. The clause remained except for the requirement of an agreement in writing, which was deleted. Then Benjamin Clymer signed the will. He died of pneumonia a year later.

"After the funeral, my father sent Otis Hackett a copy of the will. Hackett replied immediately. His letter was brief and flowery; he extolled Clymer though he really didn't know him and went directly to the main point: wanting to know when the college would get the money. When the estate was settled in the spring, my father sent him a deed to the land and a bank check, together with a letter reiterating the terms of the will: within one year Axton College was to establish a suitable meeting place where writers could gather to discuss their craft.

"It was a while before he heard from Hackett, and when he did, Hackett made no mention whatsoever of Benjamin Clymer or the purpose of the gift. The omission bothered him, so he made a note on his calendar to visit the Clymer property in the fall."

"Before he died, Dad talked about the day he went to see the property," Ingrid said. "He had to park his car and go on foot. The road was impassable, and the land was completely overgrown, wild with trees and underbrush. There wasn't a sign of building on the land! It was clear that Hackett had taken the money with no intention of honoring the terms of the will."

"He was furious," Gustafson said, continuing seamlessly, "so he made an appointment to see Hackett and knew from one look at him why Clymer had been so impressed. Otis Hackett was sitting like an emperor behind the largest, most ornate desk he'd ever seen. We believe Clymer had done the carving on it. Probably Hackett had sent him a note of appreciation inviting him to stop by to see the desk, one of those *toss-away invitations*, as my mother called them. And Clymer, being unsophisticated, a farmer turned carver, took it literally and happened to show up on graduation weekend when Hackett was hosting an open reception in his office."

"A toss-away invitation?" Leila said.

"You know, those invitations people issue that they don't really mean, like 'stop by and see us if you're in the neighborhood,'" Ingrid explained with a chuckle. "Invitations which are meant to be tossed away."

"My father had to really press Hackett before he finally confessed that he had used the money from the estate for a new science building. He had the audacity to say that he'd personally nail a plaque with Benjamin Clymer's name on it outside the largest laboratory, as though hammering a few nails into a wall would more than compensate for his misappropriation of the funds. My father was livid. He told Hackett that there would be only one plaque with Benjamin Clymer's name on it, and that plaque would be on a building on the land in Cattaraugus County. He told us that Hackett sniveled and whined like a thief trying to make a deal to get himself off.

"A few weeks later Hackett was waiting for my father outside his office early in the morning; he hadn't slept in days. The stock market had crashed since their meeting and the country was in a state of panic. Hackett revealed that the college had funds invested in stocks and that it would be impossible for him to replace the money."

Gustafson paused, then turned to his sister. "Maybe you should tell them the rest of the story. You were closest to Dad at the end."

"You're giving me the difficult part," she said with a sigh. "That morning my father convinced Hackett that the conference would work. He sold him on the idea that it would make money for the college because people who wanted to be published writers would be eager to attend. And he never stopped regretting that Hackett accepted his argument."

"But he was right," Pierce said.

"He felt he was wrong, absolutely wrong. For years after the Workshop opened, he watched and waited for the college to break the terms of the will so he could close the place down. The sale of the books would have been grounds."

"Why did he want to close the conference?" Leila said.

"It was Benjamin Clymer's intention that the Workshop be a nurturing place for writers, a haven for them in which they could share ideas and learn from each other, not a cold-hearted business. He would have been deeply troubled if he knew of the suicides and attempted suicides that have occurred there. He wanted his gift to be positive, not destructive."

"What suicides?" Pierce said.

"Most of my father's clients were ordinary working people; some of them had jobs in hospitals, others drove ambulances. As the Workshop started to become well known, word of the suicides leaked out. The conference was adept at hiding the deaths, but the locals knew and they talked about it."

Pierce's expression became defensive. "Honestly, I didn't know about any suicides; this is the first I've heard about them. They're tragic. All I can say is that some of the people who come to the Workshop have unrealistic expectations. They assume that the writers on the staff hold the keys to their dreams, that we'll read their work and lead them directly to a publisher," he said, thinking of Dynarski. "It's almost as if they're setting themselves up for disappointment."

"In his last years, my father dwelled on the suicides," Ingrid said. "He felt partially to blame because he had convinced Hackett that the conference could be a money-making enterprise when what he should have done was sue for the return of the land and the money after the year stipulated in the will had lapsed. He wanted to beat Hackett because he detested him. He knew that Hackett was arrogant and self-focused, yet he entrusted him with Benjamin Clymer's dream. My father was a proud man. It wasn't easy for him to live with his decision.

"And there was something else, which was even harder. My mother died twenty-seven years before he did. He had a busy practice and he often worked nights. He promised her he would make up for the evenings she spent alone; they would have plenty of time to travel after he retired. But then she died, and their happy plans never came to pass. My mother was his most trusted friend, the one person in whom he could unhesitatingly confide. He once told me that on nights when he couldn't face the empty house, he'd think of Benjamin Clymer going to that book-lined room, and he'd feel ashamed. He and my mother had had full years together, and he had two children raising families of their own. He said his family kept him going. Benjamin Clymer's books were his only company, and books aren't enough to keep a man alive.

"So now you know about Benjamin Clymer," Ingrid said. "In a sense, his story is a family heirloom for us. Now we're telling it to our children."

Leila rose, her eyes bright with tears. "Thank you for sharing," she said, shaking Ingrid's hand and then Gustafson's. "You've been most generous."

"It has been a pleasure," Ingrid said, reaching for a book on her brother's desk. "Mr. Pierce, I would be honored if you would autograph your novel."

"I'll wait for you in the car," Leila said after Pierce started writing.

They were parked several blocks away. Pierce ran to catch up with her. There was finality in her step and a defeated slope to her shoulders that made him impulsively reach for her hand. She pulled away as though his touch hurt and continued walking. He stopped, his mind reeling with indecision, until it settled on one thought: she was his best friend.

He sprinted up to her. "I'm sorry," he said. "I... I was wrong."

Her face was distant and mistrustful. "About what?"

"The baby."

A glimmer of joy rose in her eyes, then died. "Do you mean it?"

"Yes," he said, drawing her to him. "I mean it."

***

Dee Dee stood in the circular driveway watching the last van leave. She'd been outside most of the day seeing that the departures went smoothly. Her supervision wasn't necessary, but it was the only acceptable alternative to staying in the office with Talbot. The day had been unexpectedly pleasant. Individuals whom she had helped had come up to her and thanked her warmly. People were relaxed and smiling; their last minute exchanging of addresses and promises to write to each other had reminded her of youngsters on the last day of summer camp. Not once did she feel the strain of the intensity that had marked each day of the conference.

As she walked to Melville, she thought about the years she had given to the Workshop, all the effort and aggravation it had taken to bring two hundred people together each summer. With the exception of today, the memories she had of most of those people were of anxious faces straining to hide disappointment. Almost any job she took now would be positive in comparison. And she would get a job, a good job. Her experience and skills were excellent. This was a perfect time to leave Axton. She could sell her furniture to students setting up apartments for the school year; except for her mattress, the stuff had been secondhand when she'd bought it. She'd call her parents tonight to ask if she could stay with them until she found an apartment and a job. She still had some friends in Baltimore, and she'd make new ones. She'd make a whole new life.

A breeze was coming in through the open windows in her bedroom. She took a small canvas bag which contained her cosmetics into the bathroom. When she came out, the strap of the bag was over her shoulder. She closed the windows, took her keys off the maple dresser, and grabbed the handle of her suitcase.

On her way out, she paused in front of Talbot's door. "Bastard," she said.

***

Talbot had been drinking behind his closed office door since he had returned from taking Aaron and Amanda Greene to the airport late in the morning. Greene's parting gift had been a kick in the groin: the elderly poet had informed him that he was not coming back to the Workshop. Pierce, Greene, Nettles—Talbot had had a drink for each one. He'd had a drink for Polly and his daughters, a drink for Dee Dee, and had wept over his unpublished manuscript. While he could still speak coherently he had called the hospital: Douglas Webb's condition was unchanged. He had poured more scotch into his glass, wishing for the blessing of unconsciousness for himself.

The crunch of tires on the gravel driveway made its way through his ears to his liquor-numbed brain. He guessed that the car was Dee Dee's, and a drunken sob escaped from his throat. He couldn't replace her; she had run the entire Workshop with the exception of hiring the staff. Now she was gone and he had no staff. If Webb died, there would be a police investigation and publicity. He was finished. His book would never be published and he didn't have a home or a family to return to. He'd lost everything, he thought, covering his face with his hands.

Frank Stryker came into the office at six thirty and found Talbot asleep with his head on the desk. "Mr. Talbot, Mr. Talbot," the caretaker said, shaking him by the shoulder with a beefy hand.

Talbot's eyes opened, bloodshot and blank.

"I have to take my wife to Ellicottville," Stryker said. "We just got word that her aunt passed on. If it's all right with you, I'll stay the night and come back tomorrow after the arrangements are made."

"Huh," Talbot grunted.

Stryker tilted his head at the empty bottle of scotch. "Looks like you tied on a good one. You're in no condition to drive to Axton tonight. I'll help you to your room."

The caretaker half-dragged, half-carried Talbot to Melville and deposited him on his bed. He's going to have a painful head tomorrow, Stryker thought, debating if he should leave a light on.

Talbot started to snore, making the decision unnecessary. It made no sense to waste electricity on a man sleeping off a bottle.

***

Diana arched her back and stretched her arms. Her limbs were stiff, her mouth dry. She'd been talking to Webb continuously for hours and had had no response. Nurses had come to take his pulse, and to replace the intravenous bag which was feeding him, and to replace the container into which his catheter drained. The zigzag green line on the cardiac monitor had remained constant, peaks and valleys of mechanical life. He hadn't moved; not a muscle had twitched. His face beneath the turban of gauze was as still and unchanging as a mask except for the dark stubble of his beard growing heavier with the hours that passed, hair growing as hair grows on the dead. Doctors had raised his eyelids with their thumbs and had aimed pinpoints of light at his pupils as if they were trying to see through a dark tunnel; they had let his lids drop and had put their pencil-slim flashlights into the pockets of their white jackets, their impassive expressions telling her that they had found the tunnel empty.

She had asked the doctors questions for which they didn't have answers. They didn't know if Doug would regain consciousness. They couldn't determine the severity of his injury. They had no idea of what his prognosis would be, if he would hear, see, think, live. They had spoken to her as if they were reading from a textbook: *the brain is soft, floating in fluid... the skull is hard, unforgiving... the blow to the head caused compression of the brain when it hit the skull...*

The brain. All that Doug was, all that he could be or would be depended upon the damaged tissue in his damaged skull. If he didn't regain consciousness soon, the doctors would make the official textbook declaration of a coma.

The sun was setting and the light in the room was growing dim except for the thread of light on the cardiac monitor. She rose stiffly and switched on a lamp next to the bed. His gauze-covered skull rested like a hollow egg on the white pillow. Never had she known anyone so vital, so full of life. He had to be in there, she thought; he had to come back.

She had been talking to him since late in the morning; a woman who was leaving the Workshop had kindly offered to drop her off at the hospital on her way home. She had talked about the plants in the forest, about the escarpment where they had made love, about movies and books, about food and the weather. She had talked about pleasant things, positive things, about anything and everything she could think of that would make him want to grab at life. A tear dropped from her cheek onto the white sheet covering him. "Try, please try," she begged, wanting him back as he was— agitated, irrepressible, explosive with energy. Oh, how she regretted the times she had chastised him for speaking out at the conference.

That was it! she thought with a gasp. She'd been saying the wrong things! She'd been talking to a shell on the pillow instead of the fighter pushing that damn green line.

"William Carlos Williams was wrong in his opposition to

symbolism," she said. "Williams' poems are full of symbols that he was too stubborn to acknowledge. Think of his trees. His poems are full of trees—elms, locusts, poplars. And flowers—daisies, roses, anemones, tulips, Queen Anne's lace."

She thought she saw movement beneath his eyelids. *Please God*, she prayed. "Williams went too far in asserting that the imagination is everything in poetry. I think he used imagination as an excuse for work that was unpolished, for letting words simply tumble out of his head onto paper."

Webb's mouth twitched.

"Williams' use of common language is his only contribution to modern poetry."

"Nnnnnooooo," Webb muttered.

The sound was slurred and barely audible, but it was definitely a sound. Laughing and crying, Diana squeezed his hand. "Williams' scorn of classicism was an affectation. He…"

Webb's eyes opened. "Doug!" she cried, letting go of his hand. She wanted to hold him, to tell him how glad and relieved she was that he was all right.

His arms shot out. "It's dark, I can't see! Diana, turn the light on."

She looked with alarm at the light next to the bed, which was shining into his unevenly-dilated pupils. "I will," she managed to say.

The stubble from his beard scratched her face when she kissed him. "I'll be right back," she said. "Please don't move until I come back."

A resident examined Webb first; then Dr. Hamilton and the neurologist were called. Diana was waiting in the hallway when the two doctors came out of the room. "What's wrong? Why can't he see?" she said.

"There may be damage to his optic nerve," the neurologist said. He was a portly man who had small hands and feet.

"How much damage? Will he be able to see?"

"At the moment, we don't know," the neurologist said.

"When will you know?" she said, fighting hysteria.

The neurologist shrugged. "I'm sorry, young woman," he said. "All we can do is wait."

***

Dynarski drove his black SUV through the campus to a spot between the Shed and the Circle Theater. He had gone to Jamestown and Olean, and the back of the vehicle was packed with plastic jugs filled with distilled water, thirty-minute highway flares, masking tape, three packs of cigarettes, a box of matchbooks, newspapers, and containers holding charcoal lighter, turpentine, and kerosene. He had purchased the items at supermarkets and drugstores, a K-Mart, paint stores, and a hardware store. To ensure that he wouldn't be remembered by clerks, he had made only a few purchases at each place he had stopped; he had been a typical Friday shopper, an anonymous stranger buying familiar items for everyday use.

Talbot didn't hear the black SUV moving slowly through the campus. He was asleep. His snores were loud and liquid, as if he were gargling scotch. He didn't hear the SUV stop; he didn't hear the car door open.

The sky was overcast, the Shed barely visible in the blackness. It was a perfect night: breezy, dry, and starless, Dynarski noted as he switched on a lantern flashlight. He couldn't have asked for better conditions. There wasn't a light on anywhere; the buildings were all empty, every one as he'd expected. If it went the way he planned, everything would go up at once. Too bad he couldn't stick around to enjoy it. Not even the worst tenement deserved to be leveled more than this place.

He opened the trunk, took out the plastic jugs that contained distilled water, which he emptied and then refilled with charcoal lighter, turpentine, and kerosene; he taped a thirty-minute highway flare against the side of each jug. After he put a pack of cigarettes in his shirt pocket, he placed the additional packs, matchbooks, and the roll of masking tape on a stack of newspapers. Then he picked up the stack and hurried to the Shed.

The door was unlocked. Smiling at his luck, he went inside and started working with swift efficiency. First he opened all the windows. Then he lit a cigarette, tucked it into a matchbook, and placed the matchbook on newspapers which he rolled and taped, allowing sufficient air for the cigarette to burn. When he left the shed, nests of newspapers with cigarettes burning inside were resting on the dry wood floor against each of the four timber walls.

From the Shed he went to the Studio, then to the Circle Theater and the shack-like structure that housed the laundry. In each building he repeated the procedure—opening windows, lighting cigarettes, leaving newspaper nests from which threads of smoke curled. The men's residences were next. He worked in Thackeray, Tennyson, and Dickens, then crossed the bridge over Barrier Creek where Whitman, Hawthorne, Melville, and Clemens waited like tinder under the starless sky. He didn't go to the second floor in Melville, where Talbot snored; in each two-story building he placed an ignited nest by the stairwell.

At last he parked the SUV between the Tabard Inn and Tabard II. He went into Tabard II first, carrying three plastic jugs on which highway flares were taped. Again he opened windows, planning where he would set the containers as he moved. He lit the flares after he placed the jugs, discarding burning matches on the wood floors. The matches, he knew, would go out. But the flares taped to the containers would burn, melting the plastic in their path until the liquid inside the jugs ignited an explosion of spray and flame.

The massive front door to the Tabard Inn was locked. He ran to the back entrance, forced the lock with a credit card, then dashed from one wing to the other, opening windows. His black T-shirt was soaked with perspiration when he ran back to the SUV. There were six remaining jugs in the trunk. The thick muscles in his arms bulged as he carried the containers and his flashlight, his fingers and thumbs looped through the handles, into the Inn. Within minutes he was behind the wheel of the SUV. The motor responded immediately when he turned the key in the ignition.

Dynarski glanced one last time at the hulking timber-and-stucco building. He made a farewell salute with his middle finger and drove off into the blackness.

***

The first flames were visible on the windward side of the Shed, where tongues of fire lifted by the breeze arched against the dry siding. Flames poked through the cedar-shingle Studio, then the Circle Theater and the laundry, as if in a chain reaction. Brilliant spears of yellow and orange shot through the men's residences, through Whitman, Hawthorne, Melville, and Clemens, lighting the campus like jewels in a necklace. On a black hill, trees began to creak and sway. Leaves flipped like fans, stirring the air, feeding the breeze. Soon all the hills were creaking, sending gusts of wind into the valley like a message which the flames answered in leaps toward the sky. An explosion ripped the night air, then another, the second rocking the earth. The wind grew stronger, sweeping down from the hills, sweeping the land clean.

There is a prequel to *The Writers' Conference* entitled *Benjamin Clymer's Gift*. You are welcome to visit my website to get a free copy.

www.mariandschwartz.com

www.ingramcontent.com/pod-product-compliance
Lightning Source LLC
Chambersburg PA
CBHW070530120726
47909CB00007B/2087